Walter Soellner

KALVARIANHOF

THE PERILOUS JOURNEY

A FAMILY SAGA

Book One of Four

Gossip Park Books

Kalvarianhof
The Perilous Journey
All Rights Reserved.
Copyright © 2015 Walter Soellner
v2.0

Gossip Park Books

Paperback ISBN: 978-0-578-15600-2
Hardback ISBN: 978-0-578-15610-1

Library of Congress Control Number: 2015940718

PRINTED IN THE UNITED STATES OF AMERICA

Jesus met Levi and said to him,
Follow me, and I will call you Matthew.
(In German, Mathew is Mathais).

This book is dedicated to the many historical fiction writers and historians whose books I have enjoyed and that have inspired me.

Acknowledgments

THANK YOU TO my many friends and family, who have, over the past eight years, assisted, consulted, proofread, and edited this first in a series of books tracing the lives of Markus and Levi.

I especially want to thank my wife Sandra for endless hours assisting with conceptual ideas, and both the actual proofreading of text and her computer application skills necessary to bring book one to the point of editing.

High on the list of dedicated assistants were George and Gilda Forrester, who patiently read various iterations of this manuscript, dotting *i*'s and crossing *t*'s at every stage.

Eve and Ken Reid, another pair of minds of true value, contributed insightful margin notes throughout.

Laurie Klemme offered weeks of critical advice on formulating the draft manuscript, along with her editing and formatting skills and untiring patience, a big thank you.

Kay Pollard edited the text line by line to its final print-ready form. Many thanks, Kay, for a professional job well done.

Edward Rooks, artist and designer: Thank you for your creative talents on the book images.

Last but not least, I thank my daughter Anna Soellner for her ongoing support and confidence in keeping my spirits from flagging, encouraging me onward over the long process of my writing, and her proofreading assistance.

There are also unnamed friends and colleagues who have encouraged, supported, and inspired me here and in Europe, in this wonderful endeavor. Warm thoughts and many thanks.

A final word, to Out Skirts Press, publisher, your many professional services are much appreciated in realizing book one of my four book series 'Kalvarianhof'.

Table of Contents

Chapter I...1
   The Beginning: East Asia 1900
Chapter II 21
   The Peitang Cathedral
Chapter III..40
   Passage to the Lakes, Spears in the Sky,
Chapter IV..59
   Alone
Chapter V 69
   The Iron Rice Pot
Chapter VI..77
   Li Ling
Chapter VII 82
   The Siege, The Iron Cross, and Liaisons
Chapter VIII 90
   A Battle in Africa, a Message from the Chancellor
   of the Imperial Observatory
Chapter IX..107
   Sadness and Tears and the White Lotus
Chapter X 126
   The Imperial Mail Boat
Chapter XI..144
   The Imperial Guards and the River
Chapter XII 157
   The Battle of Peking

Chapter XIII 165
Sun on Deck
Chapter XIV 167
Reunion
Chapter XV 171
Departure, September 17, 1900
Chapter XVI 176
German New Guinea
Chapter XVII 184
German Samoa
Chapter XVIII 193
October 22, 1900 Coronel, Chile
Chapter XIX 199
The Encounter, Montevideo, Uruguay
Chapter XX 203
December 5, 1900 Five Hundred Miles North of Antarctica
Chapter XXI 210
December 11, 1900 Tristan da Cunha
Chapter XXII 217
December 22, 1900 Christmas in Africa
Chapter XXIII 226
A Whole New Century
Chapter XXIV 230
The Trip Home Continues
Chapter XXV 238
January 1901 Arriving and Departing
Chapter XXVI 242
Farewells
Chapter XXVII 245
Laying Plans

Chapter XXVIII 247
  Kalvarianhof
Chapter XXIX 256
  The Turning of the Tide
Chapter XXX 260
  Uruguay
Chapter XXXI 264
  Honey and Salt
Chapter XXXII 270
  The Past Is Prologue
Chapter XXXIII 280
  Into the Maelstrom
Chapter XXXIV 283
  Verboten
Chapter XXXV 286
  Katherina's Dream
Chapter XXXVI 291
  Herr Doctor Professor Adelmann
Chapter XXXVII 293
  The Accident
Chapter XXXVIII 296
  Eastbound
Chapter XXXIX 300
  Jerusalem and the Desert
Chapter XL 305
  The Dig and the Bedouins
Chapter XLI 313
  Secrets Revealed
Chapter XLII 319
  Return 1908

Chapter XLIII...325
    Love in the Night
Chapter XLIV 333
    Christmas 1908
Chapter XLV 339
    The Letter Unfolds Before the Crash
Chapter XLVI..352
    Potsdam
Chapter XLVII 356
    Flight
Chapter XLVIII 365
    Ambitious Plans, Distant Fears
Chapter XLIX 371
    Bye to What Was

GERMAN TSINGTAO, KIAOCHOW, CHINA

Prologue

1900 AT THE center of the universe of the ancient Middle Kingdom of the Chinese Ch'ing dynasty, and the lands were in revolt. Much of the population, up in arms, had joined the rebellion against foreigners, their religious missionaries and trade zones. The rebels were called Boxers, so named because of the mystical dance-like ritual they practiced in the belief that it would protect their warriors from European bullets. They needed every advantage they could get.

The general uprising was triggered by arrogant economic exploitation and by foreign religions foisted upon the Chinese people by various European countries. Foreigners had swarmed into China from 1850 to 1900 as the ancient kingdom weakened. The Japanese were there, and the Dutch, French, Spanish, British, and Portuguese. The Austrians, Italians, Americans, Russians, Belgians, and Germans were also there. Most of these countries had "concessions" with Imperial China, and some even had colonies within the vast, ancient country. The British had Hong Kong, and Imperial Germany had a ninety-nine-year lease on Kiaochow, and the city of Tsingtao, on the coast of the Yellow Sea.

All of them coveted China's natural resources: tea and timber, coal and precious materials, and highly skilled artisans' wares of magnificent silks, porcelains, bronzes, paintings, and sculptures. Ancient objects, thousands of years old, were bought or looted, and then they were shipped back to the grand palaces and manor houses of Europe and Japan.

The Chinese finally had had enough of the *foreign devils* who demanded the best goods for trade but who would pay only a pittance and sometimes only in opium. Opium had become the scourge of many villages and towns in China. It was time for revenge. It was time to drive all foreigners out of the country. The Boxer Rebellion was about to begin.

**EMPRESS DOWAGER OF CHINA IN THE FORBIDDEN CITY,
PEKING ABOUT 1900.**

BAVARIAN ARMY HELMET CREST

CHAPTER I

The Beginning: East Asia 1900

SEARING EAST ASIAN winds blew across the Forbidden City, sweeping sands from the Gobi Desert up the red fortress walls. Lancer Solomon Levi of the Imperial German East Asian Expeditionary Force galloped furiously toward the German Legation Headquarters near the towering walls, his best friend Lancer Markus Mathias clinging to his back.

German Kaiser Wilhelm's patrol had not seen the hordes of Chinese irregulars until it was too late. The rebels had come out of nowhere, and ambushed Lancer Levi and his two companions: Sergeant Brandenburg and Lancer Bauer.

Lancer Levi's sword slashed furiously at the attackers as they swarmed around the three mounted troops, each fighting for his life. Out of the corner of his eye, Levi saw Bauer's horse rear up in fear and agony as Chinese spears, swords, knives, and hatchets pummeled the flanks of the horse and Bauer's legs. Hopeless against the overwhelming enemy force, the three German soldiers' only hope was flight.

Sergeant Brandenburg shouted, "Warn the legation!" Those were the last words of this veteran warrior of the Franco-Prussian war of 1870 and longtime volunteer in the Imperial German East Asian Expeditionary force in China. Blades and knives and finally a deep hatchet chop into his left thigh brought him down into the Gobi dust.

Bauer was the next to fall, pulled from his horse by eager hands bent on revenge for crimes against the Chinese people. Levi pulled out his newly issued M1879 *Reichsrevolver*, wheeled his horse around in a circle, and fired all six shots into his attackers. *Bam bam...bam, bam bam, bam!* The rapid fire and thundering sound startled everyone momentarily. Levi found an opening and spurred his horse forward. He whipped his mount with the flat of the blade of his sword and bolted out of the pack of stabbers and slashers. He gave a quick look around for his two companions. They were already down and being beaten to death as Levi rode for his life in the direction of the legation.

As he spurred his horse along the Meridian Road south of the Forbidden City, he saw a lone dismounted horseman. Seeing the uniform and German *Pickelhaube* (spiked) helmet, he pulled up abruptly. It was his friend Lancer Mathias, his barracks mate.

"What happened? What are you doing here?" Levi shouted in an anxious voice.

"I could ask you the same thing, and what's the hurry?"

"We have to get out of here. There's a rebel army just over that rise, and they're heading for the legation. They just killed Brandenberg and Bauer! Get on your horse! Let's go!"

"Sergeant Brandenburg and Bauer dead?" Mathias asked in alarm, looking apprehensively down the road where Levi had just come from.

"*Jesus*, and I can't ride Max; he just broke an ankle bone on this damned road. How close?"

"Too damned close! Don't you hear them?" Levi exclaimed. The low rumble of a thousand angry voices was just audible and getting louder. "Come on. Get on! Get your rifle and the dispatch pouch, and let's get outta here!" Levi's voice was rising in pitch with every word.

Sweat was streaking his face, made even more evident because of the layer of dust completely covering him and his horse. Deep burgundy wine-colored bloodstains soaked through the dust on his cavalry pants. Markus quickly grabbed his things. "What should I do about Max?" he asked.

"Leave him! Come on, come on! We've got to warn the legations!"

Levi stood up in his saddle, peering through the midday haze as Mathias slung his rifle across his back, the leather rifle strap firm against his chest. He grabbed the dispatch pouch from his saddle and slung it over his head, the two straps forming a leather "X" on his uniform. He ran over to Levi.

"*Jesus*, Levi!" he blurted out when he saw Levi's blood-soaked uniform and his severely injured horse. "Will he make it with the two of us?"

"He'd better!" Levi said, slipping his foot out of his left stirrup so his friend could use it to mount.

Levi extended his arm down and helped Mathias swing up behind him. Wheeling the horse around in the direction of the Forbidden City, he spurred him hard to get the exhausted horse moving into a trot and then a canter. Sensing how weakened his horse was from exertion and loss of blood and the added weight, Levi said in a stressed voice, "I'd better not push him too hard, or the three of us will never make it."

They saw him coming from the lookouts high on the Chinese Tower built into the walls of the Tartar City. Peking in 1900 was not just one city. It was a city within a city, within a city, within a city.

Fortified walls separated the four cities, each city more exclusive than the last.

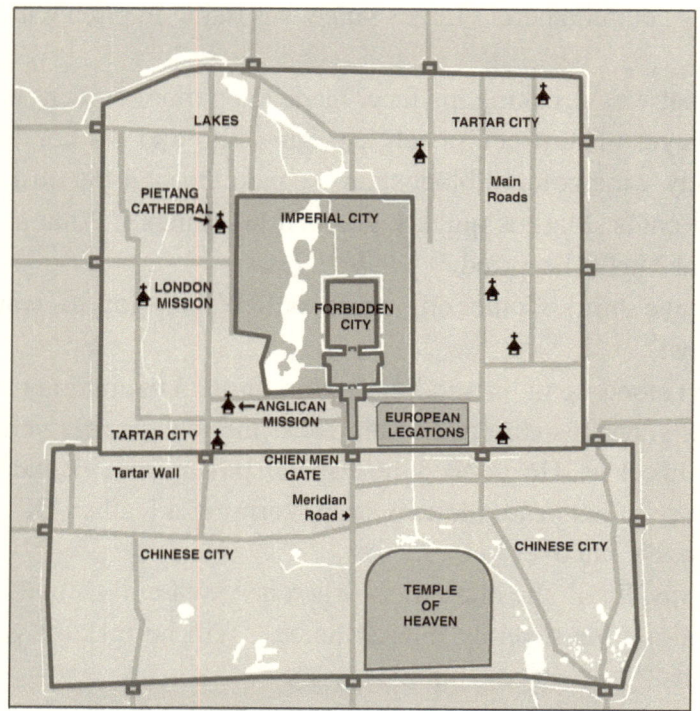

PEKING AND THE FOUR CITIES, 1900

The outermost city, Chinese City, housed merchants, traders, and craftsmen and the Temple of Heavenly Peace.

The next city, Tartar City, housed the Manchu, Mongol, and Han aristocracy, and the foreign legations of the Europeans toward which Levi and Mathias headed. The third city, surrounded by Tartar City, was the Imperial City. It contained the lavish palaces of the royal administration and the princes of royal blood. Finally, the fourth and innermost city was the Forbidden City. Hidden behind its high walls, the unseen emperor in unimaginable splendor ruled as the earthly representative to the gods.

The lookouts could see the lone rider far off, trotting a stumbling, obviously tired horse toward the Chien-Men Gate leading into Tartar City.

"Rider coming," shouted the Italian officer, Lt. Angelo Olivieri, commander of the Bersaglieri (light infantry), who just happened to be visiting his men assigned to guard duty in the tower. All the legations rotated military duties among themselves, in spite of some language barriers.

"Yes, sir," answered Corporal William Gregory of the British Royal Marines, who was at the base of the tower. "I'll notify Commander MacDonald."

Sir Claude MacDonald, British Minister to Peking, had assumed command of the legation's assorted military units and its defenses. Since the assassination of Baron August von Ketteler, Imperial German diplomat, by Chinese Imperial Guards on June 20th, and the savage massacre of dozens of missionaries and Christian Chinese throughout northern China, all legations had strengthened their defenses and formed a very loose central command under MacDonald. He could only "ask" other foreign nationals and their military units to cooperate. However, the reports of Catholic priests and nuns, Protestant ministers and their families, and flocks of Christian Chinese slaughtered by the thousands in isolated communities had spread panic throughout the European population in northern China. That had brought a remarkable sense of cooperation and camaraderie among the usually feuding Europeans. When detailed word came of the horrific killings at Taiyuan, a mere fifty-five kilometers from Peking, in which all the men, women, and children were stripped to the waist, lined up, and beheaded one by one, the legations came together as one for their own survival.

Olivieri swung back toward the oncoming rider. Lifting his binoculars, he sighted in and adjusted the focus.

"Two riders," he announced. "That horse looks like it's going to drop! Prepare to open the Chien Men Gate."

Levi slowed his horse to a fast walk, knowing that a slow trot might cause his horse to collapse. Froth dripped from the horse's mouth with each heaving breath, its nostrils flaring, its eyes glaring in a dazed stupor.

"Looks like we'll make it, but not by much. I just want to get through Chinese City before I'll feel safe," he shouted over his shoulder to Mathias. Levi urged his horse on as they approached the Tartar walls fifteen hundred feet ahead.

Courtesy of the American Museum of Natural History

THE TARTAR WALLS IN PEKING 1900

The South Meridian Road passed through each successive city and ended at the gates to the emperor's palace. Even after seeing the city walls from far off many times, Levi and Mathias were awed by the sheer scale of the fortifications.

"I don't like the looks of all these Imperial Chinese troops crowded into this city," Mathias said. "Look at their uniforms. These are General Tung's Moslem Kansu braves. I've seen them before…up the Yangtze. They're the ones that massacred those missionaries a few weeks ago. They are the most virulently anti-foreign, anti-Christian group in China. In addition, they are the best-disciplined Chinese Imperial troops the empress has. If they are here to attack the legations, we're in for a real fight. You think they'll let us through, Levi?"

"I don't know, but you can tell they hate us and are looking for a fight. Those rebels down the road may just push these bastards over the edge. Come on, boy! Hold up for just another thousand yards," Levi whispered in a slurred voice to his horse.

The huge bronze-studded wooden doors of the Chien Men Gate began to swing open as Levi's horse passed dozens of surly, strutting Imperial troops just yards from the two German soldiers. Levi, with a sinking feeling, realized he had not reloaded his revolver since the earlier attack. Mathias could feel the hair on the back of his neck prickle with tension as they narrowed the distance to the passage.

"These men are ready to kill us. You can see it in their eyes," Mathias muttered to Levi. "Just get us through that gate!"

They rode their sweating mount toward the red, white, and black Imperial German flag flapping in the wind beside banners of the other legations, high up on the walls. Finally, as the massive doors finished the outward swing, the exhausted Levi and his companion passed through the gates. His horse loped unsteadily along Legation Road. They went past the American encampment, past the tsar's Russian troops, and on directly toward the British commander's quarters. When the mighty gates swung shut, they heard thuds and clatter as the doors were bombarded by rocks.

Officers, enlisted men, and dozens of civilians watched with intense interest as Levi pulled back gently on the reins as his horse finally halted. Clouds of dust swirled around the exhausted horse.

What a sight it was. Levi and Mathias' spiked helmets with silver eagle plates on the front gleamed even in the dusty air. Most shocking for the crowd to see: both flanks of the horse covered in bright red blood from dozens of cuts inflicted during the battle.

Mathias was the first to slide off the horse. Levi slid out of the saddle to the ground. His thighs and boots were covered in blood. He had multiple puncture wounds, and partly staggered, partly stumbled a few paces before strong arms came to his aid. His German commander, Captain Bernhard Mayerling, accompanied by Sir Claude MacDonald met the two lancers at the portal to the inner chambers of what once had been the eunuchs' palatial apartment complex for the emperor's servants. It had been commandeered for the British delegation, from the throne of the Middle Kingdom. The other legations had likewise assumed quarters in and around Tartar City.

Levi, half walking, half carried, shuffled into the commander's great room and into a chair. Upon seeing Levi's injuries, MacDonald commanded, "Get a doctor and medical staff here immediately."

With so many officers, diplomats, missionaries, and businessmen pushing in, the opulent room swirled thick with pipe and cigar smoke that tinted the bloodred dragon painted on the ceiling a bluish-magenta color. A dozen different military uniforms, of various colors and styles, showed the many nationalities present.

Only when Levi sank down into the offered chair did he notice, as the gasps in the room indicated, that a broken sword blade was sticking completely through his right boot and leg. Eighteen inches above the heel, about three inches of broken blade protruded from one side of his boot and one inch of steel tip from the other. Levi sat staring a moment at the boot. He knew it had pierced his calf.

"Funny, I don't feel a thing," he said, almost to himself.

On seeing the pierced boot, the startled commander shouted, "Get those medics in here! So, Lancer, Lancer…" MacDonald hesitated a moment.

"Levi," offered Captain Mayerling.

"Yes, right, Levi," MacDonald continued. "We will see to your injuries immediately. But you must give me your report on the situation outside the walls. And tell me what happened to the other two troopers with you?"

"Sergeant Brandenburg and Lancer Bauer," Mayerling offered again.

"Yes, yes, Brandenburg and Bauer."

"They're dead, sir. And the Boxers could attack within a couple of hours. They're three or four kilometers out along the South Meridian road. That's where they ambushed us," Levi said in an exhausted tone.

"How many?" the commander asked.

"Hundreds, maybe thousands…and that's not counting the Imperial troops just outside the walls…those Kansu."

MacDonald stared at Levi for a long moment and said, almost with an air of confidentiality, "I don't think we have to worry about the dowager empress's troops. It's inconceivable that the empress would attack the diplomatic legations of, what is it now, sixteen nations? No, our concern is that rebel band of Boxers. You say they're four kilometers out? But will they actually attack, or just demonstrate?" He spoke almost to himself.

"An undisciplined rabble like that could do anything."

Turning to the other officers present, MacDonald gave them orders: "I am implementing our defensive plan we all agreed to earlier. You know your assigned positions and duties around the perimeter. Captain Hall, take a contingent of your American troops and double-check our civilians living immediately outside the walls, including Sir Robert Hart's house. We don't want any of our nationals unprotected."

"Yes sir," Captain Hall said and with a salute, he hurried out of the room.

"Sub-Lieutenant Commander Henri," MacDonald continued, "how many of your sailors are fit for duty? I know some of your men were in sick bay."

"All twenty-nine of my men are ready for duty, sir," replied the French naval officer, recently reassigned from the light cruiser *Chantilly* to strengthen the French legation.

"Good. As agreed, you are to move your men to the Peitang Cathedral. Bishop Favier and the nuns and hundreds of Chinese converts are already there. I understand more may be coming. Continue fortifying the defenses. We know it's our weakest defensive position. I'll send the Italian troops over if necessary. Someone fetch Lieutenant Olivieri."

"*Oui, Monsieur Commander*," Sub-Lieutenant Commander Henri said, saluting smartly, stamping his foot, rotating around and with sublime military elegance, marching out the door.

"Now then, we need to round up all the livestock pastured outside the walls and any and all provisions, hay, grains, that sort of thing. There's no telling how long we may need to supply ourselves. Count Molenofski, see what you can do about rounding up the livestock. If you need wagons and teams, get them from the British stables. Keep a sharp lookout. Fortunately the rebels are south of us, and the pastures are to the northeast. Good luck." He exchanged salutes with the Russian aristocrat, whose striking white uniform was crisp and bemedaled, as only a distant cousin to Czar Nicholas II would have it.

All these commands took only minutes, and Levi sat patiently listening in a half-conscious way, watching a small but growing pool of blood around his boot. A German surgeon and several stretcher-bearers arrived just as Commander MacDonald reached over and put his hand on Levi's shoulder.

"Well done, Lancer Levi. You're a brave, tough soldier. I am sorry you lost your brothers-in-arms. I will formally write to your commanding officer, Captain Mayerling here, and request that you and your two comrades receive recognition for your bravery today."

The crowd that had gathered around the two men burst out in exclamations of approval while the medics laid Levi on a stretcher. Before they were out of the room, Levi had passed out.

Markus stayed quietly in the back of the room as the dramatic return of Levi and his story unfolded. He went about his duties after hearing Levi tell of his misadventures after first delivering his dispatch case to Captain Mayerling, who relayed it to MacDonald.

More graphic news came in of missions overrun, Chinese Christians killed, and missionaries burned alive, and in some cases buried alive. Horror stories all. MacDonald decided not to share these tragic details with the general population of the legations.

"It is enough to let people know that many murders are taking place across northern China and that we must be prepared to defend ourselves with every available man for an eminent and inevitable attack here," he told his war council.

The council was made up of the chief military officer and, if available, the diplomat of each legation and several prominent clergy and businessmen. They agreed to keep the details of the attacks quiet, but with a group that big, news of the atrocities spread fast. All able-bodied men had already been assigned duties commensurate with their skills and were now given rudimentary rifle training. Many wives also insisted on handgun training, after hearing rumors and stories of massacres of women and children. Many still felt the stories had to be exaggerated. Only later was it determined that among Catholics alone, some 30,000 Chinese Christians and clergy died during those terrible months.

Several days passed before they let Markus visit Levi in the German medical ward across the street from the Japanese legation. He had been very busy the last forty-eight hours since that desperate ride up the South Meridian road on Levi's horse. The Boxers did mount a feeble attack of sorts late that first afternoon. Against the high walls and barricades, the noisy but poorly armed rebels were no match for the defenders, well stocked with arms and ammunition. The attack was handily repulsed by the international forces aligned along the top of the Tartar wall and the various lower walls, rooftops, windows, and barricades thrown up inside Tartar City to protect the legations.

Markus, fighting with his comrades, managed to kill several attackers. He thought about this first real combat as a soldier. He was surprised at how scared he was. It was thrilling and exhilarating. What a sense of power, shooting at those bastards. It was like playing God. It was being God! The noise and smells of all that gunpowder! The shouts and screams! It was great to be a soldier. He loved it.

It seemed almost dreamlike to him—this great adventure in an exotic land, with all his fellow Europeans and the incredible fortress city he now called home.

But even in the midst of all the danger and chaos, Mathias' mind was often somewhere else. He dreamed of a little village only a long day's walk north of the outer wall. There, his heart's delight lived with her father. Li Ling was his precious, most precious secret. Only Levi knew about her, but even Levi didn't know everything.

Li Ling had just turned eighteen, and she was the most perfect woman Markus had ever known. Innocent as a child, she seemed as pure as the Bavarian snow back home. Kind and gentle, she spoke in a loving way that was music to his ears. He could not get her out of his mind for more than a few minutes.

He dreamed of her eyes—slits of mystery and desire and of intoxicating beauty. He yearned for her, to be with her, to see her move, to hear her happy laugh at the little things that seemed strange to her; to touch her skin, only gently, gently, like a whisper, like a warm breeze under the plum tree in her father's garden.

He imagined her long, black hair brushed against his face. He could almost smell her ever so slightly, and he swelled with desire.

To lay his head on her chest, her soft warmth soaking into his body, it was more than he had ever experienced. She was a goddess, a child, and a woman. He did not care about the danger. He only knew he wanted to be there, to see her look at him with acceptance, a wondrous trust of love and vulnerability.

That was why, in spite of extreme danger, he was going outside the walls. He would go by himself at night. He'd somehow pass through the entrenched Boxers, the angry villagers, the Imperial troops camped by the thousands within Tarter City and within Chinese City and even beyond the outer wall, to her village. First, though, he had to tell Levi.

They were good friends, best of friends, childhood teammates, his most trusting brother-in-arms, and the one who would understand. Even if Levi didn't understand, he would accept Markus' truth as his truth, and would advise him, counsel him on the best course, the safest course, and sometimes the only course.

He walked briskly up the steps of the dispensary, now a hospital for the wounded military and civilian casualties. So far only a dozen occupied beds. Miraculously within the walls no one in any legation had yet been killed in the ongoing battles and scrimmages. The most seriously injured was a civilian who had backed up too far and fallen backward off the ramparts. There were several with gunshot wounds and some with assorted cuts and bruises from flying objects.

He passed several rooms with the injured. Visitors were cheering up the ones who could tolerate a conversation, and some even found flowers to bring. In a month or so, people would be eating the bulbs of those flowers. Markus found Levi in a semi-private room, spotless and cheerful and with a picture of Kaiser Wilhelm II in his Commander of the Guard De Corp uniform, in a golden frame on the beige walls. A Methodist missionary whose heart was giving out occupied the other bed.

"*Guten Tag, mein* General!" Markus said with a broad smile as he approached the bed. "I see they're giving you the royal treatment. You look great except for your bandaged leg...bandaged hand... bandaged ear...and what else? I hope nothing too important down there! Ha!" He chuckled. "So when can you get on your horse again? By the way, your horse is in worse shape than you are, last time I looked in on him down by the stables. But he, too, will recover."

"Good!" said Levi with a grin. "I'll need him to rescue you the next time you go out riding."

They both laughed.

"It won't be the last time I'll need rescuing, so get well fast."

"I aim to do just that. Herr Doctor Reiter wants me walking around a little in a day or so, and by the sounds of things out there, I'll be needed on the line. How bad is it?"

"You're needed on the line, or will be soon," replied Markus. "The rebels are getting bolder, aiming straighter, and there's a lot more of them every day. They need wild boar hunters like you and me up on the walls. We'll pick off a dozen of 'em at a hundred meters...if the wind's not blowing too hard!" Again, the two had a hearty laugh.

"So, can I get you anything?"

"Is there any mail? Has any gotten through lately?" He stared at Mathias' expression for signs of a positive answer. None was coming.

"No, no mail since the siege began, but we've had some dispatches get through. The Christian Chinese help with that. They just blend in with the rebels. And as long as they aren't caught with dispatches, they are okay. If they do get caught, well, that's it for them."

"*Ja*. It's dangerous work for volunteers," Levi sighed. "I sure would like to hear from Papa and the family."

"Me, too."

"Everything is green," Levi began in a reflective mood, "and beautiful and growing this time of year back home. The smell of the hay, when we go out and cut it, I like that." He paused. "This country is amazing, but it's not as beautiful as back home in Munich and the Alps. You ever been up in the tower of the *Rauthaus* (city hall) in Munich when it's not cloudy and you can see the mountains? That's the most beautiful sight in the world…the snow and the jagged peaks and the Zugspitze towering over all of it."

"Of course I've been up there. Who hasn't? And I've climbed to the top of the Zugspitze, too. Now, there is a view for your Jewish soul to contemplate. It's as close to heaven as you'll ever get, Levi!"

Levi just smiled as he gazed off into his own thoughts.

They sat there for a while in silence, both thinking about home and loved ones and the good times of their youth. Here they were in China, in the middle of a desperate battle, fifteen thousand nautical miles from home, one of them nineteen years old, the other twenty-one. They had already experienced a lot, and they knew it.

"Does it still hurt…your wound?" Markus inquired.

"No, not so much anymore. I think it's healing up pretty fast."

"So, Levi, tell me again why you want people to call you by your last name and not your first name like everybody else?"

"I told you before, Solomon just sounds pretentious…I never liked the name for myself and Mama and Papa knew it, so they just started calling me Levi. I like it that way. Any other questions?"

"Yes, as a matter of fact. Do Jews believe in heaven, you know, life after death, like us Catholics?"

"What? Why are you asking me that for?"

"I don't know. I was just curious. You know Li Ling believes in reincarnation. That's where you come back as another person or something. Your soul just keeps on coming back for a long time, 'til it gets really pure. Then it goes to heaven, I guess. That's what Li Ling told me."

"I know what reincarnation is, and yes, most Jews believe in heaven, and no, I don't believe in reincarnation. I believe that when you're dead, you're dead. You're not coming back as a person or a bug or anything, and as for heaven, most Jews don't think about it much, at least I don't, and Papa doesn't either, as far as I know. We figure it's better to be good in this life and let God decide about heaven. What is all this talk about heaven? You planning on dying soon? It's going to take a lot more than a bunch of Boxers to kill you off, that's for sure. By the way, what have you heard from your Li Ling? Is she okay?"

"I haven't heard anything. That's why I wanted to talk to you. I need a plan. I'm going out. I have to see her. I have to know she is okay, and I need your help to do that." Markus was sitting on the edge of the bed, and although it was hot in the room, the beads of sweat were not from the heat. "What do you think, Levi?"

"Well, you've really got it bad for her, I can see that. But going outside the protection of the legation forces is pretty much suicide. There are thousands, maybe ten thousand enemies out there. There are the Boxers, and Imperial troops, who may or may not be controlled by the empress. Nobody knows what side the empress is on. She may not even protect the diplomatic missions! It's really…"

"I know all that," Markus interrupted, the sound of exasperation in his voice. "I just need a plan to get out of here."

"Are you planning on coming back?" Levi asked, looking skeptically at his friend.

"I don't know, I haven't gotten that far yet. I've just got to see her, that's all." Markus sat down on the bed, slumped down, and propped himself up on his elbow. He looked miserable.

"Well, you're not going any place without help from some friendly Chinese, that's for sure. Let's think about this for a minute. When were you thinking of going?"

"As soon as possible. I just can't wait any longer. I've got to go."

"*Ja*, I understand. Just don't make any moves 'til we work out a plan so you have a chance of surviving, and that's not even thinking about you being charged with desertion. Even Captain Mayerling, as good a man as he is, would have you shot for deserting in the face of the enemy. That's something to think about. Li Ling would not be better off if that happened. And speaking of Li Ling, she will be in real danger if any of the hostile villagers finds out she's friendly with a European."

Mathias stirred. "I'm not going to desert. And some of her villagers are Christian, so I think she's pretty safe there. At least for now."

"Well, that's good news," Levi said, staring across the room. They were both silent again for a while. They could do that, be silent in each other's presence. There wasn't a need to entertain or feel an awkwardness in silence.

Before they enlisted in the army, when the two young men went hunting on Levi's vast family estate of Kalvarianhof outside of Munich, a half day could pass without a word between them. They had been boyhood friends through their earliest years when the Mathias family still lived in the small village. Even after Markus' family moved to their beautiful apartment in Munich, the two remained very close.

Finally Levi spoke. "You know, I think I may have a plan or at least a way to get you out of the legation on official business, and even partway across Tartar City." He twisted around in his bed, gingerly moving his bandaged leg with both hands. "Remember when we were in Commander MacDonald's headquarters just after we got back?"

"*Ja*, I remember, so?"

"Remember what he said after he ordered the French navy guys to go to the Peitang Cathedral…about sending the Italians over there to help out?"

"*Ja, ja*, I remember. I was standing in the back of the room, and I heard him say he was going to send the Italians if things got bad over there."

"Well, I bet you a stein of beer that he's going to send them, and soon. Things are getting really bad here, and you can imagine what the situation is over there. The Italians will probably even have to fight their way there. Okay, so here is what you have to do. First, you have to find out if and when the Italians may be going. Then, if you can get yourself attached to their unit temporarily for some kind of special duty, or something like that, you could get out of here without deserting!"

"I see what you mean. I like it, your plan, but what kind of special duty? And once I get to the Peitang Cathedral, then what?"

"That, my boar-hunting, beer-drinking, lovesick friend, is what you have to figure out for yourself. That only gets you halfway across the city, assuming the Italians, and you, don't get killed first." Levi could almost see the wheels in Markus' mind turning.

"Special duty?" he said, mostly to himself. "You know, I speak pretty good Italian and French, and I can get by with Li Ling in Mandarin. I've always been good at languages. Remember when we went to Africa last year before we enlisted, and we came across those Boars? I pretty much picked up on their sentence structure and a few words and phrases in a few days. Maybe I could go as an interpreter over at the cathedral. What do you think, Levi?"

"It's a possibility, assuming they need an interpreter and Mayerling goes along with it. I just think you need something else. Some other reason…"

"What if I tell Captain Mayerling that I want to volunteer to defend the Catholics at the Cathedral because…because…"

"Because you're Catholic, and you just feel compelled to help them? Do you really think Mayerling will buy that bucket of oats?" Levi asked.

"It's worth a try. I could add that if I died in battle, my mother would feel better if she knew I died defending fellow Catholics. What do you think?"

"I think Captain Mayerling will throw you out of his office and assign you to latrine duty if you go in there with a story like that!" Levi couldn't help laughing and wincing at the hurt caused by his laugh.

Markus, seeing Levi's reaction, started to laugh, too. "Well, I'm just trying to think of every angle."

"Your Jesus wouldn't be happy with you for using his religion to perpetuate a lie, and for lust no less. Better think of something else," he said, smiling.

"But my mother would be happier knowing I died at the cathedral instead of here with a bunch of Anglicans and Methodists and Japanese Buddhists!" They both had a good laugh.

"And with a Jew thrown in!" added Levi between chuckles.

Events moved quickly and in Mathias' favor. A badly injured Chinese civilian managed to make his way from the Peita'ng Cathedral to the fortified legations and, before he died, brought news that the defenders were desperate for ammunition and reinforcements. Sir Claude MacDonald immediately ordered Lieutenant Olivieri and his men to resupply and reinforce the cathedral. He also called for a volunteer to accompany the Italians to the cathedral and return with an assessment of conditions there and whether an evacuation was possible. On hearing the call for a volunteer, Mathias reported to Captain Mayerling with his request to volunteer and emphasized his command of Mandarin. Mayerling tried to dissuade him but in the end, he forwarded his name to Commander MacDonald. While several other soldiers volunteered, none spoke Mandarin. MacDonald considered that fact the tipping point in assigning Lancer Mathias the task. There were still many Chinese who were simply neutral in the conflict, or were secretly Christian and supporters of the Westerners, and these civilians could prove essential to the courier's survival.

By early afternoon the Italian troops were provisioned, and extra ammunition, medical supplies, and food were loaded on a half-dozen packhorses. After Markus received his final orders from Mayerling, Markus hurried over to the hospital to see Levi one last time.

"Here is a letter for my parents in case the worst happens," he told Levi. "And I'm not deserting you or the army. I'll be back, sometime, somehow."

Levi gave him a hug from his hospital bed and said, "Take care of yourself. And get a Chinese to accompany you out of town when you leave the cathedral...and leave the spiked helmet in the church. Wear something that looks Chinese! Farewell, my friend, and give my greetings to Li Ling. She's a lucky *fräulein*!"

European and Japanese Legation Compound

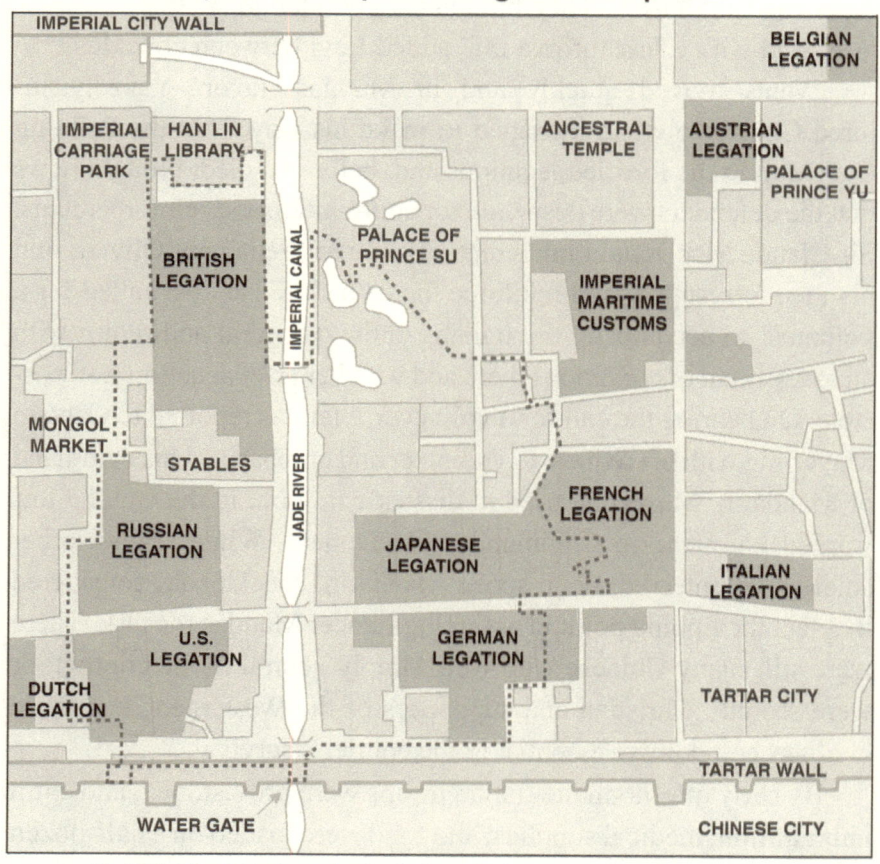

----- The dotted line indicates defensive limits of the legations during the seige, summer, 1900.

0   500   1000 feet

EUROPEAN AND JAPANESE LIGATIONS COMPOUND

THE PEITANG CATHEDRAL BEFORE THE SIEGE, SUMMER 1900.

CHAPTER II

The Peitang Cathedral

"HE'S RIGHT, I'M going to need all the help I can get," Markus mumbled to himself as he left Levi's hospital room. He hurried down the steps into the bright, hot afternoon sun and saw the Italian sailors. They were down Legation Street across the south bridge over Jade River and beside the Russian legation, forming up in preparation for the march to relieve Peitang Cathedral. Markus had won his spot in the relief expedition on the strength of his linguistic skills in French, English, and Mandarin. He marched quickly over to his gear: rifle, cartridge belt, military pack, and canteen, watched over by one of his comrades.

"Good luck, Markus! We'll look for you in a couple of days."

"*Ja*, thanks, don't fall asleep on the wall!" He grabbed his gear and marched in quick-time over to Lieutenant Commander Olivieri. Coming to attention, he saluted and reported in.

"Good to have you join us, Lancer Mathias. Captain Mayerling speaks highly of you. Join up with my marines. We will be leaving shortly." Markus joined the Italians, who had already formed up.

"*Buongiorno*," he said with a smile. Several Italians exchanged greetings with him and seemed glad to see an additional national from the legations, even if it was a lone soldier.

The Peitang Cathedral, on the western side of Tartar City, was over two miles from the legations. The neo-Gothic church, reminiscent of Notre-Dame in Paris or Westminster in London, was more than just an extravagant, white, cut-stone church. A twelve-foot wall surrounded part of the cathedral compound, which included a hospital, rectory, nunnery, and orphanage for five hundred children, storage sheds, and even some tightly packed housing for Chinese parishioners. The church stood very close to the great wall of the Imperial City that towered over part of the compound. A vexing reality arose for the Catholics when the Boxers besieged the cathedral. Armed with rifles supplied by sympathetic Imperial troops, from the great walls they could shoot directly into the church compound.

Lieutenant Commander Olivieri called his company to attention. Markus was quite able to understand his words.

"As you know, we have been asked to assist in the defense of the Peitang Cathedral and its Christian community until the relief expedition arrives from the coast…" He spoke to his troops in a forceful voice as a gathering of onlookers formed.

"There are continuing reports of Boxer attacks against the Catholic church there. Our French allies and fellow sailors are hard pressed to defend Peitang Cathedral with so few men. We Italians may very well rescue them from certain death. As Italians, as Catholics, and as brothers under the sail, it is our duty to assist in their defense. Are we ready, men?"

"Yes sir!" rang out the reply.

"Very well, my soldiers. Here are your marching orders. The cathedral complex is approximately two miles from here. We march that distance in an expanded column of fours, spread out, to have room to maneuver and fight if necessary. We will not fire our weapons unless I give the order or if under a general attack. There will probably be random shots heard from the enemy. Do not return fire. We want to move through the city as quickly and quietly as possible. Remember, our mission is to defend the Peitang Cathedral's inhabitants, not engage in combat with the Boxers or Imperial troops at this time." He paused.

"Sergeant, have your men load rifles and fix bayonets. Are the pack horses ready?"

"Yes sir. Fix bayonets! Lock and load." A clatter of steel against steel rang out with the sound of sliding bolts and cartridges slamming into firing chambers.

"The men are ready, sir," shouted the sergeant. Thirty or forty people gathered to watch the Italians, including soldiers from various units and an assortment of civilians. All were reluctant to see the marines leave the legation, thereby reducing the men available for defense, but most knew from rumors and general talk that the people at the cathedral were in desperate circumstances.

The Italians, led by Olivieri, marched in quick-time north through the British stable courtyard as a faint refrain of an Italian opera could be heard being played on an Edison gramophone cylinder. They passed through a small gate into the Mongol market and on into the vast Imperial Carriage Park. It housed stables, carriage barns, corrals, and a large, open, grassy assembly area three hundred yards long. It was deserted...eerily silent. All eyes apprehensively scanned the walls surrounding the carriage park.

The formation turned left upon leaving the wide doors of the park and headed west along the road just below the Imperial City walls. Chinese civilians, busy with their own concerns, looked up, startled to see the European sailors moving quickly down the dusty road. They stopped and stared. Some scurried away, sensing danger. The heat was oppressive, and the men were soaked with sweat. Olivieri knew he would have to rest his men several times before reaching the cathedral and in a least exposed spot. Heads could be seen peering from the top of the redbrick wall they paralleled. *We are perfect targets from that height*, thought Olivieri. He just hoped they were gone by the time the Boxers realized they had passed.

The small military unit jogged in step as they passed vegetable and fruit stands, tarpaulins laid out on the ground with foot-high mounds of spices of all varieties and colors. Exotic smells filled the air. They passed merchants with piles of water jugs, pans, buckets of all sizes, oil lamps, candleholders, and kitchen ladles, knives and prongs. Rug traders and chicken farmers with piles of white and brown eggs, crates of live chickens, roosters, and what appeared to be week-old chicks, hundreds of them, crammed into small crates, spread out along the road. All eyes were on the foreigners as they passed. Not a smile or greeting emanated from the crowd. The aroma of open cooking fires from dozens of small food vendors rose up in clouds of oily blue smoke. The soldiers could not help but salivate at the sight of all those roasting chickens and pigs.

"If I wasn't so scared," sighed a young Italian seaman between gasps, "I'd stop for some of that!"

"*Sì*, but just keep moving, or they'll have you for dinner!"

Having just passed the food merchants, as they approached the southern end of the great wall, from their backside, a rain of tomatoes, fruit, and rotting vegetables showered down on their white uniforms. The packhorses' heads stretched their tether lines reaching for the vegetables.

"*Scheiße!*" Markus blurted out.

"Jesus, Mary, and Joseph!" an Italian voice was heard calling.

"We should shoot those bastards!" another angry Italian exclaimed. Several gunners at the end of the column wheeled around and shouldered their weapons.

"Hold formation! Hold formation!" shouted the sergeant. "Back in ranks, you two! Now!" The gunners did as they were told among grumbles from their comrades.

"Sergeant!" commanded Olivieri. "We will stop at the Anglican Mission just ahead. As soon as we are through the gates, post two men on each of the four corners of the courtyard. Remember, no shooting."

"Yes, sir," the sergeant shot back.

Leading his sailors at a quick pace, Olivieri was panting when he looked up to see thin black smoke swirling above what had been the roof of the Anglican chapel. The eight-foot-high wooden gate to the mission lay by the side of the road. The Italians marched in quick-time into the small courtyard and collapsed on hearing, "Fall out." Men were dispatched as lookouts, and Olivieri and the sergeant, with several sailors, quickly surveyed the compound and outbuildings. All had been looted, ransacked, and vandalized. A dozen or so Chinese bodies, bloated and black, lay scattered through the ruins. The nauseating stench forced most of the seamen as far away as possible.

The chapel had probably been burning a day or two, as only the outer stone walls and facade remained standing. The Boxers used young teenage girls to carry firebrands to torch European property. They called them "the Red Lanterns" because they carried their glowing loads in lantern-like containers.

It was strange to see what appeared to be the ruins of a small Norman Romanesque church in China. *This is like something out of the Middle Ages or Dante's Inferno*, thought Markus. He leaned back on his pack on the ground and took a swig from his canteen. He would have given ten marks in silver for a mug of beer.

It seemed he had just closed his eyes when he heard "All men on deck!"

"Doesn't that sergeant ever stop giving orders," he muttered.

"Call the company to attention, Sergeant."

He did, and Olivieri continued: "At ease, men. I know you're tired, but we can't rest long. It gives the Boxers time to rally their troops. From here, we will proceed north to the London Mission. It's probably in the same shape as this Anglican Mission, but it has an enclosed courtyard that is defendable, assuming the Boxers or Imperial troops aren't occupying it. If we have to, we will bypass the mission and continue directly to Peitang. You just felt the anger of some of the civilians as we passed through the market area. We will be lucky if soiled uniforms are all we encounter.

"Remember, no shooting. In this dense population, we do not want to battle in place. We'll be surrounded quickly with little chance of retreat. Remember, our mission is to get to the cathedral.

"All right, Sergeant, have the horses been watered?"

"Yes, sir."

"Good. Have the seamen form up, column of fours."

From the Anglican Mission to the London Mission was half the distance of the entire march. Most of it was on dirt roads through the ancient crowded city. Some stretches, however, passed through narrow, twisting rabbit warrens with overhanging roofs blocking out the sun. The stench of humanity was overwhelming. The Italian sailors and Markus literally brushed shoulders with assorted Chinese flotsam and jetsam. A few objects bounced off some of the troops without effect.

Olivieri and his men were forced to slow to a fast walk in the steaming heat. Dust and sweat mixed in rivulets down foreheads, necks, and backs. Each sailor carried his military gear, weighing about fifty pounds, depending on how much ammunition he was given. Ammunition was always very heavy. For these sailors, with extra cartridges for the French, had packs of over seventy pounds each, a bone-crushing burden in a Peking summer, and especially for seamen not accustomed to forced marches.

The lieutenant scanned ahead for the turn east onto the broad road leading to the London Mission.

"It's ahead two long blocks on the right," he huffed to his sergeant.

"I'm glad we're out of those narrow streets. I did appreciate the shade for the men though."

"And the smell, sir?" They both managed a smile through clenched teeth.

"At least there's no smoke ahead, sir."

"Yes," Olivieri replied. Very few people were on the road, and Olivieri sensed the unnaturalness of a deserted street in an otherwise crowded city. He grew increasingly uneasy as his company drew to within one hundred yards of the mission.

"Halt!" he ordered. "Sergeant, form the men in two rows twenty abreast, and spread them out. Quietly."

"Yes sir." The order passed to the squad leaders of each of the five deck rifle squads. The sailors extended in a double line completely across the road and up to the edge of the walls and closed doors that lined the streets. All rifles were at the hip, bayonets pointing toward the mission gate.

"Advance at a walk, Sergeant." The order and the Italians moved forward to within twenty-five yards of the open gate. In a burst of savage humanity, dozens of screaming Chinese poured out of the gate running full speed toward the sailors, and swords, spears, knives, hatchets flashed in the sun. Olivieri and his men were stunned for a split second by the sheer audacity of the Boxers.

"Fire!" The order was drowned out by a fusillade of shots from dozens of rifles as the leading Boxers closed to within fifteen yards of the front-row seamen. The sounds of the chanting, screaming war cries of the Chinese mixed with exploding rifle cartridges creating one continuous ongoing explosion of sound. The reverberation against the walls lining the street was deafening.

The sailors fired volley after volley from crouching and standing positions. Chinese wounded and dying littered the street—some twisting, squirming, screaming—and still others came charging on. Reaching the nearest gunners, they engaged in hand-to-hand combat, with Italian bayonets plunging into bellies and chests. Hatchets and spears flew through the air, striking the hard-packed dirt mostly, but some finding a leg, a shoulder, or other vulnerable spot.

Olivieri fired his Remington .38 revolver, reloaded, emptied its six shots, methodically reloaded, and continued, his sword in his other hand thrusting at the charging enemy. Markus fought with the rest of them, bringing down several enemy soldiers, and plunging his French-made German bayonet into the thigh of man wielding a long knife and hatchet. His thrust was so strong it drove the blade completely through the leg and up to the muzzle of his rifle. The enemy screamed and fell forward onto Markus, who could not extract his blade. He dodged the clumsy swing of the axe, grabbing the arm of his opponent in a brief, intense struggle. The man collapsed into unconsciousness as Mathias struggled to free his rifle from the man's leg.

The entire street, shrouded in dense gun smoke, muffled the cries of the wounded. Most of the combatants on both sides were momentarily deafened by the thundering noise. The attack ceased almost as abruptly as it had begun. The remaining Boxers faded away into doorways and side streets, leaving a moaning pile of injured and dying.

"Sergeant, form a defensive perimeter, move the wounded into the compound, and shoot any Boxers that show themselves. Medic! Give me a report of the condition of the wounded after you tend to them. Sergeant, reconnoiter the compound before we move the wounded in and post lookouts."

Olivieri whirled around, looking down both sides of the road. This was exactly what he did not want to happen. A fixed battle! Damn! It would be dark in an hour. All the advantages were with the Boxers. He stepped over dead Chinese and hurried to the medic.

"What's the situation here, Giuseppe?"

"One dead, sir, two unconscious from the shock of their wounds. They won't be able to walk unassisted for a day or two. There are seven walking wounded, mostly stab and slash wounds…no broken bones among them."

"Can the seven carry their packs and rifles?" the lieutenant inquired.

"Yes sir, if they get help putting on the packs, but no double-timing, and they'll need lots of water and breaks in this heat."

"Very good, Giuseppe. Who was killed?"

"It's Deckhand Alfredo Facchinetti, sir. I got his papers."

Olivieri reached for the dead man's military papers. "Thank you. Carry on."

"Comandante," the medic continued, "the German, he's very good with the wounded. He knows a lot of first aid, sir."

"That's good to know, sailor. I'll make note of it." Olivieri turned to look for Sergeant Saldinari, who, aboard ship, was a quartermaster. Saldinari was a true professional military man, very proper, very thorough, and very good with the men, who thought of him in a fatherly way. Olivieri saw him coming out of the gates of the mission on the double. As he came up, he said, "It's all clear, sir, and I've posted the guards."

"Good, Sergeant. We need two stretchers made up and a burial detail. One grave, inside the compound."

"Who is it, sir?"

"Deckhand Facchinetti. Did you know him, Sergeant?"

"No, only by name. He's a new replacement, and I issued him his hammock and gear."

"Okay. Get the men inside the compound. We'll regroup there and plan our next move. See if there is a well and if the water is still good. Make sure the gate can close and can be barricaded."

"Yes, sir. What about the Chinese, sir, the dead and wounded?"

Olivieri scanned the street, littered with dead and moaning wounded. "We don't have enough medicine for our own wounded, and we could be attacked again at any time. Okay, Sergeant, form a detail and move all the Chinese wounded to the far end of the street, by that gate. We'll let their comrades deal with them. Leave the dead where they lie."

"Very good, sir."

A half hour later, all the men were inside the compound, most resting and talking among themselves about the day's fighting. The packhorses had been watered and their feedbags were in place. Although the London Mission had been ransacked, it had not been burned. The well was still good, which was a major break, as the sailors' canteens had long been empty.

The lieutenant and his quartermaster sergeant, realizing no immediate further progress could be made toward the Peitang Cathedral, devised a defensive plan. All the men except the double guards on the walls and gate moved into the stone church, along with the packhorses.

"It's a strong defensive structure, sir, with the added virtue of having the well immediately next to it."

Fortunately, the Boxers were primarily armed with what amounted to medieval weapons: spears, swords, knives, clubs, and hatchets. They had few firearms. However, if the Chinese Imperial troops joined in, they were well armed and trained. Ironically, the Germans trained them, having been hired by the empress several years earlier. So far, for the most part, the empress's troops stayed out of the fighting. The Europeans knew that warlords controlled many units of the Imperial Chinese army. They were powers unto themselves and had the forces to act independent of the empress's wishes. Some, like General Tung, were virulently anti-European.

Olivieri turned to his quartermaster sergeant. "How are the provisions holding up, Sergeant?"

"Well, sir. We have plenty of ammunition, given our resupply for Peitang. Almost all our medical supplies are used up. We packed two days' rations per man, so that is not a problem yet. Our water had completely run out but now with the well," he gestured in the direction of the mission well just outside the side door of the church, "that's not a problem. Transport of the wounded and the walking wounded will slow us down considerably and make us more vulnerable to attack, but morale seems very high, sir."

"Very good, Sergeant. The good news is that we're only five streets over from the cathedral. They certainly heard the sounds of the fighting. The bad news is that the Boxers are probably rallying their troops as we speak. We should assume that we'll be surrounded by morning, if not attacked tonight."

Just then, Bugler Panelli, assigned to guard duty, rushed in with a thin, elderly Chinese man in tow.

"Sir, he's come over the wall in the back of the compound. We nearly shot him. He's got a written message from the cathedral. At least that's what it looks like. I don't read French." He handed it to Comandante Olivieri, who studied it closely in the dim candlelight.

"Very good, Panelli. Back to your post." The Chinese man stood silently nearby, awaiting developments.

Olivieri: "The French know about our battle. They had several Chinese Christians infiltrate the Boxers who saw the fight. They know we won this scrimmage and that we are held up here. Sub-Lieutenant Commander Henri is prepared to meet us halfway with a force of fifteen *fusiliers-marins*. He's included a map with the best route and where we could meet. He said for us to send a message back with this man giving our estimated rendezvous time. Sergeant, call Lancer Mathias over here. He speaks Mandarin. I've got several questions for this courier."

Sergeant Saldinari got up, moved across the stone floor of the church, and gave Markus a gentle tap on the shoulder. Markus was sound asleep.

"*Ja, ja, vas is das?*" he mumbled.

"Lancer, the comandante wants you to interpret for him with that Chinaman over there. Quick now. On your feet. No, no, leave your gear here. This won't take long." They stepped over sleeping sailors and made their way to the far end of the dark church where a few candles were burning.

"Sir, you wanted to speak to me?"

"Yes, Lancer. How's your Mandarin? I have a few questions for this man. He's one of ours."

"I generally can get by in Mandarin, sir."

"Good. Ask him about the Boxers. How many are around this part of the city? And are there any Imperial troops that appear likely to join the fight against us? Ask him."

Mathias greeted the Chinese man in the formal, proper way of greeting elders in China. The man showed a slight surprise and warmed to Markus readily.

Yes, he told Markus, there were at least several hundred Boxers around this neighborhood; and yes, they were recruiting more every day. The relatively small number who were at the London mission at the time of the fight just happened to be encamped there. That's why it hadn't been burned down. Yes, there were Imperial troops all around the city, but so far they had not joined the Boxers in the fight against foreigners, at least not in formal units. However, a number of individual Imperial troops had joined on their own. The French lieutenant said it was only a question of time before the Imperial troops joined up with the Boxers.

No, there was no food shortage yet, but everybody at the Peitang Cathedral thought they were going to die, except the French. There were about two thousand people at the Peitang Cathedral, under the care and supervision of Bishop Favier, and more Chinese Christians were making their way there every day. Most were terrified after being hounded out of their homes and driven from village to village, some beaten, raped, robbed, and murdered. Some villages were friendly to the Christians, some were neutral, and some drove them off into the countryside. This madness was sweeping the country.

The questions kept coming, and Markus tried to keep up with the rapid answers in Mandarin.

Finally, Olivieri said, "Okay, that's enough. I think we have the picture of what we're up against. Sergeant, give this man some food and water and send him back over the wall with my reply. But quietly. We don't want him intercepted by the enemy."

"Yes, sir. Anything else, sir?"

"No, Sergeant. Get some sleep yourself." Markus turned to go. Olivieri spoke up again. "Lancer, you did a fine job translating. I understand you also were quite a help to Medic Giuseppe today. Thank you for assisting my wounded sailors."

"Oh, that, sir. It's what I was trained to do…we were trained to do, back in Bavaria. The crown prince took a special interest in making sure all troops were trained in first aid for the field."

"Really?" replied Olivieri.

"*Ja*, well, it was mostly how to stop the bleeding and splinting broken bones and protecting a wound, sir."

"I see. You've become quite an asset to my unit, Lancer Mathias. What other talents do you have?"

"None that I can think of, sir." They both smiled.

"Now get some well-deserved sleep. We've got a big day ahead of us tomorrow."

"*Gute Nacht*, sir." Markus slipped into German as he stepped back to his place by the wall.

"*Buonanotte,*" replied the commander. Both men, at opposite ends of the church, were asleep in minutes.

The night passed quietly, with the guards changing every two hours so that every man got some sleep. Just before dawn, a thud was heard in the deserted courtyard. Guards could be heard scurrying around. They burst into the church as Olivieri and several other sailors awoke.

"What is it? What's going on?" he inquired.

One of the guards exclaimed, "It's the Chinaman, sir. His head has just been thrown over the wall!"

Oh my God, thought Olivieri. *They have the note and the map. Now what are we to do?*

The sergeant was awake and heard the news. He quickly went into the courtyard to confirm the identity of the man.

He returned, and he gave his report. "It's him, all right, sir. Now what are we going to do? They've probably got the map and letter. They'll be waiting for us and the French."

"Right," said Olivieri. "We're in a strategically strong defensive position here, plenty of ammunition and water, but only one day's worth of food. But this is not our objective. We've got to develop another plan to get to the cathedral. It may require us to simply make a break for it, but the wounded will really slow us down, and if we get into hand-to-hand combat, we'll be hard pressed to protect the wounded."

Dawn broke while the sailors ate their breakfast, visited the latrine, such as it was, and packed their gear and filled canteens. Suddenly, they could hear a great deal of gunfire from the direction of the cathedral.

"Sergeant! Get someone up into that belfry and see what's going on. Form up the company and be prepared to move out. Put the stretcher-bearers between the horses. If we can't move out we'll move the men to battle stations, as we discussed." Everyone jumped into action.

"What do you see, sailor?" Olivieri called up to the man wedged into the tight rafters of the bell tower.

"There's gun smoke and shooting about three blocks away in a line between us and the Peitang, sir. I think it's the French... It *is* the French...I just saw a uniform between the buildings. Looks like they are fighting their way here, sir."

"Are you sure about the uniforms, sailor?" the commandant asked.

"Yes sir. I saw at least three of them...they're wearing red trousers."

"Good! Sergeant! I'll address the company. We're moving out! This is our chance and we're taking it!"

"Yes sir!" The stretcher-bearers prepared the wounded, while the packhorses were loaded and the rest of the Italians fell into four columns facing toward their leader. They waited expectantly for Lieutenant Olivieri.

"Men, the French are battling their way here as I speak. This is our chance to complete our mission to get to the Peitang Cathedral. We will be moving out and marching in quick-time in the direction of the French, who are about five long blocks away. Plan on considerable enemy action as we go. I have assigned six riflemen to each of the two stretchers for their protection, and two men for each of the walking wounded. We must avoid being strung out too far. We want to be able to concentrate fire if need be. The enemy probably suspects we will try a breakout. You are authorized to fire at will, but we do not want to slow down or stop. Keep moving forward. Sergeant, are you prepared to move out?"

"Yes sir."

"Okay then. Move out!"

The Italians marched in quick-time through the gates and turned east toward the cathedral. Rounding the wall at the end of the block of buildings, they immediately encountered a group of armed men, surely Boxers. Spears and hatchets flew through the air toward the sailors as the Boxers charged.

Olivieri shouted, "Front rank fire!"

The four sailors in the front of the column of fours opened up on the onrushing, shouting crowd, a hundred feet in front of them.

"Sergeant! Bring your men abreast of the front rank, sixteen across! Fire at will and keep moving forward!"

The Boxers seemed disoriented with firing in front of them and now behind them. Some of the enemy began to seek shelter in doorways and behind gates that lined the street. Some appeared on rooftops, throwing assorted objects down onto the sailors. One of the stretcher-bearers, hit with a spear in his thigh, collapsed and his corner of the stretcher collapsed with him, almost dumping the wounded man onto the ground. Several of the guards quickly grabbed the stretcher and the stretcher-bearer.

"Medic! Medic! Over here!" One of the guards took it upon himself to pull the spear out of the man's leg just as the medic arrived and applied a thick bandage to the wound.

"Stay on your feet, sailor. It's going to hurt, but it's not too serious, and you didn't lose very much blood. You two," nodding to two in the guard detail, "help him move along and keep him up. He'll be okay."

The firing continued, with Olivieri directing several men to fire at the roofline to keep the Boxers' heads down. Fortunately, a morning breeze was blowing the heavy smoke from the guns through the ranks and back down the street, which helped protect the rear guard.

Markus was in the front ranks firing into the diminishing opposing forces when he saw the blue and red uniforms of the French *fusiliers-marins* coming around a corner three hundred feet in front of him. As the shooting died down, he began to shout in French: "Comrades, comrades, over here!"

The French commander of the fifteen *fusiliers-marins* came charging up the road toward the Italians as the Boxers quickly melted away into doors, gates, and narrow side streets. More Boxer casualties sprawled in the street up and down the site of the scrimmage. Most of them were young, scrawny men from the countryside. As the two military units met, there were handshakes and slaps on the backs and broad smiles all around even though most of the two units didn't speak the other's language.

Olivieri and the French Sub-Lieutenant Commander, Paul Henri, greeted each other and conferred briefly. They formed a joint rear guard and prepared a defensive marching order. The French officer led the combined soldiers through deserted streets toward the Peitang Cathedral, leaving behind the dead and dying Boxers. Sporadic shots were heard from the rear guard as a few angry Boxers kept up a harassing pursuit.

Ahead, they could see the gleaming white stone cathedral towers looming up above the one- and two-story Chinese buildings surrounding the Catholic church.

Cheers rose up into a wonderful crescendo of welcome as the French and Italian men marched quickly through the gates into the relative safety of the walled community.

Bishop Favier was waiting for them in front of the large Gothic edifice, the sun piercing the magnificent stained glass rose window over the south portal. Hundreds of Catholic and other Christian converts and dozens of European civilians crowded around to hear the priest make a short speech and give a blessing to all who gathered there.

"These are the times that try men's souls," he began dramatically in his melodious voice, quoting Thomas Paine, an American revolutionary war pamphleteer.

"But God, in his infinite mercy, has sent us these brave men, soldiers of Italy, yes, and soldiers of God also, to protect and defend His chosen people, we here, gathered together, on this sacred ground. They have come to shield us from the Godless hordes without. Pray for our deliverance," he continued, "so we Christians can continue our holy work among the multitudes so deserving of our care."

The crowd was spellbound by the bishop, famous for his inspiring sermons, and they were now, more than ever, in need of reassurance. Bishop Favier continued for a few more uplifting minutes and then concluded with a general benediction, before stepping down and moving through the crowd to greet Captain Olivieri and his men.

Bishop Favier heard the reports of attacks on rural missions and the intimidation of converts months earlier and warned the European authorities that the situation was getting dire and that defensive actions must be taken. Virtually all he approached ignored him. He took it upon himself to gather large quantities of rice and other grains, all the medical supplies he could get his hands on, even a number of old rifles with ammunition.

He also got his parishioners to strengthen the walls of the compound and in several places even raise their height. Since a road ran completely through the church compound, he crudely barricaded both ends. This foresight was remarkable and of crucial importance. With the continuing arrival of refugees from the surrounding countryside, resources were strained to the limit. Everything was scrupulously rationed: food, medical supplies, ammunition, even living space. He had done all he could do before the gathering storm, and now that storm had hit his swelling community. It was up to God, his frightened parishioners, and these meager troops from France and Italy to hold back the unforgiving tide of enraged Boxers.

Markus was happy to have made it this far on his own secret

mission to see Li Ling again and to hold her in his arms. But he knew he was less than halfway to Li's father's walled home out beyond Tartar City. He surveyed the interior of the cathedral compound and reflected on what he had experienced in just getting this far. And with a company of Italian sailors no less. He'd come to realize that his goal was more than ambitious. He had to figure out how to move on. He couldn't wear this uniform, let alone his spike helmet, outside of these walls. Levi was right.

Meanwhile, Captain Olivieri was shown where to billet his sailors by Captain Henri; and after stowing his gear, Markus and the other troops used their one-hour "leave" to look around and get the feel of their new erstwhile home. Markus sat down on the steps in front of the church, his ever-present Mauser rifle leaning between his legs. He was already thinking of ways they could traverse Tartar City and the great beyond.

A few moments later, he was jarred back to reality by the bark of rifle fire coming from high up the redbrick walls of the Imperial City that overlooked Peitang Cathedral.

"Oh, brother. Here we go again," he shouted to no one in particular as he dove for cover against the hand-carved stone blocks of the building. He could hear return fire from inside the compound and saw the pings of bullets hitting and chipping the upper edges of the great crimson ramparts before him. It was over as fast as it had started. Silence, silence except for the moans of one Chinese and one Frenchman, withering in the sun, by the side of the cathedral.

Markus scrambled up and ran to assist the wounded, keeping one eye on the upper edge of danger. He could see that this was going to be a lot harder than even Levi thought.

CHAPTER III

Passage to the Lakes,

Spears in the Sky,

AFTER THE BRIEF scrimmage, Markus, the Italian and French sailors, and leaders of the civilian defenders assembled in the heavily fortified cathedral. Bishop Favier began by defining what life had been like in the compound the last few weeks and concluded, "Constant dangers are expected in the days to come."

"When he isn't ministering to his growing flock, he's a cool, efficient administrator, and a realist and pragmatist all rolled into one," someone offered. The bishop knew what would happen if the Boxers overran the compound. He was ready to fight on the barricades if need be.

With a nod from the bishop, Captain Olivieri and Captain Henri addressed the troops, assigned battle positions, duty rosters, and other essentials and then dismissed the soldiers. Olivieri called Lancer Mathias aside.

"Lancer, I want you to report to Bishop Favier's office in the sacristy off to the left side of the altar for a meeting in half an hour."

"Yes, sir," replied Markus as the captain turned to engage in other conversations. *I wonder what that's all about?*

All the key people were at the meeting: Favier, Olivieri, Henri, a half dozen of the civilian leadership, the store's clerk, medical doctor, eight priests and missionary ministers, and Lancer Mathias. Bishop Favier, calling the meeting to order, quickly turned the meeting over to the two captains.

"Gentlemen, I asked Bishop Favier to call this meeting because of a very important assignment that must be carried out to assist in the survival of the Peitang Cathedral community," began Olivieri. "Accompanying my sailors on our journey here is a young Imperial German soldier who volunteered for the assignment I am about to describe to you. He is standing before you now…Lancer Mathias. At ease."

Markus relaxed his stance as everyone in the room stared at him for a moment.

"The assignment is to send back to the legation a detailed accounting of our position here and our probable needs in the near future. No one knows how long this rebellion will last, of course. We, the defenders of the European community and our Chinese friends, have a better chance of survival if the legations know our condition. We have two tasks before us at this meeting; one is to document our resources, all our resources, and create a report of our status here that will be transmitted back to the legations. After conferring with all of you in your spheres of responsibility, Captain French will prepare the report. As we all know, the situation outside this compound is deteriorating every day. Therefore, speed is of the essence in compiling the data and conveying it back to the legations." He paused.

"Our second task today is to devise the best way to send the information back to the legations in the quickest possible time. Now Lancer Mathias here has volunteered for this dangerous task," he nodded toward the German, "but it is for us to decide the best strategy to accomplish our mission, and whether Mathias is the best man to do it."

Captain French was already assembling the list of existing resources while Olivieri continued.

"I will entertain suggestions from you all as to the most secure means of communicating with the legations."

The group commenced a lively debate on how to get the information across Tartar City without it being intercepted and the courier killed. No one thought it could be done easily, and most thought it was suicide. Markus, listening to all these discussions in French, Italian, English, Russian, and Mandarin, didn't like what he heard. The assorted group did not know that he could understand their languages, except Russian, so they spoke frankly of his slim chances. Markus felt they looked at him as if he were an innocent man being led to the gallows.

After considerable discussion, a night attempt was agreed to be the most practical time to make the attempt because of the advantage of cover of darkness. Tartar City was not like most European cities where strings of lights were rapidly going up, illuminating the urban night. Most of this city was black as pitch on a moonless night. And in the narrow, winding streets, even moonlight barely penetrated.

The discussion turned to who should go and under what conditions. Many options were suggested: one man, no, two men, preferably Chinese, our fastest runners, no, a casual drunk in peasant dress, no in Boxer dress, in merchant's dress, no, in monk's robes. He or they must be unarmed, no, armed with knives, no, guns, but revolvers only, with a tiny document hidden on his person, no! Inside a vegetable that could be thrown away, no! Memorized! Olivieri and French listened to it all, discounting one idea after another.

From the side of the gathering, a man rose to speak. He raised his hand for silence. The Chinese in the group immediately fell silent and seemed to pay great respect to this middle-aged man who had not spoken earlier. He was dressed in the finest silks and in aristocratic fashion. So fine was he dressed—in crimson, gold, and deep blue embroidered robes down to the floor—that he could have been one of the Imperial princes, of which there were many. Heads turned as the room grew silent. Bishop Favier stood up and was about to introduce this nobleman, but sat back down in response to the slightest of gestures which he alone noted.

The mysterious man greeted the group formally, first in Mandarin, then in French, followed by English, Portuguese, and Japanese. Everyone in the room was at rapt attention, including the two captains. Markus, standing nearby, could smell the sandalwood perfume of the fan held in a perfectly manicured hand on which a pure yellow gold ring held a huge green jade stone. The fan hand swayed back and forth slowly, which drew attention to a grotesque four-inch-long, curved fingernail. Markus was transfixed.

The man began to speak with an almost instant simultaneous translation, as he spoke first in Mandarin and then in French. Many of the Europeans knew enough French to understand him.

"Please forgive my people," he began in a slow, methodical tone that could have had the slightest French accent, "for the discomfort they have brought you. Most are lowly peasants easily swayed by clever rhetoric and magic. While they have certain, shall we say, grievances with their European guests, their perchance for violence does them great discredit, as they are, in most cases, a gentle people. Be that as it may, your needs are great, and a solution to your present circumstances requires immediacy.

"May I suggest a possible route and method for this enterprise you are contemplating? I live on the other side of those ramparts, in Imperial City."

Everyone in the room looked at each other, and a noticeable murmur could be heard.

"It may be possible to have your courier enter Imperial City and travel by boat at night, south through the three lakes that flow south to the south wall. That is half your adventurous trip to the legations." A slight smile passed across the stranger's face. "Once inside the ramparts, I have a boat that may be of use. It can be rowed to the southern end of the waterway and the south wall. From there, under disguise and with bribes, your courier travels east to the far corner of the Imperial City ramparts. It is several hundred yards over the wall to the Imperial Carriage Park and the Han Lin Library, which backs up to the British Legation. It can be done in one night. I would estimate four hours if everything goes smoothly." His fan continued to move in undulating sweeps.

The room was quiet for several moments until everyone began to talk at once about what they had just heard, eyes glancing continually at the regal visitor.

"Do you believe him?" "Do you think it would work?" "Can we trust him? Who is he?" "Where did he learn all those languages?" "What if he is a spy? He'd give our position away to the Boxers!" "It sounds like a good plan to me." On it went for a few minutes until Bishop Favier stood up and stretched to his full height as a show of authority. The room quieted down.

"Thank you, Your Excellency Chou Lee, for offering your enlightened assistance in our hour of need. You have always been a friend to our community here at the Peitang Cathedral."

Captain Henri looked at Captain Olivieri. Their eyes met in immediate recognition of a golden opportunity. After a further brief discussion among all in attendance, they agreed the military leaders would work out details and make the final decision.

As the others filed out of the sacristy, the nobleman Chou Lee approached Bishop Favier and the two captains.

"Lancer Mathias, stay for this," Favier said.

"I offer my trusted eunuch servant, Chang Pao Fu, as a guide for your courier," Chou began as he slid his hands into the silken sleeves of his crossed arms. "I will guide them both through a very secret route into the Imperial City. I regret I cannot reveal this route to you." He paused. "It is an Imperial secret, punishable by death to me and my entire household if revealed. I myself have used it only once, to come here to retrieve my servant who succumbed to your Christian ways. He has been with me a long time and is my most trusted and able servant." Chou Lee hesitated a moment.

"Of course, I am assuming you will accept my plan for your courier." He spoke in a very quiet voice and with a raised eyebrow. "It is the safest plan. All other plans require traversing Tartar City, which, as we speak, is filling with my angry countrymen. Your courier would be in grave danger of discovery."

Captain Henri spoke up. "And when do you advise this mission to take place?"

"Tomorrow night. If we leave here by eleven, your courier should be at the legations before dawn, at the latest. That departure gives you time to complete your status report for the legations." The two captains looked at each other again.

"Have you seen your servant Chang here in the compound?" asked Olivieri.

"Yes, he is pleased I came for him. He is ready to return to my household and his duties," said Chou.

"Good, that's very good," said Olivieri. "We will discuss your proposal and get back to you shortly. Thank you for your offer, Chou."

"Yes, thank you for your help," said Henri.

Bishop Favier got up from his heavy wooden chair, came around from behind his desk, and ushered Chou Lee deeper into the cathedral back rooms, speaking to him in a quiet murmur.

He returned shortly.

Markus stood quietly listening to the entire conversation,

fascinated by the strange Chinese nobleman and his eunuch and the plan to go through the Imperial City. It seemed so exotic, he didn't even think of the danger.

This was so different from Germany. He'd never seen Kaiser Wilhelm. He had seen King Ludwig the III of Bavaria and all the royal regalia at parades near the Nymphenburg Palace in Munich, but it wasn't anything like this. Markus had forgotten for a moment where he was as he daydreamed of home.

"So, Lancer Mathias," said Olivieri, with a slight smile on his face, "what do you think of Chou's plan? Are you up to it, soldier?" The two captains were staring at Markus.

"Yes sir. I think it's a good plan. Better than those narrow streets out there with all those Boxers. Yes sir, I'm ready."

"Good, Lancer Mathias," Captain Henri said. "However, Captain Olivieri, Bishop Favier, and I will discuss the details before we make a final decision. You're excused to the barracks… no discussion of this to anyone."

"Yes sir." Mathias saluted, turned, and left the room. He walked down the aisle of the church after first genuflecting before the altar. Before he reached the massive wooden doors, he dipped his middle fingers in the holy water basin and made the sign of the cross. His mind was racing; he was not thinking of the Imperial City secret route back to the legations, but of his still unknown route to see Li Ling.

Events moved rapidly.

"The decision has been made to go with the plan Chou Lee advanced," the bishop announced. "Some concerns about Chou Lee's trustworthiness were resolved, and the report by Captain Henri is complete."

All agreed that Mathias should be the courier as he had been in on all the discussions and saw, firsthand, the circumstances at Peitang. He was ordered to remove his uniform and assume local garb for the mission that night.

"You'll be given double rations today, and we advise you to get some rest."

As he lay on his bunk in the crowded barracks, he heard occasional gunfire but no major battles.

Bishop Favier commandeered the Mongolian packhorses used by the Italians, one being slaughtered for food to feed the growing number of refugees arriving at the cathedral. For most Chinese, meat was a luxury, but here in the compound for the next two weeks, horsemeat soup was the staple. Favier, ever conscious of resources, was not about to feed six horses for long.

It was almost dark when an Italian sailor shook Markus awake.

"The captain says for you to get ready and report to the bishop's office at nine. And bring your pistola, *bang, bang*! Ha!"

Ha, yourself, Markus thought with a smile. He was getting out of there that night, and on his way to see his *fräulein*.

Markus spent the afternoon poring over a detailed map of the Imperial City from the bishop. It included the Forbidden City, the Inner City, and the Chinese City. All four made up the greater city of Peking. One other feature of the map of particular note for Markus was the extended countryside outside the outer walls. To his delight, he even found Li Ling's village, An-Tsun, lying close to a tributary of the Hun Ho River. He spent two hours studying the map, to the great satisfaction of the two captains, who were impressed with Markus' dedication to the mission. Markus smiled as he noted the three lakes linked together leading south through the Imperial City. But he also saw that the lakes also extended north to and through the northern walls of the Imperial City all the way through the northern part of Tartar City and even out beyond the furthest wall!

That's my way out of this dragon's den! he almost said out loud. *It's perfect. Chang leads me to the lakes, Chang finds the boat, I dump Chang, I head north out of this mess and into the arms of my*

Li Ling. Levi would be proud!

Now, he gathered the meager gear he was told to bring. Reflecting on the daring adventure he was about to undertake, he knew he could not let down the legation by not delivering the report, but his goal lay in the opposite direction of the legation.

He assured himself that now he was going to An-Tsun village. How to get the dispatch pouch, now slung under his shirt next to his revolver, to the legations, was his dilemma. As he passed out of the barracks, he handed his military pack to the Italian supply sergeant.

"Here are my clothes and helmet. Take good care of them. I'll be back when this is all over."

"Okay, German. Good luck!" the sergeant said cheerfully as he took the bundle.

Markus shuffled off to the rendezvous point with the two captains, Chou Lee, and Chang. His smelly peasant's costume, a pile of rags commandeered off one of the locals, revolted him with its smell and greasiness. All the money he borrowed from Levi, most in gold and silver coin, was stuck in a deep pocket he mended himself that afternoon. *My mother would die if she could see me like this*, thought Markus.

The departure took place as scheduled at eleven o'clock that night, after the two captains and the bishop exchanged final strategies. Captain Olivieri wished Lancer Mathias good luck. Bishop Favier blessed Mathias and Chang and wished them God speed. Chou Lee led his servant Chang and Markus out of the compound through a narrow breach in the convoluted perimeter wall.

Once outside, Chou walked briskly but quietly down several side streets, his head held high as he passed assorted characters milling around in front of shops, gates, and doorways. Faint orange and yellow lanterns were all the illumination available as Chou's two "servants" followed behind him with their heads down. Turning into a narrow passageway, he whispered over his shoulder, "Take hold of the end of my fan, Chang. And you, soldier, take hold of Chang's arm. It's going to be pitch-black ahead and for the next hundred yards or so."

The three of them slowed as it grew darker. Markus sensed he was in a confined space as they passed through one creaking door after another, tripping up several stone steps, the scent of recently burned candles in the still air. It was hot and muggy in his ragged clothes, and the heavy pistol scraped his chest as it swung back and forth. He had packed the numerous coins tightly so at least they didn't jingle as he walked.

More turns, the sound of a heavy iron latch moving, whispers he couldn't make out. The surface became very smooth for walking; it was wood, polished, and all of a sudden a strong smell of incense.

We must be in a temple, thought Markus, *or in a wealthy home with a polished floor*. He couldn't believe how dark it was. He heard the grating of stone sliding on stone. Some grunts. His heart beat faster. The air became cool, a breeze in his face.

"Now we descend a long flight of stairs. It may be slippery. There's a low ceiling," Chou whispered. They all stepped gingerly at first down several stone steps. Behind them, they could hear the grating of stone on stone and a final bang as the passage they were in was sealed behind them.

Mathias thought it was like a tomb. More steps down and then a flat floor. He heard a match scratch against stone. A glorious burst of yellow light, and then a flicker illuminated Chou Lee's face. He smiled, stooped down, and picked up a thick stick. In a second, it burst into flame and lit up the damp walls of the passageway. The staircase descended into darkness.

"Here we can use light," Chou said, "but at the other end it must again be dark." He turned, and they continued downward.

Being able to use a torch lifted Markus' spirits. After what must have been fifty or sixty steps, he heard Chou step into water.

"When I came three days ago, it was dry. There must have been a storm in the mountains. During the rainy season, I have heard this passage is completely flooded. The underground water level rises, just like in our wells," said Chou.

He lifted the hem of his magnificent robes. Chang quickly lifted the back. Chou finally placed his foot on the tunnel's floor. They were all standing in six or seven inches of water. There was no breeze now, only a heavy, damp, musty cold…colder than any of them had felt since early last spring, as the final snows melted in northern China.

Markus pulled his ragged shirt closer around his neck. "Fifteen minutes ago I was sweating, and now I'm freezing! Let's just get out of here," he said.

Chou set the pace. They moved quickly, and bits of the burned torch hissed as they hit the water. The water was now a foot deep, and there was a lot of splashing as they progressed.

Sound is amplified down here, thought Markus. The two men in front of him were breathing heavily.

"The water's getting shallower; the floor must be rising," Markus said excitedly.

"Yes, it is," said Chou.

"Thank God for that!"

Ahead lay a long, narrow, sweeping passageway that began rising rapidly, but without steps. It curved in and to the right in a tighter and tighter arc.

"We must be above ground by now," Markus said aloud. "The air is warmer, and the walls aren't damp." No one responded. They were now in a four-foot-wide spiral staircase, the steps of which abruptly ended at a wooden door.

Chou spoke. "I must blindfold you now and put out the flame. You and Chang will be led to a portal in the garden by the lake. Remain completely quiet and cover your head, soldier. I will meet you there. Stay out of sight. There are many Imperial troops here in Imperial City who favor the Boxers and hate Christians." He looked on Chang with what Mathias thought was sorrow.

Chou put the torch in a wall sconce and blindfolded the two. He rapped gently on the door, and soon someone was on the other side. Another iron bolt slid, and the door creaked, and there were more whispers. Suddenly, Markus felt firm hands clasp both his arms and direct him forward.

Fifteen minutes later, their blindfolds were removed, and Chang and Markus were firmly pushed out into the night.

They found themselves standing in the shadows of a secluded doorway overhung with vines and other foliage. A quarter moon shone low in the sky as they looked out onto an undulating landscape, narrow, next to a lake. Trees, shrubs, and large stones protruded from the ground like tall sculptures in a park. Markus had seen these strange and gigantic rocks before, mostly in temple gardens. These strange shapes, many times with deep, natural holes, some passing completely through, were called philosopher's stones. Since ancient times they had been highly revered for their aesthetic qualities. The air, warm and refreshing, had the smell of jasmine. Across the lake lay the fabled Forbidden City, its walls rising out of the mist.

Markus was awed by the significance of this place. *No one gets to see this. Nobody in our whole company has ever gotten beyond these massive ramparts, not even Captain Mayerling. No one gets in except the highest officials*, he thought. *The German ambassador might get to go in there, or maybe the crown prince could, if he ever came to China.*

Uneasy with the legendary mystery and the massiveness of what lay before him, he fidgeted with the dispatch pouch inside his shirt. Chang, standing beside him in silence, seemed almost serene. He stared off into the distance, into a mysterious world Markus knew nothing about.

As they both waited for Chou, two figures appeared along the edge of the lake heading in their direction. Two tall spears silhouetted against the moon's light reflected in the water. Chang's hand slowly rose in front of Markus' body and pressed him back against the wall in the deepest shadows. The two figures grew larger. There were sounds that were barely audible. The two stopped almost directly between the portal and the lake. They turned and looked back. Chang's eyes followed their line of sight. Chang's hand again pressed Markus.

Four more spears appeared as thick black needles against the creamy moonlight in the lake. Markus held his breath. Sweat ran down from his temple, coursing in front of his ear and down his neck. He could feel it pass his dispatch pouch. The four caught up with the two and exchanged muffled comments.

Suddenly three of them turned, looked in the portal's direction, and started walking toward the hidden intruders. Markus moved his hand up toward his gun, his body rigid with tension. Chang pressed hard again. Markus stopped. Absolute stillness. Between the six armed men and the portal stood one of the giant standing stones. The three men stopped just on the far side of it. He could hear the clatter of steel spear tips against stone.

What are they doing? He could hardly breathe as he listened for them. It was barely discernible, but he could hear a familiar sound. His shoulders slumped from relief. They were pissing on the philosopher stone!

The three laughed as they gathered their spears and rejoined the others. Markus was less amused. It had been too close. And where was Chou? The six Imperial Guards moved on down the lake out of sight. More waiting. Chang had lowered his hand and was casually leaning against the portal door, when, seemingly out of nowhere, Chou appeared.

In a very low voice Chou spoke:

"So, you see, you have arrived safely in the Imperial City. I was detained some distance away to allow our brave Imperial Guards to pass. If it were only my servant Chang and me, the guards would not disturb us, but a third person might have required some explanation. The risk of detection must be minimized. The boat is tied near the Moon Viewing Pagoda up the shoreline three hundred meters ahead. Chang and I will walk along the shore. You, German, walk along the edge of the wall until you are directly across from the pagoda. Watch me. If I move my fan at my side like this…you must stop and remain perfectly still. I will signal you when to come. Don't run. Walk in a humble fashion, as I am sure you have seen many servants and slaves do. It is our custom here in China." Chou smiled at Markus. "It appears the guards have moved on sufficiently for us to proceed."

The Chinese aristocrat, with Chang following, strolled out from the shadows of the portal and headed north along the lake. Markus followed instructions and crept along the wall as best he could, dodging branches and bushes in the dark, and dreading the sound of every snapped twig. He could see the tower of the small pagoda. It actually sat in the lake with a short, ornate stone bridge arching out to it. Minutes later Markus was opposite the appointed spot. He waited.

Chou hadn't told him what the signal was! Markus waited, and he watched.

The pagoda had open sides on the first level so one could see through to the lake. Chou moved his arm in a wide, circular motion, and as he was standing in the moonlight, Markus immediately understood. He walked hunched over the way he thought a Chinese servant would. Over the bridge and a few short steps brought him to Chou's side. Chou's attention was elsewhere. He held up his fan to his lips in a signal of silence. He pointed up. Chou, Markus, and Chang looked up into the darkness of the staircase by the wall.

Sounds! What sounds? The three stood there perfectly still. Movement! There *was* movement directly above them. Scuffling and groans, and moans and gasps, and the group realized that they were hearing lovemaking on the second floor! They looked at each other.

Chou approached Markus very closely, bent near his ear, and whispered instructions. Markus slowly but steadily undid his ragged shirt, slid the dispatch pouch over his head, and handed it to Chang. Then he silently stepped to the edge of the pagoda on the water side, climbed over the railing, and slipped into the water. He submerged himself up to his neck and clung to the rough, stony edge of the temple-like structure.

Chou and Chang began talking, chuckling and scuffling around the stony floor, commenting on the beauty of the lake in moonlight, the sweetness of the air, the gracefulness of the night birds wheeling over the water. More sounds from above. This time sounds obviously intended to be heard on the first floor. Two figures emerged from the shadowy staircase.

"Good evening, sir," the first one said in a manly voice. "A lovely evening."

"Oh, we have company here, Chang, for our moon viewing," Chou exclaimed enthusiastically. "It's always a more enchanting experience when shared with others."

"We can't stay, sir. We were just on our patrol duties, and it's a good vantage point to observe up and down the lake. We must continue our duties, sir."

"Of course, your duties come first," Chou replied cordially.

The two Imperial Guards quickly crossed the bridge and headed south along the lake. Chou smiled as he leaned over the railing and signaled Markus. Chang hurried to assist.

"A short interruption, and now, how was the water?" Chou asked.

"Warm, really warm, not like back home. I'm used to Alpine

lakes, cold Alpine lakes…and the air is so warm, I'm sure I'll dry quickly." Chang handed back the dispatch pouch to Markus.

"You keep it for now, Chang, until I dry out," said Markus.

The three climbed into the rowboat and shoved off.

"German," Chou commanded. "You must lie down on the floor. Those two guards saw two people at the Moon Viewing Pagoda, not three." They moved out into the center of the lake equal distance from both shores, Chang pulling steadily on the ores. The boat had two sets of ores and was quite long with a flat bottom and square ends fore and aft. Chou sat quietly thinking of all the potentialities ahead. Markus shifted his revolver to the side of his waistband to be more comfortable.

There was a general current south, so the rowing was smooth and easy. There were, in fact, three lakes to traverse. Two arching stone bridges, like the Moon Viewing Bridge, separated the three. All went well until they passed under the first bridge. Chou had carefully scanned the shoreline leading up to the bridge and the three-arched structure itself to make sure no one was near. They glided under, and Chang began rowing again.

Chou was the first to see it, another boat, similar to theirs, to the right, just pushing off from the shore four hundred meters ahead. Again needles in the sky. How many? Five! Chou quickly tapped Markus on the leg, leaned down as Markus curled around, trying to stay below the gunwale of the boat.

Chou: "Another boat ahead, over the side, on the left, quickly. If they come up on us, stay under the boat."

Markus said nothing. He slipped over the left side without a splash, and slid into the inky water. With his pocket full of gold and silver coins and his heavy pistol in his waistband, Markus had no trouble staying low in the water. He wondered how deep the lake was. Only the fingers of his right hand touched the boat. They pressed into the top edge of the stern.

The two boats were on a collision course two hundred meters ahead, and it was obvious the Imperial Guards intended to intercept them. Markus worked his way around the side of the boat so he could see without being seen. He saw the five spears pointing skyward on the oncoming boat. He worked his way back around the boat to put Chou between the guards and himself. He rose out of the water high enough to whisper over the stern: "Chou! Chou!"

"Silence!"

Markus ignored him and said in a very low voice, "Chou, promise me you will get the dispatch pouch to the legation if anything happens to me, promise!"

"Yes, yes, of course, now get down and be quiet!"

Markus slipped back down into the darkness just as Chou started to recite poetry in a soft but audible voice.

"On a night of infinite beauty,

I sense your forbidden touch,

As the moon caresses the mountaintop."

Markus knew he was covering for the possibility that the guards had heard them talking. Chou continued his recitations, and Chang continued a rhythmic sweep of the ores. In a matter of minutes, the two boats met and the Imperial Guards pulled alongside.

"Good evening again, sir," a familiar voice said as one of the guards stepped into Chou's boat. It rocked back and forth, and Chou steadied himself with his hands on either side. Several of the guards used their spears to steady the two crafts. Chang sat silently staring down.

"And good evening to you. The Empire appreciates its professional soldiers doing their duties so diligently, and on such a beautiful night."

"Thank you, sir." The guard looked at Chang and then back at Chou.

DETAIL OF A PAINTING OF 'THE MOON VIEWING PAGODA'.

"It's quite late to be boating, sir, and I see you have some water on the floor."

"Yes, my servant is not a particularly good oarsman, but on such a night I ignore such inadequacies."

"Are you going far, sir?"

"Just down to the far end of the lower lake. I have several more poems I enjoy reciting in this cool night air. Now, we will be moving along and allow the empress's guards to proceed."

The guard continued: "I see you have a second pair of ores and ore locks. Your servant seems tired. Several of my guards will serve Your Excellency as rowers and return your boat to the Moon Viewing Pagoda." The guard stood within a meter of Chou and towered over him. He had a slightly menacing tone of voice. Chou had to make a quick decision on how to proceed.

Since the stern of the boat cantilevered a meter out over the water, Markus was able to keep his mouth out of the water as he faced straight up, his body floating directly under the boat as Chou had instructed. He heard the entire conversation.

Jesus, they are going to stay with the boat all the way to the end of the third lake, thought Markus. *What's going to happen when we get to the shallows? I can't stay under this boat in two feet of water the whole way!*

Chou said, "That's a kind offer, but I prefer to drift, and Chang can continue to row slowly. I am in no…"

He was cut off.

"I insist on escorting you to your destination, sir. It is an honor to serve the nobility." He turned and stepped into Chou's boat and ordered two guards in as rowers.

"They will proceed at whatever pace you prefer, of course. Good evening, sir." The spear-bearers pushed off before Chou could formulate a plausible rebuttal.

"As you wish, your guards are most welcome. I do enjoy a small audience for my poetry." Chou watched the guards' boat pull ahead of them and head for the opposite shore.

"Proceed," Chou ordered in a quiet voice, and the two guards, sitting next to each other, pulled on their separate ores. Chang sat motionless, his ores dragging in the water.

LANCER BANNERS

CHAPTER IV

Alone

MARKUS FELT THE boat surge forward with the first pull and saw the tips of the ores slice into the water. His feet were pointing toward the bow, and he immediately doubled over at the waist, his head hitting the underside of the hull with a thump. Chou heard the sound and instantly shifted his body and feet noisily. Markus' hands had been gripping the two sides of the boat just below the waterline. As the boat moved forward, his body rolled over itself, and his precarious hold began to slip away. In an instant, his hands, lubricated by the water, slid along the sides of the hull and off the end of the boat!

He was still under water and knew instinctively that he had to stay under as long as he could. He rolled over and breast-stroked in the opposite direction. With his lungs about to burst, he rolled over again and floated on his back with only his nose and mouth out of the water. He took in long, deep breaths. Every time he filled his lungs, his chest rose to the surface.

Markus resisted looking back toward the boat for fear of being detected, but finally his curiosity overcame his fear and he looked back. Chou and the boat were diminishing in size as they drifted south, two spears pointing to the sky. He rolled back onto his back to conserve his strength and to think.

What was he going to do now? He was in the middle of a lake with no boat!

Markus was not afraid of drowning. He knew he was a good swimmer, an excellent swimmer actually, and he felt that while on his back like this, it would be very hard to detect him from shore.

I wished I could have dumped Chang and gotten the boat. But what would that leave me? Maybe the boat wasn't a good idea after all, he thought. *With Imperial Guards out in boats, I'd be caught for sure, and probably end up at the end of one of those spears. Could I actually swim all the way to the north wall? I don't even know how far it is. And what time is it? Maybe one in the morning. The moon is way over there already.* Markus looked directly up into the night sky. It was a brilliant blaze of millions of stars. He recognized the Big and Little Dipper and few other constellations.

This feels like being in the Alps, he thought. The sky was comforting. Everything else in the world was gone for a few moments as he slowly moved his hands back and forth in the warm water to give his body propulsion against the mild current. He rolled onto his side and began to do the crawl stroke so he could search the shoreline for trouble.

He knew he could easily stay out in the lake for several hours making progress back toward the pagoda.

Moon Viewing Pagoda. The Chinese use such beautiful language to describe things.

He rolled onto his other side to survey the opposite shore. Nothing. He could see the pagoda ahead. He could stop there to rest and decide what to do.

In a few minutes, he pulled himself up onto the floor of the building. He lay there on his back resting. Rolling over onto his stomach, he sighted up and down the shore and across the lake. It was very quiet and quite dark now as the moon was below the horizon. Only starlight blazed down.

Maybe I should see how far I can make it in the water. He'd thought about moving on land, possibly along the wall, but if he were detected, he would have no chance of escape. In the water, he had a better chance. He closed his eyes and he could see the maps he'd looked at earlier.

He had to be near where the north lake went under the Imperial City wall. That was his next objective. Once past the wall, he'd be back in Tartar City, then several more lakes north to the northern wall of Tartar City. Beyond that, he should find open country, more lakes, and from there, he'd go on to Li Ling's.

He was beginning to feel confident. Now that he had a clear objective, he was ready to go. Taking one more close look around, he slipped into the warm black waters and headed north. Swimming for about thirty minutes, he could now detect the towering ramparts of the north wall. Several weeping willow trees clung to the shoreline with branches hanging in the water. He was soon under them lying in six inches of water. Even the mud was warm as he regained his breath and let his arms relax.

Now, would there be guards on the wall looking down, maybe on both sides, and a barrier of some kind in the water? Well, he'd soon find out.

After fifteen minutes of rest, he crawled on his hands into deeper water. No one was on the ramparts as he approached a very long, low arch that was the opening in the wall into the northern lake and beyond. The brick arch was at most five meters high and fifteen meters wide. He slowly approached the opening, doing the breaststroke and trying to keep as low in the water as he could. It was very dark near the wall and as he approached, he decided he'd aim for the very edge of the arch as it came out of the water.

Finally, he reached the wall, his fingers finding a good hold. He rested, looking all around, listening. It was very dark but he could see the starlight reflecting off the water. He listened for several more minutes. As far as he could see, there were no obstructions or barriers blocking his passage under the wall.

Pushing off, he kept very close to the arch as it emerged from the water. It was within an arm's length, but he sensed that the water was deep. The thickness of the wall, approximately fifteen meters, formed a virtual tunnel. He swam slowly in the pitch-blackness, reaching up constantly to touch the roof of the arch to keep his bearings. More than halfway through, he began to see starlight again on the water.

Suddenly, a stabbing pain in his groin! He slapped the water and reached the slimy surface of a submerged tree branch. He floundered around in the water trying to untangle the branch from his clothes. The branch broke, and he surged backward, hitting his head on the arch roof. He was making a terrific noise in his struggle, but he regained his senses and ability to stay afloat.

"Jesus!" escaped from his lips. A two-foot section of water-logged branch snagged his shirt and pants. He had no choice but to drag the branch with him as he made his way toward the far opening. As soon as he was out from under the arch, he saw, thankfully, more weeping willows and headed for them.

His eyes searched the top of the wall and the shoreline as he tried to stay as low as he could. This time, hitting mud, he dragged himself up onto the shore under the tree. He looked around rapidly as he fumbled with the damned stick. He reached down and touched his lower abdomen. It really hurt but he didn't think it was too serious. Again, he breathed deeply, closing his eyes for a few seconds.

"I'm out of Imperial City; hopefully there are fewer guards out here," he muttered. "*Ja*, but there're probably going to be more people…just as dangerous."

Another fifteen-minute rest, and Markus was ready to go again. And again visualizing the map in his mind: There was a causeway of some kind that bisected the next lake at a diagonal, he recalled, a road or footpath or something. *Well, let's find out. Let's see, it must be about two in the morning. Dawn is around five-thirty, but first light is maybe five. I'm not going to make it through Tartar City before dawn. I'd better start thinking about staying in this lake like a turtle.* He knew he couldn't stay in the lake all day, even if the water seemed warm to him now. He would soon get cold and sapped of strength.

Optimistically, he plotted that by swimming at a steady pace, he would be beyond the Imperial City arch by daybreak. The causeway should be just ahead, and if all went well, he could beach himself and climb into the tall cattails growing along the shore, which he hoped were there.

Just before dawn, he reached the causeway. Sure enough, thick vegetation grew in the shallow water. Markus peeked out of the grass and found an oxcart path two meters above the waterline. It ran the length of the causeway as far as he could tell. No one appeared to be in the tract, so he decided to walk cautiously along it, heading north. The tall water grass, mixed with bamboo, rose at least a meter above the road and in some places towered over the causeway on both sides, forming an arch of foliage. In these, the path was very dark. Markus picked up the pace and knew he was making quick headway toward the outer wall of Tartar City.

Emerging from under one of the overhanging arbors, he neared the end of the causeway. He stopped abruptly, perfectly still. A large mass blocked the road ahead. Slowly, listening carefully for any unusual sounds, Markus crept closer. He studied the broad form that seemed to take up the full width of the tract. As he quietly approached, he realized it was a cart stacked high with cut bamboo and cattails. He stopped instantly when the cart moved!

Hearing familiar sounds…stomping hoofs in the dirt. There must be someone around. Markus pulled out his revolver. He peered into the brush on each side of the road. Nothing. He looked around the front of the four-wheel wagon and saw a harnessed horse patiently waiting. *Someone's around here*. He strained to see the road out beyond the horse. He heard sounds he thought he knew. *Scratching sounds?* No, dragging sounds, and voices.

Markus eased into the foliage out of sight with his head just above the level of the road. He waited. Two men dragged cut greens around to the back of the cart and began stacking armloads of bamboo and cattails onto the wagon. It was piled almost three meters high and appeared to Markus as surely a full load. The two Chinese, talking casually, climbed aboard the front of the wagon and clicked the horse into a slow walk.

Markus had to make a decision, climb aboard and under their load for a free ride, continue the walk north, or return to the water. The wagon was moving away. He'd just follow behind the wagon. There was no way those two could see him, and if they stopped he'd just disappear into this roadside jungle. He pushed his pistol back into his waistband. As he walked, he stayed constantly alert to any possibility.

The roadside bamboo seemed denser as he continued north. Unbeknownst to Markus, he had passed the end of the causeway and was now passing through a swampy bamboo forest. The cart traveled on for at least a half hour and then came to a stop. Markus stopped, edged toward the foliage, and waited. Hoof beats! Definitely not the wagon horse. Two horses. He slipped into brush and was surprised to find there was no slope down to the water. In fact, he was standing in a foot of water that was almost level with the road .

What the Jesus was this? I must be beyond the lake!

The horse sounds grew louder, accompanied by strong voices. There was an exchange between the two men in the wagon and the two riders. In a moment, the horses walked around the wide load and within ten feet of Markus. He could smell the horses and heard the last fragment of their conversation:

"Remember, those who help the Christians will be treated like Christians!"

"No, no, we just cut bamboo."

The horseman rode south.

Boxers! And it wasn't even dawn! Again, Markus was confronted with choices: Stay with the wagon, disappear into the landscape, or…or what?

As long as it was dark, he had a good chance. He had to hide before light, that much was certain. He'd stay with the wagon, at least for the time being. The wagon had already started up again, and Markus hurried to catch up. He examined the back of the load and figured he could wiggle in and under the load. In a few moments, he was safely embedded deep beneath the mound of bamboo and assorted grasses.

It was safe, and he was happy to be off his feet, out of the water, and lying down. He realized for the first time since he left Peitang Cathedral how tired he was.

Don't fall asleep, he told himself, *don't fall asleep*. He strained to listen to the two brush cutters riding in the wagon. He caught a few comments but nothing of value. Again, he estimated the time. It had to be near dawn, maybe four or four thirty. He was getting nervous about where they were going and what he should do. What would Levi suggest? Take longer and be safer.

The decision was made for him, as the wagon turned abruptly

into a low-walled pasture with Mongolian ponies, probably what the two Boxers were riding. It was still dark as the wagon pulled up near a barn and stables. The two Chinese got down and walked around behind the wagon. One of them was about to climb up onto the load, but the other one said, "Wait, let's go have our tea first."

"Yes, good idea." The two walked away from Markus' hiding place and turned the corner around the barn. Markus could see them depart. As soon as they were gone, he slowly worked himself out of the load, stopping every few moments to listen. No one was apparently around. He figured it would be at least ten minutes before the two returned to unload the wagon. That gave him time to look around and get his bearings.

"I wonder where I am…where the lake is…how far to the final obstacle, the great outer wall of the Tartar City," he muttered under his breath. He stood in front of a two-story stone barn with stables on the ground floor. He peered in through the large doorway. No light, only the sound of a few horses and the heavy smell of horse barns, manure, hay, straw, or what passed for straw here in China. He slowly crept around the interior, finding a built-in ladder to the hayloft. As he explored, he noticed, through a glassless window, orange streaks in the sky.

Time to find a hiding place for the day. For sure, it would be above his head.

He backtracked to the ladder and climbed. There were window openings at either end of the barn, with wooden shutters, and in the center of the wall above the big door was a large opening, obviously for loading hay into the loft. He felt the hay.

It was feed stock, not silage, so they probably wouldn't be going up there, he reasoned. Climbing over stacks of loose hay, he surveyed his surrounds in the ever-growing light. He walked over to the big opening, looking out carefully. Beyond the pasture walls were rows of small, low buildings, most with tile roofs, but some with thatch. This had to be a part of Tartar City for servants of the town's elite.

Looking up, Markus saw another built-in ladder near where he stood. It ran up the wall at least six or seven meters to a small opening near the roof. He looked back out the window in the direction of the two tea drinkers. No one and no sounds. He swung around and starting climbing, careful not to make noise, through cobwebs and dust and heat. The higher he climbed the hotter it got.

All barns were the same: hot and dusty in the summer, and warm and cozy in the winter. He reached the opening and looked out. To his left the town spread out in rows of streets with mostly two-story buildings. He could see a few carts and several people far below and far away. Directly in front of him, in the distant mist, he was sure he saw the top of the outer wall. To his right, when he strained his neck, he could see dawn's colors coming up fast in the east and below the horizon. It was just what he was looking for, the last lake, just south of the wall. "Great, now I have my bearings again. Time to hide," he whispered. As he descended the ladder, he heard the two wagon men talking, just outside the barn.

Hunger gnawed as he burrowed deep into the hay pile, which seemed like a luxury to him compared to the bamboo wagon he rode in earlier. He chose a location in the high-stacked hay he felt would probably not be probed in feeding the animals below. He was fast asleep as the first rays of golden sun shone through the upper window.

Markus woke several times during his ten-hour snooze, and at one time crawled out of his hiding place to relieve himself. Early in the morning, he had heard horses coming and going and voices chatting farmyard concerns. He had already planned a potential food source.

"Those two men on the wagon last night went for tea. Where there's tea, there's probably food," he mumbled. Near dark, he crept to the far end of the hayloft and peered out the far window that was just above a hut where stable hands seemed to hang out.

"That's probably it." He could just see into the hut from his vantage point. The edge of a crude table had teacups on it. The moon was rising by the time everyone had left. Leaving the hayloft, he climbed down the ladder and peered out the door. No one. Walking along the edge of the barn, he came to the corner and peeked around. Again, no one. He walked directly toward the hut, stopping a moment to listen, and stepped in. Sure enough, a teapot stood on a cold stove. He picked it up and drank deeply, directly out of the kettle. Quickly searching around in the darkening room, he found dried rice cakes and a large cast-iron pot half filled with cooked rice. He scooped up a handful and stuffed his mouth, washing it down with more tea. Finding a cloth, he dumped the remainder of the rice into it and tied up the rice ball, stuffing it into his shirt.

CHAPTER V

The Iron Rice Pot

"SAVE SOME OF that for me," he heard over his shoulder, in a dialect of Mandarin. Markus froze! His heart raced. He grunted in reply. His hand reached toward his revolver.

No, he thought, *too much noise.*

His left hand moved toward the half-filled teakettle as he heard the stranger approaching. In his garb, from the back, Markus probably looked like one of the poor stable hands. The man went directly to the rice pot. He lifted the lid and peered in. Markus, standing just one meter away, hesitated a split second, and then swung the teakettle with all his might at the stranger. He was taller than Markus had thought. The kettle caught the man in the upper shoulder and bounced into the side of his head. He yelled and fell to the floor. Markus was on him with a second powerful blow that struck an elbow, glanced off, and hit the man smack in the face.

He's an Imperial Guard! flashed through Markus' mind as a powerful hand grabbed his ankle and jerked him off balance. He felt himself falling, but on the way down, he latched onto the thick wire handle of the empty iron rice pot. He completely spun around, the pot making a wide arc through the air. This time the pot dealt a crushing blow to the side of the man's head. Blood gushed from a fatal wound, carrying with it white bone fragments. Markus lay there breathing hard, staring at the Imperial Guard's body and uniform.

"Good God," he said aloud, "what am I going to do with him?"

Quickly regained his senses, he jumped up and looked out the doorway to see if anyone was near. He saw the guard's pony tied to a hitching post nearby. Returning to the body, he was already formulating a plan.

Imperial Guards wore distinctive uniforms, a white, loose-fitting tunic with large calligraphy covering the entire chest area, baggy pants down to mid-shin, and a distinctive sort of headscarf.

"If I take the uniform and the pony, I might get pretty far before anybody finds him. I might encounter other guards, but I'll worry about that if and when it happens." He spoke to himself as he pulled the clothes off the dead man and put them on over his peasant outfit. The tunic was bloody on one side and smelled of death. *What to do with the body?*

"Leave it. You've got to get out of here. Use the darkness," he heard Levi saying in his mind. *Where to? Back to the lake...leave the horse in the woods...bury the uniform... Ja, that's what I'll do... unless something else happens first.*

He was surprised when he stripped off the guard's uniform and saw he was naked from the waist down. Markus felt it was somehow obscene to leave the dead man naked like that. Before he left, he dragged the body deeper into the shadows, found a saddle blanket, and threw it over him. Mounting up, he headed toward the lake, taking the same road he had come down on in the wagon. Markus sat well in the saddle but walked the horse through the trees, in some areas on dry ground, some soggy, and in a few places the horse splashed through water. He soon came to the lake. The moon was up and it shone a faint light on the landscape.

Should he leave the horse and uniform there or follow the lake north on horseback?

He'd stick with the horse for now—faster progress, less tiring, and faster escape if need be.

The shoreline soon transformed from swampy woods to open fields and soon, small docks and houses. It had to be ten or eleven. The houses were dark except for those few faint glows in several windows. He had a good chance of not encountering townspeople. He didn't want to encounter the Boxers and the Imperial Guards.

Markus ventured on toward the northern wall, hoping for a large unobstructed opening where he could pass through. He walked his mount at a quick pace along a dirt road parallel to the lake. *These lakes must be the water supply for the four cities*, he speculated. Within half an hour, he saw the mighty ramparts that protected the inner cities. Still no guards. His eyes strained toward the upper wall, searching for the silhouettes of trouble. He dismounted about fifty meters from the wall and stopped.

"You moved me along at a good pace. I hate to leave you," he said into the ear of the horse. He began walking the horse toward the wall and the opening, clearly visible ten meters from shore. Again, he scanned around and down the lakeside.

Nothing. Good. He hoped he could pull off his next maneuver.

He led the horse into the water and began swimming toward the arched opening. He tugged on the bridle gently, and the animal responded and swam alongside Markus. He had to go further out from the arch to give the horse more headroom, but the beast was surprisingly cooperative.

This is one well-trained horse, he thought as they swam into the darkened opening. Before long, he and his mount were climbing the muddy bank beyond the Tartar City.

Markus was always surprised that a city could end so abruptly. On the other side of the wall was a city. On this side, nothing but open land and further out farms and rural life. In Bavaria, the town extended far beyond the city walls and gradually melted into agricultural land. Here it was city, a wall, rural. Strange!

Now, head for those trees and good cover. Next, I've got to figure which way to Li Ling's village from here. He dismounted under willows near the river that fed the city lakes. Markus sat down. *Visualize those maps*, he told himself.

"*Ja*, I'm positive this is the Hun Ho River. An-Tsun village is up this river about four or five kilometers. We should make it there tonight if all goes well," he said to the horse.

He remounted and walked his horse at a good clip along the bank, passing through a stand of trees. Emerging from the dense foliage, he saw ahead of him a log fire burning on a low bluff above the river. Several men with torches were casting nets into the shallows. The fire illuminated their surrounds and the slowly swaying trees. It was both beautiful and ominous.

"So now is a good time to see if my bluff works," he said, leaning to the horse's ear. Riding at a steady pace, sitting tall in the saddle, skirting the blazing fire on the opposite side from the fishermen. They heard his horse and stopped what they were doing. They turned and stared at him. He kept going, looked at them, and made a slight gesture in their direction. They nodded deeply and slowly raised their heads. He continued on his way, realizing they were probably happy to see an Imperial Guard leave them alone. He glanced back over his shoulder. They were still looking at him.

Wonderful! That went perfectly. The horse plodded on. *It's after midnight judging by the moon, and so far so good*, he thought. He wondered if Chou and Chang got through with the dispatch pouch. He hoped so. It was his responsibility. And he wondered what they thought happened to him. Did they think he'd drowned or been captured? What was Levi thinking? Maybe that Markus was dead.

He hoped not. Levi shouldn't give up on him. He'd make it back. Somehow.

He followed the river as the moon crossed the sky, thinking about Li Ling and how he would greet her, and whether she would even be at home. He hadn't seen her, held her in his arms, in—how long had it been, six weeks, eight weeks? He told her he wouldn't be able to be back for a while, but he doubted she thought it would be this long.

Markus reveled in the beautiful thoughts: her smile, her eyes looking at him, her smell, the soft skin beneath his hands, her lips, oh those lips, how sweet, how impossibly wonderful.

He felt himself getting an erection as he thought of her body, of lying with her in the silent dark. Markus swayed in the saddle, the horse pretty much leading the way along the path.

And then he stopped himself. He had to get back to what was going on here. He had to pay attention or he'd ride right into trouble. He peered around both sides of the trail, straining to see into the dark night shadows.

As he rode along, he soon slipped into speculations about his arrival at Li Ling's residence. What would her father say when they met again? He seemed to like Markus and enjoyed their talks about Europe and about how China had to modernize. They'd even discussed how foreigners were resented by most people because they were rich and took too much and didn't give anything back.

Markus considered Li Ling's father to be a very wise man, a good man and a good father. As far as Chinese went, he was exceptionally well educated, very progressive, and he had even been to Paris years ago. Markus was so surprised when he found that out. He remembered Mr. Ling having told him that he was an assistant to the magistrate in charge of the astronomical observatory in the Forbidden City. It was a very important function within the massive bureaucracy of the Imperial Household. Astrology and astronomy were the basis of much decision making. The delegation, authorized by the emperor himself, traveled to Paris to purchase new telescopes and other astronomical apparatus. It opened Wan Ling's eyes to a wider world few Chinese knew anything about.

Now Li Ling lived with her father in a small walled compound in An-Tsun village. He supported the two of them by being a scribe, a letter writer for the community of mostly illiterate farmers, tradesmen, and shopkeepers. He was also a painter and calligrapher and had a local reputation as the finest artist along that part of the river. Several prosperous landowners patronized him, and so, at the local spring and autumn fairs, Mr. Ling sold his painted scrolls and calligraphic poetry. Wan Ling never told Markus why he had a falling out with the Imperial Magistrate of Astronomy. And Li Ling would not tell him either.

It was about three in the morning when he approached the village. He could just make out familiar landmarks he recalled from previous visits. The village sat on a shallow embankment above the tree-lined river. Its tiled and thatched roof buildings were clustered together along a half-dozen narrow dirt lanes. Several two-store buildings and one three-story temple projected above the hamlet. Small farm plots with primitive thatched dwellings were scattered across the landscape. Several prosperous farmers had walled compounds of three or four buildings. Markus remembered the peach, pear, plum, and apple orchards he had seen near Li Ling's home.

He had been thinking about what to do with the horse, and now he had to make a decision. He dismounted in a stand of ancient maple trees. He was still a considerable distance from any of the dwellings. He'd bury the saddle, the bridle, and the horse blanket there and turn the horse loose. He patted the horse's neck and ran his hand through the stubby mane. As a cavalryman, Markus genuinely appreciated this mount and whispered to him, "You've taken me far. I thank you for that."

He had examined the horse earlier for any markings. All Imperial German horses were branded and easily identifiable, but these Mongolian horses had no marks.

Should he keep the Imperial uniform? No, that would cause more attention than his peasant rags. Better to bury it, too. The next half hour required digging, scraping, and gathering leaves and branches to cover the shallow grave. When he finished, he gave a sharp slap to the rump of the horse, to get him moving in the direction opposite his own course. Markus headed out on foot.

The moon was long below the horizon, but the sky was a sea of sparkling crystal specks of light as he approached the nearest homes. It was dead quiet. Li Ling's home was actually just on the outskirts of the far side of town. He contemplated skirting around it to avoid risk of detection. But now, being so close, and at night, and so quiet, and being so tired, Markus uttered, "What the hell, I'll be through there in ten minutes." All went well as he passed by one darkened dwelling after another and onto the lane of shuttered shops. He heard several dogs barking far off and nightingales heralding the oncoming dawn.

It had to be about four. It would be light in about an hour. He'd be there before that. He made his way down the dusty tracks that served as streets in such villages, until he was startled to hear a voice in the dark.

"Go away, beggar! We don't want vagabonds around here." He stared hard into the darkness but couldn't see anyone. A rock skipped past him in the dirt. He picked up his pace and hunched over like Chou had told him.

"Jesus," he muttered and kept going. Up ahead, isolated from neighbors by the twenty or so assorted fruit trees, was the Ling family compound. The second story of the house loomed only as a dark mass above the two-meter-high stone walls. He approached the gate with both eagerness and trepidation. He searched for the small hidden recess in the wall and pulled on the rope that lifted the gate latch. The beam wasn't barring the portal, so the gate swung with a slight push. He stepped inside.

I made it. His eyes misted up. After all he had been through in the last forty-eight hours, no, in the last week, he was actually standing in Li Ling's courtyard. An eighteen-year-old soldier, he had participated in more fighting and danger than most troops see in ten years. He stood perfectly still for a few moments in the still night air, regaining his composure.

CHAPTER VI

Li Ling

"ARE YOU GOING to just stand there until dawn?" A familiar voice spoke quietly off to his side. Markus jumped back a step, banging his head against the gate. He immediately recognized the voice.

"My God, Mr. Ling, you scared me," Markus managed to scratch out in a dry voice.

"You sound exhausted," Ling observed. "Come inside and we will prepare for you some tea." Mr. Ling turned and led Markus across the small courtyard and along a series of stepping stones through a flowering garden to the round portal leading into the house. A wood framed lantern with frosty white paper screens glowed on a table. It barely illuminated a dining area surrounded by walls of books and hanging scrolls of paintings and calligraphy. In the corner, a shrine with a bronze Buddha and a white porcelain sculpture of Quan Yin stood behind an offering bowl of peaches. Unlike most Chinese homes, where the smell of wood smoke was in the air, the Ling home had the sweet smell of soft coal.

"Sit down, Lancer Mathias, and rest yourself," Mr. Ling said in a quiet voice.

"Li Ling, whom your journey is about, is sleeping in her room.

You must have had an arduous trip here." He poured tea out of a cast-iron pot into a cup in front of Markus. The German soldier lifted the cup, nodded his head, said thank you, and drank the tea. Ling refilled the cup.

"You must tell me your experiences in getting here from the German Legation, but not now. Li will want to hear your story also. I regret she will be very happy to see you again. For me, I want to understand what you intend to accomplish in this adventure." His voice was kind but had an edge of sadness to it.

"As you have surely found out, it is very dangerous for foreigners to be traveling anywhere in northern China at this time. I am surprised you arrived safely, although the young always seem to find a way to accomplish their most precious dreams." Ling seemed to stare off momentarily. "I assume you were not followed or seen by villagers?"

Markus put down the porcelain teacup. "No, I don't think so."

"Yes, I see your humble clothes became a necessary and successful disguise. You will need a bath and clean garments, but first you must rest. Day will come soon and Li will be eager to greet you."

Ling led Markus to an alcove with a raised bed. It was a very ornately carved, wood-paneled and canopied four-poster sleeping platform. It was also where Markus had first kissed Li. He collapsed onto the thick quilt and was asleep in seconds.

It was midmorning before Markus stirred awake. Li Ling had been watching him for hours as she prepared the midday meal. It was already getting hot, but the thick brick and stucco walls and the many full-grown fruit trees around the home helped make for a pleasant atmosphere. Mr. Ling had left earlier on one of his mysterious errands. Even Li didn't know their nature. As Markus turned over on the quilt, Li was by his side. She reached down and touched his face with a cool, damp cloth.

"You are finally back, Markus. I was so waiting for your return."

He sat up and took her hand from his face. He gently pulled her in and kissed her lightly on the lips, lingering. She stayed a moment and then pulled away, her eyes down, a smile on her lovely face. She looked toward the doorway.

"My father will be back soon."

"Yes, I know." Markus pulled Li to him again, this time with a much more passionate kiss. She responded as he had remembered her, setting his whole body on fire with passion.

She broke off. "No, no…you must get up. My father will be back any moment." She got up, her hand smoothing her hair. "You must take a bath. Father has given me clothes for you. Those Imperial Guard clothes you were wearing will be burned in the stove." She smiled at him as he got to his feet. "I'm so happy you are here again," she said.

"Yes, I am too. I just had to come, Li. I just had to see you." It was obvious they both felt the same way. "But your father is not happy I'm back."

"You must understand my father. He just wants to protect me from a broken heart, he says. He really likes you. I know it. Now, here is a towel and soap. You know where the water tub is, outside by the garden. No, wait! Take these clothes with you." She laughed.

What luxury, thought Markus as he sat on the little wooden stool, his feet in a deep, wide, bucket-type thing that served as a bathing tub. He couldn't quite fit in it. He sat down first and now his feet were in. His smelly disguise lay in a pile. He had pulled the coin-filled pocket out of the pants. Now it was simply a bag. His revolver lay on top of the bag. He heard Mr. Ling talking to Li.

He thought he had better get dressed. His outfit was similar to the Imperial Guard's uniform he had worn just ten hours earlier, except this one didn't have the calligraphy on the front, and the material was of much finer quality. He strolled into the house and greeted Mr. Ling and Li.

"Lunch is just ready."

Li's voice was like music to Markus. He smiled broadly and sat down at Ling's urging.

"You must be hungry. How long were you on the road from your legation? And how did you get permission to come visit at a time like this, with Boxers on the streets everywhere?" Ling didn't hesitate to question Markus, but Li interrupted.

"Father, let poor Markus eat his lunch; look how hungry he is."

Markus eagerly ate the cold vegetable soup, rice ball, fresh carrots and cucumbers from the garden. He stopped eating long enough to respond to Ling. "A week, I've been working my way here for a week. I'll be happy to tell the whole story after lunch if you like."

"Yes, of course, of course," said Li. "A week? It took a week to get here? You have done that trip in a good day's walk! What happened on the road?"

"Do you really want to know?" he asked.

She did. After lunch, the three of them walked into the garden, under the rapidly ripening fruit trees. They sat down on a wooden bench, and Markus spent the next two hours relating his exploits in getting to An-Tsun. He debated whether to tell that part of the story concerning killing the Imperial Guard and using his horse. He modified the story slightly so the guard attacked him in the teahouse, so it didn't seem like a cold-blooded killing. He enjoyed telling the story, and elsewhere he was truthful.

Markus noticed that when he mentioned the nobleman Chou Lee and his eunuch servant Chang Pao Fu, Mr. Ling seemed startled. Markus caught Li glancing at her father apprehensively. He let it pass as if he hadn't noticed, but he had noticed and he made a mental note to ask Li later.

Li and her father asked for details and then Mr. Ling glanced at his watch. "You are fortunate not to have been killed two or three times during the past week. Now, I must leave for the afternoon." He rose from the garden bench and started for the gate.

"What time shall I prepare dinner, Father?"

"Don't wait for me. My return may be quite late, child." He passed through the gate and was gone.

"Where is your father going, Li?"

"I don't know where he goes all the time. He doesn't want me to accompany him, unless it's just to visit a friend or to purchase provisions. He is doing something out there, and it makes me concerned." She stared at the gate across the garden. "These are terrible times, with the people very angry and doing cruel things, especially to Christians. As you know, we have some villagers who have taken up with the Christian missionaries. They are very frightened that the Boxers will come and hurt them. It's so sad."

Li Ling looked down at her hands and was silent for a moment. Markus put his hand on top of hers. They both leaned in toward each other.

"Father told me to tell you that not under any circumstances are you to leave our compound. And if anyone comes calling, you should not be seen. He said it would be very dangerous for all of us."

"Yes, I realize that. I'm sorry I've put you both in danger. But Li, I just had to come, to see you, to know you are all right…and your father."

"I know. I am so happy you're here."

They turned and kissed, a wonderful, long, sweet, soft kiss, passionate but unrushed, both feeling a perfect rightness to that sublime moment. His hands slid over her garments as they sat on the garden bench…up her sides to her shoulders, to her neck, holding her head gently, and then down the back to her waist. His hand swept tenderly across her thigh to her knee, down to the hem of her wrap. The fine feel of the silk of the hand-stitched cloth as he moved his hand slowly up and under her garment made them both breathe deeply in mounting passion.

She stopped his hand and took it as she rose from the bench and pulled him toward the house and the ornate bed.

CHAPTER VII

The Siege, The Iron Cross, and Liaisons

DOWN THE HUN Ho River from Li Ling's compound, across the farmlands to the city walls, word spread. The battle raged at the foreign legations with one assault after another. The Boxers surged against the fortified barricades, sometimes in waves of enraged peasants, scrambling over their fallen comrades. Many of the rebellious Chinese had by now acquired firearms of one sort or another. From primitive single-shot hunting rifles to the latest 1899 European military issue, the intense fighting ebbed and flowed as the days and weeks passed.

The nobleman Chou Lee and his able servant Chang, true to their word, managed to deliver the dispatch pouch to the legations and with it the harrowing account of Markus' fight, first to get to Peitang Cathedral and then his watery exploits under the boat. Chou told this story to Commander MacDonald and to the German commander, Captain Mayerling. Others listened in, too, eager to hear any news from outside the walls. Chou Lee appeared as mysteriously within the legation compound as he had in the Peitang Cathedral. He re-counted his efforts to return to look for Lancer Mathias along the lakes. For days he sent Chang out to search the thick reeds and wil-low trees and finally to search for Markus' body in the eddies of the lakes…all to no avail.

Markus, deemed a hero, was praised and blessed at his memo-rial service at the headquarters of the German Legation. The ser-vice was packed with soldiers and civilians from all twelve nations represented in the besieged community. Both Catholic priests and Protestant missionaries prayed for his safe return or his blessed as-cension to heaven. Captain Mayerling recorded the heroic details of Lancer Mathias' mission in the official company logbook with a recommendation to award Lancer Mathias, posthumously, the Iron Cross First Class.

King Frederick William of Prussia first bestowed the Iron Cross, a meritorious award for bravery, in 1808, during the Napoleonic Wars. It was still the highest Imperial German military honor a sol-dier could receive.

Levi was distraught for days after the memorial service. He questioned Chou in detail several times, trying to understand, try-ing to see how his dearest friend might possibly have survived. Levi regretted agreeing to Markus' plan soon after he left for the Peitang Cathedral, and especially on hearing the guns of the two battles. He blamed himself for sanctioning the highly dangerous mission. But as time went by, Levi somehow just could not accept the almost uni-versal belief that Markus had drowned or been killed by the Imperial Guards or Boxers.

Levi thought they would surely have heard something, or Chou would have heard something. Especially since Markus' body had not been found, and he had been a good swimmer. Levi poured over maps of the ancient city, the lakes, and surrounding villages. With as much hope as belief, Levi thought that Markus had somehow survived and made it to Li Ling.

"If he is with Li Ling, and her father doesn't turn him in, he's safe for now." Levi talked to himself while pacing back and forth in a quiet corner of the barracks. It was a comfort to think this, but he also wondered how Markus would get back to the legation. Would he come back? He said he would. How could Levi find out if his friend made it? Maybe that character Chou could help, but could he be trusted if Levi told him the whole story? Would he consent to help and find out if Markus was at Li Ling's? How could Levi approach Chou? He'd stayed in the legation compound for days after delivering the dispatches, but now he was gone. Levi determined that if he saw Chou again he would try to get his help.

Levi recovered from his injuries, but his noticeable limp reminded everyone of his sword wound. He, too, had his name and deeds recorded on the official company log and had been recommended for the Iron Cross, in this case second class. He had assumed full duties, mostly on the Tartar Wall and the barricades protecting the German Legation and their neighbor, the Japanese Legation directly north of them.

Since the siege began, the Boxers had overrun the Austrian and Italian legation buildings and most of the French quarter. The magnificent Han Lin Library—containing vast quantities of ancient scrolls—which abutted the British Legation, had been burned to the ground. Most of the Mongol market was captured, and a large section of the Chinese Christian neighborhood, part of the greater legation compound, was destroyed by fire. It became a military necessity to shrink the size of the legation compound in order to defend the extensive walls and barricades with the ever-diminishing fighting force. Even wounded men were put back on the walls if they could be of any use at all in the prolonged battles.

At the Peitang Cathedral, Bishop Favier continued giving half portions of food rations and overseeing the medical needs of the growing numbers of casualties. Every civilian had a job and every resource was carefully husbanded. The Mongolian ponies had long since been eaten, their bones boiled and re-boiled to gain every nutrient.

At the legations, all tobacco had long since been consumed, so those in desperate need of a smoke had to crush dried leaves, grass, and straw from the barns. The only alcohol officially known to exist was in the dispensary, although a bottle of schnapps could probably be found in the German Legation and likewise wine in the French and Italian quarters.

"Levi, I'm sorry about Markus. I never thought of him as a hero; he was just one of us. *Ja*, just looking for some adventures. So, here we are, so far from the fatherland, battling these peasants, and he's maybe still out there somewhere. You still think he could be in hiding, maybe with the Christian Chinese?" Hermann asked the question, while peering through a gun hole in the broken wall.

"Hermann, I don't know what to think. I feel he's still alive somewhere. Watch it! Movement on your right! Third window. Rifle barrel."

"I see it!" *Bang!* Hermann squeezed off a shot. A puff of dust and stucco burst off a window frame of the burned-out house that used to be part of the French Legation a mere fifty yards in front of them. They resumed their conversation, each still looking out their individual gun holes.

"Have you written to his parents yet? I know your two families were good friends. *Ach!* What am I talking about? No postal service anymore! Ha!" He half laughed in embarrassment at his stupid question. Hermann was one of the half-dozen young Bavarians who enlisted with Levi and Mathias, mostly to get away from home and see the world. He, too, at nineteen, was the lowest rank above recruit in King Ludwig's Bavarian Army.

Since the German Empire was proclaimed in 1872, the various

armies of the kingdoms, duchies, city-states, and principalities that made up the Imperial German Empire retained their loyalty to their local sovereign but had also pledged allegiance to the emperor, who was also the King of Prussia. It made for colorful pageantry at court, each army retaining the splendid traditional uniforms of their local sovereign's army.

"We should be relieved soon. I hope they don't pull another night attack. I want a good night's sleep."

"*Ja*, me too. Here's our relief now," Levi said. One last look out the gun hole, and he and Hermann headed down the ramp to their meager dinner, a quick cleaning of their rifles, and then to their bunks. And so it went for weeks on end, each day a struggle to get through for the civilians and military. It was hot, day and night. The food was monotonous and never enough. Everyone was getting thinner and worn down emotionally. Danger lurked every-where. One of the beloved missionaries, Reverend Stonehouse, was standing in front of a gun hole when a shot through the seven-inch opening snuffed out his life.

The Boxers, reinforced by certain Chinese Imperial Troops un-der several warlord generals, operated semi-independently of the empress. This caused great anxiety among the military leaders in the legations. They knew that if the Chinese Imperial Army's artil-lery were brought to bear on the embattled foreign legations, they would be overrun in days. For some mysterious reason, the Imperial cannons had not assaulted the legations so far. The ongoing threat of the artillery was kept a strict secret from the general inhabitants so as not to cause panic or further depression among the already weary refugees.

On July 8 Commander Claude MacDonald sent an urgent tele-graph message to Admiral Edward Seymour, who was stationed at the international settlements at Tientsin. He described the desperate situation at the Peking legations and requested an immediate relief expeditionary force be sent to rescue them. All telegraph lines to the outside world were cut the next day.

The informal council of war at the legations, chaired by Commander MacDonald, considered ways to reestablish communications with the European forces at Tientsin:

Could a well-armed dispatch unit mounted on our best horses make a surprise dash for the coast? Could a single rider or two do any better? We don't have any "best horses." We've eaten most of our mounts. What if we sent Chinese loyalists? No, this is similar to the Peitang expedition, so why not send a real fighting force of a company of troops? Would that weaken our legation defenses too much? Yes. Should we just wait, just hang on here and hope that reinforcements get through before we run out of food and ammunition…and able-bodied defenders? We're losing one or two good men able to man the barricades every several days from death, wounds and illness. We can't keep up that loss rate forever. So what should we do?

On and on it went for days. Discussions, debates, raised voices, pounded fists on tables and slammed doors. Even the military leaders were exasperated, knowing what the worst would bring. And the Chinese Christians were in even more desperate straits than the Europeans. Food was not fairly distributed. The Chinese got less than everybody else, and what little they got was of poorer quality.

"Well, everyone knows the Chinese can live on very little—next to nothing really, but we have needs of a special nature. It's just common sense." It was the unspoken and quietly spoken opinion of many.

Levi volunteered to try a breakthrough. Everyone praised his bravery, particularly with fresh memories of his desperate dash to warn the legations of the Boxer onslaught, but: "You're in no shape with that bad leg of yours. Thank you for offering."

"The council," MacDonald announced, "decided to delay a

decision on what to do, with the expectation that a relief column will arrive soon."

An unusual and disheartening event occurred early one morning when a Chinese Christian messenger made the daring trek from the Peitang Cathedral to the legations. He brought word of the desperate circumstances at Peitang and that the Boxers were tunneling to penetrate the barricades.

"It's a medieval technique known to all military minds. Tunnels are packed with explosives and detonated under the walls of besieged fortifications, either blowing up the walls or exploding within the compound," one of the officers explained. The messenger, in a grieving voice, related how one particularly gruesome blast killed over two hundred Chinese Christians, mostly children, because the blast occurred under the church orphanage. Everyone was horrified, and immediate orders circulated to watch and listen for any signs that a similar effort was being made here.

"How long has it been…" Levi was talking to himself again, "four weeks? No, five weeks since the siege began? How many men have we lost so far…and ammunition…and food…and smallpox? I can't believe there's smallpox in the legations. So far, it's only among those kids, those poor Chinese kids in the hospital. God in heaven, I hope I don't get it. If I survive, I'll have all those scars on my face! I have to keep up my diary. When we get home, Mama and Papa will be amazed at all the dangerous adventures I've had over here. When I get off duty tonight, I'll update my writings." He was emphatic.

Levi shifted his weight to his good leg as he leaned into the wall on the eastern rampart. Midday was the worst shift. Heat and dust, and dust and heat. It had been unusually quiet all day so far. Something was up; he felt it. Probably another night raid was coming.

He stood with the other mixed ranks on the catwalk, peering out the gun loops on occasion, like the others. From this vantage point, Levi could turn around and look back down on the legation streets and buildings. It was very quiet. Between the heat and the exhaustion and short rations, everyone was trying to conserve what energy they had.

Everyone was waiting, waiting for the next meal, the next attack, the next death. But mostly they waited for rescue, for the relief column that was sure to come—but when? *Can we hold out? Will we be over run before aid comes?* Rumors were that there had already been a relief force sent out from the Taku forts on the coast, and then up the rail line through Tientsin. British Admiral Seymour with his Royal Welsh Fusiliers, along with an assortment of Russian, German, Italian, and American troops were thought to have attempted a rescue. But where were they? Had they been defeated or driven back or something of the sort? That distant thunder of battle heard last week, was that Seymour's forces fighting their way here? If it was, they obviously failed. Anxiety raised, despair set in among many.

Levi heard the talk, the rumors of the strange phenomenon of the so-called moral breakdown by a growing number of legation individuals: sexual affairs, liaisons, one-night stands, quick flings in the dark corners of the night. No one said anything publicly. It seemed either people didn't know what was going on, or they turned a blind eye to it. It was as though some people needed something emotional. They grabbed at life, and at love, to escape for a few fleeting moments of hungry pleasure. Even in the barracks, at night, Levi heard the sounds. Masturbation seemed endemic.

CHAPTER VIII

A Battle in Africa, a Message from the Chancellor of the Imperial Observatory

"LEVI," GÜNTHER CALLED from two gun loops down, "you started to tell us about that battle in Africa that happened about a dozen years ago. Those British fighting the blacks, the Zulu, right? And they were outnumbered by, how many was it? And they won, right? I mean the Brits won this big battle, right? Come on, Levi, finish the story."

"*Ja*, they won all right," Levi said, still fantasizing about the passions bubbling throughout the legations. He turned toward his three weary companions. They were slouched against the barricade wall, trying to stay out of the sun.

"It was probably one of the greatest military victories in British history, I mean, for such a small unit against such a massive force of enemy. A dozen of those troops got the Victory Cross for heroism.

Ja, that battle made their careers as soldiers!" He paused.

"Well, if you want to hear the story, I have to start at the beginning, which started with one of the most appalling defeats in British military history. Fifteen hundred British soldiers and officers were wiped out down to the last man, in less than half a day, by a force of over four thousand Zulu warriors. They say there're lots of reasons for that disaster, but mainly the Brits failed to fortify their camp with entrenching, or breastworks, or even a laager, you know, a surround of wagons. So," Levi continued, "when the Zulus attacked, they charged straight into the camp with no obstacles in their path. The Brits all got massacred because of poor defensive planning by their officers."

"Good thing we got Mayerling," Günther blurted out. "He's a smart one!"

"And we got these walls!" said another.

"*Ja*, we are in much better shape than those Brits," Levi offered reassuringly. "So all this took place in '79, in Natal, in Southern Africa. That's east of our colony in Southwest Africa and south of our East African colony. Anyway, at a place called, I think, Isandhlwana, they all got wiped out, all fifteen hundred of them." He paused for a moment.

"But what was really amazing was that just twelve miles away from this bloody disaster was a little Christian mission and river crossing called Roark's Drift. There were only about 125 troops stationed there," Levi continued to his enraptured audience. "When they heard about the battle at Isandhlwana, they quickly built a breastworks and a redoubt. The next day, most of the four thousand Zulus attacked Roark's Drift. Imagine four thousand against 125! It was a stunning battle. The fight lasted all day and all through the night and into the next day; the Zulus attacked in waves. There were mounds of dead and wounded Zulus all around the mission perimeter. Most of the British soldiers were wounded in some way, but they kept beating them back, time after time. Finally, they were forced into their last stronghold. But the ingenious redoubt was so constructed that four ranks of troops could fire one above the other with such firepower, they were able to beat off the thousands of warriors. Finally, you know what happened?" Levi slowed for effect, as his little audience closed in to hear.

"The Zulu chief called a halt to the battle, and lined up his thousands of warriors on the hills above Roark's Drift. He had them all salute the British soldiers for their bravery. Then they sang a Zulu song and marched off across the veldt. The Brits were astonished because they thought they were done for, for sure. That was one of the most extraordinary military victories in British history."

The three German lancers just stood there in silence, envisioning the tale they had just heard. Their eyes focused on something far out beyond the horizon. To them, a story like that wasn't really about the British and the Zulus. It was interpreted by the four German lancers on the barricades—high on the walls of an embattled legation in a strange foreign kingdom—as every soldier's battle with an unknown enemy. It was every soldier's fear of defeat and death, and hope for victory and life. They had just heard that overwhelming odds could be defeated. Bravery and dedication and determination and discipline did mean something in battle. It could and did mean survival and honor and glory and all the things for which these young men joined the ranks. The four young German soldiers seemed reinvigorated by the tale as they resumed their battle stations on the dusty barricades.

A month into the siege of the legations, everyone was malnourished. Some were stoic, others depressed. Constant shooting and every several days, an attack, first this side of the compound then the other, unnerved the strongest. No additional word from the Peitang Cathedral, but the sound of battle reassured everyone they were still holding out. Then a strange silence fell across the legations. The

Boxers stopped their assault. Only a few enemy could be seen, but far off. The embattled Europeans stopped firing unless attacked. It became a wait-and-see game with everyone wondering who or what had caused this turn of events. Were the Boxers tunneling? Was the relief force approaching the city? Did the allied forces convince the empress to intervene and stop the fighting? No one knew.

For Levi, undisturbed sleep was a welcome change. Everyone's hopes were buoyed. The cessation of fighting lasted one week before firing into the legation began again. But for Levi, an amazing event occurred during the lull, and a possible opportunity. The nobleman Chou Lee slipped through the barricades one night and surprised everyone with his presence. He immediately went to Commander MacDonald's headquarters, as always crowded with assorted military nationals.

"I am pleased to see your strong determination and excellent generalship of these past ill-starred weeks, Commander," the nobleman said in his clear English. "I have been informed that a second military force is coming to your assistance as I speak."

The crowded room, growing even more packed as word spread of the aristocrat's return, burst into noisy chatter on this news.

"When…when will they get here, in days, in weeks?"

Chou surveyed the many faces staring at him, ignoring the question.

"Unfortunately the first expedition sent out for your relief was defeated, and its remnants returned to the coast. How regrettable as they were less than ten miles from your gates."

"I knew it!" someone shouted from the back of the crowd. "We heard that fight."

"This new expedition is encountering much resistance from my countrymen. However, their resistance is an ill-fated effort, I believe, as your compatriots have gathered a formidable international force. The fortress city of Tientsin has fallen to your advancing army, but still, there are many Boxers and many Imperial Troops that will impede their progress." Chou, standing regally in the midst of the crowded room, fell silent. The gathering buzzed with excitement.

Levi leaped off his bunk on hearing Chou was back and squeezed into the headquarters room to catch the last half of Chou's remarks.

Commander MacDonald rose from his desk. "Thank you, sir, for your efforts on behalf of the legations, and for your most heartening report. I'm sure I speak for all the people here besieged when I express my feeling that you are a true and valuable friend." The crowd cheered and applauded, in probably the most uplifting few minutes in weeks.

Levi was moved by Chou's words, but most especially by the simple fact that he had returned. He was not going to lose this chance to talk to Chou about Markus. Levi had only to decide how much he was going to tell Chou, how much he would *have* to tell him to gain Chou's assistance. Levi couldn't let Chou disappear again before he'd tried.

Commander MacDonald asked the room be cleared except for the senior commanders of each delegation. Levi hung back as long as he could and then swiftly approached Chou. He stopped very close to Chou so as not to be heard.

"Your Excellency," he whispered, "may I have a few minutes with you in private, at your convenience? I am Lancer Levi. Lancer Mathias is my best friend. I think I know where he is."

Chou heard the German's words. His eyebrow rose ever so slightly as he turned to inspect the stranger. A moment of silence hung heavy in the air between them. Chou's eyes glanced to either side as his bejeweled hand fanned slowly in front of his face.

"Tonight, your barracks, late," Chou said and slowly turned and strolled away.

Levi was transfixed for some seconds as those four words sunk in. Several senior officers glanced toward Levi. While they admired the young soldier, military protocol required that Levi leave the room immediately. Levi became aware of himself again and quickly departed.

Outside, in the open air, in the hot August sun, Levi leaned against the shadowed wall, closed his eyes, and thanked God for intervening! He would see Chou tonight! And he'd be off duty, thank God again. Perfect. Now, what should he say? How much should he tell Chou? This may be his only chance to get Chou's help finding Markus. Maybe he could even bring Markus back with him. Markus had better have a damned good story to explain this whole mess. And it would surely be a strange story.

Levi ate his meager dinner in silence away from the others. It was stale rice in a kind of broth with green leaves of some sort floating on the surface. If he were in Germany, he'd say they were linden leaves, but this was a Chinese lookalike, and it was edible. Without seasoning, it was about as bland as bland could be, but taste was his last concern. His thoughts raced. Chou must be able to find some way to communicate with Markus, assuming he was at Li Ling's. What was the name of that village? Sang-Tsun? No. An-Tsun. *Ja*, that was it, on the Hun Ho River, or near it anyway. Chou would know all the towns around Peking. He'd lived there long enough. *What time is it? Sun's down, better get some sleep.*

Levi did doze off several times, but by eleven o'clock, he was awake, dressed, and sitting on his bunk amid the snores from a score of dark forms. Levi saw a dark shadow seem to float down the central aisle of the barracks in complete silence.

"Come," there was a whisper. It was Chou.

Levi followed the nobleman out the back door and into a stillness broken only by the muffled sound of a few rifle shots, far across the battlements. Chou kept a brisk pace along Legation Street. They crossed the South Bridge over Jade River, a sewage canal. Levi wanted to know where Chou was taking him. They turned north along the walls of the Russian Legation, and then turned into a stable yard, now bereft of all but a few skinny ponies. No one appeared to be around. Chou motioned with his fan toward a long, wooden bench against the stable wall. They both sat down.

"So, German, we meet again. I had the esteemed pleasure of meeting your friend Lancer Mathias. It is with great sorrow I was not able to bring him safely here. Now, you say you may know his whereabouts? This is an extraordinary statement, Lancer Levi. How could you possibly have this information?"

Chou's demeanor was not as aloof as Levi recalled from the group meetings. Levi felt awkward and stumbled in his first attempt to speak his thoughts. "I, that is, we…Markus and I are best of friends. We come from the same place in Germany, the Kingdom of Bavaria. We talk about everything…our families, our country, and, well, everything."

Chou could see Levi struggling to say something difficult to reveal or admit. "Yes," he interrupted gently, "and your friend told you something that you prefer not talking about. But you know you must disclose this now, to me, because you want me to help Lancer Mathias…if he is still alive. Is this not correct?"

Levi breathed a sigh of relief, for Chou seemed to know, seemed to understand what he wanted. "*Ja*, that's right, sir, that's what I want to talk about, what I want your help with, if you would be so kind, Your Excellency…but it's complicated, very complicated. There's a lot that nobody knows, except me, about a lot of things, about the mission to the Peitang Cathedral, and why Markus wanted to go, to get out of the legation. I mean his reasons. And the thing is, I approved. When he asked me…he always asks me before he does something, and I said yes, and I helped him. And now he's out there, I just know he's still out there."

There was growing tension in Levi's voice. Emotions he had suppressed for weeks were bubbling up in his consciousness.

Chou could read Levi's state of mind and took on a fatherly tone as he asked: "You are good friends, truly brothers. And we are here to see if I can find him and guide him back to the legation. Is that correct?" Chou waited for an answer.

It was long in coming, but finally Levi said, "But, the thing is, I'm not sure he wants to come back. He said he would be back, but there are complications, things that might cause him not to come back."

Chou was startled to hear this and inquired, "Do you mean because it is too dangerous to travel, or did he do something for which he will be punished? Or is there some other reason that causes him not to want to return? Here in the legation, he is considered a hero. He will be welcomed back with great enthusiasm. Now, you must tell me why he may not return and where you think he may be."

Chou was emphatic, and Levi knew he had to tell him the truth, the whole story, because only part of the story would not make sense and would be a lie. "You're right, sir. I'll tell you everything, and hope you will understand and help Markus." Without looking up, Levi took a deep breath and began.

"My friend has a friend…a very close friend whom he has been visiting at her home north of Peking. Since the siege began, Markus could not visit her. He became desperate to see her and know she was safe, so he began looking for ways to get out of the legation compound.

"When we heard about the mission to reinforce the Peitang Cathedral, I suggested that he find a way to join the troops going there, as a way to get out. You see, it's my fault Markus is in this mess. I thought up this scheme. And since he speaks Mandarin and several other languages, he was accepted as a courier to bring back the dispatch, the dispatch pouch that you brought back. I'm sure he was torn between his desire to return with the dispatch pouch and his wish to see his…" Levi hesitated, and Chou finished the sentence for him.

"His lover."

"Well, yes, but I'm sure he truly loves her."

"I now understand the situation your friend is in, but you have not told me where his 'friend' lives. Do you know where she lives?" Chou looked at Levi with a keen eye for any unspoken truth.

"Yes, I do." Levi began again, now with enthusiasm. "She lives in a little village up the Hun Ho River named An-Tsun and..."

Chou interrupted him. "Are you sure that's the name of the village? An-Tsun?"

"Why, yes, that's the name. I'm sure of it. Is there something special about it?"

"No, no, continue," Chou said as he leaned in closer to Levi.

"She lives with her father in a fruit orchard, or something like that. At least that's what I remember Markus saying."

Chou turned away from Levi, and Levi continued.

"Her name is Li Ling, and she's about seventeen or eighteen and Markus..." Levi stopped on seeing Chou get up and turn away from him.

"Your Excellency, is something wrong? Did I say something that..."

Chou held up his closed fan, still facing away from Levi. He slowly turned. Levi was staring up at him in the dim moonlight, expectantly.

"I must leave you now. We will continue this discussion later perhaps."

Levi was startled as Chou began walking away. "Your Excellency, you are going to help me, aren't you? Aren't you?"

Chou said nothing as he disappeared into the shadows.

Levi was beside himself at this turn of events. What did he say? What upset Chou to the point that he just walked away without an explanation? Was it something about that village, or about Li Ling? Levi scratched his head in bewilderment. He slowly got up, still trying to understand what had just happened, and headed back to the barracks.

For two days and two nights, Levi worried and waited for Chou Lee to return or to contact him. On the third day, Levi was relieved to see Chou talking with Captain Mayerling near the Spanish Legation. Mayerling gave his departing salutations, and Chou turned and walked briskly away. Levi hurried to catch up to the nobleman. Chou stopped and turned on hearing Levi's greeting.

"Yes, Lancer Levi," he began. "Your commander has some news for you. Are you off duty this evening? If so we shall speak again on issues of mutual interest, but now you must seek out your commanding officer."

"I can meet you at the stables at midnight. My shift ends at eleven. But have you heard anything...I mean about Markus, I..."

"Not now, tonight," Chou said in his aristocratic tone. With that, he tipped his fan and walked away. Levi watched Chou's silk robes billow as he strove off, trying to figure out the man he saw departing. Wheeling on his heel, he headed straight toward the German Legation compound and Mayerling's headquarters.

Levi knocked and entered his commander's office and then saluted.

"Yes, Lancer Levi, you look as fit as can be expected under present circumstances. How is your leg?"

"My wound has healed, sir. Thank you for inquiring. Sir, I was told to see you by His Excellency Chou Lee. He said you had some..."

"Yes, Lancer, I was about to send for you, as I know you and Lancer Mathias were...are good friends. Chou has told me a strange story that seems almost implausible. I want to hear your opinion of this story. And if you have information to aid me in evaluating the truth of this tale."

"Yes, sir. I'll help in any way I can, sir."

"Good. Chou told me that his informants told him, there is a German soldier holed up in a village north of Peking. He doesn't know if it's Mathias or one of our other missing troops. You know we have several men unaccounted for since just before the siege, including Sergeant Brandenburg and Lancer Bauer, both of whom you believe were killed while on patrol. Could one of them somehow have escaped that attack?"

"No sir. I saw each of them pulled off his horse with at least six or eight Boxers attacking each of them. There is no way they could have survived, sir."

"You're sure of that, are you?"

"Absolutely. Yes, sir."

"All right then, do you know any possible reason why Lancer Mathias would or could end up in this village...let me see," Mayerling shuffled through papers on his desk, "ah, here it is, a place called An-Tsun, An-Tsun village. Ever hear of a village by that name, Lancer Levi? Levi? I asked you a question." Mayerling sat up in his chair, staring at Levi with a rapidly growing suspicious look in his eye.

"You hesitated, Levi. What do you know about this village? What's going on here?" His voice was harsh and demanding. "Now. I want to know what you know!"

Beads of sweat formed on Levi's forehead as his thoughts raced. How much should he tell? Could he get away with telling only part of the story? Would Mayerling believe him if he...

"Lancer, you're hesitating again," said Mayerling, rising from his desk. "You talk now, or I call the Sergeant of the Guard."

"Yes, yes, sir. I have heard of the village...from Markus. You see, sir, he has, or had, a lady friend who lived there. And..."

"When was the last time you personally know of that Lancer Mathias visited this 'lady' friend?" By the tone of Mayerling's voice, there could be no misunderstanding of what he meant by "lady."

"No, no, sir. It wasn't like that. Mathias really loves her and… well, the last time he visited her was when we got the three-day passes, about a month before the siege began, sir."

"Good, now what is this 'lady's' name?" The commander sat back down and picked up his pen.

"Li Ling, sir. Her name is Li Ling. She lives with her father. He used to be some kind of astronomy scholar. That's what Markus told me."

"Have you ever been to this…An-Tsun village?"

"No, sir. I've only heard about it from Lancer Mathias."

"Do you think that Mathias could have somehow gotten from under that boat in a lake in Imperial City and made it all the way to his girlfriend's… his lady friend's house out beyond the outer walls of Peking? Do you think he could have done that, Levi?"

"I don't know, sir. It's a long way, but he maybe could have, sir."

"Why wouldn't Mathias have tried for the legation, I mean, if he managed to escape the Imperial Guards in the middle of that lake? Do you have an answer to that, Levi?"

"Well, sir, he might have tried to make it to the legations, but couldn't because there were so many Boxers surrounding us here. Maybe it was easier for him to go north than to go south, sir. He needed to go somewhere, and he knew Li Ling would take him in, and he knew how to get there, sir."

"Yes, that sounds logical," Mayerling had to admit. "So you actually believe Lancer Mathias made it to, to this family, Ling, in An-Tsun?"

"Yes, sir, that is, if Chou, I mean nobleman Chou says there is a German soldier there, one of ours, who else could it be but Markus? I don't think any of the other men knew the Lings or even An-Tsun village, sir."

"Well, whoever it is, there's a German soldier out there, and we have to get him back safely. That's going to be tough with us under siege here in Peking."

The commander leaned back in his chair and looked up at Levi. In a more conciliatory tone he asked, "Since Mathias is your friend, do you have any ideas for getting him back? And I don't mean you going out there on your own… You were lucky to have survived the Boxer attack out on the Meridian Road."

"Sir, if I may offer a plan? Well, it's not really a plan exactly."

"Yes, what is it?"

"It's the nobleman Chou, sir. Somehow he was able to discover that one of ours was at the Lings, and…"

"How did Chou know to look in An-Tsun village?"

"Sir, I asked Chou to see if he could find out if Mathias was there. I…"

"You started your own investigation, without informing me?" Mayerling laced his tone with mild irritation. "That is highly irregular, Lancer. You must know that."

"Yes, sir."

"We will overlook that for now. What is the next step in your 'plan'?"

"Well, sir, I am meeting Chou this evening…after I get off duty at eleven, and I hope he will assist me…assist us, in getting Markus back."

Mayerling shook his head and couldn't help but smile at Levi's resourcefulness. "So, were you planning to inform me about all this? Never mind, I know the answer. But from now on I expect to be kept fully informed, and you must seek my approval before any undertaking. Is that clear?"

"Yes, sir." Levi hesitated for a moment then added, "There is something else, sir."

Mayerling looked up expectantly. "Now what?"

"It's about Chou. When we talked three days ago, he seemed willing to help, even caring. But when I mentioned the name of the village and Ling's name, he turned on me and abruptly got up and left. I thought it was very uncharacteristic of him. Do you think that means anything, sir?"

Mayerling thought for a moment. "I don't know, Levi, but I'm glad you shared that with me. Who knows the inscrutable mind of a Chinese nobleman." Mayerling seemed to be staring into the unknown, while Levi stood waiting. "Your concern for your fellow comrade is in the finest military tradition, Levi. You are dismissed, but report to me first thing tomorrow morning. I want to hear what Chou has to say."

Levi saluted, made a smart about-face, and left.

He felt nervous and excited at the same time as he sat waiting on the stable bench. The evening air seemed cooler than the usual sultry late night atmosphere. There had been no night attacks for almost a week, but the random shots meant it was still dangerous to be out in the open anywhere the Boxers had a clear shot into the legation's grounds.

As Levi sat in the August moonlit stable yard, he saw a figure approaching from the western perimeter wall, beyond which lay the smoldering ruins of the Mongol Market. The shadowy figure walked hunched over, like a servant or a slave.

That's not Chou Lee, thought Levi. He sat upright, pressing his back to the wall and raising his rifle so the barrel pointed in the direction of the oncoming figure.

As the stranger approached, he slowed down to a careful walk and Levi recognized the gait and proportions. It was Chou Lee's eunuch Chang Pao Fu. Chang spoke first.

"Greetings, Lancer Levi. My master, Chou Lee, sends his greetings."

"*Ja*, greetings to His Excellency Chou Lee." Apprehension was in Levi's voice. "I expected Chou himself to be here. Is something wrong? Should I go to him? Is he still going to help me?" Levi had risen from the bench and had moved into the shadow of the stables to be less of a target in the bright moonlight. Chang had also moved into the darkness.

"My master has sent me to deliver a message to you." Chang pulled a folded letter out of his wide sleeve and handed it over. In the dim light, Levi knew he would not be able to read the message, but he could feel the wax of the seal on the heavy folded paper. It smelled of sandalwood.

"I can't read this here. Does Chou expect a reply from me? We could go back to the barracks and I…"

"No, sir. That will not be necessary. My master said there is no need for a reply from you, that you will understand the…" Chang hesitated a moment, "the conditions, I should say, the circumstances. That is all." Chang hesitated again to be sure Levi understood. "Now I must return to my master. Good night, Lancer Levi." He stepped into the moonlight again and was about to leave when Levi grabbed his arm.

"No, wait. I have to know. Will I see your master, His Excellency, again? I need his help!"

"I understand," Chang said in refined Mandarin, with an edge of sympathy. "It is not for me to say. It is my master's wish that decides all things." With that, Chang moved swiftly across the stable yard and disappeared into the darkness of the Mongol Market wall. Levi was dumbstruck by this turn of events. He stood there staring after Chang, into the blackness and the bleakness of his disappointment, still clutching Chou's letter.

He slowly turned and proceeded back toward the barracks. His head was down as he shuffled along, oblivious to the danger of walking slowly in the moonlight, or of the constant smell of either burning buildings or gunpowder. Levi crossed the stone bridge along Legation Street without a thought to the stench of the open rivulet of sewage. He was completely focused on what lay scribed on the stiff paper in his hand. His pace picked up as he neared the one place he knew would be lit at this time of night, Captain Mayerling's office.

"*Guten Aben*, Levi," the guard said as Levi approached the circular opening to the German Legation.

"*Ja*, and you," he replied absentmindedly. He entered through the heavy wooden door and quickly closed it. A lantern was glowing on a table in the empty room. Levi thrust the letter near it as he broke the wax seal. It was a longer message than he had expected. Beautiful calligraphy covered the page. Levi was surprised at Chou Lee's elegant Gothic German script. He began to read in the dim light.

> *Lancer Levi:*
>
> *The message in your hand suggests my able servant Chang has successfully delivered it to you. My presence was not necessary for communicating our mutual concern for your comrade Lancer Mathias. Through my inquiries, it has been determined that the German soldier at the Ling compound is Lancer Mathias. He is uninjured and being well cared for.*
>
> *However, it is extremely dangerous for him even to be in the village of An-Tsun. My agitated countrymen are even now attacking Christians and burning homes in that and other surrounding villages. Therefore, no attempt to rescue or even contact him is advisable at this time. An unfortunate but necessary circumstance. When your enemy is stronger, it is best to wait longer. However, your fellow soldier should be safe with the family Ling.*
>
> *When the time is appropriate, I will attempt communication and inform you of my success.*
>
> *There is another issue of singular importance. You must destroy this letter as soon as you have consumed its message, as it is a grave threat to my continued existence.*

There is another matter of a most delicate nature but of equal importance. The girl Li Ling and her father, Wan Ling, must never know of my assistance, and must never hear my name from your lips. Events of the past require complete anonymity.

Chou Lee, Chancellor of the Imperial Observatory.

Levi stared at the red Chinese chop next to Chou's written name. How did Chou find out it was Markus and that he was uninjured? He must have an amazing network of spies or agents or something. And what was all this secret stuff about not telling the Lings his name? Levi wondered what their past connections had been. He wondered what had happened. He'd have to ask Markus next time he saw him, whenever that would be. It looked like he'd just have to wait, as Chou said. He knew Mayerling would want to see the letter in the morning, and then he'd have to burn it.

CHAPTER IX

Sadness and Tears and the White Lotus

SMOKE LINGERED IN the still morning air, and it wasn't from cooking fires. Boxers on foot and Imperial Guards on horseback had visited An-Tsun village several times since discovering the horse from the imperial stables wandering near the village without a saddle. No one seemed to know how it got there, but when the body of a fellow Imperial Guard stripped of his uniform was discovered several kilometers away, the search was on. Most of the guards and Boxers suspected Chinese Christians and took their brutal revenge on any person with even a slight association with Christians. Their families and their property also suffered swift retaliation, and the smoke was evidence of that rampaging anger.

Wan Ling hurried down the back alleys of his village trying to avoid anyone he knew or knew him. He had been too visible of late in local disputes and with strangers. It caused eyes to turn. Until recently, he had maintained the illusion of the quiet life of a scholar, artist, and scribe. Lately he was seen intervening to protect his

Christian neighbors and even defending missionaries fleeing south toward the coast.

As he rounded the back wall of his home, he thought of his people and his ultimate efforts. He was completely sympathetic with his fellows' frustration and anger with the foreigners. He knew he needed to somehow damp down this self-destructive violence. The killings and burnings were counterproductive to their efforts, and now they'd been swept up in an ill-conceived, ill-timed revolt. Wan was furious that the White Lotus was not leading the uprising. It had slipped from their hands again.

He shook his head in exasperation. Sun was going to have to flee, again. The Imperial authorities would be looking for a scapegoat if the effort collapsed, when it collapsed, and it would be the White Lotus.

He reached the front gate and pulled the cord, and Li Ling hurried out to greet her father. She looked stressed.

"Father, I'm so glad you're home. I was worried about you. I've prepared the additional bed for your friend. When will he be arriving?"

He quickly swung the heavy gate closed and heaved the beam into the brackets. "Thank you, daughter, I'm fine. Sun Yat Sen will come tonight sometime, possibly late. Have a meal prepared for him," Wan sounded tired.

At thirty-five, Sun Yat Sen was a youthful-looking, energetic, and forceful personality. He had already done battle with the Chinese authorities and was on constant alert for fear of arrest. As a liberal rebel and political conspirator advocating parliamentary monarchy or better, the complete overthrow of the empress, he was thought of, by the ultra-conservative government and nobles, to be a very serious threat. He was always in grave danger.

"Where is our guest, Mathias?" asked Wan.

"He's working in the vegetable garden. It's his favorite place.

It gives him something to do." Li Ling followed her father into the house. Pouring cold tea into his cup, she sat down beside him at the table.

"Father," she began, "I must talk with you. I'm so worried about us, all of us. You know how I feel about Markus and how he feels about me. But what can we do? What's going to become of us? What if the Boxers come here to the house? If they find him..." Her words trailed off. Tears brimmed in her eyes. "All these fires and beatings of our neighbors, why has everything gone crazy?" Tears streamed down her face as she rocked back and forth. "When will it end?"

Mr. Ling put down his drained teacup and looked at his daughter. He knew that even in the best of times, a serious relationship with a foreigner carried a great stigma except for the most loyal or closest friends, especially for a woman, and especially in a small village like An-Tsun. In these lawless times, the discovery of Markus within the household would be fatal to him and could be fatal to all. He reached out and took her hand.

"My most precious daughter, no one knows when this madness will end. You must be patient and very careful. As long as no one knows Mathias is here, we should be safe. I sadly understand how you feel toward this man, but remember, he presents a grave danger to you...to us, if he is discovered. You know that."

She nodded her head slightly, looking down.

He paused, thinking about what he had to tell her.

"I must ask you to be strong and brave at this moment, as I have to tell you something. Can you be strong for me, my daughter?" He looked into her tear-streaked face with his gentle eyes. She seemed so young.

She nodded again.

"Sun Yat Sen will be arriving sometime tonight, as I said." Wan changed the subject to what was most pressing on him. "He is fleeing from the Imperial Guards and must soon leave China for a period.

It's just too dangerous for him here. It's similar to the last time…and the time before that too. Do you remember when you were a little girl and he stayed with us? And he had to leave for several years?"

"Yes, Father, but why does he have to flee again? Did he do something wrong?"

Mr. Ling thought a moment on how best to answer.

"It's very complicated, child, and the less you know the better it is for you."

She followed his comment with a perceptive question. "Is it about all those meetings you go out to? Is he there? Did you and he…"

"Enough, Li." Wan raised his hand, and she fell silent. "Sun Yat Sen is a very brave and honorable man, and he has a great mission in this world, for China and for all its people. I can see in your eyes you need a greater explanation, so I will reveal to you our…his plan. He and others want to better our kingdom, our country. They want to modernize China, change China so the people have a better life. Do you understand? But the empress and others don't want change. Don't want to help the people. That is the problem and that is why he must leave for a time. Because we, the White Lotus, are not strong enough; we are not strong enough to overcome the forces against us. And that is why it is so dangerous for Sun and all who support him."

Li looked up. "The White Lotus? What's the White Lotus? I've heard of it but not much."

"You know it from your history lessons, don't you? It's a very old spiritual league, going back well over a thousand years to the Tong dynasty or even before. For many centuries, it was devoted to attaining the Pure Land of Buddha, Amitabha, and seeking salvation through the Eternal Mother Goddess."

"Quan Yen," Li said, almost to herself.

"Yes," her father responded. "She is a direct descendant of the Great Mother." He continued:

"In the fourteenth century, the White Lotus Society revolted against the monarchy, believing the apocalypse was at hand. Since then it has been both spiritual and militant, particularly during the Ming dynasty and now during the Ch'ing. It's a secret society of true patriots, made up of many people. Nobody knows how many, because we must mostly remain anonymous to each other for our own protection. The Imperial government has many, many spies. There are spies everywhere, even in this village."

There was a long pause as they both thought about the implications of all these facts.

"And to complicate our efforts, the Boxers have started this terrible purge of Christians. They have very legitimate complaints against the foreigners, but their violence is damaging our efforts for governmental change."

Li Ling sat up and looked intensely at her father. "Governmental change...changes the government? You and Sun and the White Lotus Society want to change the government? You mean a new emperor? Who? Who would this new emperor be and from where?" Li stared at her father as she waited for him to reply.

Wan Ling finally smiled and looked at his daughter, and with a grin, said, "So many questions, so many questions; perhaps I educated you too well. Now I must explain everything. In our new government there isn't going to be an emperor or empress. We want a government for the people, for all the people, similar to America. A republic, with a president or prime minister, similar to England, and a legislative body and..."

Markus, passing through the door from the garden, interrupted them.

"Li, I've picked some carrots and onions and... Oh, *Mr.* Ling. Good evening to you, sir."

He looked at the two of them sitting close by each other at the table. Something was up. They looked very intense.

"*Ja*, so, is there any news beyond the walls?"

Li Ling looked at her father. Wan looked back at her.

The exchange was just long enough for Markus, already sensing something, to blurt out, "Li, Mr. Ling, what is it? What's going on?"

Silence filled the room.

"Father, you have to tell him. Markus has a right to know. He is in just as much danger as all of us, probably more…and…and maybe he can help," she added as she rose from the table and walked to Markus, taking his arm.

Mr. Ling looked up at the two of them, so young, so fresh, and so happy with each other. He had dismissed the idea that Markus could somehow help the situation. He was simply another complication, but he knew Li was right. Markus did have a right to know what was going on.

"Yes, my daughter, Lancer Mathias should be informed of the circumstances he, and we, find ourselves in. Let us enjoy our dinner together and talk about our future."

On hearing her father's decision, Li smiled broadly. Wan knew that the discussion, and his decision, would bring danger, sadness, and tears to Li, and probably to Markus, too.

Steam rolled off the rice pot and teakettle as Markus and Li chopped carrots and other garden vegetables and sliced a smoked fish and peaches.

Markus was looking forward to a wonderful meal, unlike anything Mama ever cooked at home. He was getting used to this Chinese food. He'd heard there was a Chinese restaurant somewhere in Munich, which he'd have to find when he got home. Whenever that would be.

"*Ja*, so, Li, what's this big conversation your father is planning for us? What's it all about, as if I can't guess?" He smiled at her and she glanced at him, returning a smile. "It's about us, right? And, and what else? It's what's going on in town, on the other side of these walls, *ja?*" He rolled his head as his eyes scanned the great beyond.

"Yes, that's part of it," Li offered. "But there's more, lots more." She hesitated. "It would be better to let my father explain...let him tell you the whole story." With that, she took the dishes to the table for dinner. Markus followed her, came up behind and kissed her on the side of her neck, saying, "Ooh, all very mysterious!" They both chuckled as she pushed him away with her hip while glancing toward her father sitting in the garden.

It was a very good dinner. They talked about the food and the weather and Markus almost mentioned the Chinese restaurant in his hometown, but thought better of it, so he talked about his mother's cooking, and the food he got in the army. Li was both enjoying the conversation and waiting for her father to begin the extraordinary story she had heard earlier. Finally, as the teacups were filled for the third time, Mr. Ling began.

"We are going to have a visitor tonight, a very important visitor." With that, he commenced to relate the facts of the present situation and the story of the White Lotus Society and Sun Yat Sen's efforts for a better China. He also revealed the plan to get Sun out of China to safe haven in Japan.

"There are already many Japanese in China," Ling explained, "as they, like the Europeans, have designs on various parts of the country. The intent is to make contact with the Japanese or other foreigners, with the help of friendly Chinese, to secure the escape. Sun will stay here for a few days or as long as it takes to make the necessary arrangements."

Wan paused. "Li, you must prepare a bed for Sun. Markus will move into the garden shed. A most comfortable bed can be made for you there."

Markus, looking at Wan, nodded in recognition. "Of course," he offered. All of this was fascinating to hear. Both sat at the table in rapt attention as Mr. Ling continued.

"Now I must disclose the final necessary element of this enterprise. It is truly not what I wish, but what must be done. It is for your safety, Li, and for the safety of Lancer Mathias, and for the very safety of this household. Markus must accompany Sun Yat Sen."

Li gasped. "He has to leave? Markus has to leave? Now, with all this fighting going on all around us?" she protested. "It's too dangerous. You can't send Markus out there, Father! There must be a better way, a better time, but not now!" Her voice rose in emotion. She looked back and forth between Markus and her father.

Markus sat there with a stone-cold look on his face. He did not want to go, to leave Li, his one true love, his only love …but he knew almost immediately that Mr. Ling was right. He did have to go, he did have to leave and get back to his unit. This was probably the safest way to make it out of An-Tsun village, and to one of the European concessions where he would be safe and could reestablish contact with a German unit.

Markus looked up. "You are right, Mr. Ling, sir. I must leave… and now. I have put you and your daughter in danger by being here. I apologize to you… to you both. I will go with Sun."

Li was beside herself with a sense of impending loss.

"When…when will this happen?" Li asked her father as she wiped away a tear on her cheek with the knuckle of her index finger.

"Probably in a few days, my daughter…a week at most. It depends on Sun and the arrangements we can make. Until then, we must just wait…and keep out of sight, and hope the Boxers and Imperial Guards don't do a house-by-house search. They are doing that in several nearby villages."

Wan Ling rarely misspoke, but he immediately regretted mentioning the other villages being searched. *What is the point of upsetting everyone*, he thought.

Li and Markus looked at each other with worried eyes.

"What will we do if they come here, Father?"

"Yes, what should we do, Mr. Ling? Maybe I should leave now. I could sneak out at night and…"

"Don't be impulsive, Markus. You would be caught by dawn. No, it's best to stay here and wait for Sun."

"Is there someplace Markus could hide here if they come?" asked Li.

"I know where I will conceal myself if they come," said Markus without hesitation.

His self-assurance startled his companions. Li and Ling looked at each other and asked almost simultaneously, "Where?"

"In your koi pond," he said with a grin. "I've already tried it. While you both were out, I put on those dark purple pajamas you gave me and carefully sank into the deep end of the pond below the lily pads and water grasses. There's a bit of an overhang, and I just about fit. I've prepared a breathing straw, and I put it just where I'll need it," he said triumphantly.

"Oh Markus, you're so clever!" Li bubbled, looking lovingly at her lover.

"My wish is that your 'clever' hiding place may never be needed," said Ling.

Sun Yat Sen was due to arrive well after midnight. Mr. Ling waited in the garden while Li and Markus made up a bed in the garden shed. They moved the tools and ceramic pots around and stacked wooden boxes to extend the length of the workbench on which a beautifully printed quilt was laid.

"*Ja*, this will do fine for me…fine for us! Ha!"

"Quiet! My father will hear you on this calm night," whispered Li with a smile. They stole a quick kiss before returning to the side of Mr. Ling. They were sitting together listening to the crickets and watching the night swallows swoop back and forth catching insects. It was very still with just a few wispy clouds tracing across the half moon. At an almost inaudible rapping, all three heads turned toward the barred gate.

"Inside, light out," Wan whispered to Li. All three got up, two headed for the house.

Wan Ling slid the bar from the gate, and a stealthy figure quietly passed through. Wan could just make out two other men, Sun's comrades, scurry away in the darkness.

"Greetings, friend."

"Yes, and to you…come." They entered the house and were met by the two young lovers, who closed the door to the garden behind them.

"It has been a long and treacherous day. We lost a man to the Guards in the last village… They are very thick hereabouts, these Imperial Guards and Boxers." Sun spoke breathlessly as he looked around and glanced at Markus. "A new recruit to our cause?"

"Not precisely," replied Wan. "He is visiting Li. This is Lancer Mathias of the Imperial Germany Army. He has come from the besieged legations in Peking. He has his own interesting story to tell when you have the time or inclination." They shook hands firmly and exchanged slight smiles.

"Yes, but not now." Sun looked back at the gate, and then nodded toward Markus. "He got here, from the legations, in one piece? Remarkable!"

They sat at the table and Wan struck a lamp. Li brought dinner for Sun, and tea for all as Sun related the difficulty of making it to An-Tsun village.

"They are searching the villages and beating and killing scores of innocent peasants. Sometimes our people are their own worst enemy." He shook his head. "The masses are so angry and frustrated, they lash out at even their own kind. We must bring change…big change. And this is the price of that change. Some of us will be consumed by the fires of our own revolution."

Silence lingered over the little group. Finally, Sun spoke cheerfully. "Wan Ling, your fine house and garden look splendid. I haven't been here in, how long has it been?"

"Almost two years now," Mr. Ling replied.

"Yes, and Li is a lovely young woman now, and with an admirer, a European! Just like I've seen in Hawaii. Well, well, is this part of the new China we are creating?" he said with a big grin on his face. He burst out laughing at his own joke, and the others could not help joining in. It was a lighthearted moment in an otherwise bleak situation.

"Now to business," Sun said. Wan made the slightest gesture.

Li read her father's command and got up. Turning to Markus, she said quietly, "Let's finish making up your bed."

Mr. Ling's eyes followed them out until they disappeared into the darkened garden.

They were in each other's arms on their first step into the garden shed. Markus was intoxicated by the feel of Li's body pressed against his and her passionate kisses. She could feel his hardness through her light summer dress. She reached down and under his shirt and slid her hand down to grasp his cock, while his hands slid up her smooth skin and cupped her breasts. His hands continued upward and pulled Li's gown over her head. His trousers crumpled in a pile by his feet. They separated for only a second while she helped him out of his top. With an urgency of intense passion, she grabbed him again as he lifted her up, his hands on her buttocks. She slid onto him as her legs wrapped his hips. He began an ever-increasing rhythm.

"I love you, I love you," she breathed into his ear as they both culminated their lovemaking in a flurry of kisses.

"No, no, don't move!" he whispered. "Not yet."

"I'm not going anywhere." She giggled and they remained locked together, leaning on the gardener's workbench in an almost pitch-black corner of heaven for them.

The next morning Li was up early preparing breakfast, and Markus walked in from the garden shed to find Wan and Sun seated in close discussion.

"Good morning, everyone," Markus said with a respectful nod to the two and a smile to Li.

"Yes, good morning, young man," Sun responded.

"Come join us here." Wan gestured toward the bench at the table. "We have plans to make, and you are a part of that."

Li listened to this apprehensively as she placed a half-dozen bowls of assorted foodstuffs on the table and handed around chopsticks and spoons. They ate heartily between light conversation.

When they finished, Mr. Ling said, "I will leave now to reconnoiter the village. I should be back by noon." He glanced at Li as a gesture of reassurance. "We shall see if travel conditions make it possible to reach the coast safely. The White Lotus has been preparing possible routes and safe houses for your trip." He was looking at Markus.

"Thank you, sir," Markus offered, then looked at Li, who appeared almost childlike in her vulnerability. He walked over beside her as her father made his way to the gate with Sun. The two men talked briefly, and Wan opened the gate just wide enough to slip out. Sun returned to the two young people and, with a lighthearted air, asked, "Did I ever tell you about my visits to Europe? And tell me, Lancer Mathias, about your country, Germany. I've not been there yet!" They sat back down, poured more tea, and Sun did his best to cheer up the two star-crossed lovers as they awaited the return Mr. Ling.

It was a hot early afternoon. Wan had not returned for the lunch spread out on the table. All three were resting on benches in a shady part of the garden, waiting. Sun was reading a book of poetry he had selected off a bookshelf. Markus and Li held hands as they sat silently watching the koi lazily drift through the roots of the water plants in the pond. Markus stretched his arms and yawned and looked up into the ripe peaches overhead.

"They smell so good...good enough to eat," he said, smiling.

Li looked up with a smile and answered, "Yes, and the plums over there are ripening, too."

They both turned around to look across the garden to the dozen trees within the walls. They sat transfixed for a moment as their eyes widened at a thick black cloud of smoke towering into the sky. Their backs stiffened and Li squeezed Markus' hand.

"Oh, no! It's the village...where Papa is!" They stood up and Li called out, "Sun, Sun!"

Sun swung around and immediately saw the menacing cloud billowing in a diagonal across the sky. "Li," he commanded. "Get me some clothes I can wear into town. I can't be seen in these western clothes...and a hat. I'm going to look for your father."

Markus asked, "Is there anything I can do?"

"Yes, stay here, out of sight, in case someone should come searching. Li should probably be all right here as long as you are not seen, so be vigilant."

Markus hurried into the house and returned moments later as Sun was slipping into traditional Chinese garb. "Here, take this, you may need it." Markus handed his military revolver to Sun. Li's hand was at her throat, watching. Sun took the gun, looked at it a moment, then handed it back.

"If it comes to that, I don't think, what is it, six shots? I don't think it would be enough. Besides, I'm going as a simple villager swept up in the commotion." He gave a resolute smile to them both and headed for the gate. "Only Li should answer the gate. You stay out of sight."

Markus unbarred the door and Sun was gone. He stuck the revolver into the front of his belt and headed for the house. "I'm going to slip into those purple pajamas, just in case. Li, I think it would be a good idea to remove from sight anything that shows more than two people living here. Start with the table settings."

Li quickly gathered up the extra place settings and Sun's cigarettes and clothes.

"What are we going to do? Do you think Sun can find Papa?" Li's eyes were glistening.

"Your father is a wise man, Li, a smart man. He knows how to take care of himself…and Sun will probably find him, or they will come back separately. From what I've heard about your father's involvement with the White Lotus, he surely knows how to take care of himself…and he has friends around here who will help him, too."

She was in his arms, and he held her for a long time.

"I want to do something." He broke away from her and went to the garden shed and returned with an auger.

"What are you going to do with that?" she asked.

"You'll see." He headed to the gate and started boring a hole about four and a half feet off the ground. The auger rotated through the old thick wood, and soon the clean hole was finished. He found a stick, broke off a three-inch piece, and stuck it in the hole.

"Now, when you want to look out onto the lane in front of your gate, you can. Just take out the stick. See?" Li leaned into the door as she pulled the stick out. "I made it for your height." Markus smiled. Now you can check who is knocking before you let them in. And you notice I drilled the hole over to the side so most people won't even notice it's there.

"Let me have a look. *Ja.* Good. Just one thing, step outside for a minute and rub your hand over the hole to knock off any loose shavings; then no one will see it." He unbarred the door and she stepped out and was back in seconds.

Taking his hand, she said, "Let's go inside and wait. We can watch the smoke from there."

It was after dark when they heard rapping at the gate. Markus moved to the side of the pond as Li raced to the gate, pulled the plug out of the hole, and peered out. She quickly unbarred the gate and Wan and Sun hurried in. Both stepped quickly into the house and sat down. They appeared sweaty and exhausted.

"The Boxers are everywhere and in numbers," Wan started, gulping down a cup of tea. "Food, please, Li, for our guest." She had dishes already prepared and brought them out immediately for everyone as Wan continued.

"About fifty Christian villagers were being harassed when I arrived at the river road. They put up a fight and sought sanctuary in the temple. They barricaded themselves in and fought a pitched battle most of the afternoon. I watched the whole thing from the second floor of the herb shop. There was nothing I could do to help them. Somehow, the temple caught fire, and soon the Christians had to run for it. Most were killed by those club-wheeling thugs." He shook his head.

Sun had eaten quickly and continued.

"I think many villagers who were not with the Boxers initially were incensed that their Buddhist temple was burned down because of the Christians, so they pretty much joined in. Now the whole village is looking for any Christians that escaped. They are going door to door and will surely search the outlying houses and farms like this one tomorrow. We are going to have to leave before dawn."

"Before dawn!" Li blurted out. "Before dawn…where will you go, where can you hide!" She clung to Markus' arm, her fingers digging into his bicep.

"We're not going to be 'hiding' anywhere," said Sun, "We're going to be running, and the sooner the better. I've been through this before, and I've found that there is a time to fight, a time to hide, and a time to run. And this is a running time. Our contacts haven't arrived here yet with the escape route to the coast, so we had better make contingency plans ourselves, if they don't get here in the next few hours, and that doesn't seem likely."

They sat for a few moments in silence. Finally Mr. Ling spoke:

"Since you don't have the use of the route plan and safe houses, you could head north to the Great Wall and then follow it east about twenty miles, then turn south toward the coast. There are fewer villages on the other side of the Great Wall and they are smaller, so the missionaries haven't established themselves there very much. The country folk have probably not joined the Boxers. It might be a fairly safe route. I believe you would turn south at the fork of the…"

Wan was interrupted by rapid knocking at the gate. Everyone froze. They all looked at each other for a second. Markus blew out the light and reached for his revolver. Sun also pulled out a small Smith and Wesson 1884 model revolver from his belt.

Wan said, "Let's hope that's your route map arriving." He got up as Makus headed for the pond.

Li followed her father, overtook him, and pulled the plug out of the spy hole. Peering out, she whispered to her perplexed father, "It's a nobleman, from the look of his dress. Whatever could he want?"

Mr. Ling pressed his daughter away from the view hole and looked through intently. He slowly withdrew and turned, staring at nothing at all. "What is he doing here?" he muttered audibly but to himself. "I told him…" Wan broke off. He slowly, almost reluctantly pulled the bar from its brackets, and the gate swung open.

An aristocrat of obvious birth stepped through the gate, followed by his servant. Wan stared at the brocaded man before him. Chou Lee stared back. Both were silent. Li looked back and forth at both of them, wanting to know what was going on.

Finally, Chou spoke. "It's not wise to leave your gate open like this when some of our misguided countrymen are on a rampage even as we speak."

Wan Ling motioned silently for the two to enter the compound. For another awkward moment, there was silence. Wan stepped toward Chou, very close. "You promised never, never to come here," he whispered sternly. Li looked intently at her father, her brow furrowed. Sun, having put his pistol back in his belt, came forward and spoke.

"Ah, Your Excellency Chou Lee, it's good of you to come. But was it necessary? The risk! I thought one of the others would bring the route maps."

"They are not coming," Chou said. "Fate has ordained their deaths at the hands of our enemies…and we must assume the route maps are in their hands. I fear the White Lotus safe houses are being burned as we speak."

"Come in, sir. Come in," Li said graciously, leading everyone into the house. Chou followed Li, looking intently at her.

Sun led the way back to the table and struck a light. Mr. Ling offered Chou a large chair at the head of the table; the others sat down on the benches. Chou's eunuch, Chang Pao Fu, stood behind the chair.

"This is quite a…" Sun began to say.

"Chou Lee and Chang! Am I glad to see you!" Markus burst in. "I mean, sir, Your Excellency, it is so good to see you again! Li, these are the men who helped me get out of Peitang Cathedral and to the lakes in the Imperial City!" He approached Chou, bowed, and extended his hand.

Chou did not get up but did take Markus' hand in a very light handshake. "It is through divine providence that you have accomplished your objective and arrived here at Mr. Ling's home…and Miss Li. It was a significant accomplishment. And now you must reverse your travels and again in a most treacherous time. May fortune bless your efforts."

"Thank you, sir, thank you," Markus said with a big grin. Turning to Chang, he again extended his hand.

Chang bowed low and held his bow a few seconds, indicating

there would be no handshake. He did, however, respond to Markus' greeting by saying, in a very soft voice and with the slightest smile, "I am happy to see you well, sir. You have had an arduous journey."

"*Ja*, so," Markus demurred.

"Come sit down, here," Li directed.

Wan cleared his throat. "These are dreadful times, dangerous times to be on the roads, or to be associated with westerners or reformist ideas. Am I to understand, Chou Lee, that you are assisting Sun Yat Sen and the White Lotus? That you are assisting in our efforts to bring China into the modern world?"

"As you have said it, I do lend my assistance when it is perceived to be of value. We are a small wave in a stormy sea, but we can move the ship in this direction or that. The Middle Kingdom, in its ancient glories, relies on the magnificent achievements of the past. There are some, even in exalted positions, who perceive a need to evolve and progress, to bring China into the modern age. These are noble aims and require noble deeds. Sun Yat Sen and others, and you, Wan Ling, are the vanguard of the changes that must occur. But now, we must husband our forces, to keep alive our leadership. I have only come to your home, Wan Ling, because of these most dire circumstances." Everyone was at rapt attention, staring at Chou.

"The route maps are gone. The safe houses are probably gone. Your escorts are gone. That is why I am here."

Sun spoke up with all eyes turning to him. Li clung to Markus' arm. "Do you have an alternate route and other safe houses for us, Your Excellency? Wan has just suggested making north to the Great Wall, following it east, and then turning south to the coast. What do you think?"

Chou Lee was looking at Li as Sun spoke. He hesitated a moment, sitting erect in the great chair, his eyes turning to Wan. "Your plan is a good one, Wan Ling. It is surely the safest land route to the coast, given that there are no completely safe roads or villages. And we cannot know the shifting forces that may oppose our progress. All routes will be hazardous at this time. However, I have a plan that may take you directly to the coast in the shortest distance and, barring obstructions, the least time in passage."

All four listeners were startled by Chou's bold statement.

"Truly, a different route?" Sun asked.

Mr. Ling added, "But all other routes are through much more populated villages or Peking itself, and they all will have great numbers of hostile villagers and Boxers…and probably Imperial Guards. We have had word that some units of Imperial Guards are directly joining the Boxers. It seems we must go north to avoid these hostile populations."

CHAPTER X

The Imperial Mail Boat

"I DO NOT propose a route through villages or Peking," The tense atmosphere was quelled by Chou Lee's steady aristocratic tone.

"I did not come here on horseback or palanquin or walking. I came by the Imperial Mail Boat. I boarded west of Peking on the Hun Ho River. It travels twice a week up the Hun Ho and turns off onto your tributary. As you know, it stops here once a week going north and once a week going south." He paused. "My plan is for you to commandeer the boat on its southern route. As I have just transported myself here on that craft, I know its crew, its layout and schedule."

Sun burst in: "What a brilliant plan. Take over the ship and sail all the way to the coast! Brilliant! We probably won't even have to go all the way to the coast. We'll probably run into an American or British or German gunboat along the way."

"Or you may run into a blockade," Wan offered in warning. "In the past the Imperial Guards have suspended heavy ropes and chains across the river to catch pirates. They could do the same if they find out you are coming, not to mention other boats that the Boxers or Guards could commandeer. I'm sure others are fleeing downriver, also. Our people who have taken up with the Christians, and missionaries too, and probably all sorts of Europeans are just trying to get out of harm's way. It's not going to be easy. We are a long way from the coast."

This monologue by Wan dampened down Sun's enthusiasm. Li rested her head on Markus' shoulder as everyone sipped tea. It was almost midnight and moths flew in descending circles around the lamp in the center of the table.

Markus asked, "When will the mail boat be passing An-Tsun?"

"Some time midmorning," Li offered. "At little villages like An-Tsun, it only stops to drop off and pick up mail, passengers, and freight. It's usually here for only an hour or two, or as long as the crew take for lunch and such."

Chou pulled from his heavy long sleeve a stiff sheet of paper. He showed the drawing as he described the boat. It was a graphite drawing of the side view of the mail boat. The image itself was about twelve inches long. Below it was a top view of the boat, actually only the deck with dotted lines indicating the below-deck compartment, which consisted of a very tight engine room in the stern, too small to stand up in. Amid ships was the coal-fired boiler that drove the steam engine. A large pile of wood and coal was stacked nearby. Forward, just behind the bow of the wooden-hulled riverboat, was a pilothouse large enough for four people. A canvas canopy covered the entire deck back of the pilothouse, with the large funnel poking through the canvas.

"The crew consists of three navy men: a pilot and two deckhands that feed the boiler. There were two Imperial Guards on board on the upstream journey. I assume the same number coming downstream. That is what you will have to deal with."

"Chou Lee, sir, do you also have a scheme to take over this boat that has two armed guards and three Imperial Navy men?" Markus asked. "Maybe Sun could approach the vessel without raising suspicions, but there is no way I could get near. I would be spotted right away. And even if both of us could get near, how could we overcome five military defenders?"

"As I have stated, that is what you will have to deal with." Chou paused and nodded his head slightly in the direction of the two men. Unfolding his fan with a smart snap of the wrist, he continued. "However, I suggest you eliminate the two Imperial Guards before you get on the boat."

"And you have a plan to do that?" Markus asked, knowing by now that Chou would have a plan already worked out.

"Before I got off the mail boat in An-Tsun, I took note of the actions of the crew. After tying up, the two Imperial Guards went into the tavern by the dock. I also went into this establishment. It was empty except for the two and the barman. An excellent opportunity to overpower part of the crew, take their uniforms, and get aboard and subdue the remaining crew. The captain also got off and walked to the village temple to deliver the mail. That should eliminate a third foe." A momentary silence. "Are either of you familiar with boilers?"

Markus spoke up. "*Ja*, I am. My friend Levi has a farm, and they have a big steam-driven thresher. He and I would help sometimes and run it. I don't imagine this boiler," he pointed to the drawing, "is much different than a thresher."

"Excellent," replied Chou Lee.

Mr. Ling had been silent during these discussions but now he spoke up. "I propose those leaving," looking at Sun and Markus, "leave soon, take over the tavern tonight, and wait for an opportune time to carry out the plan. In daylight it will be very difficult to get to the dock undetected."

"An excellent suggestion, Wan," Sun offered. "How soon do we leave?"

"There is no need to hide in the tavern all night," Li said urgently.

"You only need to get to the dock before dawn." Li looked plaintively at Markus and then her father.

Sensing her anguish, Wan offered, "Li is correct, there is no need to spend the night in the tavern. Better to finish up here and for us to get some rest."

"Another excellent point," Chou said.

"Then it's agreed? We take over the boat tomorrow," Sun offered. After several more minutes of discussion, and sleeping arrangements made for Chou and Chang, it was agreed to rise at three o'clock in the morning. The two men would be out the gate by 3:45. The dock was a brisk ten-minute walk away.

Markus and Li Ling stepped into the dark garden arm in arm. "We knew this time would come, my darling," Markus began. "I must get back to my unit. I have an obligation to my country and to my fellow soldiers." He turned and held her tightly. "You know I love you. You know I want to stay, but…"

"Shh," she whispered. "I know all that. I just want this moment to go on forever. I want to remember you just as you are this moment." Tears were streaming down her cheeks. She turned toward him and their lips touched. His tears mingled with hers and each of them sobbed quietly.

They stood there in the silence of the night for a long time, gently swaying until they were both drained of emotion. Finally, she said: "You must get some rest, my love. Come, I will lie with you while you sleep." She led him, not to the garden shed, but to her room upstairs.

By three in the morning they were all up. A faint smell of smoke still lingered in the air. Li was preparing tea and a meal. Mr. Ling, Sun, Chou, and Chang were conversing. It was agreed Chou Lee and his servant would leave first to scout the path to the tavern. Sun Yat Sen and Markus would follow ten minutes later.

Wan Ling handed back the small bag of coins Markus had given him when he first arrived in An-Tsun village.

"You may need this as gold and silver sometimes smooth a dangerous passage."

Markus checked his revolver and the extra cartridges. Sun adjusted his gun in his belt. Li assembled a set of clothing and a hat to make him less conspicuous. Sun also wore non-western clothing. After a quick meal and farewells, Chou and Chang slipped out into the darkness.

Mr. Ling and Sun found a distraction to leave Li and Markus alone for a few moments.

"Be safe, my love," she whispered.

"I promise," he said.

Sun, knowing it was a difficult time for them, joined them. "Time to go, it will be light soon. Come along, let's go."

The four walked to the gate, where Wan Ling stepped forward. "Lancer Mathias, I bless your journey back to your people. Li and I have gained much from your visit with us."

Li brought forth a small cloth bag with a long shoulder strap. "Food for you and Sun." She reached up and kissed his cheek. "Good-bye, my love." The bar was slid aside, and they were gone.

It was all a blur as Markus sat inside the dark tavern, stale beer smell permeating the air. They had just broken into the empty building by a back window. Chou Lee and Chang were gone. Li and Wan agreed to wait behind their barred gate until after the mail boat left, in the event that if the daring plan failed, Markus and Sun might be able to return.

She's there, and I'm here, leaving for, who knows how long. There is so much I wanted to say to her, so much I wanted her to know...and now I'm going, I'm... Markus was cut off by Sun.

"Heads up, someone's coming," With drawn guns, they crouched low on either side of the door. Streaks of light came streaming in through the dirty windows. A lone male rattled a set of keys and unlocked the heavily carved ancient red door. He stepped in and let out a yelp as the cold nose of a gun was stuck into his back.

Sun spoke. "Not a sound, and you won't get hurt!"

"Sun? Is that you? It's me, Peiho!" the startled man blurted out.

"Peiho? Peiho? May the ancients be praised!" Sun practically shouted. "Ha, what luck we have today, Markus. This is Peiho. He's one of us. Oh, Peiho, I am so glad to see you! So, is this your tavern?"

"Yes, but what are you doing here, Sun? You scared me to death. I thought you were Boxers. I thought I was a dead man."

"We're on the run again. This is my friend Lancer Mathias of the Imperial German Army... It's a long story for another time. So, they haven't caught on to you. Good, good. It has gotten too dangerous here for me, and for my friend."

Peiho was looking at Markus with a mix of surprise, disdain, and revulsion. "How has he not been killed a dozen times over?"

"He's been, shall we say, visiting friends...ha, another time, Peiho."

"What are you doing here? What do you want? It's very dangerous. If you are seen...and him, we are all dead. Quick. What do you need? Money? A gun? You can't stay here. You have to leave quickly, before light."

"Peiho, we can't leave." And with that, Sun related the plan to commandeer the Imperial Mail Boat and escape downriver. Peiho was not impressed. He was angry and appalled at the audaciousness of the plan.

"You're going to get us all killed. You've got to leave now. Take one of the fishing rowboats. You still have time. You could be long gone before the boat is found missing."

"No, Peiho. That's not fast enough. We're going all the way to the coast if we have to. Listen, listen! Peiho," Sun clasped his arm, "we can stage it so it looks like we held you captive. A little cut on your head, a little blood, and you tied up… You'll be seen as a victim. I know we can pull this off…and remember what we are all working toward, what you have sacrificed and labored for. The White Lotus must regroup, the struggle must continue. I have much to do and you can help me, help all of us. We can win this—we just have to keep trying."

"Do you really think they will believe me, even if I'm tied up?"

"Yes, I know you can do this." Sun looked into Peiho's eyes and through Sun's sheer force of personality, Peiho agreed.

The black smoke above the trees and the sound of chug chugging out of the single stack indicated the Imperial Mail Boat was just upriver. It slowed down and drifted with the mild current in the blue-green water. It came about so that the bow of the boat faced upriver as it bumped the rickety wooden dock. Its whistle blew three times, and two ropes secured the fore and aft to the dock.

The dock and village were unusually quiet after the previous day of rampage. The villagers were either dead, burying the dead, or looking aghast at the damage to so many buildings in the town. The captain of the mail boat swung the mailbag over his shoulder as he hopped over the gunwale of the boat onto the dock. Only two porters had outgoing packages. These were handed to the crew, the porters' receipts were stamped, and they went back up the cart path toward the village.

No one had visited the tavern that morning, which wasn't unusual. All three men inside peered out the windows at the goings-on down by the river.

"Out of sight, someone's coming," Peiho exclaimed. "It's the mail boat captain. He's heading for the temple to drop off the mail, but the temple's a burned-out shell. I wonder where he's going to leave the mail." He wiped grime off the glass to get a better look. Turning, he retreated to behind the bar, lying down quickly as Markus bound him hand and foot with a nearby rope.

"Usually some of the crew come for a beer. Let's see if they do today," Peiho offered.

"Yes, we'll see," Sun said. "Now this is going to hurt, but it's just a glancing blow…just enough to draw blood, sorry." With that he struck Peiho a swift hit across the edge of his forehead with the butt of his gun.

"Ouch. That hurt, but not too much." Peiho grimaced. Sun, knowing his clothing would disguise his identity, moved to the windows. The captain walked by with his sack of mail. Markus joined Sun after he'd gone, and they continued in silence scouting up and down the path.

"Imperial Guards with rifles. Let's get out of sight," Markus said excitedly.

Sun added, "I'll give the signal when we jump them. Have the rope and gags ready." They all waited, with guns drawn, for the red doors to open.

Nothing happened for several minutes. More time passed.

"Where are they?" Mathias whispered. "I'll go see what's up."

"No, I'll go." Sun got up slowly and walked to the windows. No one was coming. He looked back down the path toward the boat. Nobody in sight. He leaned in close to the glass and looked up toward the village. He just caught three figures as they rounded the path by some trees.

"They're heading for the village! Three of them. I just saw three of them disappear around that clump of trees up the path."

Markus came forward and looked. "Are you sure?"

"Yes, yes, now's our chance. They're probably curious to see the village after the fire. There can't be more than one or two on board the boat. Let's go!"

"What about Peiho?" Markus questioned.

Sun spoke quickly. "Nothing's changed. Peiho will be all right. He knows what to do."

Sun and Markus hurried around the bar.

"We're leaving now—are you set?"

Peiho gurgled through his gag and moved his head up and down. Markus knelt down beside him. "Thank you, Peiho, and would you tell Li Ling we got away on the boat, that is, if we get away on the boat?" Peiho again nodded his head.

"Come on, come on, no time to lose." Sun was already opening the front door. They both looked uphill and quickly but casually walked toward the dock.

The path was dusty in the noonday sun. The wooden boat gleamed white in the brightness. It was hot and dragonflies and gnats buzzed above the water as the slow current swirled in small back eddies near the shore. The stems of willow trees hung in the water and were pulled in the direction of the current downstream.

Sun led as Markus, a step or two behind, slouched with his head down below the brim of his hat. Both men, conscious of their pistols out of sight but at the ready, approached the boat. The back of a head could be seen just above the gun wall. No one noticed the two as they neared the ropes securing the vessel to the dock. Two other men were far to the side, lying in the shade asleep. Sun looked back up the path. "Now!" he said.

With a quick jerk, the pistols were drawn, and both men jumped over the boat railing, landing with a thump on the deck. The first deck hand peering into the engine compartment swung his head around in fright and almost fell into the dark space.

Markus pointed his revolver directly at him with an outstretched arm. "Quiet!" He grabbed the sailor by his white uniform collar and pushed him down on the deck. The frightened seaman lay on his stomach, his fingers spread out palms down on the planks.

Sun had moved quickly to the engine opening and peered in, his pistol sweeping back and forth.

"Don't shoot, don't shoot! I'm coming out!" A young,

high-pitched voice rose from the dark shadows.

"Hands up, sailor," commanded Sun. "Out."

The young man, no more than eighteen, emerged with greasy hands. He was stripped to the waist.

"Down on the deck, quickly…by your friend."

"What do you want? The mail pouch is already gone. We have no money."

"Silence!" Markus poked the barrel of his pistol into the back of the talker. Sun ran to the pilothouse and flung open the door. No one. He quickly looked up the path. No one in sight.. His eyes scanned across to the men in the shade. No one stirred. "I'll get the lines and shove off. You keep them down and quiet."

"Right," Markus replied in a low voice.

It took a mighty push by Sun, but the small but heavy boat eased out away from the dock as Sun jumped back aboard. The craft was pointing upstream, but as the current caught the bow, the boat, on its own, began to swing around with the current. Sun ran to the pilot-house and spun the wheel so the rudder was hard to port. He called back to Markus in a tone just loud enough for him to hear: "We'll let her drift downriver before we coal her up. They won't be able to hear the engine or see the smoke."

"Sounds good! What about these two?"

"Tie them up. Here's some rope." He flung a coil of hemp back toward Markus. "No, have one of them stoke the boiler. Do you know how to start the engine?"

Markus took his eyes off the two on deck and looked into the engine compartment.

"I'm sure I can figure it out…but better to get one of these to show us. They can be persuaded. How long should we drift?"

"Just a few more minutes. It's a good thing the boiler has a good start on a head of steam; we don't have much control under way without power." Sun paused. "Let's get that engine started. There's a bend in the river up ahead."

Markus ordered the men to their feet. "Which one of you stokes the boiler?"

The shirtless sailor pointed to his chest. "I do. He's just in training."

"*Ja*, so, get started." He motioned toward the boiler. "You," he pointed to the second seaman, "put your hands behind your back."

While the boiler stoker descended into the well in the middle of the boat and began shoveling coal into the firebox, the second crewman stood with his hands behind his back waiting for Markus to pick up the rope on deck. Markus took a few steps toward the rope and heard a splash.

"Jesus Christ, he's gone!" Markus yelled as he lunged for the sailor, fast slipping toward the boat's wake to the stern. Markus raised his gun and took aim at his rapidly disappearing target.

"No, don't shoot, don't shoot. They might hear us!" Sun yelled to him. The other seaman was raising his shovel and stepping away from the firebox. Markus turned in time to see him raising the shovel.

"Don't!" he said coldly as he pointed his pistol at the man. "Back to work." On second thought Markus shouted, "I'm going to tie this one up and get that engine started. There's enough coal in the box for now."

In no time the engine was chugging, and the sweet smell of soft coal filled the air aft of the smokestack. The sailor was sitting next to the pilothouse door while Markus and Sun conversed inside.

"That had to be the easiest board and seizure of a naval boat I've ever heard of," Sun exclaimed, smiling. "Now let's look at this nautical map of the river. There are a lot of small ports of call between here and…and, let's see. This must be the homeport for this mail boat. Fengtai, it's the nearest town to this mark." They both studiously bent over the map.

"You see this? It's heavily underlined, that's probably it. Well, it doesn't really matter because we're going to steam right past it, right?" asked Markus.

"Yes, that's the plan. They aren't going to be happy seeing their mail boat sail by. Maybe we should wait until dark. What do you think?"

They both scanned the shoreline on the An-Tsun village side of the river as they talked.

Markus thought for a moment and said, "If we wait, it gives them time to alert downriver Imperial Guards and the Imperial Navy. They're sure to throw everything they have at us. If we race at full speed, we may be able to stay ahead of them. What do you think, Sun?"

"I like the idea of outrunning them if we can... Look, we're losing steam! We need to fire the boiler again. Should we use the sailor?"

"*Ja*, let's save our strength. I'll take the wheel. You want to get him going on the shovel?"

Sun untied their captive and got him working the coal pile. Markus found a short cord next to the wheel and secured the wheel to steer a straight course down the middle of the river. He came to where Sun was sitting, watching the shore and their prisoner.

"I secured the wheel. I want to look around the engine room. Maybe I can get up a little more speed." He came back in a few minutes smiling broadly, with two bottles of Tsingtao beer.

"It may sound Chinese, but us Germans brew it right here in China! Ha! There're a few more down there and some fruit and rice. Did you notice the two rifles in the pilothouse?"

"Yes, and we may need them...better get back to the wheel. We're heading in toward shore up ahead...and let's check out those rifles."

They sailed on uneventfully for an hour or so, coaling every fifteen minutes. There was a naval lieutenant's dress jacket and hat in a small closet in the pilothouse and an assortment of other naval gear. Their prisoner had not said a word, but sat down on the lowered deck of the coal bin. It was mid-afternoon and a few fishing boats were out with nets on the river. Sun had managed to squeeze into the officer's jacket and with the hat on, he looked official enough to pass any casual observer. One village they passed had a dock, and several people were obviously waiting for the downriver mail boat. Even sailing at full speed, the Royal Navy boat was relatively slow. Fortunately, sailing with the current increased their speed. Sun guided the boat near the opposite shore as they passed the startled onlookers. Several shouted to the boat, but Sun merely stepped out of the pilothouse and gave his best crisp naval salute. A cluster of frustrated villages just stared at the passing vessel.

"We'll be coming up on another village pretty soon, and then it's the home port of call. We must have been found out by now. I hope the telegraph is out; it was out in Peking last I heard. What time do you make it out to be?" Sun asked.

Markus automatically reached across to his wrist. No watch. He had left it at the Peitang Cathedral with the rest of his clothes.

"I'd say it's about 1600 hours…four o'clock. What do you think?"

Before Sun could answer, the side window of the pilothouse exploded in a shower of glass, followed by the delayed sound of a rifle shot. Sun ducked and stumbled backward, blood streaming from half a dozen cuts on his face and arms. A fuselage of shots rang out from three horsemen on shore, two with rifles.

"Imperial Guards!" shouted Markus as he ducked behind the gun wall of the boat. Drawing his revolver, he returned fire. "It's the lieutenant and his guards!" Markus scrambled forward to the pilothouse and grabbed a rifle. "Mother of God, are you all right?"

Sun was already raising a rifle to fire… "I'll live!" he said as he squeezed off a round. On shore, a horse pitched forward with a bullet in its neck. The rider hurtled over the head of the horse and toppled down the embankment, his rifle landing in the water. More shots zinged though the air, chips of white paint bursting off from impacts. Markus kept up a steady rate of fire at what he thought were five shooters. The other two horsemen had dismounted and were firing from behind trees. As the boat continued at full speed, the gun battle rapidly dwindled out. Markus stopped returning fire and, crouching low, made his way to the pilothouse. Sun had steadied the helm with rope and was tending his wounds. Markus flung open the closet and pulled out a small medical kit he remembered seeing earlier.

"Better check our prisoner, Markus." Sun nodded his head sideways.

"I did. He's sprawled on the coal pile dead. He caught a shore bullet right to the head... Now let's see how badly you're hurt, Sun."

"It looks worse than it is. You've never been beaten by the empress's guards?" Sun managed. Markus finished bandaging Sun's cuts. "Thanks for your speedy response to the attack. You Germans are well trained, and a good shot, too." He smiled.

"*Ja*, thank you for helping me get back toward my outfit. So far so good. What are we going to do with the dead seaman on the coal pile? Maybe we could pull ashore and drop him off. Someone will find him."

"Yes, we could do that, but I think it's too risky. If we hadn't been moving downriver when we were attacked, those five or six on shore could have overwhelmed us...better for us to keep moving as fast as possible. We'll just dump him overboard...he will almost surely be found."

"All right."

Sun moved to stoke the boiler. Markus slipped into the engine room. He picked up an oilcan and squirted several moving parts and checked to see that there was enough water in the boiler. The two of them lifted the limp body of the young sailor off the blood-soaked coal pile and moved him to the gun wall of the boat.

"Shouldn't we do something; I mean just dumping him..." Markus' voice trailed off.

"There is nothing to be said," began Sun. "He is a casualty of war, and this is a kind of war. He is a victim of the times, this young countryman of mine. What a waste of youth, this beautiful body here...and now," he paused, "I'll take his legs, you get him under the shoulders."

It was a small splash. The body bobbed several times and then almost submerged as it drifted toward the stern. The two men went back to the pilothouse, swept the glass away, and reloaded the rifles.

"How much ammunition do we have for the rifles?" Sun asked.

"I'll check, and let's see if this searchlight on the roof works. We may need it at night. *Ja*, she's working. And let's see what food my lovely Li has packed for us."

It was almost dusk when they heard a loud thump against the hull of the boat.

"Whoa, what was that?" Sun moved quickly to the starboard side of the boat and looked over. A large tree trunk with several branches was scraping the side of the vessel.

"Snags. It's just snags. But we'd better be careful; one of those could sink us."

Back at the helm, the two of them talked about maintaining the boiler pressure, checking the water level in the boiler, keeping alert for further attacks, and working out three-hour shifts through the night.

"I wonder how far downriver we have to go before we encounter some of our comrades?"

"That remains to be seen, Markus. Right now, I'm mostly concerned about Boxers, Imperial Guards, and the Imperial Navy. They surely have other boats, gunboats on this river, and they'll be alerted, from here to the coast soon enough. We'd better think up some alternatives. So far we've been very lucky."

"Get some sleep, Sun."

Just before dawn, while the last darkness hung over the river, Sun manned the wheel. There was enough moonlight on the open water to navigate between the foreboding shorelines of impenetrable blackness. The engine's four-stroke rhythm was the only sound besides the crackle of the damp coal, burning off the dead seaman's blood. The river had widened to almost a quarter mile in some places, and the mail boat had passed only a few lights on shore all night. A small lamp next to the maps in the pilothouse was the only illumination on board. Sun clicked the light on and off every so often to check the map.

He was just prodding Markus awake when the boat seemed to slow down. Both men felt the vessel shudder as if it were pushing an ever increasingly heavy load.

"What's that?" Mathias said in a sleepy voice.

"I don't know, but we had better find out fast." Before the two men got to the bow of the mail boat, it had ground to a halt.

"Sandbar! We hit a sandbar! Reverse engine...quickly!" Markus raced to the helm and threw the engine into reverse. It took several long seconds for the engine to slow to a stop and then slowly start in the opposite direction. Markus gave it full power and the boat shook from the vibration and the churning in the shallow water.

"We're in the middle of the river, damn it, and I couldn't see a thing," Sun stammered. Markus moved the wheel hard to port and then hard to starboard, trying to wiggle the boat off the sandbar. "She's really run herself up pretty good," Sun exclaimed while hanging over the bow.

"Take the wheel, Sun, I'm going over the side...see if I can shove her off."

"Right."

Markus took off most of his clothes and his shoes and slipped over the side near the bow. The water was only four feet deep, but the boat wallowed in the sand. It was truly hard aground. All the force Markus put into his shoulder didn't budge the heavy boat.

"That's not going to work," he said, climbing back aboard.

"Can we lighten this thing? Or shift weight to the stern?" Sun looked around.

"There's really not much that's movable on board except the coal…and we're not going anywhere without that."

The two continued to swing the wheel back and forth, trying to nudge the vessel loose. Neither of them noticed two small boats approaching from port side. They didn't hear the faint bump as one of the boats stopped. A head appeared above the gun wall.

"Good evening, sirs," a soft voice spoke. Sun and Markus lunged for the rifles and spun around.

"Don't shoot, sirs, don't shoot. We only offer our assistance to the Imperial Mail Boat, sirs. We just want to help," the nervous voice continued. "As you see, it's dangerous to sail at night, sirs. Too many sandbars for big boats."

Sun and Markus straightened up and slowly lowered their rifles.

"I think it's safe enough," Markus offered.

Sun approached the man and only then realized there were two fishing boats with three men total in them. "Two boats," he called back as Markus slowed the engine and came forward. Sun said, "Looks like we have some help." In the dark, the three fishermen climbed aboard and did not notice Markus' telltale features immediately.

"Big trouble for big ship," one of the fishermen said.

"Yes, it is. It is kind of you to offer your assistance in helping get us off this bar," said Sun.

The fishermen looked at each other in bewilderment.

How foolish of me, thought Sun. The Imperial Navy would not be so polite. They would expect these peasants to help and would not have extended any undue courtesy.

"So, let's get the four of us to the stern. Helmsman! We will try weighing the stern...give her full steam." The three fishermen and Sun stood at the very end of the boat. The engine roared into life. Sun had the four jump up and down. No luck. The four went overboard and tried pushing, also with no luck. After a half hour, the exhausted foursome got back in the boat. Sun offered the three a beer, and while they passed it around among themselves, Sun went forward.

"We are really stuck...and it doesn't look like we're going to get off this damn sandbar. It's going to be dawn soon, and we'll be seen for miles around. They'll catch up with us for sure if we stay here. What do you think?"

Markus responded, "You're right." He nodded toward the back of the boat. Without waiting for an answer, he continued: "Can we trust them? We could take one of their boats, or buy it from them. But would they tell, alert the Imperial Guards? And what do we do with this boat? Just leave it?"

"Good questions, Markus. I don't know, but we better think of something fast; it'll be getting light in an hour."

CHAPTER XI

The Imperial Guards
and the River

THEY BOTH WERE silent for a long time.

"I think they're getting suspicious. Look at them. Are they getting ready to leave? We can't let that happen!" Sun exclaimed.

"I've got an idea!" Markus said. "We buy one of the boats from them and send them on their way. Then we set fire to this boat and leave. I know the fire will attract attention, but the navy is going to find this boat anyway in the morning. They'll come out here to investigate…to make sure we aren't aboard, burned up. With the fishing boat, we can blend in with the other river traffic and make it to shore if we have to. What do you think?"

Sun looked at him and smiled. "Now I understand how you were able to make it all the way from the Peking legations to Li Ling's. You're a clever man. Let's do it! I'll go back and negotiate with the fishermen. I'll make up some story. You stay here."

"Here, take this," Markus said, handing Sun the bag of coins he had brought all the way from Peking.

Sun came back with a grin on his face.

"Not only did I pay a handsome price for the boat, I paid the other fishermen very well, too. They were all happy and smiles as I shoved them off."

"Very good, now we better get going. Let's light this boat. We can just shovel glowing coals in here and the coal pile and engine room. That should do it. What do you think?" He looked at Sun for a reply.

"Hand me a shovel!"

"I'll help but first we load the rowboat with the rifles and food... anything else?"

They waited long enough to make sure the mail boat was well on its way to destruction as fire crackled in several places. Having thrown everything moveable either into the engine compartment or the pilothouse, including the mailbags, uniforms, ropes, grappling poles, and crates of unknown supplies, the inferno roared as the two pulled hard on the ores. They were away from the boat when a small explosion sent debris and ambers into the air.

"There goes the boiler. I shut off the steam escape valve, so it was just a matter of time before she blew," Mathias exclaimed as they both stopped rowing to watch for a moment.

"That'll be seen for a quarter mile at least up and down the river," Sun warned. "We'd better put our backs into it while it's dark."

Markus and Sun spent the day steering to the center of the river and not overdoing it on the oars, especially when other boats were near. They kept the fishing nets plainly in sight. They headed toward shore when an Imperial Navy boat appeared, steaming full speed north. When it passed, they headed out again. It was oppressively hot for the next two days. Little conversation passed between the two. Both men waited impatiently for the breezes of nightfall. They rationed their food, but the last of it was gone by morning of the third day.

"We've got to head into a village and get food and more beer," Sun offered in a scratchy voice.

"*Ja*, we can't afford to drink this river water. Sickness could be fatal and not just from the water. I'll stay a bit off shore while you go get supplies. There should be some Chinese coins left in the bag. It's too risky to use those German gold marks."

With fresh provisions, Sun and Markus continued their escape down the Hun Ho River. It seemed an easy exit from the turmoil around An-Tsun village and the greater Peking area. The gently flowing river widened and narrowed as they sailed past farmland and forest, with villages spaced on either side. On the evening of the fourth day, the sky clouded over and by late evening, a cool shower soaked them.

"Let's head in, turn the boat over, and get some sleep. I need to stretch out; sleeping in the bottom of this boat is killing my back," Sun suggested.

"Good idea. There're some willows up ahead."

In no time, the boat was out of the water, the rifles and their other meager provisions under cover, and both men plunged into much-needed sleep. It was well into morning, with fog hanging heavy in the air, when Markus opened one eye to see three kids sitting on their haunches, smiling and staring at the white man. Markus reached behind him slowly and shook Sun gently.

"Yes, yes, time to get moving again. Let's see what food we have for…" He spotted the kids. Sun greeted the three and slowly emerged from under the rowboat. The willow tree was at the edge of a village with a good-sized dock. No one was near. Sun nudged Markus and nodded his head toward the village. He spoke, not in Mandarin, but French.

"Let's get out of here. Don't give the kids anything. They'll just run back home with it. Come on, let's go!"

They righted the boat, loaded the supplies and the rifles, all of it covered in fishing net, and pushed off. The three kids ran along the bank shouting and laughing. They ran down onto the dock and jumped up and down, waving and calling to the strangers. Up the dusty path from the dock to the village, several horsemen were leaning down out of their saddles talking to a group of villagers.

"Pull hard! Pull!"

The horsemen sat up in their saddles and looked toward the river.

"They've spotted us! Ease up a little and play with that net."

Sun looked over Mathias' shoulder. "Imperial Guards! Two! They're walking their horses down to the dock."

Sure enough, the soldiers stopped next to the kids and again bent down. Both sat up and looked intently at the slowly receding boat. One of them stood up in his stirrups and yelled out and waved his arm. "Come to shore! Come to shore!"

Markus tried to keep rowing as he reached for one of the rifles.

"Head for the center, pull," said Sun.

He slid the bolt back and forward, sliding a cartridge into the chamber. "Keep it down, Sun...for now."

Both riders pulled hard on their reins, forcing the two horses to turn their heads downriver. With swift kicks of their spurs, the horses forged forward along the shore. "Come to shore, now!" The call was given several times. Both horses pulled up abruptly. The riders swung out of their saddles as they slid their rifles out of the saddle holsters. With well-trained skill, they landed on the ground and raised their rifles.

A shot rang out and dirt kicked up near the two Imperial Guards. It delayed their return fire, but not for long. Both fired and a skimming bullet not three feet from the boat danced across the river arcing off to the left, like a skipping stone on water. Sun fired again, resting the rifle barrel on Markus' shoulder as the German plugged his ears against the next shot. One of the guards dropped his rifle and grabbed his thigh. The other's shot tore a chunk of wood out of the upper edge of the stern. One last shot from Sun struck the saddle of one of the horses and sent the two animals scattering in opposite directions. Both men rowed hard for the far side of the river, at a diagonal downstream.

"That did it, they're on to us now," Sun grunted as he labored on his ore.

"*Ja*, maybe it's time to get off the river," Markus said between deep breaths.

"At the next village, maybe we can steal some horses. What do you think?"

"Maybe…the question is, how soon can that Imperial Guard get a boat and cross the river, get a horse, and catch up to us with the rest of the Chinese army or his Boxer friends? Then there's the Imperial Navy, either coming upriver or coming downriver, with us in the middle. I'll sure be glad to see nightfall!"

At this point in the river, several small islands were strung along the eastern shore where the rowboat was heading. Scrub trees and other foliage covered the erstwhile sandbars, and the two men beached their boat between the shore and the island.

"Let's pull it up out of sight." With each on either side, they dragged the wood hull through the thicket of branches. Flies buzzed around them as they sought shade and a chance to rest.

"Now what?" Sun wiped his forehead with his blood-smeared sleeve.

"Maybe this is a good place to leave the boat," Markus said. "It looks like we can probably wade to the shore from here. The river is too dangerous for us. They'll be stopping every fishing boat for the next day or two."

"Yes, I'm sure you're right. But if we leave the boat, we have to leave the rifles."

"*Ja*, but we have the revolvers, and quite a bit of money left." He paused. "We won't do well in a standing gun battle. That I can promise you. Let's wait for darkness…that's about two and a half or three hours from now. Then we ford the river and head south. We'll find a village and maybe horses or other opportunities. What do you say, Sun?"

"Splendid, Splendid! More opportunities, wonderful. I am amazed at your optimism. Do all German soldiers exhibit such positive attitudes…and why are you not an officer?" Sun, always smiling, looked at his comrade, and continued:

"I always thought I was the most optimistic person I knew, but you, you seem to believe that, of course, there is a way, a successful plan. I need you to join my movement! What do you say? Herr Mathias. I'll make you a general in the White Lotus!" They both laughed. It was a great emotional release from the last four grueling days.

"*Ja*, so make me a general, but let's keep the noise down; there may be someone nearby." They both looked around, trying to see through the thick foliage.

They waited well into darkness before wading out into the shallow stretch of river that separated the shore from their hiding place. The water was warm and only up to mid-thigh. Crouching low and moving at a quick pace, the two made for a low bluff and a cluster of trees. Each carried a fishing net over his shoulder. Markus had the food bag Li gave him. It was stuffed full. They followed the well-worn path through the trees, stopping every so often to listen. An hour of walking brought them to the outskirts of a cluster of homes and outbuildings. They saw dim lights in several. It was about ten o'clock and the moon was high.

"It doesn't look very prosperous…I doubt they have any horses," Markus said, scanning through the dim moonlight.

"Maybe we should just keep going," Sun suggested. "Destroying an Imperial Mail Boat might not have been such a good idea—even the empress will hear about that."

"Well, too late to worry about that now."

A dog barked as they passed between the river and the houses. The men were soon beyond the hamlet, following a path along the river. Seven hours of walking, with numerous breaks, brought them to the outskirts of a much larger village. It was a town really, and from the top of a small rise, they could see a long dock projecting out into the Hun Ho. Several larger boats and a cluster of smaller fishing vessels were tied up or moored off shore. They could see out across the sleeping rooftops to a four-story pagoda towering above the one-story homes.

"Are you thinking what I'm thinking?" Sun paused.

"Steal another boat, one of those bigger ones?"

"Or take our chances on land. What do you think?"

"The boat's faster, but on the open water, with other mail boats and the Imperial Navy and all, I think we can blend into the landscape better…but it's slower going."

"Yes, neither is very appealing right now…and I'm tired…not like you young soldiers."

"This spot we could stay in, plenty of brush for cover and we have enough food and beer for a day, and it's almost light," Markus said. "Maybe we should rest here through the day."

"You think it's safe enough?"

"Well, we have a good view all around from up here, and we're off the path. *Ja*, I think it would be a good bet." They searched around for the densest area.

Light rose from the east, spreading across the South China Sea. As the sun began burning off the mist over the river, they settled in. A beer, some fruit, and both men drifted off to sleep, their revolvers at the ready. While it was another hot day, their deep, shaded beds were cool, and they only heard voices twice as people traveled along a path twenty yards away.

Late in the afternoon, Sun got up and crept to an opening that overlooked the river and town. They saw half a dozen fishing boats, and the Imperial Chinese Naval flag flying on two ships. One appeared to be a government mail boat and Sun recognized the other as a naval gunboat. The mail boat was heading upriver and the gunboat, just leaving the dock, was heading north. Sun, ever watchful, crept back to the "nest." He told Markus what he saw, and they discussed its implications and what they should do next. Digging around in the food bag, Markus brought out the last big bottle of Tsingtao beer and a hard ball of damp rice.

"We've got a few smoked fish left," he said, handing one across to Sun. Both men were thirsty after a long day of sleep, and that last beer seemed like the nectar of the gods.

Markus got up and stretched and said, "I'm going to take a look at the river."

Sun settled down in the comfort of his bed of leaves in the shade. Minutes later, Sun heard Markus breaking through the brush rapidly and rose on his elbow. "What is it? Someone coming?" He sat up.

"No, no, but a boat…it looks like a Japanese gunboat, just off shore from the town. I think it dropped anchor!"

"Wonderful! It's our chance!" exclaimed Sun. "Can we get to it? What do you think?"

Markus knelt down on one knee. "If we can get to that dock and use one of those boats, we could be out to it in a five-minute row. Let's hope the Japanese stay put. The question is whether we should we wait until dark."

"No, no," Sun exclaimed, "it's our chance. We have to take it. That gunboat may not stay that long. We should be able to walk right down along the shore by those buildings near shore and to the dock. We keep the nets up on our shoulders, and you keep that hat down over your eyes, and we'll be all right."

"Okay then, let's go!" They gathered up their few possessions and headed back to the path leading down to the shore, fish nets draped over one shoulder. Walking out of the trees and down from the bluff, it seemed like a half mile stretched out before them to the dock.

"Just a steady pace; walk like those other fishermen we've seen," instructed Sun in a quiet voice.

Most of the villagers and townspeople in China never ventured far from home. They knew each other and recognized strangers in their midst. Knowing that, Sun and Markus avoided every possible encounter. However, chance and the unexpected sometimes intervene to endanger and challenge the simplest plans. As the two walked with the amble of men off to work, they heard the hoof beats of horses behind them. Coming around the side of the hill from the north, Sun, glancing over his shoulder, saw seven Imperial Guards.

"Imperial Guards! Seven of them! Just keep going!"

"Holy Mary Mother of God," Markus mumbled inaudibly. The horsemen thundered past, no more than twenty-five feet away. A dust cloud obscured the riders immediately after they passed.

"Let's see where they're going...I hope it's not the dock," Sun whispered.

"Look, they're turning in toward town...that gives us time." The two picked up their pace. Now they were in among the scattered fishing sheds and shanties. Several men bent over nets, mending them, coiling rope, and sorting fish in baskets. As the two fugitives passed, the men looked up and stared. After they passed, the men leaned in toward each other and whispered. It was all Markus could do to stop from turning around to look back at them.

"Just keep going, keep it steady," Sun insisted. They were a hundred yards from the dock when Markus grabbed Sun's arm.

"Look! The guards are back and talking to those fishermen. They're looking this way! Run for it! Run!"

Both men leaped into flight, no pretense of stealth. The Imperial Guards, seeing the men run, wheeled their horses, spurred them harshly, and broke into a trot, a canter, and then full gallop. They were closing fast, but the two runners were almost to the dock. Fishermen and townspeople within sight of the commotion stopped in mid-step and stared at the unfolding drama. Several of the Imperial Guards had already slipped their rifles out of their saddle holsters and raised their guns. *Bam...Bam...* The shots rang out. A splinter of decking flew into the water from the dock. Seeing this, the fishermen on the dock dove into their boats.

On board the Japanese gunboat, several officers and crew, startled by the gunshots, stared toward shore. Someone on board began clanging a bell, and the whole ship seemed to spring into action. Black smoke belched from the single stack as steam surged to the engine. The clatter of anchor chain being reeled in, mixed with orders shouted in Japanese, were heard.

Sun was breathing hard as they mounted the dock. Markus pulled him up.

"Come on, come on...right to the end, we'll just jump!" The dock itself was fifty yards long, and it was all Sun could do to stay several yards behind Markus. The Japanese gunboat's bow turned sharply in toward shore, the entire craft leaning hard to port. Markus' eyes fixed on the gunboat. In a blur, he could just make out four Japanese marines pulling a canvas cover off a gun mounted on a post in the bow. On shore several horsemen slid to a stop, dismounting on the beach next to the dock, and were kneeling to fire at the fleeing men. More shots fired! The two men, hearing bullets whizzing around them, lunged forward. Markus, moving at a full run, was the first to dive into the river with Sun plunging in behind him, just missing a rowboat tied to the end of the dock. It was none too soon as several Imperial Guards clambered onto the dock, their rifles firing down the dock. Heads broke water as Sun gasped for air. Markus, the good swimmer that he was, made a perfect dive and came up far ahead of Sun. He turned around, seeing his companion's head bob on the surface. The cool water shocked them both as Sun vigorously splashed toward Markus.

Across the water, they could hear the loud chattering of gunfire as the Japanese fired the Gatling gun mounted on the bow of their ship. A Japanese sea marine hand-cranked the unwieldy gun, while another marine took aim. One of the Imperial Guards collapsed on the dock, and several others turned and ran back to shore and the side of the dock. Markus treaded water as he waited for Sun to catch up with him. The Japanese gunboat was a hundred yards from the swimmers.

"I'll never make it. I can't go on!" Sun called to him.

"Yes, you can, Sun. Come on! We're almost there! Just keep swimming!" Bullets splashed the water around them, and Sun's feet kicked up out of the water.

"Ahhhh, I'm hit!" Sun had stopped swimming, and he was thrashing wildly in place. Sun's head went under. Markus swam furiously toward him. He came up under Sun and pushed him to the surface, but not before seeing a cloud of red river water around Sun's foot. They both burst to the surface, gasping for air.

"I can't make it! Go! Go!"

"Roll over on your back, I'll help you. Roll over!" Sun simply stopped, his arms floating out from his body. Markus slipped his arm into position, sweeping the water with his free arm, swimming on his side, and towing Sun behind him.

The Japanese kept up a barrage of fire, now joined by riflemen shooting from amidships. Several sailors lowered a skiff, with two marines in the bow firing their rifles, as the boat headed toward the two men in the water. The Imperial Guards, completely outgunned, retreated behind nearby sheds and overturned boats on the beach. They fired sporadically, but the shooting rapidly died down to random shots.

Finally, Markus collapsed on the deck of the gunboat, while

several officers and medics attended to Sun.

"On behalf of the Chrysanthemum Throne and the Imperial Japanese Navy, welcome aboard the IJN *Sapporo*," a tall Japanese officer said in heavily accented Mandarin. "I am Captain Shiba Goro, commanding, and this is Warrant Officer Okada Takitaro. We have been looking for you since we received word from the Imperial German Navy of your flight south along the Hun Ho. That was a very close encounter with Imperial Guards. Most men do not escape their pursuit."

Markus looked up at the Japanese officers in their impeccable blue uniforms.

"Yes sir, they almost had us. Thank you very much, sir." He nodded to them both. "And we thank your gun crews. It was a miracle you were anchored off shore and that you spotted us when you did." He rose to his feet, stood at what passed as "attention," and saluted the two officers. He looked over to Sun and saw him lifted onto a stretcher.

"Yes, those Imperial Guards pursuing you are the best trained soldiers of all the Chinese army, compliments of their German instructors." The two navy officers smiled haughtily.

"We, too, have had the assistance of your kaiser's military training." The captain paused. "And you are, I presume, Lancer Markus Mathias of the Kingdom of Bavaria. I have seen pictures of your alpine mountains, much snow, like in Hokkaido." Smiles crossed their faces.

"Your esteemed companion, Sun Yat Sen, is well-known to us. He has been our guest in Japan several times, studying military tactics and planning his 'revisions' of the Chinese government. Our emperor encourages him in his endeavors." Again, a smile crossed Captain Goro's face. "But now, you must rest, nourish yourselves, and clean up. You and Sun Yat Sen will share one of my officers' cabins."

The bunk was so welcome to Markus that after a quick wash, a meal of soup, rice, and smoked eel, he was soon asleep. Several sailors carried Sun to his bunk across from Markus. After his injury was treated, he ate heartily and soon sunk into deep sleep. Fortunately, for him, the bullet had simply grazed the side of his foot. After several days on crutches he walked close to a normal gait.

The Japanese gunboat *Sapporo* turned south and was fifty-five nautical miles from Tientsin near where the Hun Ho River flows into the Pei Ho River and then to the sea. Tientsin, a walled city heavily fortified by the Chinese, had been overrun July 13 and 14 by a combined force of Russian, Japanese, French, British, and American forces. It was the staging area for a massive rescue effort under way, consisting of over fourteen thousand troops of the five nations. As the *Sapporo* sailed south, intermittent fighting raged for days just south and east of Peking as the foreign armies encountered significant resistance. The besieged legations, again under constant attack, fought on desperately.

CHAPTER XII

The Battle of Peking

LANCER LEVI, ON the barricades, strained to see any evidence of the relief column. Heavy fighting, heard for the past two days off to the east and south, marked this hot August 15, 1900. Everyone in the legations was in a state of turmoil and agitation. Levi, with field glasses, swept the battered landscape from east to west. He abruptly stopped and refocused.

"I can see a flag!" he blurted out. "There, to the southeast!" He rose up and pointed over the parapet. "Can you see it? Is it French? Is it Chinese? They look so damned similar. Can you make it out?" he shouted to his comrades along the wall.

One of them grabbed the glasses from him. "Let me see." As he raised the glasses to his eyes, two bullets struck in quick secession, blasting red brick chips and dust up into Levi's face.

"*Scheiße*!" he swore as he ducked down. "I don't need a bullet now when we can hear the relief column a mile away. Keep down, keep down!" he yelled as several more bullets zinged over their heads.

"I've lost it," the soldier with the glasses said. "I can't see through the haze and gun smoke… Wait, there to the left…that looks like a

British flag! And that's an American flag, for sure! Look, the red stripes on white! It has to be the relief column; they're in sight at last! We've got to tell Captain Mayerling. Pass the word!"

One of the German soldiers ran to the staircase that led off the battlements. Levi and the others cheered and shouted and grabbed each other, big grins on their sweaty, dusty faces. Several people in the compound close enough to see the excited soldiers stared at the cheering a moment and then ran to surrounding buildings.

"It's not over yet, boys," someone shouted, " they're still thousands of Boxers and Imperial Guards out there, but the relief troops are here at last!"

Tears flowed from many an eye of the hearty soldiers as cannon fire pierced the air far to the east.

"They must be trying to blast the Tung-Chih Gate into Tartar City," someone exclaimed. "Or the Ch'eo Yang Gate," shouted another. "By God, it's taken them two months to get here, two months!"

The spaces along the high walls were filling up with many of the legation's officers, including Captain Mayerling and Commander Sir Claude MacDonald. With his usual authoritarian voice tinged with emotion, he shouted over the din. "We must be very diligent along the entire perimeter for the next twenty-four to forty-eight hours. The Boxers may try one last desperate attack on the legations in hopes of wiping us out before the relief column arrives in strength. Every able-bodied man on the barricades. We want to avoid an untimely disaster."

They stood scanning the burned-out buildings and the mobile defensive timber walls the Boxers had ingeniously built during the siege, and behind which many of them still lurked. Two burned-out, movable towers, now mere piles of lumber, lay crumpled on the ground. They had been built over a month ago and used in unsuccessful attempts to breach the high walls. After an hour or so of trying to ascertain the strength and nationalities of the advancing relief forces, most of the military not engaged in wall defenses retired to safer locations within the legation's buildings. A steady fusillade of enemy bullets continued to pierce the stagnant air. For the rest of that late afternoon and into the night, continuous battle sounds exploded around them. Only in the early hours of the morning did the shooting die down to a sporadic crack of a rifle shot here and there beyond the towering ramparts.

Levi lay in his bunk exhausted after getting off duty, weak from poor nutrition. All the people trapped in the crowded quarters of the various legations were in the same state. Whenever he closed his eyes, he thought of food, the food of his youth, what his mother cooked in his beautiful home in the forest in Bavaria. There were dumplings and sauerbraten, wiener schnitzel and sausages…and bread, fresh-baked rye bread with caraway seeds, hard-crusted rolls, and salty pretzels…and beer, lots of beer. He could almost taste this banquet in his dreams.

"Do you think we'll be shipped out of here after this is all over?" Günther spoke from the next bunk over. "I'm ready to go home, how about you? We signed up for overseas duty, but I've had enough of China. I don't mind the fighting so much, but all this heat and dust and dirt, and they hate us here. They can give this…this middle kingdom back to the Boxers for all I care. Levi? Are you listening?" Günther craned his neck to look over to Levi.

"*Ja*, Günther, I'm ready to go back, too; but not before we get Markus back. And according to that aristocrat character Chou, when the relief column gets here, maybe Mayerling will send out a search party. And if he does, I want to be a part of it."

"*Ja*, me too, of course."

"As for China," Levi continued, "well, I think it's a pretty amazing empire." He thought for a moment. "We're fighting them now, but it's like when Prussia was attacked by the French in 1870. The Prussians beat them good, even laid siege to Paris, but now the

French are our allies here in China. Maybe someday the Chinese will be our allies, too." Levi rolled over, facing Günther, propped himself up on his elbow, and continued.

"I mean, think about it. This country goes back, what, four or five thousand years, maybe more. All these amazing temples and castles and palaces…and the clothes of the rich…I've never seen so much silk, not even on the ladies of the court in Bavaria."

"Oh, when have you ever seen the ladies of the court?" Günther jabbed with a chuckle. "The only ladies you've ever seen were your mama and sister…and that milkmaid on your papa's farm! Ha!" He threw what passed for a pillow at Levi.

"I've seen some, I've seen some, more than you!" They both laughed.

"I want to take home a lot of treasures from here," Levi mused. "Like some of that stuff we saw in the markets, before all this fighting. I want to get some of that blue and white pottery, you know, that porcelain with dragons on it. It's really popular back home. Mama has some, all the way from China. And a Buddha and some ivory carvings and some of those old bronzes…and some paintings! I could fill wagons with all the stuff I want to take home." He rolled back down and stared at the ceiling before drifting off to a sleep filled with dreams of home.

At four the following morning a wave of thunderous cannon fire, rifle salvos, and the screams of the attackers seemed out of the ground itself. The full force of the multinational relief troops engaged the Boxers and Imperial Guards, now numbering in the thousands. The onslaught of battle outside the walls of the embattled legations brought all the able-bodied defenders, including the walking wounded, to the ramparts in minutes. French, Russians, and Belgians, Spanish, British, and Dutch, Germans, Americans, Japanese, Austrians, Italians, and Chinese all fought side by side through the deafening roar and thick, choking gun smoke.

The Boxers, Imperial Guards, and Chinese Army units put up a simultaneous fanatical defense and attack. For them, it was no longer a simple but protracted siege of the legations driven by hatred of all foreigners. It was now a defense of the Imperial City and especially the Forbidden City itself. The empress and the throne of the Middle Kingdom were in immediate mortal danger. Even the generals of the Imperial Guard and army units that had stayed out of the fray came to the aid of the empress and poured their troops into the battle.

Lancer Levi was among the German, Belgium, Austrian, and other troops who fought along the wide Tartar Wall, overrunning barricades the Boxers had formed. The battle seesawed back and forth, but finally the legation's soldiers were in full retreat with many casualties.

"We can't afford to try that again," Levi gasped in frustration as he slid behind their makeshift defenses. "Drag him in, drag him in, for God's sake," he shouted. "We'd better just hold them off here!" He aimed his rifle at the enemy down the wall and shot off a couple of rounds in frustration.

It was utter chaos as the tide of battle shifted back and forth all around the perimeter with more and more enemy and allied casualties piling up. Throughout the day, the fierce conflict continued as a blistering sun beat down on friend and foe alike. Levi's shirt was soaked with sweat. With the constant dust, he and his fellow fighters were coated with a thin layer of mud.

The relief column had fought their way north through stifling heat all along the Pei Ho River, encountering stiff resistance at Changchaiwan and the towns south of the walled city of Tungchow. As the Boxers retreated under heavy fire, they poisoned the wells, causing great hardship to the advancing allies and inflicting many casualties. Japanese forces were the first to breach the gates to Tungchow. After clearing the town, the other forces, Russian,

French, British and American, were able to march through without resistance and bivouacked six and a half miles from Peking. All allied forces had moved up to a line that was held by the Japanese. The next day, the troops rested and reconnoitered each nation's line of advance for the assault on the city. The combined forces held one last meeting of the commanders, under the leadership of American General Chaffee, where they agreed upon the final battle plan and the timetable.

The next morning, General Chaffee was startled to hear heavy artillery fire. It was soon evident that the Russians had advanced during the night and were attacking the Tung-Pien-Men Gate on the west side of Tartar City, with the objective of receiving the honor of being the first to liberate the legations. The Russians found heavy resistance, even with the assistance of French forces that had moved up to reinforce them. Chaffee immediately ordered the full assault on Peking to begin. The British broke through the south Sha Kou Men Gate into Tartar City, occupying the Temple of Heaven before battling up the Meridian Road to the Chien Men Gate. Meanwhile the Americans managed to scale the exterior wall of Tartar City while under direct fire. This was considered one of the most audacious and heroic feats by individual soldiers in the assault. The Americans, the French, and the Russians advanced in fierce fighting westward along the top of the Tartar wall ramparts, while Levi and his comrades held off the Boxers midway down the sixty-foot-wide battlement.

The fighting raged in hand-to-hand combat for hours along more than a half mile of wall. Levi and the others were thrilled to see the first European flag raised at the southeast corner of the Tartar City. It was an American flag, soon followed by the French tricolor and the double-headed eagle of Imperial Russia.

Levi slumped back behind the barricades, coughing from the heavy gun smoke. He thought of Markus and how he wished Markus were here for this great battle. The moment had finally come, the liberation of the legations after fifty-five days. From his position, he was overcome with joy to see the first relief troops, British Colonial sikhs from India, and American infantry shipped in from the Philippines. They came sloshing through the water gate under the Tartar wall, that stinking open sewer still called the Jade River.

Fighting continued fiercely throughout that day and into the evening. The following day bloody clashes resumed with the entire Imperial City still in Chinese hands. Two days later, Peitang Cathedral was finally relieved by Japanese forces. Italian Captain Olivieri personally delivered Lancer Mathias' uniform and personal belongings to Captain Mayerling and was surprised and delighted to hear that Mathias was still alive. Days later, word came over newly strung telegraph lines that a Japanese gunboat had pick up Mathias and another man along the Hun Ho River.

When the Imperial City finally fell to the combined forces of the relief column, the Imperial court fled to the far western provinces. Empress Dowager Tzu Hsi and her court would only return to the Forbidden City a year later, after an agreed-upon armistice.

Most of the military forces and many civilians that defended the legations in Peking and at the Peitang Cathedral were relieved of duty by fresh troops and, over the next several weeks, transported back south to the coast for rest and recuperation or a ticket home.

Levi and the others traveled south by wagon train to the newly repaired railhead north of Anping. Levi commented:

"It's a happy bunch, this high-spirited international group of soldiers, sailors, and civilians. Thank God for these newly laid rails." There were threats from wandering bands of Boxers along the route of the heavily armed train, but the food was plentiful. Fresh fruit was wondrously delicious after nearly two months of the most meager rations. Levi, anxious to find Markus, wanted to be assured he was safe and healthy. He wanted to exchange heroic tales, and to show him the three large wooden crates of artifacts he had purchased and otherwise picked up. He daydreamed often on the three-day ride to the coast. What fun it would be to present Mama, Papa, and his sister with exotic Chinese presents when he returned home to Kalvarianhof. He had asked Captain Mayerling if he could personally care for Markus' gear. With his commander's approval, Levi had everything washed, and he personally polished all the leather and brass.

Swift breezes blew in through the open train windows. They were pure heaven after the stifling, stagnant heat of the legation compound. Levi watched the rolling countryside pass away hour after hour, mile after mile, and thought of all the experiences he had had in China. He knew he was going home with Markus at his side. Germany was months away, two oceans away, on the other side of the world, but this was the beginning of the long trip home.

CHAPTER XIII

Sun on Deck

LANCER MATHIAS AND Sun Yat Sen, enjoying the formal hospitality and good food of the Japanese officers and crew of the IJN *Sapporo*, had a chance to talk at leisure.

"How's your foot feeling today, Sen?"

"No pain…just stiff, and I'll be walking with a bit of a limp for a while."

"What are your plans when we get to the coast?" Markus continued.

"I must get to Hong Kong. A friend is in trouble, and he needs my help. From there, probably Japan. They are a big supporter of our efforts, but for all the wrong reasons." He looked around and lowered his voice.

"The Japanese desire the raw materials of northern China. Manchuria to be exact. Therefore, a weak Imperial throne here is a big advantage for them and for the Russians, too. They have been expanding down into northeast Asia from Siberia. Those two monarchies are going to clash one of these days, and China is going to be in the middle." He shook his head.

"We have to be ready with a reform government that will strengthen China so as to resist both of them. It's not going to be easy, but we must try." He fell silent as the two of them sat in deck chairs on the stern of the gunboat, watching China slip away in the churning brown waters of the lower Pie Ho.

Markus looked sideways at his companion for a long time. He was only a nineteen-year-old German soldier out for travel and adventure with his friend Levi. Here was a man with a cause so much bigger than anything Markus had ever dreamed of doing. He wanted to reform a whole country… change an ancient civilization threatened by two powerful neighbors and full of Europeans with their own agenda. *What are the Europeans doing here*, he wondered. They weren't helping the people. He wasn't helping Li Ling or her father.

Markus was disturbed by his thoughts, torn by his self-interest and the realization that he and his fellow Europeans and the Japanese were just hurting this beautiful country and the girl he loved.

"Sen," he finally said. "I really admire you and what you are doing for your country. I've never met a man like you, with your big ideas about helping other people. We Germans talk a lot about patriotism, and we have lots of parades and flags and such. But you, you are a true patriot, Sun, a true patriot." He hesitated, his voice tightening. "It's an honor to know you, sir. I just know you will succeed someday. You're surely going to change China."

Sun looked over to the young man sitting next to him.

"Those are kind words, and coming from such a brave soldier. Thank you." He smiled. "I hope you're right, but it will take many people all working together to accomplish our goals. People like Wan Ling and Chou Lee, and even Li Ling, too. We need women to help in the struggle. But I'm afraid this Boxer uprising has set us back who knows how long. With more and more European armies flooding into the country, who knows what will happen? However, one inescapable thing is clear to me." He paused. "With change comes opportunity. That is why I am an optimist. We revolutionaries have to be optimists!" He turned toward Markus and chuckled. "There is always opportunity!"

CHAPTER XIV

Reunion

THEY NAVIGATED THE Pei Ho River all the way to the Taku forts on the Chinese coast. The small port city was teeming with Europeans who had fled from the interior or had been rescued by one contingent or another. Naval vessels of a dozen nations, most painted white, glistened in the crowded coastal waters. They waited their turn for a berth at one of the few docks, or simply ferried their human cargo out in assorted shallow draft tugs, lighters, and junks, for the long journey home.

The railway line carrying the Peking legation's survivors did not go directly into Taku, but curved north a mile from the coast. Most passengers got off and traveled by horse carts to Taku. The rest stayed on the train, whose final destination was Port Arthur, around the coast of the Gulf of Chihli. As the weighted-down carts piled high with luggage, furniture, crates of treasures, souvenirs, and their passengers slowly pulled into the crowded port, the separate legations said their good-byes among tears and kisses. Each group headed for their designated areas for embarkation.

Levi climbed to the top of the pile of crates in his cart and stood tall, scanning the crowds. Spotting the German heavy cruiser

Kanonenboot Ilti, he shouted, "Look!"

His buddies strained to see where he pointed in the harbor. The Imperial German Naval flag, flapping in the breeze, caused the wagonload of Germans to let out a "hurrah!" Examining the ship more closely, they were shocked to see the massive damage she had endured in the bombardment of the Taku forts two months ago when the forts were still in Boxer hands.

"It's amazing she's still afloat."

"There's no chance we'll sail back home on that wreck," Günther burst out.

"Look over there, further out. Isn't that one of ours? Is it another cruiser?" He searched for his binoculars.

"It's the SMS *Hansa*…and she's not damaged."

"That's our ticket, boys, or one like her. That's our ticket home!"

The soldiers maneuvered their cart toward a building with a German flag flying, and soon reported in to the port officer.

"Yes, the SMS *Hansa* has just come from refueling," he began. "They are preparing to steam south with several other German ships. They will resupply our colonies in the South Pacific. A flotilla of other nations' ships is doing the same for their colonial outposts. The *Hansa's* eventual destination is Bremerhaven, Germany." His audience listened intently. "You won't be sailing for a few days, but you've been assigned berths aboard the SMS *Princess Eugenia.*"

The port officer instructed them: "Take your gear and report in when she docks. She's been given priority berthing, so you can board her this afternoon…four berths over."

The sun beat down on the congested town, but a refreshing breeze came in off the gulf. Leaving their military gear and crates of souvenirs at the German Consulate, Levi and his friends began exploring the market square and the streets near the docks. The food stands and small shops were doing a brisk business with all the foreigners vying for last-minute purchases before shipping out. There were many bars with tea, rice wine, and lots of Tsingtao beer and lots of pretty prostitutes available in every price range.

"Let's see if we can find the Japanese consulate. Maybe they have information on that gunboat Markus is on. It's sure to arrive here. My God, will he have some stories to tell us, uh?" Levi laughed with the others.

"And we also have stories, *ja*?" Günther said. "Let's get some beer."

Markus and Sun Yat Sen were indeed arriving at the mouth of the Pei Ho River. However, the two men transferred to the flagship of a small Japanese flotilla, on orders of the Japanese admiral. One of the Japanese officers announced:

"Our noble admiral wants the pleasure of presenting the rescued German soldier to his German commanding officer. Captain Mayerling is also returning to Germany and is in Taku and will be present. However, Field Marshal Count von Waldersee, the overall commander of the relief efforts, has just arrived in port, and as commander of the allied forces, including the Japanese, Lancer Mathias, the Japanese admiral will present you to him. A formal military ceremony is to be held tonight, on the deck of the SMS *Empress Augusta*, the German cruiser."

Captain Mayerling informed Markus, "And the troops under my command during the siege, including your friend Lancer Levi, are invited aboard, along with Sun Yat Sen and a contingent of Japanese officers."

At the splendid banquet, with a naval band playing lively martial music celebrating the victory over the Boxers, Markus was awarded the Iron Cross second class. Officially, it was for his heroic efforts involving the Peitang Cathedral mission, but on hearing the details of his long and daring escape, it also recognized those attributes that best exemplify the German soldier: ingenuity, fortitude, and perseverance. It was his second Iron Cross in little more than two months, an almost unheard-of occurrence. Other officers and men received awards of assorted medals, including all the soldiers who fought in the defense of the legations.

Levi found Mathias at last, just before the ceremony. They fell into each other's arms, with long hugs, laughter, and slaps on the back. Günther and the others joined in at seeing their long-lost comrade, given up for dead by most of them. The boisterous merriment continued late into the evening with schnapps and beer, real German beer from home. Later that evening, Levi, Markus, and the others boarded a launch to their assigned berths on other ships. After more hardy slaps and drunken hugs, the sweet sleep of united friends finally fell over them.

CHAPTER XV

Departure, September 17, 1900

THE SMS *PRINCESS Eugenia* left the port of Taku early the following morning while the exhausted partygoers were still sleeping, as the ship slipped away from the mainland of China. One person peered through the mist of the approaching dawn. He gazed out beyond the quiet docks and the town buildings to the brown hills and rolling land west to the horizon. Tears were streaming down his face, and his body convulsed as he sobbed quietly. The finality of his leaving Li Ling was just now a profound realization as the mighty naval vessel churned out into the Gulf of Chihli toward the Yellow Sea.

How could he possibly leave her? He loved her more than anything in the world, and he knew that she loved him too, and he'd just abandoned her. She was so kind and so loving, so precious. He clung to the railing as he buried his face in his arms.

Levi had noticed his friend's absence from his bunk as he slipped out of their cabin. Now he followed at a distance. He knew his friend had to be alone for a while, and so he followed along more as a protector than a companion. He stood in the gangway, behind the windowed door, and just kept watch.

A German missionary and his wife, out for an early stroll, noticed the man at the railing in obvious distress. As they approached, Levi stepped out of the doorway, waved his hand slowly back and forth, and then raised his finger to his lips in a quiet gesture of silence. The couple understood and walked past, only to pause a moment to turn around and look back. Levi approached his friend, said nothing, and gently put his hand on Markus' back. He patted him softly. Finally, he said, "I know you love her very much. You have opened your heart to a lovely girl." He fell silent for a moment. "Life can be cruel, and for some inexplicable reason God causes us great and cruel pain, sometimes without any explanation or logic to it. I know one thing, my dear friend. From all you have told me, Li Ling is a strong girl and will go on to have a good life."

Markus sniffled. "I know. I know. I knew I had to leave her, to get back to our unit, to go home. But I feel so empty, so guilty in just leaving like that. One moment she's on my arm, and the next moment I'm out her gate and gone."

They both stood there for a while looking across the choppy, deep blue water…the taste of salt in the air and the mournful cry of seagulls. It seemed to echo Markus' mood.

Finally, Levi said, "Let's go back to our bunks and get some sleep; we're both still exhausted."

The two of them would have many opportunities to talk about their uniquely different China experiences as they sailed through the South China Sea toward the first stop on the long trip home. The Imperial German Colony in Northeast New Guinea lay over three thousand nautical miles south southeast of Germany's China possession, the city of Tsingtao in Kiaochow.

Imperial Germany began colonial empire building in the late 1880s, which was relatively late compared to other countries. Even so, they acquired colonies and "concessions" in various territories. German holdings stretched from the Imperial Colony of Kiaochow,

China, through far-flung islands in the South Pacific, purchased from Spain in the 1880s. They included the Mariana Islands, Carolina Islands, Marshall Islands, and parts of the Samoa Islands. Germany's largest land mass in the Pacific was northeastern New Guinea, called Kaiser Wilhelm's Land. In Africa, Germany had Cameroon, Togo, German Southwest Africa, and German East Africa.

The navy band, on board, played rousing tunes most evenings as the chief form of entertainment on the crowded ship. Discipline was relaxed for the returning troops, and the opportunity to dance with the civilian women cheered everyone. The trauma and sorrow of many seemed to slip away in the cool breezes and leisurely sunny days. They ate generous portions of traditional German food, which brought smiles and pure contentment.

Markus talked to Levi a lot about Sun Yat Sen. "What he is doing for the Chinese people to make China strong again is remarkable, Levi. Sun is inspiring and dogged in his determination to succeed." He paused. "I want to do something with my life, something grand, something meaningful, something that will mean something to me and others. I don't know what it is yet or even where I should look, but when I see a man like Sun Yat Sen, I see myself as not doing much of anything." He stared out over the crowded stern deck to the ships of several nations following in the wake of the SMS *Princess Eugenia*.

"What are you talking about?" Levi replied with a grin. "You're in the finest army in Europe, and you just lived through, actually fought through, how many battles and adventures? And, don't forget we both won Iron Crosses. You got two of them, for God's sake!" he said with an air of good-natured consternation. "We've both done a hell of a lot since we joined up just over a year and a half ago. Think about it, we're going home heroes. Won't our parents be proud... and the girls in town!"

"*Ja*. You're right. We had a hell of an adventure in China, didn't we?" They were both beaming broadly as they slid down in their deck chairs for an afternoon nap in the warm South Pacific sun.

"And remember…you're only nineteen!"

Steaming through the straits of Formosa, the British ship HMS *Good Hope* departed the flotilla on her way to Hong Kong. Two days later and further south, the American ship USS *Newark* broke off and sailed east to Manila to resume the suppression of the Philippine insurrection. A day later Levi, Markus, and dozens more crowded the railings on the starboard side of the ship and watched the French frigate *Marseille* turn gracefully westward toward the deep-water port of Cam Ram Bay in French Indochina. Ten days of calm waters and blue skies brought the voyagers just north of British New Guinea and into the Bismarck Archipelago.

At eleven in the morning, September 30, 1900, on a breeze-less day two hundred nautical miles south of the equator, the SMS *Princess Eugenia* dropped anchor just off the town of Herbertshohe, on the German island of Neu Pommern. For several days, all on board watched lush green jungle islands slide by in mysterious silence. It seemed intensely beautiful and foreboding, so different from anything they had seen in northern China. Canopies roped above the open decks shaded the passengers. Most everyone stripped down to the minimum of clothing that modesty and decorum permitted, while young men ogled the carefree female passengers in their sheer white summer dresses.

"Markus, you know those books we used to read in school about our colonies here in the South Pacific, and about all those native girls in grass skirts and nothing else? Well, we're going to find out if those authors were writing fact or fiction, right?" He laughed at his enticing suggestion.

"Well, I'm sure you'll find out, knowing you. We may both be in one of those grass huts before nightfall, if they have any!" Again laughs. "But none of them could be as beautiful as my Li Ling." Markus' last comment had just the slightest air of regret, but he said it with a big grin on his face. With the balmy sea winds, on a ship full of happy Germans, and green tropical islands all around, China and his regrets were fading from his immediate consciousness.

The only dock, with its wide wooden planks, was crowded with many of the German colonials of this island just off the coast of German New Guinea. Mixed in among them were the blackest people Levi and Markus had ever seen. They were natives, men with big, bushy black hair that appeared to never have been cut. They looked like fierce warriors.

The view from the high railings was of a most exotic sight. Even with sun-baked tans, the Germans were so white in contrast to these strange black people. With the pure turquoise blue of the shallow, sparkling water and the vividly green foliage in the background, most people on board simply stared in happy fascination and wonder.

GERMAN NEW GUINEA

CHAPTER XVI

German New Guinea

"LADIES AND GENTLEMEN...YOUR attention please. This is the captain speaking. We will be here in Herbertshohe for two nights. The lighters will take you to shore if you wish. We will lift anchor promptly at 7:00 a.m. on October 2 and sail across the bay to Kaiser Wilhelm's Land. Please do not stray too far into the hills, as some native peoples are not particularly friendly. The last lighter back to the ship this evening will leave the dock at 8:00 p.m. Have a good day ashore." With that, people began scurrying around in preparation to disembark.

"Let's go ashore and stretch our legs, look around and find some shade," Levi offered.

"God in heaven, it's hot! We're almost sitting on the equator!" Markus grumbled to no one in particular. "Let's go for a swim."

By two in the afternoon six naked German soldiers were frolicking in the dazzlingly clear water off a wide deserted beach, a half mile up the shoreline from the ship.

"I can't believe we're here. This is a million miles away from that dusty hellhole of Peking. Look at the fish! It's like you can just reach out and pick them up…but they're ten feet down!"

Markus, by far the strongest swimmer of the group, swam out beyond the underwater reef that protected the island from the big breakers. Several of his companions watched him as his powerful arms emerged from the water in slow, methodical strokes.

"He's like a fish! He should be in the navy! Ha," someone shouted over the pounding of the waves.

"Günther, you're getting red. You should see your back. Better put on a shirt or you'll be sorry," offered one of the swimmers.

Suddenly, one of the soldiers, Heiner, stopped cold. His arm went up as he pointed straight out to sea. "What is that?" His nearest companions stopped their splashing around, ran their hands through their hair to get the water out of their faces, and squinted in the bright sun.

"Shark. It's a shark…and a big one!" someone yelled. They turned almost in unison and looked out to the distant swimmer. He was far from the predator, but it did not give any comfort to his friends. The group began to move out of the water and trot down the beach in the same direction as Markus was swimming. Constantly looking back toward the blade cutting the water, they all were gauging the distance from it to Markus. The shark seemed to weave back and forth in slow curves as it moved in the same direction the soldiers were moving. They were surprised at how close the creature came toward shore. At times it was in only six feet of water and appeared to be a frightening ten or twelve feet long.

"Jesus, Mary, and Joseph, look at that thing! We've got to get Markus out of the water, and fast." Some of the men, trying to alert their friend, yelled and waved their shirts and pointed toward the shark. The black fin curved away from the shore and headed toward the white object out beyond the reef.

"Oh my God, it's heading toward him," Levi blurted out.

"Markus! Markus! Look out, look out!"

Markus finally did notice the men waving their shirts and raised his hand to wave back. Then he noticed the pointing and looked back in that direction. As he rose on a swell, he immediately saw what they saw. He stopped and treaded water slowly, watching the fin and the dark hump of the back of the shark as it approached. As it grew near, he pulled in his legs, took a deep breath, and wrapped his arms around his shins. He sank below the surface and watched as the long, round-eyed black form swam by him a mere three feet away.

On shore, Levi was beside himself with fear. His hands were in his hair, pulling.

"My God, he's gone under! Can you see him? Can anyone see him?" he yelled in panic as he paced back and forth in a foot of water. The others were also in a dreadful state of fear and helplessness. "We've got to do something, anything!"

Several men began throwing shells, driftwood, and anything they could find on the beach out toward their friend. Several others waded out into four-foot surf, slapping the water with their wet shirts to distract the shark.

Markus held his breath and bobbed just below the surface, watching the sleek and deadly shape make a wide circle around him. The shark flipped its tail sharply, propelling itself directly toward its prey. Markus saw it coming, held tight, and closed his eyes. A second later, he felt the rough-scaled creature slam into his shoulder and side as it plowed directly over him. He had to come up for air as the jolt knocked some of the air out of his lungs. He knew he was bleeding. The shark's skin felt like a board full of protruding nails dragged across his body. He burst to the surface, gulped air, and began swimming toward shore at a furious pace.

No one had noticed the dark prow of the outrigger canoe or the three black figures slicing their paddles forcefully into the water. They were riding a deep trough from up beach and burst into sight fifty yards from Markus, on a course that put them between the on-coming shark and the swimmer.

"Come on, come on! Faster, swim faster!" they shouted to Markus from the beach. He was still a hundred yards out.

"Look!" All eyes were now on the racing canoe and the black fin coming directly toward Markus and shore. The swift boat was on an interception course with the shark. Just as the two crossed paths, the great fish dove under the canoe at the same moment a black body rose in the canoe and in a lightning-fast motion thrust a thin fishing spear directly down into the leather tough skin beside the dorsal fin. The great predator of the deep disappeared into the murky depths of the bay. With a skilled maneuver of the paddles, the canoe assumed a parallel path with Markus and was quickly beside him. One of the natives dove overboard and soon Markus was lying in the canoe, panting and bleeding and holding his side.

Within moments, the Germans pulled the outrigger up to shore and profusely thanked the three New Guineans with pats on the back, broad smiles, and bows. The terrifying ten-minute ordeal had drained the soldiers of everything, except great exuberance for the dangerous encounter.

"How do we thank these guys? We can't even get their names out of them," Heiner said, looking at the others. "Can we give them something? What do we have?" They all looked around at their mea-ger possessions, Shirts, belts, some German money, cigarettes, and a pocketknife. That was all. They offered the natives the knife and a shirt, but the rescuers waved them off with a smile and climbed back into their outrigger. Several of the Germans helped push the canoe off the beach and waved to the departing strangers.

Levi was tending Markus' massive abrasions along his side and shoulder. He had torn up his shirt and bandaged the bleeding wounds as best he could. The others gathered around and joked nervously about the near catastrophe.

"You're one of the luckiest bastards I know." Levi grinned. "Those guys came out of nowhere in the nick of time to save your beer-soaked ass." He paused as he tied a knot in the long sleeves to secure the bandage. "And they just smiled and left. I don't know what the captain was talking about earlier," he went on. "These natives are as friendly as can be. Now let's get you back to the ship and the doc. Can you walk all right?" Several companions took each side of Markus and guided him slowly back toward the dock, as the conversation became more boisterous with jokes and comments.

"I'll say one thing; you're one hell of a swimmer, but not as fast as a shark!"

Markus was completely exhausted by the time they got back to the dock, and as soon as the officer in charge saw his condition and the blood-soaked bandages, he ordered a lighter to take the swimming party back to the ship. The captain and a medical team met the returning soldiers, having received a wireless from the port officer.

"You men seem to attract danger," he began with a half smile. "I'm just gratified the outcome was so fortunate. And by the way," he looked down at Markus on a stretcher, and in a voice of both slight arrogance and condescension said, "those natives you say rescued you, they're cannibals...or they were cannibals until His Majesty the kaiser took over these islands."

For the next several days, the shark attack story was the talk of the ship. Markus stayed in sickbay through the raising of the anchor and the short trip across the bay. His shipmates went ashore and decided to spend their time in the small town of Alotau, at the far eastern tip of German New Guinea. They reported to Markus that the native women were bare breasted all right, but that the customs of these people isolated the females most of the time, and they had strict rules of no premarital sex.

"Well, if that doesn't beat a horse to death!" Markus laughed. "I was wrong, Levi. You're not getting into any grass shacks after all."

They shook their heads in amusement.

"Well, one more island to go. Samoa. We leave as soon as the ship is provisioned," Günther added. "And that's tomorrow for sure."

For the next week the beautiful white naval ship plowed southeast through the oncoming south equatorial current in the Coral Sea. They could see the Vanuatu Island's peaks but sailed past without making landfall on the British colony.

"They say these islands are really the tops of undersea mountains—hard to believe, isn't it?" Heiner offered as his friends lounged on deck after a vigorous calisthenics drill. It was pretty much their only strictly military duty on board, as the navy men took care of the ship.

"Well," Levi spoke up, "I understand that some professors found seashells up in the Alps some time ago. So maybe Bavaria was at the bottom of an old ocean way back. What do you think, Markus?"

"After all I've seen since joining the army, I'd believe most anything. Remember we just passed that smoking volcano on… what was the name of that little island? I am just glad we are having this beautiful weather. Remember when we came out here in early spring…those high seas and winds and rocking back and forth, and up and down and getting sick all the time? Now is the best sailing we've ever had, but I'm still looking forward to sinking my boots into some good old black German soil, *ja*?"

"Of course," they all agreed.

"What are you all going to do when we get home? Re-enlist? We'll all get more rank and more pay. Our tour of duty will be over in less than a year. Levi, how about you?" Markus, said.

"Mama and Papa want me to go to university. I think I've had enough of the army for now. University life, I think, will suit me fine." He looked over to Markus. "And you? Are you going to make a life for yourself serving the kaiser in uniform, like your father?"

Markus looked up and out to sea. He was wistful as he related, "My father was a great man, at least to me, my sister, and Mama. But that 1870 Franco Prussian War is what killed him. Well, not right away, but slowly. The wounds he received took years to heal." Markus paused with an ironic grin on his face. "And, you know, he wasn't even in the Prussian army at the time. He was just an observer from Bavaria for King Otto. He was wearing the Bavarian uniform when he was hit. So when I think about what we've just been through," he looked around at his friends, "well, it's been a mighty adventurous time for all of us, but I think I've seen enough of fighting for a while. The university sounds pretty good to me, too. Besides, I want to stay home and not be sent out to another one of our colonies somewhere. I like Bavarian weather!"

There was silence for a while as the young men napped in the shade. "So Günther and Heiner, what about you two? Got any plans?" asked Levi.

"Günther and I talked it over." Heiner looked at Günther. "We're staying in. There's not a war on anywhere now, no one is shooting at us, and we'll get more pay, more rank, and more girls! Ha! They love boys...*men* in uniform, right, Günther?"

"*Ja*, right, and I've been thinking about Wilhelmina. I think she likes me...and I aim to find out, soon as we get home."

"You've just been dreaming about getting your hands, no, your lips on those big tits of hers! It's all right, Günther, we've all been dreaming about Wilhelmina's tits!" said Heiner. More laughs.

Günther looked flustered and threw his cap at the others. "You guys keep your eyes off my girl when we get home!" Again, they all laughed heartily, including Günther.

Markus' deep gashes from the shark were healing well according to his last checkup from the ship's doctor. "You'll have those scars on your side for a long time, but they shouldn't give you any further discomfort. You were a lucky soldier. The natives lose several people a year to shark attacks." As Markus was putting on his shirt, the doctor continued: "You may not know this, but most of the time, the shark takes a bite and lets his victim bleed to death. Then he goes in for the feast, and usually the bite comes on the second pass. You were very fortunate."

"Thank you, sir. I'm staying out of the water for a while." With that, he saluted and passed through the narrow passages to the mess, where Levi was waiting.

"What's the word from the doc?"

Markus slipped onto the narrow bench. "He says I should be fish food and that I was damned lucky…well, he didn't say 'damned.'"

The ship steamed on through smooth blue seas and the passengers dreamed of lovers, loved ones, and home. Few were sad to leave China, except for a few missionaries, fretting over lost souls, and a few businessmen who left business behind. By and large those aboard simply looked forward to the next island, Samoa, the next pause in their long voyage home.

GERMAN SAMOA CREST

CHAPTER XVII

German Samoa

THE SHIP'S CAPTAIN ordered a general meeting of all passengers in the great room, serving as a lounge and dining hall, as the *Princess Eugenia* neared German Samoa.

"We will be arriving at Germany's newest outpost in the South Pacific, Samoa," he began. All eyes were on this elegant naval officer as he pointed to a cluster of islands on a map tacked up for viewing.

"I should think a bit of local history would be appropriate to you as we will be in port for approximately a week. It has been only seven months since we have taken over full administration of a cluster of islands in the greater Samoan Island chain. Dr. Solf is our first governor of these islands. He assumed his duties just this past March. You may have the opportunity to meet Dr. Solf during our stay here. It should be noted," he continued, "that the native peoples of these islands have asked us to intervene in their long-running tribal conflicts, to govern them peacefully and assist their king and village chiefs. Great Britain and the United States have also been asked to assist in the administration of other islands in the Samoa group in order to stop the incessant tribal wars. They have assumed their duties on their islands as we have here. The kaiser's treaty of Berlin allowed for this mutual governance of all the Samoan Islands. You will find the peoples of these islands quite friendly and in many ways quite different from the natives of our other Pacific possessions. I encourage you to enjoy yourselves and get plenty of exercise on land, as the next leg of our trip home will be a long one. Next landfall will be Chile, in South America. If there are any questions, my first officer here will answer them. Good day."

The room was abuzz with questions and comments as Levi led his friends out onto the deck.

"One week in port. Enough time for you three to find some trouble, *ja*, Heiner?"

Heiner gently punched Levi in the arm. "*Ja*, and I heard the native girls are not hidden away like in New Guinea."

"We shall see, Heiner, we shall see."

The tall mountains appeared far out to sea, as the great cruiser approached the small islands, which emerged from a dazzling turquoise ocean that extended as far as the eye could see. The sight was otherworldly, pure enchantment. The cry of seabirds circling the ship was like primitive music. Snow-white beaches, leading to a garden of Eden of tall palm trees, were so close to the breaking waves, they hung over the water. Intense deep green foliage, almost black in contrast to the beach and sky, seemed impenetrable.

"Oh my god, look at this island, will you? This must be the most beautiful place in all creation," Günther sighed, as he and most of the others on board gazed at yet another exotic tropical isle of singular beauty.

The boats were away soon after dawn, the coolest part of the day. Landing at the little port town on Mulinau, on Upolu, one of the two largest of German Samoa, the voyagers were met by Dr.

Solf himself and his small staff. Surrounding them were large brown people, many larger than the largest German on board the ship.

"Look at the size of them natives," Günther murmured. "Are they all this big?"

"So, Günther, you still want to bed one of these girls? She might kill you!" His friends had a good laugh.

"Let's find some beer and cool off," Levi offered. "We'll save the swimming for later!"

They found a café of sorts, right on the beach near the docks. There were green coconuts, dozens of them, strewn all over the beach. Near the café, out in the water, were thatched houses, built on stilts. Immense clamshells, some of them three feet across and with the lid on, two feet high, were piled nearby.

"Mary Immaculate! Have you ever seen anything like these? I'd love to see the size of a pearl that came out of one of them! These are gigantic! What a place this island is. Big people, big clams...I wonder what else is to be found further inland?" said Günther.

Markus intervened. "We'll have to see about that after a stein or two of beer."

The next day, again landing early from the ship, the four comrades decided to venture inland. Following one of the winding paths lined with grass and palm-thatched houses, they soon were beyond the village. As the path rose in elevation, it narrowed and forked off toward terraced lands cultivated in strange plants.

"Breadfruit, I think it might be breadfruit. I read they eat breadfruit...whatever that is."

"Maybe it's like our potatoes. We make potato bread. Maybe they make bread from breadfruit...and dumplings!"

"Stop, stop with the talk of potatoes and dumplings, you're making me hungry."

They chuckled as the little group ascended higher along the forested trail. Their route paralleled a swift flowing stream that tumbled over rocks and formed crystal-clear pools at intervals.

"Let's stop in the flat area ahead—pee break!"

The four halted and stood shoulder to shoulder as they urinated in unison off the side of the path. Some aimed their yellow stream in a high arch; others washed the nearby wide-leafed plants. Out of nowhere, all of them were startled to hear high-pitched giggles and laughter. The soldiers turned toward the sounds and beheld a group of native women in brightly colored skirts and nothing else, looking and pointing and laughing.

"Will you look at that? Jesus, Mary, and Joseph, we've gone to heaven, boys!" , Heiner said.

The two groups stared at each other for a few moments until the women scurried off through the trees.

"Let's follow them," Günther insisted.

"*Ja*, of course," Heiner responded.

They left the path and made their way through knee-high ferns in the direction of the Samoans. Before they could see it, they heard the thunder and crashing of water on rocks. Through the canopy of trees, the mist from a waterfall guided them. Several bright colors—red, orange, and yellow—flashed into view when they approached a large pool at the base of the falls.

The women were on the opposite side of the fifty-foot-wide natural basin of water. Some were washing clothes; others were sitting, talking, and staring at the strangers with smiles and whispers. The two groups, each on opposite sides of the water, sat and stared at each other.

"Look at those bodies. Oh Jesus, what I wouldn't give to..." Heiner trailed off without finishing.

Finally, Markus slipped into the water, treaded water, and floated on his back, keeping clear of the women's side. Levi was next to pull off his shirt and boots and dive in. He swam up to the falling water and stood under the pounding shower. "Wow, this is fantastic! Come on in, boys!"

Günther and Heiner peeled down to their pants and walked gingerly into the cold mountain pool. Soon they were all paddling around and looking at the women.

"Come in, come in," they shouted merrily and signaled with hand gestures. Soon several women slipped into the water and swam and laughed, but still stayed their distance.

Günther finally swam up close to a lovely young native, and they both swam a sort of crawl stroke parallel to each other, smiling. His companion rolled onto her back, her breasts just breaking the surface. "My god, I never swam with a naked lady before. Will you look how her breasts float!"

His friends burst into hilarious laughs. The late morning drifted into early afternoon with the four Germans and five native girls swimming and frolicking in the water, sunning themselves and warming up in the intense brightness of a cloudless sky after the cold swim. The women had no sense of modesty that these Europeans always experienced back home. Some of their skirts were thin and loosely draped, revealing their thighs and dark hair. Their happy innocence made them even more alluring.

Heiner lay on his belly to hide his stiff erection. It was all he could do to not climax from his moving and joking and kidding around with two lovely full-breasted natives sitting and lying within arm's reach. Several women got up and made gestures with their hands like eating and pointing in the direction they began to walk. The other girls got up and prodded the men to follow.

Heiner called to Levi, "Throw me my shirt, will you?" As he caught his shirt the beauty nearest him took his hand and pulled him up. She pretended not to notice the bulge in his pants Heiner vainly tried to cover up. The touch of her hand and her forceful pull caused a huge open-mouthed, goofy smile on his face as he turned his head back toward his friends, who followed closely behind him.

A short three-minute walk brought the jolly party to a flimsy thatched shelter with four-foot-high walls and a wide opening for entry. Four women went inside and soon emerged with mats and several baskets of fruit and gourds of fruit juice. They set out the baskets, and soon all were enjoying bananas, melons, and other strange and wonderful delights. They laughed and pointed and somehow communicated in a primitive way. Finally, the group quieted down and they all lay on the mats in the mid-afternoon shade.

After a while the woman nearest Heiner, the one who had taken his hand earlier, slowly rose and picked up her mat. Heiner was watching her watch him as she took a few steps toward the shelter. She stopped and with a silent smile nodded her head toward the entrance. Heiner hesitated a moment, then rose up and followed her into the shadows of the structure. The other men pretended not to notice, but the women were nonchalant.

Günther glanced at the hut and looked at his two female companions. He propped himself up on his elbows, smiled, looked around, and fidgeted as he gazed from one to the other. As each young woman moved, even slightly, her full breasts swayed and jiggled in a most erotic way. He reached out and touched the foot of the nearest. As he gently rubbed her ankle and then calf, he scooted closer. The other girl reached over and ran her hand through his hair and giggled. He reached up and touched her nipple. The two women looked at each other and held the look a second. Then they both slowly got up, pulling their mats with them. Günther rose with them. The two turned and walked behind the shelter with their newfound friend behind them.

Markus and Levi were taking in all this, watching the playfulness and the disappearance of their two friends. There was a sexual tension in the air and the remaining individuals could not help hearing the moans of delight and sighs of pleasure. The remaining beauties became quite playful, tossing banana peelings at the two men and trying to provoke an active response from them.

Soon, Levi was up on his knees, returning throws with whatever was around. A merry food fight began with the girls up and dodging the attack and responding with their own well-aimed rinds and luncheon debris. All were laughing and dodging and running in circles. Levi got up and chased one of the girls, caught her, let her escape, and chased after her into the forest.

The other girl, still laughing and breathing hard, plopped down beside Markus. They were lying on their backs, she with her hands coursing through her hair, both smiling and giggling. She turned and threw her leg over Markus as she rolled onto her side. She rubbed her leg back and forth across his stomach and soon they were kissing. The rest of the afternoon the playful group of newfound friends spent seeking pleasures and finding them.

Markus was sound asleep, entwined in his lover's legs, as twilight approached. Levi strolled up and nudged his friend and then walked over to the hut and slapped the side of the palms that made up the wall.

"Time to head back, boys. It'll be getting dark soon."

"*Ja, ja*, we're coming, in a minute" came the reply among noises and laughter from inside the hut. Heiner and Günther both emerged with their girls. Günther had his arm around his woman and was cupping her breast in his hand. Everyone was still in a good mood, but they all had quieted down from the noisy early afternoon party.

"We have to be going," Levi said to the women as he gestured toward the path they had taken earlier. "Good-bye now. See you again, we hope!"

Of course, none of the women understood the words but totally understood the meaning. Among waves and good-byes and laughs and blown kisses from Heiner, the four men tramped off downhill through the forest. They were silent for a few minutes, until they thought they were out of earshot of the women. Günther and Heiner began exchanging experiences and comparisons.

"So Günther, how many times did you do it with her? Huh? You won't believe this, but I did it three times…two with Lanea and once with Pelou. And we did it like sitting in each other's laps. It was incredible! And the other one was kissing me and rubbing my back and my balls while I was doing it to the other one! *Jesus*! That was unbelievable! So, Levi, and Markus, how was it with you two?"

"Save it, Heiner." Said Levi, "I'm not about to tell you or anybody else about this afternoon. And I suggest you not tell every guy on the ship, or we'll have a riot and a mutiny with all those sailors combing the woods looking for our lady friends. You want to get us restricted to the ship?"

"Okay, right. I was just curious about you all having as much fun as me." He was grinning and smirking and stepping high along the trail. "You think we can come back here tomorrow? How many more days do we have in port? Damn, I wish we could talk with the girls…hard to know where they'll be tomorrow. Especially my two!" He chuckled.

Back on board that evening, Levi and Markus were, in fact, comparing notes on the day's events.

"I say that was one hell of an experience!" said Levi.

"*Ja*," offered Markus. "Those gorgeous women were so uninhibited. You suppose they're all like that on this island? It's so different from what we heard about the women in New Guinea…or in China. This would never happen at home." He paused. "These islands are a wonderful place, so beautiful, so different…their brown skin and big black eyes and all that long hair with curls…they all seem so happy and carefree, it's just amazing. Back home it seems we have so many rules and restrictions."

"You're right about that," Levi replied. "This all is amazing, but you know, during the siege, when things were looking pretty bad, there was a lot of…well, promiscuousness, a lot of sex in the night, even among the missionaries. I saw it myself while on guard duty.

Wives and single women with different partners, and the officers were the worst…or I should say the most 'active.' So maybe it happens at home too; we just don't see it because it's not happening in our families." They both fell silent, reprising the day's events.

The next day Heiner and Günther were off the ship and into the woods. Levi and Markus hung around on board and in the afternoon went ashore for dinner and a walk around. They did see one of the women from the previous day, but only in passing. They exchanged smiles and went their separate ways. By the end of the week, the vessel had been provisioned and was set to sail. Günther and Heiner commented that the ship was leaving in the late afternoon.

"One last chance to go ashore. You two going to join us?"

"*Ja*, we'll come for a beer or two, but not up to the waterfall!"

They all laughed.

CHAPTER XVIII

October 22, 1900

Coronel, Chile

"THE VOYAGE ACROSS the vast South Pacific is long and hot," began the navy deckhand. "I've sailed it several times. It's pretty monotonous." Levi and his friends sat listening. "Santiago, Chile, is fifty-five hundred nautical miles from Samoa. If all goes well, the trip will take about thirteen days."

Those days passed slowly for all aboard. The great white ship plunged into mounting swells, with the occasional squall cooling everyone. The women on board still wore their lovely sheer white dresses, and all the men aboard still enjoyed watching them. The four friends, sated in Samoa, were not quite so eager to follow every movement of a skirt. Naps, cards, gambling, and gymnastics occupied the soldiers. The band played through pleasant meals, and one day a truly exciting sight appeared out of the mist—Easter Island. The isolated, mysterious Chilean island emerged from over the horizon.

The captain, in his usual official tone, announced: "As I stated yesterday, we will stop here only to take on water, deliver mail, and drop off one passenger. A single shore excursion of just six hours is approved."

The debarkation allowed a quick trip up the slopes to the immense stone sculptures that dotted the island. No one knew who carved the huge figures, all of them facing out to sea.

As the hardy group hiked across pristine grasslands, Levi said to no one in particular, "Some ancient civilization carved these, but how did they do it, and why? Imagine the manpower it took to move these things, and without any steam power. This is the strangest of all the places I've ever seen... I wonder what it all means." A wind from the sea blew constantly, causing many to turn up their collars. "I've got to read up on some of the places I've seen!"

The air grew cooler and the seas rougher as the Antarctic currents pushed north and eastward toward South America. Now seventeen hundred miles south of the equator, the SMS *Princess Eugenia* encountered gale-force winds for almost a week after leaving Easter Island. Every one of the passengers fondly remembered the tranquil South Pacific as they held tight to the railings and safety ropes strung both inboard and on deck.

"Captain says we'll be sighting the Andes Mountains midday tomorrow, and it couldn't come a day sooner. I'm sick of being sick," grumbled Günther. "You can give this tub back to the navy... and, how are we expected to sleep in hammocks for weeks on end? A deck chair is better than this." He paused. "Actually, I can sleep in a saddle easier than a hammock. Too bad there're no horses on board!"

"Oh, stop your grumbling," Markus scolded, teasingly. "You'll be ashore soon, chasing the señoritas, you and Heiner. Personally, I can't wait to practice my Spanish. It should be pretty close to Italian, I imagine."

Levi broke in, "I just hope they have a good harbor to get us out of this rough water. I never was much for open water sailing, unless it's on Schliersee or Lake Constance!"

Giggles broke out as Heiner added, "*Ja*, Markus is a natural ocean man, and he doesn't need a boat…except to get rescued, and by headhunting cannibals!" Everyone within earshot burst into hysterics.

When Markus stopped laughing, he said, "Very funny, very funny…and they weren't cannibals, at least not anymore!"

The next morning the captain announced a change in ports: "We will be harboring at Coronel, near Valparaiso, instead of Santiago. There have been civil disturbances in the Santiago area, and as many of our passengers have just been through serious civil disturbances in China, it was decided to land at Coronel for everyone's comfort. We will be in port late this afternoon."

They were all on deck, where they spent most of their time, even as each day grew cooler.

"Coronel, who's ever heard of Coronel?" Markus asked. "And I wonder how far Valparaiso is from this port? I want to buy some of those alpaca sweaters for my sister and Mama. They'll be the perfect gifts for Christmas…if I can keep the moths out of them 'til then. And if, by some miracle, we make it home by Christmas."

"I could use one right now," voiced Levi, folding his arms across his chest and slapping himself to keep warm. "I never thought I'd miss those hot days in Peking, but this is beginning to feel like Garmisch in November!"

They all nodded their heads in agreement. The southern Andes lay to the east, towering over the landscape as the ship steamed closer to shore.

When the SMS *Princess Eugenia* docked, it was too late to go ashore, but the next day most of the passengers streamed down the gangplank and spread out through the ancient former Spanish Colonial city. The main cathedral, built in the heyday of the Spanish conquest, retained its extravagant Baroque architecture.

Levi, the only Jew in the group, seemed more interested in the wonders of the paintings, sculptures, and lavish altar than the Catholics. "This is an amazing church," he exclaimed as he craned his neck to look up at the painted saints and angels that swirled above the visitors in magnificent detail. Gold gilding was everywhere on the lavish ornamentation. "This is much more elaborate than Marian Church in Munich. Of course, that's Renaissance style, so there's a big difference."

"Oooh, listen to Herr Doctor Professor Levi, the great historian!" Heiner kidded. "How come you know so much about Catholic churches? You're a Jew, for God's sake! Oh, did I make a joke? Ha!"

"Very funny, Heiner. Stick around, you might learn something," Günther chided. "But in the meantime, let's get something to eat."

Levi could not let it pass. "We Jews value knowledge and history, and I especially love art history...everyone's art history, especially this." He turned around in a circle, his hand pointing to the ceiling far above them. "Imagine a European-style Spanish Baroque church way over here in Chile." He was smiling from the pure joy of being in such a beautiful place. "But you're right, Günther, I'm hungry; viewing art always makes me hungry."

They walked the cobblestone streets past quaint cafes, lively cantinas, open-air markets, fountains, and sidewalk shrines to this or that saint.

"Chile seems a lot like Italy, doesn't it, Markus? Remember when we went skiing in the Italian Alps and went down to Lake Como? That was great fun! It's almost like here," Levi exclaimed.

"*Ja*, it was, but it seems so long ago...what with everything we've seen since then. But it's only been two years. I wonder how it will be when we get home. Do you think it's changed?"

"*Na*, nothing ever changes at home, but we sure have, don't you think?"

Markus found his sweaters, and Levi found some small pure gold Inca objects of fanciful design, probably from one of the hundreds of illegal digs in the ancient sacred places in the mountains. Günther and Heiner, as usual, were more interested in the exotic native women in the cafes than in anything else.

"They sure are short," Heiner commented. "Look at them, what, maybe four feet tall? But the young ones, they look pretty good. You sure can tell the Spaniards...I mean *Chileans* from the natives."

"Heiner, you really need to get back to Wilhelmina before you catch something you'll regret! Like Spanish fly or something," Levi jabbed.

The days in port passed quickly, each soldier getting what they wanted—sightseeing, enjoying wonderful wines and Chilean food, practicing Spanish, buying souvenirs, and in Günther and Heiner's case, chasing women. "They're a hard lot, these Incas or whatever tribe they're from," Heiner observed. "Straight black hair and high cheekbones make 'em look exotic, but the whores in China seemed softer or something. Anyway, we had a go of it, but not with any of the Spanish women. Maybe we'll have to go to Spain for that, eh, Günther?"

"*Ja*, onward to Spain, except we're not stopping in Spain."

Steaming south along the coast of Chile, the air grew colder and the weather harsher. Squalls and storms with pounding rain kept most everyone indoors as the ship approached Cape Horn.

"This is a Godforsaken place, only fit to be passed through," Heiner snarled, looking out the lounge window. His friends were sitting around a card table smoking their pipes or cigarettes.

"Well, we're only about five hundred miles from Antarctica," Levi commented casually as he threw his bad hand onto the pile of chips on the table.

"Heiner wants to stop and try an Eskimo, eh, Heiner?" Günther kidded.

"Wrong pole, Günther," Markus corrected.

The next day the four were seated in the same place until Levi suddenly jumped up.

"The Atlantic! We're in the Atlantic," he shouted enthusiastically as his friends watched the coast slip by. "The Straits of Magellan, now it's due north to Uruguay. We'll be there in less than a week." He was in an especially good mood.

"Exotic beers and lots of good food await us, boys, just like in Chile. And our people have been in Uruguay for years. I read they're some of the biggest landowners."

"When you say 'our people' do you mean Jews or the rest of us Germans?" Heiner asked with a smirk on his face.

"Jesus, Heiner! What's that supposed to mean?" Markus piped up.

"Hey, I was just asking? His people…" Heiner thumbed toward Levi, "are all over the place."

Markus jumped up from the card table, almost spilling his beer. Günther reached out his arm to restrain him. "He didn't mean anything by it…cool off, Markus," Günther urged. "Come on, sit down."

Levi then spoke up in a calm, resigned voice. "Let it be, my friend. I'm used to it." He gestured toward Markus' chair. "Sit down."

"*Ja*, well, I don't like that talk, Heiner." Markus stared intently at Heiner.

"I'm sorry, I'm sorry, Christ, I'm just sick of this boat. Levi, I'll buy you a beer in Montevideo, okay?"

"Okay," Levi said, not looking up.

CHAPTER XIX

The Encounter,

Montevideo, Uruguay

AN OVERCAST DAY, dreary and cold, found their ship easing into a berth in the harbor at Montevideo across the bay from Buenos Aires, Argentina. Diplomatic arrangements, made by the Imperial German Navy for coaling and resupply, allowed the SMS *Princess Eugenia* the use of the port. Without coaling stations around the world, no nation could sustain colonies.

Again, passengers took advantage of the days in port to explore another obscure country on the long voyage home. Markus and Levi, in their crisp dress uniforms, strolled the streets and plazas, taking in the surprising flavor of a European culture transplanted to South America. The two soldiers appreciated wearing their full dress uniforms as the chilly air was brisk.

"It's amazing, don't you think, Markus…I mean, it feels so European."

"Yes, there're lots of Europeans and even Portuguese from up north." They turned down a narrow cobblestoned street lined with small shops. "Hear that? Sounds like a polka and with an accordion, too."

"Look what we've got here. Looks German all right. Let's go in." They peeked through white lace curtains into a very familiar-looking beer garden. The sign over the door said, *Willkommen*. As they passed through, Levi noticed a *mezuzah* on the doorpost. Some dozen or so people were at light oak tables, beer mugs and platters of food in front of them. The accordionist had just finished playing and took a drink of beer from a glass on a stool. A few people applauded. Most of the people in the restaurant turned and looked at the two strangers in their field gray dress uniforms with red piping and spiked helmets, the coat of arms of Bavaria on the helmet plate.

A blond, smiling woman wearing a green dirndl and low-cut white blouse came up to them. "Welcome, two beers for you soldiers?" She was carrying six mugs of beer. "Be right with you."

The two sat down on a long bench at an even longer table. Most of the seats were filled except for the bench opposite them. The beers came and were half emptied on the first draft.

"Ahh, now that's what I like. So, are you hungry?" Markus asked.

Levi replied with a nod. They ordered hot dumplings and gravy and Russian rye bread with a thick spread of butter for a perfect dinner on such a cool early evening day. As the music began again, a family of five came in, looked around, came over to their long table, and sat down opposite. The adults looked across at Levi and Markus, smiled, nodded politely, and turned facing the musician, who had struck up a lively tune.

The family consisted of parents, appearing to be in their forties, two boys, Moses and Benjamin, age ten and fourteen respectively, and their sister, Katherina, age nineteen. The entire family was dressed in black, father with a white shirt and tie, and only the daughter in a cream full-length dress and black lace shawl with small red flowers embroidered on it. Her long, curly black hair came halfway down her back and was immediately noticed by both young men. Sitting just across the table from her, they leaned in and could smell her well-scrubbed freshness. They looked at each other and smiled as the youngest boy turned to look at them.

After the music stopped, Levi formally introduced himself and Markus and were introduced to the family by the father, Herr Professor Obermaier. A warm conversation ensued, with the two soldiers relating their China experiences.

"I see you both have won an Iron Cross, and so young," the professor commented. He, in turn, told the family saga of his great-grandfather immigrating to Russia with hundreds of other Germans, at the invitation of Empress Katherine the Great.

"Free land, she promised, free from conscription into the Russian Army, she promised, and she kept her word. She was truly a great empress. Katherina is named after her." He nodded toward his daughter, who listened politely, watching the two men. "Grandpapa prospered and my father, too. But then we got a new czar. He changed everything. High taxes, Jew baiting, and worst of all, conscription!" He paused, staring vacantly at the floor. His wife put her hand on his arm. The boys were silent, watching.

"*Ja*, so that's why we're here. Lots of Russian Germans came… not just Jews, but Lutherans and Catholics, too. We get along pretty well here. It's a good life, *ja*, Mama?" She smiled and squeezed his arm. "*Ja*, and so now we go full circle," he continued, brightening. "An Obermaier is going back to Germany after three generations!" he announced proudly. "Katherina is going to Berlin, to the Jewish Academy…and her Tante Berti is going with her." The whole family was smiling and looking at Katherina with pride.

She blushed mildly, looked down a moment, then looked up with a broad grin and exclaimed, "And they accepted my application thanks to Papa's many letters and his good name." She smiled with loving eyes at her father.

The evening was filled with good beer, good music, friendly conversation, and eyes flashing across the table. The boys asked about soldiering. Mr. Obermaier talked colonial politics and inquired about Bavarian life, as he had never been there.

"So Miss Katherina, what will you be studying at the academy?" Levi managed to muster, dazzled by the young woman's beauty.

"Ancient literature, the classics, and biblical archeology. I find the Old Testament stories fascinating...especially when names and places are known to have existed. I think there is so much yet to be discovered," she said passionately. "I would like to go to Jerusalem and Babylon and Egypt. That would be wonderful." She looked wistful. "Here in Uruguay...well, it's so beautiful, but it's a long way from our roots."

"Now, now, child," her father interrupted. "We came here so your brothers wouldn't have to be Russian soldiers. I will not have my sons die so the czar can expand his empire, like when he grabbed Finland. How many beautiful young boys died for that." He shook his head as if to shake out the truth of his last statement.

"So," he said finally, "time to go. The boys have school tomorrow and books still to read tonight, *ja*? We bid you good evening, gentlemen. We may see you again before your ship leaves... If not, God bless your voyage home. *Shalom!*"

As the Obermaier family got up to leave, Levi quickly but quietly asked Katherina, "When will you be leaving for Berlin?"

"In just a few days," she replied, "on the German ship *Princess Eugenia*."

CHAPTER XX

December 5, 1900

Five Hundred Miles

North of Antarctica

ON THE OUTPOSTS of German culture, whether formal colonies or simply scattered communities on faraway continents and islands, Kaiser Wilhelm II encouraged contact with the fatherland. As a part of that policy, it was not unusual for civilians to be transported from distant ports to and from Germany on naval vessels, as long as it did not interfere with naval operations. And so it was at the port of Montevideo, Uruguay.

On a cool, blustery day, with a brilliant blue sky broken by intensely white puffy cotton clouds, Miss Katherina Louisa Obermaier kissed and hugged her family good-bye at the base of the gangplank of the SMS *Princess Eugenia*. Levi and Markus joined most of the other passengers crowding the railing on the port side of the ship, waving and blowing kisses to the people below.

"Isn't she a sight, Markus…look at that woman. What a beauty!" Levi could hardly contain himself as he watched Katherina stride up the gangplank and into the shadowy recesses of the ship.

"Levi," Markus commented, elbowing his friend as they both watched, "you are really smitten by that girl. We've only spent two hours with her."

"I know, I know, but isn't she something! And she's got a real mind of her own."

"*Ja*, and that mind is in a really pretty head, *eh*, Levi." He bumped him again. "Want to find out what stateroom she's in? Let's find the purser, he'll know."

From Montevideo, Uruguay, in South America, to the Imperial German Colony of Southwest Africa was thirty-six hundred nautical miles. The *Princess Eugenia* was swept along by the Brazilian current that flowed eastward across the South Atlantic to Africa. With good weather, the ship could make the voyage in ten or eleven days. Unfortunately, unusually cold turbulence slowed the progress eastward. Visibility was near zero as the powerful ship plunged through towering waves. Levi and most of the passengers had returned to their cabins and tried to sleep as the ship rolled rhythmically. The clang of the ship's bell struck the hour before midnight. Just the slightest vibration from the mighty engines rippled through the floors and hull as the narrow passageways grew quiet for another night at sea. They had been sailing for several days.

The initial impact was so violent, many passengers, including Levi and Markus, were thrown out of their bunks. Books and bedding, personal effects, and everything else not tied down flew to the floor. Tons of fuel in the coalbunkers shifted; stokers were thrown against hot boilers. The first officer broke his arm when tossed against the wheel on the bridge.

At first silence, then screams from civilian passengers. Shouts and commands. The ship's bell clanged general quarters. There was another impact, less violent, but more noticeable because everyone was awake and in a state of panic or at least high anxiety. In the first minutes, passengers, soldiers, and the ship's crew jammed the passageways, some injured, most scared, trying to find out what happened.

Levi and Markus picked themselves up and made for the door to their cabin, just as the ship's bow rose on another wave. Markus opened the door as a six-inch wave of water swished down the passageway floor toward the stern.

"We're taking on water! We must have hit another ship or some rocks! Get your life preserver! And coat! Quickly!" Soldiers and navy men were berthed on the lowest deck. Civilians and officers were on the upper decks.

An announcement blared over the clanging ship's bell.

"This is an emergency. All passengers are to report to the dining hall immediately. Bring warm clothes and life preservers. Nothing else. Information and instructions will be given out as needed. Repeat: This is an emergency. All passengers..." The message repeated continually.

"Let's make for the upper deck!" Markus shouted over the clamor of other voices.

"No, I'm going to Katherina's cabin. I'll meet you in the dining hall. Go!" commanded Levi.

"Need help?" Markus offered.

"No, you help the injured, if there are any." Only then did Levi notice Markus' head bleeding. "Is it bad?"

"No, go help Katherina!"

"Right."

On impact, the captain leaped from his bunk, grabbed his coat, and ran to the bridge.

"Status report!" The first officer was holding his obviously broken arm, but he was still in command when the captain arrived.

"We hit an iceberg. An iceberg!" He managed to wince.

"An iceberg, this far north?" The captain thought for a moment. "Head her into the wind. All ahead slow. Keep her as steady as possible. Double lookouts on the bow…and get someone into the crow's nest. They may be able to see something above this fogbank. We don't want another collision. Let me see the chart." He grabbed the edge and pulled it toward him on the chart table. "Light," he commanded. "My God, we're at the extreme northern limits of Antarctic icebergs! God be with us! Status update!"

"Yes sir. There's ice all over the forward deck. We're taking on water in several starboard forward compartments. Don't know how bad yet."

"Injuries?"

"No report on that yet, sir, except the first officer's broken arm."

The third in command, a young lieutenant, ran up the gangway to the bridge. "Sir, the troop deck C is flooding forward, but the watertight doors are confining the flooding to the forward quarter of the ship on the starboard side. We believe we got everyone out. Duty officer has engineers assessing the damage and making emergency repairs to help stop the leaks as best they can. We've got pumps on the way."

"Good," said the captain. "You take over the bridge, Lieutenant. First officer, see to your injury. Have the lifeboats prepared as a precaution. Do it as discreetly as possible. We don't want to alarm the passengers. I'm going below for a firsthand look." With that, he spun around and exited the bridge.

Levi dashed to the steep ladder stairway leading to the next deck up. *Katherina's stateroom is B11*, he remembered.

He made his way down the crowded passage, squeezing by passengers pushing in the opposite direction. A woman dragging a suitcase was arguing with a navy enlisted man about how important the contents were, and she simply was not going to leave them behind. Levi, blocked by this ongoing confrontation, hesitated a moment, then opened a stateroom door next to the woman's suitcase and pushed it into the empty room. As he pushed by the stout woman, she stared in wide-eyed silence.

"Finally she's speechless!" the navy man said with a smile of satisfaction. "Okay, lady. Now move along to the dining hall as the captain requested."

He found her in compartment B11, kneeling beside the bunk of her aunt. Katherina looked up as Levi knocked and then pushed open the door, which was ajar.

"Levi!" she exclaimed in a stressed voice. "Tante Berti bumped her head when she fell; she's unconscious... I got her back into her bunk, but she won't wake up." The young woman was in tears as she stroked the brow of her aunt. Levi came beside her and bent over the still form on the bed, her gray hair fanned out across the pillow.

He looked at the old woman for a moment and said, "I'll fetch the ship's doctor." His touch to Katherina's shoulder lingered a long moment and he turned on his heel and was gone.

The next half hour was harrowing; the crowded dining hall was jammed with frightened passengers demanding answers, while bundled up and in bulky white cork-filled life jackets haphazardly tied. A half-dozen naval and army officers were calming the most agitated. Mercifully, the captain appeared, and one of the officers called for quiet.

The captain began in his cool, calm voice: "Most of you have already heard that we struck an iceberg at eleven o'clock this evening. My engineers are, as we speak, stemming the flow from several breaches in the hull. We are not in any danger of sinking." He paused for effect. "Let me repeat, we are in no danger whatsoever of sinking." Pause. "I am sure many of you were concerned about that possibility."

He was interrupted with a shout from the back of the room. "Why are the lifeboats being prepared if we're not sinking...tell me that!"

Eyes turned toward the caller, and then back to the captain. "That is standard operating procedure immediately after an incident. Now we are confident there will be no need for furthering that procedure." He purposefully avoided using the word "lifeboat."

No need to raise those images in the minds of the passengers, he thought.

"After an additional inspection of the ship by my officers, the cabin stewards will escort you back to your compartments. Those few whose cabins are unfit for service will be berthed elsewhere. Please be patient for the next several hours. The kitchen stewards are preparing a midnight buffet for your pleasure...and on behalf of the entire crew, I want to extend an apology for any alarm or injury to you or your belongings this incident has caused. Lieutenant, take over."

With that, the captain departed, and the passengers were heard to say: "Thank God we're not sinking. We would have all drowned. Do you believe him? Do you think the ship is safe? Are there more icebergs out there? I just want to get home!" Some people were crying with a sense of relief.

By morning, everything was back to some semblance of normalcy. The soldiers and sailors most seriously affected were also the best prepared psychologically to deal with the dislocation. Levi and Markus found themselves berthed one deck up, crowded into a two-person cabin with two naval officers. Katherina's Tante Berti, recovering from a bad bump on the head, slept under deep sedation. Levi visited their cabin several times early that morning, and on the last time, they found Katherina finally asleep.

Through the night, the captain returned to the bridge several times and received full briefings on repair progress. After consulting with the engine room and his naval engineers, they determined that the forward port hull had been weakened, and a very severe pounding by waves or another collision could sink the ship.

"How long do you need for repairs…repairs that will allow our passage to Bremerhaven?" the captain asked.

"Three or four days in a calm harbor, sir. Or a week at sea…and in this weather it would be very…"

The captain cut him off. "I know, I know, 'very dangerous.' Thank you for your report." He ordered reduced speed and determined to make for the nearest port.

"My charts," he ordered. The chart table light focused on the mid-south Atlantic. The captain's finger traced their route from Montevideo and stopped at a speck in the vast Atlantic.

"Here! Here's where we stop for repairs. Chart a course to—to Tristan da Cunha. Give me an estimated time of arrival and any information you can find on that island."

BRITISH CREST

CHAPTER XXI

December 11, 1900

Tristan da Cunha

THE DESOLATE ISLAND of Tristan da Cunha, *the most remote place on earth*, was a British possession that lay halfway between two continents. Getting a break in the weather, the German ship sailed south-southeast and sighted land a day and a half after the accident. SMS *Princess Eugenia* dropped anchor just off shore from the little hamlet of Edinburgh on the morning of December 11. Captain's announcement:

"We will be here at Tristan da Cunha four or five days for needed repairs. We will lower boats tomorrow if the weather stays clear. Only hearty passengers will be permitted an opportunity to traverse the choppy surf for a shore excursion." He continued: "At the invitation of the local authorities, those going ashore are welcome to step foot on British Crown property for a brief walkabout. There are no historic or archeological sites of interest, and only about sixty permanent residents live here. One member of the crew has been to this island and informs us there is one pub and one church."

Almost everyone was on deck to view the bleak island, including Tante Berti, sporting a small bandage behind her ear.

"So we're going ashore, aren't we?" asked Markus to no one in particular in his small circle of friends as they gripped the railings on the rolling ship.

"It's going to be cold and damp on that island, but they have a beer hall, so let's go!" exclaimed Heiner.

"They don't have beer halls on English islands; they're called pubs," Günther replied sarcastically.

"Well, whatever they're called, they've got beer and they're on terra firma, and a stein of beer on solid ground sounds good enough for me!"

Only about thirty passengers in two longboats braved the choppy waters and the extremely rough ride through the surf to the beach and small hamlet. Some chose to wander off into the stone-walled uplands, spooking the herds of sheep. More than a dozen soldiers crowded into the little pub, and it was soon steamy and raucous with the clink of glasses of British ale. Several local women had come to the pub to help the owner. It was the biggest crowd in the little pub in months and the pub owner was happy to accept silver and gold German marks and even several Chinese gold coins of unknown denomination.

In addition to the Germans, a group of locals showed up to partake in the excitement. Most were sheep farmers or fishermen. A Scotch-Irish fiddle player struck up jolly tunes in the smoky room, and soon a soldier or two were dancing with the female help. The two buxom redheads were whirling around the floor in the arms of first one soldier and then another, all the time enjoying the drinks as much as the men. With the laughing and singing and fiddle music, and half-drunk voluptuous women in their arms, it wasn't long before hands were roaming and kisses taken. With the fiddler playing tune after tune and the women whirling dance after dance, the whole spectacle became more and more erotic and sensual for the watching men.

One of the women in particular attracted the eyes of every man in the room. With her curly red hair in ringlets flying freely, her skirts flaring out as she turned, and her blouse half-unbuttoned, revealing full, heavy breasts bouncing and swaying with her every move, at that moment she was every man's dream. The crowd quieted down and drank their beer as they watched with growing intensity and desire. The fiddler was oblivious as he tapped his foot, moving with the rhythm of his own music, his eyes closed.

She wanted to dance and keep on dancing even with sweat streaking her forehead. Her friend continued, but finally spun into a chair and collapsed, laughing and grabbing the nearest beer. The dancing woman had spun out from her partner and was now dancing alone. Her arms were out, sometimes above her head; her feet were tapping and stomping to the music.

She thrust back her shoulders, her head rolling back and forth to the tune, and she shook her body as she stepped lively around the little dance floor. The pub had grown quiet as every eye was on her shimmering body.

"My God, she's a beauty!" someone whispered. The tension in the room rose to an unsustainable level. Even the barkeep had stopped and was watching uneasily. Levi and Markus looked at each other. They, too, mesmerized by the pure uninhibited sensuality of the lovely creature, followed her every move.

Levi suddenly realized that his shipmates were ready to "explode" into action. He stopped following the dancing woman and looked around at the men beside him. They were all on the edge of their seats and leaning forward. He elbowed Markus.

"Let's get out of here."

"What?"

Again, he said, "Let's get out of…"

"That's enough, Rosie!" a voice bellowed. "Clarence! Clarence! Stop the music! Stop playing." The voice took a long pause.

"Time to go home, Rosie. Time to go back to your children." The entire room quieted to absolute stillness. All heads turned toward the big burly man in the back with a thick mustache. He had sad eyes, and his voice was not menacing.

"It's time to go home now, girl," he said in a gentle voice. She had heard the music stop, and she had heard his familiar voice. She kept dancing for a few seconds as if straining to hear a forgotten tune. She slowed and finally stopped. Her shoulders slumped. She just stood there in silence, a faraway look on her tired face. Everyone stared at her. No one moved a muscle. Tears were running down her face from eyes that seemed to be peering far away and into the past. Her hands came up to her face as she slowly slumped to the floor, sitting there for all to see, quietly sobbing.

The atmosphere of the room had changed in a matter of minutes. A pathos and sadness hung in the air. No one knew what, but everyone knew that something terrible had happened, had changed this beautiful, erotic woman bursting with sensuous life into a wounded soul crumpled on the floor before them.

The big man came slowly forward, his heavy coat smelling of sheep. Several soldiers cleared a way for him to pass through to her.

"Now, now, Rosie, it will be all right, let me take you home." He knelt down beside her and laid his work worn hand gently on her shoulder. The other woman came over quietly and put a shawl around Rosie's shoulders.

"You'll need this, Rosie, for the chill," she said in almost a whisper.

"I'll take her this time, Lil," he said quietly. Slowly he managed to get her up. Several soldiers rushed to help. They stepped back in respect once she was on her feet, her face still in her hands. The two figures slowly moved to the door, held open for them by men with downcast eyes. After they were gone, the room rumbled with low voices asking what could have happened. A dozen speculations passed from one to another, and from table to table.

The room suddenly fell silent again, and all eyes focused toward the dance floor. The barkeep had come around the corner of the bar and walked to the bare spot on the floor.

"That was Rosie Whigs," he began. "She's got four kids. Beautiful little kids, you see," clearing his throat. "You see, eight months ago…was it eight months ago, Tommy?"

"Yeah, yeah, it was eight months ago," a voice spoke up.

"Yes, well, eight months ago there was a shipwreck, up off Wagner's Cove…on the submerged rocks out a quarter mile from shore it was. Well, a group of fellas here got a longboat and headed out to the wreck. We have wrecks here ever so often, you see…and fellas go out to rescue people and to salvage what they can. Well, that's what they did that day…a day pretty much like this. I mean, the seas…it were pretty much like this." He gestured slightly toward the sea out beyond the hamlet. "Well," his speech slowed, "six of them went out and…and none of them came back."

He had lowered his head, and his hand fiddled with his apron strings tied at his waist. He was silent for a few moments.

"It was the worst thing that ever happened here in Edinburgh, or the island. Almost killed us off as a community." A tear welled up in his eye. "Losing six good men, six good men at one time. You know we only have sixty-three people here…well, we had sixty-nine…" His voice trailed off. "Rosie's husband, Ronnie, he were among 'em. So that's the story."

He was silent a moment, everyone waiting to hear if he had anything else to say.

The barkeep perked up a bit and continued. "Don't want anyone leaving our island with the wrong idea. We're a good community, a lot of hardworking folk here. We're little, but we stick together. We're going to get through this, we are. We all agreed, we're going to get through this." He lowered his eyes and seemed to nod his head to himself, in a way to affirm his belief in their deliverance. Finally, he turned and stepped firmly back toward the bar.

The soldiers at the tables, to a man, silently turned back to their companions and their beer. No one had anything to say. They slowly finished their drinks and several rose to leave. As they shuffled forward toward the bar, several reached into their pockets, and without counting, placed silver and gold coins on the counter. They nodded to the barkeep, their lips pressed tightly closed. He accepted their gesture and understood the meaning of the growing pile of coins. Several shipmates stayed for another round. Levi and Markus were among the last to leave, and they, too, added coins on the counter. The barkeep spoke up, thanking them and asking the two to thank all the others.

"This will go a long way for her," he said.

As Markus and Levi stepped out of the low doorway into the brisk, gusty late afternoon gray, the two were taken aback to see Katherina standing near the window of the pub, waiting for them.

"What are you doing here?" Levi blurted out. "I thought you were on the ship with your Tante Berti."

"Oh, she insisted she had recovered and suggested I was free to choose. I came ashore on the second longboat. It was an exciting ride. I wasn't going to miss this once-in-a-lifetime opportunity to see this island. And I didn't care how choppy the water was." She took a long look out to sea. The green-gray waters were still churning menacingly.

"I took a stroll up into the hills with the others. I came back a bit early and came over here. I sensed something was going on in the pub. I saw everything through the window. It was a heart-wrenching drama…that poor woman." Katherina's voice resonated with sincere concern. "You'll have to tell me everything when we get back on board. I couldn't hear a thing, on account of the breakers." Again, she nodded toward the sea. "She passed by me not three feet away. Was that her husband with her? Poor man."

Over the next few days, Levi and Markus, but mostly Levi, sat for long, leisurely hours on deck or inboard with their friends. Katherina joined them often. The tragic incident on Tristan de Cunha Island occupied their thoughts. Their conversations revolved around the tragedy's effect on the island peoples, their hard way of life, and what bound them to the desolate mountaintop that was the island. They talked and looked out across the sea and discussed the tragedy of Rosie Whigs.

The two young people sat on deck chairs, their feet up. Katherina and Levi wrapped themselves in multiple blankets while the chilly winds blew across the deck and the ship rose and fell, plowing her way toward Africa. They snuggled and laughed as the ceaseless gusts lifted their blankets and blew their hats. They neared the western coast of the dark continent on a cold, sunny day and were thrilled to see land again. He touched her hand, and she did not resist but turned to him and smiled.

"Time for lunch!" she said. "Hungry?"

GERMAN SOUTHWEST AFRICA

CHAPTER XXII

December 22, 1900

Christmas in Africa

IT WAS NEARING Christmas as the SMS *Princess Eugenia*, newly repaired at Tristan da Cunha, sailed northeast within sight of the African coast. German Southwest Africa, the most southern of all the Imperial German colonies, stretched from the Orange River border with the British Crown colony of South Africa eight hundred miles north to the border with Portuguese Southwest Africa. The vast, trackless wastes of the Kalahari Desert were the ill-defined eastern border of the German colony.

On December 22, 1900, after a two-thousand-mile journey from that forlorn British island in the South Atlantic, the *Princess Eugenia* eased her way into the little primitive harbor of Swakopmund. It was a small coastal town, a village really, with crude prefabricated buildings, and dry dirt streets with swirls of dust constantly in the air from steady breezes off the ocean. It was located just north of

Walvis Bay, where the only good harbor for a thousand miles north or south was located. Unfortunately, Walvis Bay was controlled by a British settlement that had established itself before the Germans arrived to claim the surrounding lands. The German captain and officers had hoped to spend Christmas in Windhoek, the capital, but soon found that the two hundred miles of rail line inland from the coast was only half built.

"At least," the captain said to his fellow officers, "we can properly inspect the ship's repairs in calm waters, and give the crew and passengers a well-deserved break after the rough South Atlantic crossing." Everyone was happy with the idea of celebrating Christmas among fellow countrymen on German colonial soil.

"Do you think they have Christmas trees here in Africa?" asked Markus as he gazed out the ship's window. "It looks like this land is solid desert, just sand, sand, sand."

"*Ja*, what I've read about this part of Africa is that there are maybe fifty miles of desert from the coast inland. Once past that it greens up, but it's still only good for grazing cattle and, guess what? Ostriches." Levi chuckled.

The gentle voice of Katherina, sitting with her aunt, said, "Isn't it exciting to be on another continent? Imagine all we've seen and experienced so far on this trip, and we still have thousands of miles to sail before we reach Germany."

Levi and Markus looked knowingly at each other, both thinking that the trip from Uruguay to Africa was a welcome respite, except for the iceberg, from what both had been through in China. They just smiled at each other as Katherina continued.

"I've been writing letters home to Mama and Papa, and I have so much to tell them…so many adventures! Do you think I can mail my letters here in Africa to Uruguay?" She looked to Levi for a reply.

"I think you should ask the purser or the captain or someone ashore. I'm sure there is a post office in Swakopmund and ships going across to South America."

Their conversation was interrupted by the captain's announcement over the ship's speaker:

"Attention please. We have several important announcements to all the passengers and crew. First: We must remind you that a state of war exists between the British forces of South Africa and the Boers of the Transvaal. While the kaiser's forces here in our colony of Southwest Africa are not engaged in this conflict, there have been incursions into German territory to the east. There is no danger here in Swakopmund at this time, but we instruct all persons going ashore to maintain frequent contact with the authorities. In the unlikely event of a change in conflict status, please return to the ship immediately.

"Second: Please realize the delicate political position His Majesty's colony is in here. Historically, the Germans of this colony have been friends with both the Boers to the east and the British to the south. Many German colonials are in sympathy with the Boers, our Dutch neighbors back home. However, it is very important that no passenger or crew is seen to support in any way the two sides now engaged in the struggle to the east. There are spies from both parties in Swakopmund. Therefore, refrain from giving or accepting any gifts or other valuables that could be construed to be assistance to either side."

Levi watched the expressions on the faces of his companions as they turned from gay, lighthearted ease, to frowns and wrinkled foreheads.

The captain continued: "Third, and now for a happy Christmas announcement. Our good ship's officers will host a gala Christmas dinner on board...and yes, we will have a Christmas tree. Members of the crew have volunteered to find, somewhere ashore, branches that our ship's carpenter has agreed to fashioned into our beautiful tennenbaum. Also," he continued, "midnight mass will be held in the dining hall…a joint Lutheran and Roman Catholic service conducted by the ship's chaplain and with the ship's band and chorus singing all our favorite Christmas hymns.

"Our fourth and final announcement: Governor Theodor Leutwein, chief administrator of this colony, in the spirit of the holidays, has generously offered to host a New Year's Eve celebration and dance at Governor's House. It will be a splendid occasion to commemorate our grand far-flung German Empire here in His Majesty's colony of Southwest Africa. Our short stay here in Swakopmund will end when we depart the morning of January 3. All passengers and crew must be aboard by noon on January 2. Passengers may disembark tomorrow for day excursions. Enjoy your visit, and a Merry Christmas to all."

"Well, that was a startling speech the captain just gave," exclaimed Katherina with a perplexed expression. "How far off is the fighting anyway?"

Günther answered, "I heard the border is about 350 miles to the east, so there's little chance of danger here." He hesitated a moment, then lit up. "The Christmas dinner and New Year's Eve party sound great!"

"Oh, won't that be fun!" Katherina beamed, and turning to her Tante Berti she whispered, "I can wear my green silk dress and Mother's pearls she gave me." A wonderful broad smile laced across her face, and that brought a similar smile to Levi's lips as he watched the young woman.

"Spies! Think of it," she said to her little group of friends. "British spies! And Boar spies right here in Swakopmund. I can't wait to get to town."

"*Ja*, well, I don't think you are going to be able to recognize any even if you happen to see one," Levi advised with a good-natured chuckle. "You'll probably see a few drunken sailors and soldiers, though."

"Yes, and I'm going to be one of them," announced Heiner. "We've got lots to celebrate, New Year, new continent, and we're headin' home...but not before we check out the local talent in town. Know what I mean? Ha!"

"Really!" Tante Berti exclaimed. "We'll have none of that crude talk in our company. Katherina, we're leaving."

"Oh, Tante, please."

"Tante Berti," Levi spoke up. "I'm sure Heiner didn't mean to offend you." He gave a hard stare at Heiner. Markus, sitting next to Heiner, gave him a nudge and nodded his head toward the older woman. All eyes were on Heiner. He realized he was being stared at with anticipation.

"*Ja*, I didn't mean anything by that." He hesitated. "I apologize if I offended anyone." He cast his eyes down.

"See, Tante, he apologized," Katherina said gently to her aunt as she reached over and touched her arm. "Now, can't we stay awhile longer?"

"Well, it's time for my nap, anyway," the woman said, getting up from her chair. "If you want to stay for a short time more, I suppose it will be all right." With that, she moved through the group and headed to her cabin.

The following day, having disembarked and strolled into the primitive village that was Swakopmund, most passengers were sorely disappointed. Before them lay a frontier hamlet in a wasteland of sandy hills, rocks, and low, barren mountains as a backdrop. Crude prefabricated houses were laid out along wagon tracks that were the streets. *Schutztruppe*, colonial European volunteer troops, were seen in their unique colonial uniforms wearing American western-style hats with one side pinned up. Some were riding camels.

In the rapidly expanding town, one of the most startling sights among the piles upon piles of building supplies being offloaded from two freighters were the Herero and Namaqua tribesmen, natives to this region, wearing modified German army enlisted men's uniforms, assisting in the work. The newcomers figured out that these men were *askari*, locals recruited into the colonial German army and police units and used to police the colony. One *askari* was adjusting an Imperial German flag that had an ox head superimposed in the center, its big, curved, golden horns indicating it was the German Southwest African Colonial flag.

"There's hardly a living thing growing around here except down by the river," Katherina observed as she strolled along the wooden sidewalk with her friends. "Why would the emperor want such a forsaken place?"

"Well, there's better land fifty or sixty miles inland, and Kaiser Wilhelm wants to establish colonial territories like the other Europeans," Levi offered. "So here we are in German Africa!"

They all trooped into a dry goods store, and in one corner of the jam-packed mercantile was an astonishing assortment of native artifacts. Levi, immediately drawn to the carved wooden masks in stylized forms of human and animal faces, asked for details. Markus picked up a steel-tipped spear and a stretched-hide shield brightly painted in geometric patterns.

"I wonder if I can get this back aboard. My papa would like seeing this! How much, shopkeeper?"

"For you, our visiting guests, a nice souvenir from darkest Africa, two marks. I'm sure your captain will allow such treasures on his ship." By the time the small entourage closed the double doors to the shop on their way out, Katherina and Tante Berti had each purchased several necklaces of strung ivory, amber, and garnet beads. Markus had his spear and shield, and Levi had loaded up with three masks and a three-foot-tall sculpture of a stylized couple, he with an enormous drooping penis and she with long, drooping breasts. Tante Berti scrupulously avoided looking at Levi's sculpture. Katherina examined the artwork out of the corner of her eye, smiling mischievously. Markus ignored the whole scene, but Günther and Heiner smirked and made unheard comments to one another followed by cackles of delight. Levi also purchased a heavy ivory cuff bracelet, exquisitely carved from one hollow piece of tusk, the most expensive item of the group, but the one that everyone completely ignored. Even Günther and Heiner got enthusiastic and purchased small sculptures and jewelry as family gifts.

Back aboard, a Christmas tree, constructed in time for Christmas Eve, twinkled to everyone's delight. Made primarily from palm fronds and certain stiff weeds found near the river, the tree had handmade ornaments from a group of missionary volunteers, and small candles that burned brightly. It met everyone's expectations.

Midnight mass was an enchanting service with all the ship's lights blazing, the band and ship's chorus performing one after another of the most beloved Christmas carols, and everyone joining in singing "Silent Night." Even Levi, Katherina, and Tante Berti enjoyed watching all the Christian rituals, some of which didn't seem that much different from their Jewish services at temple.

Off to the side, and a little drunk, Heiner whispered in Günther's ear in a slightly slurred speech, "I wonder what the Jews think of all this?" as he nodded toward Levi and the others.

"I imagine they're enjoying this as much as everybody else," Günther replied, not giving Heiner's comment much thought.

Christmas week passed in a blur of songfests, holiday cakes and cookies, and lounging around aboard ship before the big New Year's Eve party and dance at Governor House. Many ship's passengers took strolls in the desert just outside of town, and Levi even managed to persuade Tante Berti to allow her niece to go on one. Levi instructed Markus to distract Günther and Heiner one evening so he and Katherina could wander the sands alone. The sky was ablaze with stars that night. Though Jewish, the desert scene reminded them both of the Christian stories and pictures they had heard about and seen, of the first Christmas in Bethlehem.

"Your Catholic friends would especially appreciate all this, don't you think?" she said, not expecting a reply. It was an otherworldly experience as they meandered through the small hills and dunes, he holding her hand, she accepting. They talked about their families and their separate plans for the future and their adventures so far on the trip.

"Levi, you know what I'd like to do this minute?" she exclaimed in her sweet, almost childlike exuberance.

"No, I have no idea. What is it you'd like to do? What is it? Tell me this instant," he said in a gentle, compelling voice.

"I'd like to walk in the sand in my bare feet!" She hesitated a moment. "Do you want to?"

"Let's! Here, sit down on my coat."

"All right, but you must turn around. I have to take off my stockings," she said, laughing. "And don't you tell Tante, or she will never let me out again!" And again, she laughed.

While Katherina slipped out of her shoes and stockings, Levi hopped around on one foot as he, too, slipped out of his boots.

"Ooo, it's cold! Colder than I thought it would be," Katherina declared as she held Levi's arm for support. In her other hand, she held her shoes and stockings, which swayed and dangled as they strolled haphazardly in the sand. He watched her and her stockings and was overcome by the most wonderful feelings for her. It was all he could do not to sweep her up in his arms and kiss her. He finally had to look away, as his passion was rising in his loins to the point of possible embarrassment.

"Katherina, may I call you Kathi...? I heard your younger brother call you that back at the restaurant in Montevideo."

"Of course you can, silly. We're best of friends, aren't we?"

"*Ja*, I guess we are, that is, I hope we are," he said as they both stopped for a moment.

"You guess, you hope? How sweet," she said, turning toward him, and in the most unexpected gesture, she came close and kissed him gently on the cheek. His arm rose to embrace her, but she had already stepped back, turned, and said, "Let's run to the top of that dune, shall we?"

From atop the low dune, the two could see their ship at dock with all its lights twinkling in the moonlight and the little village with a few people on the streets.

"Isn't it just so beautiful! Isn't everything just so wonderful," she breathed as she turned to take in the sweep of the desert landscape.

"Yes, it is." And as she completed her sweep, Levi stepped in close and gently but firmly pulled her to him. He held her only a moment before relaxing his grasp and lowered his lips to hers. It was a soft, warm kiss that was almost perfectly still. They both stood there, lips touching, for only a moment, hardly breathing. She couldn't see the small tear in the corner of his eye, but she could begin to feel his chest rise and fall as their two bodies pressed gently against each other. She was startled for an instant at his grip but surrendered to the warmth that laced through her body. Her head was swimming with the beauty of his soft lips and his masculine smell as her tightly corseted breasts pressed against his chest. She could feel her body react to her rising passion.

"Oh, Levi," she whispered when they both pulled back, only inches separating their faces.

He responded, "Yes, I wanted to do that...and then when you kissed me back there, I..."

She put her fingers to his lips. "This is such a magical moment, such a wonderful moment."

His hands slid around to her back and she turned her head and laid it on his chest.

"Yes, it is," he said.

CHAPTER XXIII

A Whole New Century

FULL DRESS UNIFORMS were required with all medals and ribbons. As the invited guests to the New Year's Eve dance streamed into the long, two-story wooden building that was Governor House, an array of elegant and colorful military men paraded by. There were Prussians, Bavarians, Saxons, and others, and of course, naval officers, some in rich blue with gold braiding and others in tropical dress whites.

The less numerous ladies, in their most elegant and colorful full-length gowns, swept through the double doors, all eyes eager to enjoy the beauty of it all. Even Tante Berti wore a striking deep purple-black dress that was much admired. But when Katherina followed her aunt into the garland-hung hall, all eyes turned to see the stunning young lady in the emerald green crepe silk dress. Her tiny, silhouetted waist and white shoulders, gently brushed by long black hair, would have rivaled any beauty at the Imperial court in Berlin. Or so Levi thought. Markus was mightily impressed with Katherina's good looks, too.

"Levi, I hope you're going to let me have at least one dance with her this evening. After all, we are friends, and it is New Year's Eve."

"Are you talking to me, fellow? I don't even know you!" Levi responded. But it was Heiner who surprised everyone by asking her first. "Well, I'll be a son of a boot scraper!" Levi blurted out as Heiner led Katherina hand on hand through a Strauss waltz.

"Looks like you've got some real competition there," Günther goaded Levi warmheartedly. "Don't worry, I'll keep him drunk for you, at least most of the time, so he makes a horse's ass of himself, ha."

All evening there was no shortage of admirers for the lovely Jewish girl. Markus did manage to get his dance, and Levi maneuvered three dances. He and Markus also danced with Tante Berti, to her delight. Midnight and the New Year were soon upon the merrymakers, and while the time was counted down by one of the ship's officers, Levi was at Katherina's side. The New Year's cheers reverberated through the hall, and they hugged. Levi kissed Katherina's cheek ever so slightly, both knowing many eyes were on them. The crowd burst into song, singing the national anthem and God save the kaiser and the Fatherland.

"It's nineteen hundred and one, and we have a whole new century stretching out before us! Isn't it exciting?" Katherina exclaimed as she refused a dance offer for only the second time that evening. "Imagine what wonderful adventures there will be for us all. Tante Berti and I want to tour London and Paris and Rome, and…well, other places too, between my studies, of course… There will be so much to see in Germany, too."

January first and second were spent recuperating from the New Year's Eve celebration. It had ended with the last of the partygoers climbing the gangplank onto the ship at three in the morning. Everyone managed to stow their souvenirs before the *Princess Eugenia* sailed as scheduled on the third. Sixty-degree cool winds blew in gusts as the German warship sailed north toward its next coaling station in what had been British Cameroon. It was now another of the Kaiser's Crown Lands, this one, in central West Africa. The eighteen-hundred-mile voyage, due north along the African coast, consumed five January days, helped along by the north-flowing Benguela Current. The captain again announced day excursions ashore during the two-day visit.

Three days later, back aboard and in their cabin the evening before weighing anchor, Levi commented to Markus, "Did you hear those German settlers talking in the *bierstube*? The colonial army is suppressing a revolt by the natives who are claiming inhuman, slave-like treatment on the German plantations hereabouts. It sure doesn't sound right." He looked at his friend as they sat on their bunks.

"It's one thing to have colonies…all us Europeans have them, but to maltreat the natives to such an extent…it's just a violation of our standards. As you would say, it's just not Christian."

"*Ja*, well, maybe we don't know the whole story. Maybe it's just talk, you know, beer hall exaggerations."

"Do you remember me commenting to you when we were in Swakopmund?" Levi continued. "Those rumors we heard about a massacre of Hereros after a revolt down there? I find it all very disturbing. We Germans are an honorable, cultured people. Bismarck was a great and honorable advisor to the Kaiser. He wouldn't condone such treatment nor would the Kaiser."

Markus, a bit defensive, replied, "I'm sure these are isolated instances, and…"

He was cut off by Levi. "Katherina and I were talking earlier. She told me one of the reasons her family fled—…that was her term, 'fled'—to Uruguay was because of the pogroms against the Jews condoned by the tsar." His voice was forceful and sharp. "And when you think about it, the Boxers were revolting because of the way they were being mistreated by us Europeans." He thought a moment. "Yes, they were brutal and murderous, but the Chinese did have grievances, real, legitimate grievances, don't you think?" He was staring at the floor. They both sat quietly for a few minutes.

Markus spoke: "Sun Yat Sen was saying the same thing a couple of months ago about his people, except he wanted to direct the fight against the monarchy, not the Christians and Europeans."

Silence again, and then Levi concluded, "Well, it's disturbing when we step back and think about it…but we aren't going to figure it all out and the world's problems tonight, so let's turn in."

GERMAN TOGO

CHAPTER XXIV

The Trip Home Continues

AFTER SAILING FIVE hundred miles due west for a day and a half, the *Princess Eugenia* dropped anchor off the coast of German Togoland, another small Crown colony the kaiser had newly acquired from the British. There were no land excursions this time, as the stay was only a few hours, just long enough to drop off and take on mail and a few passengers.

The longest stretch of the trip home, some thirty-seven hundred miles to Lisbon, Portugal, was uneventful, with both the passengers and crew happy to sail into the bustling harbor after ten days at sea.

"Europe at last!" exclaimed Katherina with tears in her eyes, clinging to the railing. Turning to Tante Berti, she said, "Mama and Papa should see this."

"They will, child, they will," Berti said gently.

"We Obermaiers are finally going home to the fatherland after two generations. Isn't it grand, Tante? Isn't it just grand?"

"Yes, yes it is, Katherina, but we're not in Germany yet... We must sail all the way around France and up the English Channel past

Belgium and the Netherlands."

"Yes, I know, but this is Europe!" The two women gazed out into a harbor clogged with ships, many coming and going to Portugal's colonies around the world.

"How long will the stay be here, have you heard, child?"

"No, but it will…"

Katherina was interrupted by the captain's announcement:

"…five days in port, sailing on the morning of January 30."

"Let's find our male escorts and see the sights, shall we, Tante?"

"Yes, of course. You know, they are fine young men…well, some of them. They do make good escorts for our shore excursions, and such," Berti began. "But remember, you're going to university in Berlin. Your young men friends are all Bavarians, and soldiers at that. And we are Prussians… I don't want you to get too friendly with these traveling companions. Do you understand me, child? We are going to Berlin," she emphasized further. "They are going to Munich."

"Yes, Tante," the young woman said in exasperation, rolling her eyes. "I'll go get them!" she said as she leapt off her chair and scurried away.

In a matter of hours, they had disembarked near the ancient tower that guarded the harbor.

"The Moorish influence is so obvious here in Lisbon," Levi said as his usual traveling group wandered the narrow streets, their necks craning up to look at all the beautiful architecture.

Strolling along, Katherina said to no one in particular, "I wonder if there are any remnants of the huge Jewish population that once lived here…I mean before the great expulsion. All the Jews and Moslems that didn't agree to convert to Catholicism had to flee, you know."

Tante Berti spoke up as the group moved along looking for a café for lunch. "I've read about the Sephardic Jews being driven out of both Spain and Portugal in the 1200s. But I understand there is a beautiful Sephardic synagogue somewhere in Lisbon. Apparently, it was built by returning Jews several hundred years later when they were permitted to come back…and by Jews who stayed and continued to practice their faith in secret. Maybe we can find it while here."

"Yes, of course we will, Tante Berti," Levi offered.

Heiner asked in his usual way, "Why would anybody want to come back here if they were driven out in the first place? Why didn't they just stay wherever they went?"

Günther immediately interjected, "Heiner, quit with the questions!"

"No, no, it's all right, Günther," Katherina said. "It's a legitimate question. The same reason we Obermaiers always dreamed of returning to Germany. It's our fatherland, it's our ancestral home. It's like you wanting to go home after your service in China. Am I right, Heiner?"

"*Ja*, but I've only been away from home for about a year. And you, Katherina, you're Russian. I mean no offense, but you weren't even born in Germany, so you're not even German, right? You're just a Russian Jew."

Katherina's eyes widened as she stared at Heiner. The whole group came to a halt. Markus stepped into the conversation.

"What a harsh thing to say, Heiner. Sometimes I wonder about you and your big mouth. Do you even think about what you're saying?" His words were sharp as he stepped between Heiner and the two women. He added in an apologetic tone, "I'm sorry for that, Katherina and Tante Berti. He's an empty keg, that's for sure."

"I'm going back to the ship!" Tante said indignantly. "Katherina, are you coming?"

Günther immediately spoke up. "That won't be necessary, Tante Berti, I'm taking Heiner here in the opposite direction from wherever you're going." He looked sternly at Heiner, who stood quietly to the side, but with a defiant expression on his face. "There's no need to go back to the ship right now. Enjoy lunch in one of these cafes or restaurants." With that, he took Heiner's arm, spun him around, and headed off down a side street. "Beer time, Heiner."

Twenty paces down the street, Heiner spoke up in a low voice. "Well, she's not German, and just going back to Germany doesn't make her German. And besides, Germany doesn't need any more Jews from Russia or South America or some other goddamned place. Every time I say something or ask a question, they get mad. I've had enough of those Obermaiers."

"Oh, shut up with your 'Jew' talk! They're nice people."

"I'm sorry for all that," Levi said after the two soldiers left. "That was boorish of Heiner. As we well know, that kind of talk among some people is all too familiar."

Berti added, "You don't have to tell us that. You have no idea what we endured in Russia." She paused a moment. "Even in Uruguay, but not so much there really," she said thoughtfully.

Katherina, as if not hearing Levi or Berti, said in a forceful, emotional voice, "But we are German! Just because we've been gone for two generations, we speak German and it's our culture, our heritage. We never thought of ourselves as Russian or Uruguayan. We're Jewish Germans, for as far back as anybody remembers." She continued in a more controlled tone, "Everyone in our village in Russia was German…and the same thing in Uruguay. And we have family in Brandenburg and Pomerania."

"We know, we know, don't let Heiner's comments trouble you," counseled Levi. "Now let's go have some exotic Portuguese food, shall we?"

Markus chimed in, "Splendid idea, and look there, across the plaza. Doesn't that look like a charming place for lunch?"

With so many passengers and crew going ashore in the next few days, it was easy to avoid Heiner. Unfortunately, Günther was seen less frequently, too.

"We found the synagogue!" Katherina bubbled to Berti, who had stayed on board one day. "It's beautiful…and we visited the great cathedral, and other churches and the royal residence. Little Portugal has all of Brazil and those African colonies and something in Asia, too."

"*Ja*, they started exploring the world earlier than most other Europeans, so they got there first. Look at England," continued Levi. "They've colonized all of India, and I would be hard pressed to name all their territories around the world."

"So Germany now has colonies, too, and…"

Markus was cut off by Berti.

"Yes, yes, it is amazing how much of the world is ruled by European nations, but I read the paper. You know we have a nice German paper in Uruguay, and I see the turmoil here and there in these colonies. Maybe we should all stay home."

"But a great nation like Germany needs colonies…look at France," continued Markus. "They rule half of Africa, and they're in Indo-China…and then there're the Belgians; they have the Congo. Even Italy has colonies."

"Enough of politics, please," asserted Berti. "Levi, are you going to find a souvenir here in Lisbon? This afternoon is your last chance," she said with a smile.

"Oh, no, I think not. The captain probably won't let me bring another thing on board!" Everyone had a knowing laugh, as the ship was brimming with crates and baggage and boxes. Mostly of the civilians, but also from soldiers like Levi, who took a particular interest in the various cultures visited. All this was in violation of good naval procedure and onboard orderliness, of course. It was only that the good captain turned a blind eye to it all. If the warship had to go into action, a lot of what was blocking the narrow passageways would go overboard.

As the four finished their lunch, Levi, with a broad grin, leaned over toward Berti and whispered loud enough for all to hear.

"Tante Berti, you're my souvenir from this trip."

She beamed and shook her napkin at him playfully, "Oh, go away," she said with a hint of a blush on her cheeks.

The little group of travelers truly enjoyed Lisbon but were glad to see it slip away as their ship sailed north on the last leg of their long trip home. Markus said to Levi as they leaned on the railing, "I'd be happy to come back here sometime. There's a certain nice quality in the people, and we only sampled a few of their wines!"

Days later, the French coast, the English Channel, and finally, the German port of Bremerhaven loomed out of the early morning mist.

World Map

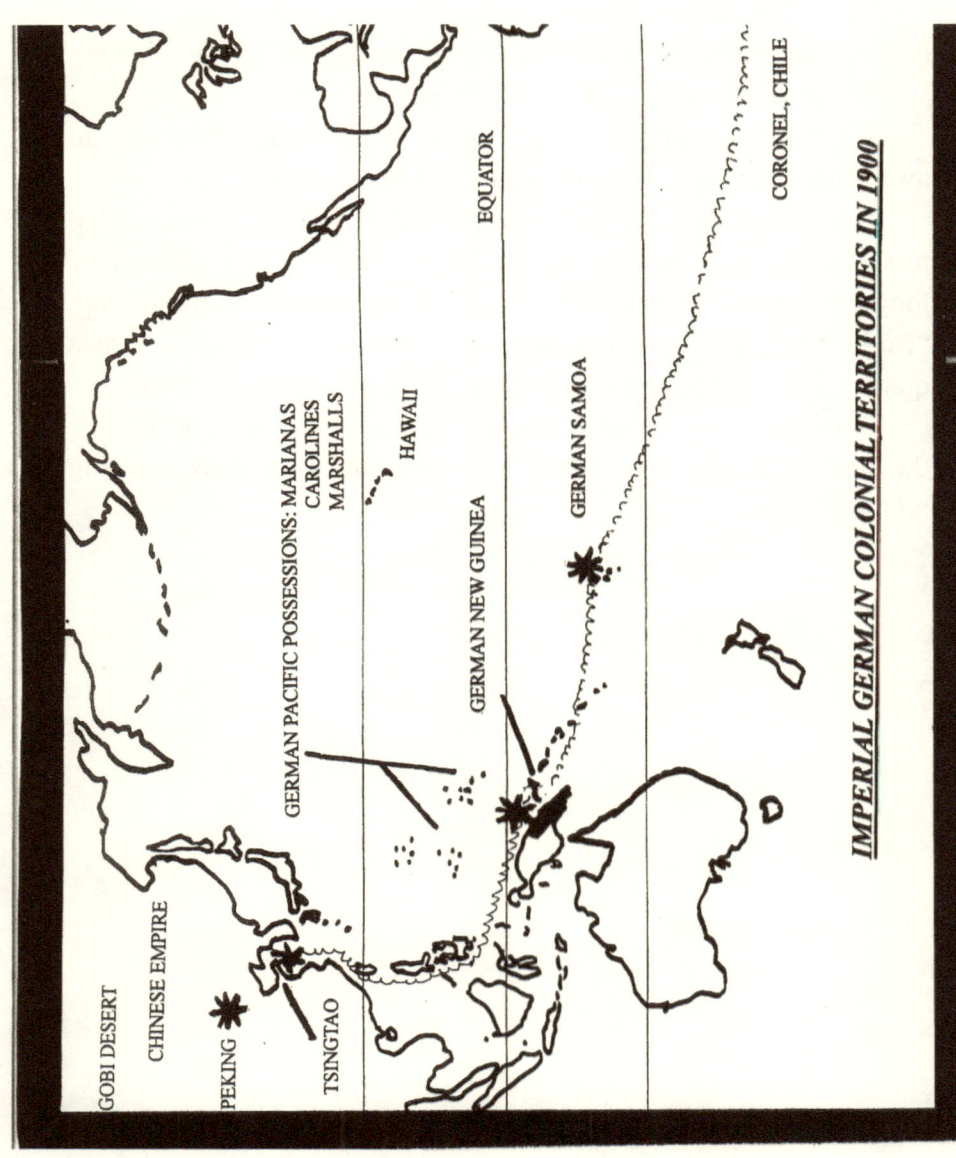

GOBI DESERT

CHINESE EMPIRE

PEKING

TSINGTAO

GERMAN PACIFIC POSSESSIONS: MARIANAS
CAROLINES
MARSHALLS

HAWAII

GERMAN NEW GUINEA

GERMAN SAMOA

EQUATOR

CORONEL, CHILE

IMPERIAL GERMAN COLONIAL TERRITORIES IN 1900

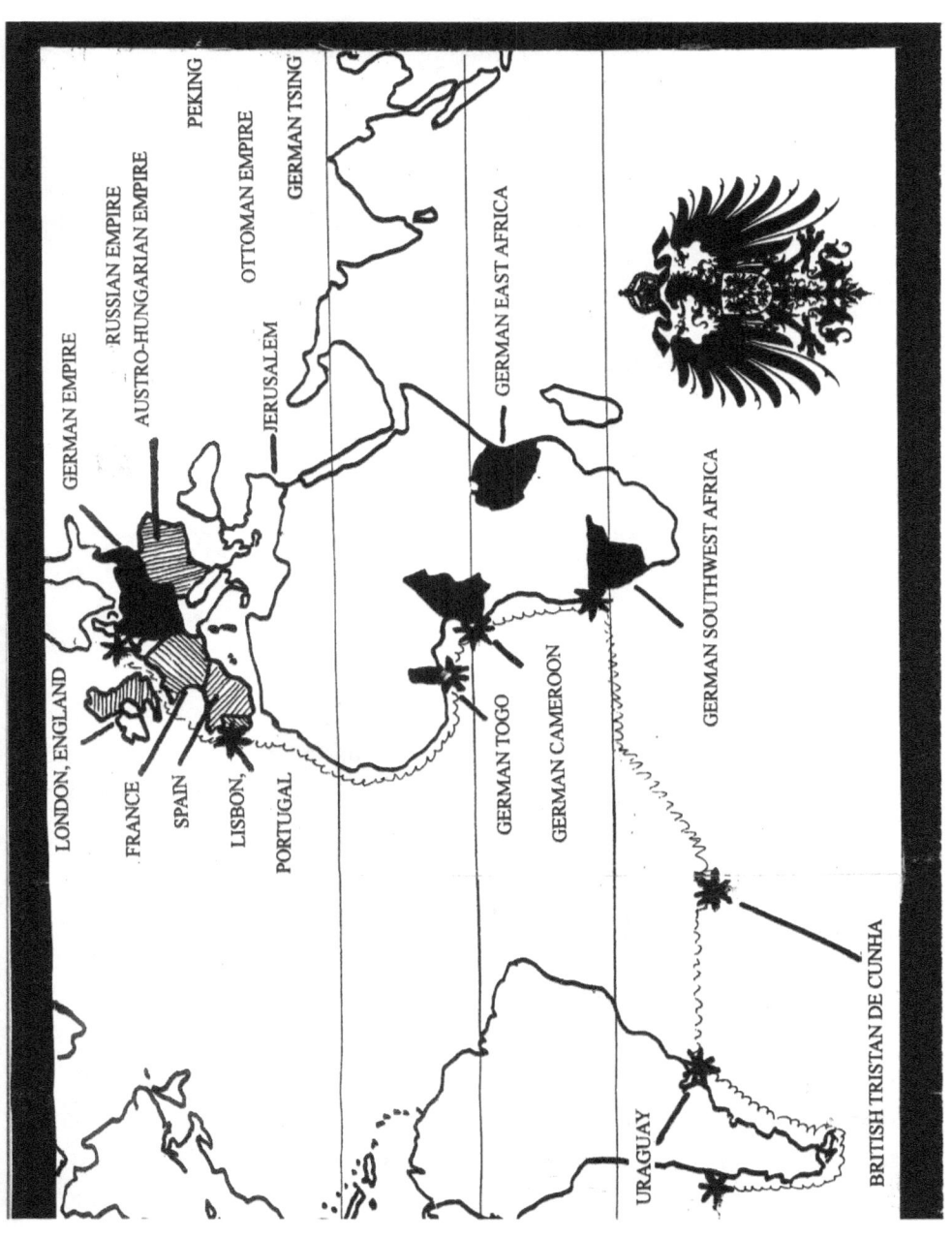

**MARKUS AND LEVI'S MAP OF THE LONG WAY HOME FROM PEKING,
CHINA TO KALVARIANHOF, BAVARIA, GERMANY. AUTUMN 1900.**

IMPERIAL GERMAN CREST

CHAPTER XXV

January 1901

Arriving and Departing

AS THE SMS *Princess Eugenia* slowly made its way toward its berth with the assistance of a harbor tug, a naval band on the dock struck up lively martial tunes. Hundreds of relatives and friends crowded near the gangplank to search eagerly for familiar faces. Most passengers again crowded the railings waving and shouting "hello."

Neither Levi nor Markus expected a greeting from family on the dock, so they spent their time collecting baggage, theirs and the Obermaiers'. Even the cold and stinging winds of January did not cool the warm and happy excitement of the debarkation. Katherina had tears in her eyes, and even Tante Berti sniffled a bit in the emotional excitement of the moment as they pulled their fur-trimmed hoods tighter around their faces.

What to say, what to do, thought Levi. In a few minutes, Katherina will be off to Berlin, and I will be bound for Munich. At least I could see her off at the train station. I could help with their bags, and we could all have lunch together or something.

His plans took a decidedly good turn. As he and Markus followed the Obermaiers down the gangplank, to his surprise and wonderful delight, he heard a familiar feminine shriek as his sister Ilsa and his papa Otto Levi, arms spread wide, swept him up with hugs and kisses.

"We took the train from Munich yesterday morning and just got in," his sister exclaimed excitedly. "Mama got your telegram from Lisbon over a week ago telling us when your ship was due. I just couldn't wait to see my big brother!" she bubbled. "So Papa agreed to bring me all the way here. Oh, Levi, it's so good to see you again!" She clung to his arm. Levi greeted his father warmly with a strong handshake and hug, finally resuming his erect military posture.

"Ah, Levi, look at you in your uniform, and what is this! An Iron Cross? What in heaven did you do to deserve this honor, my boy? But all that later...let's get your baggage."

Levi reached out and touched his father's arm. Katherina, Berti, and Markus stood just back from this reunion, but now moved forward as Levi said, "Papa, Ilsa, here is Markus."

"Yes, yes, of course. Greetings to you, Lancer Mathias, splendid to see you again. I saw your mother a month or so ago. Took good care of Levi, did you?" As he spoke, he glanced at the two strangers watching.

Markus greeted Levi's father and warmly shook hands with Ilsa. "This is the first time we've met in years, Miss Levi, but your brother has told me a lot about you." The two young people enjoyed each other's greetings.

Levi broke in. "Father, Ilsa, I want you to meet some very special friends of mine...ours." He nodded to Markus. Katherina looked expectantly to Levi and they exchanged smiles. Ilsa's eyes darted between the two. Levi continued. "We met in Montevideo, Uruguay, and we all have become dear friends," he said gallantly as he continued to look at Katherina. His sister noticed his stare.

"Father, this is Madam Berti Obermaier, Tante to Katherina." They greeted each other formally. "And Father, this is Miss Katherina Helena Obermaier, who will be attending the Jewish Academy in Berlin."

Levi's father's eyes twinkled as he took in the lovely young woman in front of him. "So, you're going to stand for your entrance examinations. Good luck to you, Miss Obermaier." Turning to his son, Otto Levi said, "I've made reservations for lunch for us at the Bahnhof Europa Restaurant. Possibly your new friends would like to join us. I'm sure it can be arranged."

"That would be splendid, Papa." Turning to Berti, Levi asked, "Would you like to join us for lunch? We can leave all the baggage here in care of the ship's steward."

Berti glanced at Katherina and turned to Levi's father. "That is a kind invitation. We are most appreciative of your offer."

With that, Markus spoke briefly with the ship's steward, turned, and joined the others as they headed through the crowd, Levi with a young woman on each arm. The two women glanced and smiled at each other while Markus caught up and took Katherina's other arm. They all followed Herr Levi and Tante Berti, laughing and joking.

As they strolled along, Ilsa noticed the small gold locket with an engraving of the star of David pinned to the high collar of Katherina's white blouse. Katherina caught Ilsa's eye and said enthusiastically, "Your brother and Markus are very brave...did you see their medals, Ilsa?"

Levi cut in. "*Ja*, but Markus here, he was awarded two medals. A real hero. Wait until you hear his stories."

"Oh, do tell, Markus." Levi's seventeen-year-old sister giggled. "I've always wanted to hear a real hero's stories, especially from one in such a handsome uniform."

The six doffed their winter coats and were soon ensconced in cozy seats in the most elegant salon in the Europa. The walls of mirrored glass with ornate gold gilding, the sparkling chandeliers and waiters in waistcoats, exuded a level of luxury not experienced by these travelers for many months. The long dresses of the women in the restaurant spread a rainbow of color in the crowded room with Tante Berti's deep blue, Katherina's cream, and Ilsa's light pink.

The happy gathering lasted well into the afternoon, continuing with a spread of north German pastries and coffee, while both families conversed and shared their own unique histories. It became apparent to Otto Levi and Ilsa that a special bond had developed between Miss Obermaier and Levi. This homecoming experience would be remembered fondly by all in years to come, but for different reasons.

"So, what are your accommodations this evening?" inquired Herr Levi.

Katherina spoke up just as Berti was about to answer. "My father made arrangements here in the city for us this evening. We'll take a hack from the boat, and then leave tomorrow by train for Berlin."

"Yes," Tante Berti added, "and it's getting on into the afternoon. It's best we take our leave and return to the ship for our things. Thank you so much for the lovely luncheon and conversation, and give our best regards to Frau Levi. It has been most entertaining." She hesitated a moment as she got up. "Herr Levi, Lancer Levi, and of course, Ilsa, I wish you all a pleasant journey back to Munich." She also smiled at Markus as her eyes went from one to the other.

"Yes, it is getting on, isn't it," the senior Levi noted, pulling the gold chain out of his vest pocket and squinting at his watch.

"Let's all go back to the ship!" offered Levi. And they were off.

CHAPTER XXVI

Farewells

"OH, LOOK AT all these boxes!" exclaimed Ilsa. "Did you bring me a present from China, dear brother?" She laughed.

"Yes, of course. One for you and one for Mama, one for Papa and one for everybody, but you'll have to wait until we get home. I don't really know which crate yours is in." He grinned, examining one container after another.

The Obermaiers, the Levis, and Markus finally said their good-byes, with Katherina and Levi managing to slip into the freight room on board. Behind a tall pile of luggage, they said their farewells. It ended with a sweet, short kiss as they held hands and promised to write as soon as they got to their separate destinations, and surely, they would see each other again soon.

"Maybe I could come to the train station tomorrow to see you off," Levi said with desire in his voice.

"No, no, you have too much to do and you're all leaving tomorrow, too, and early, as your father said."

Otto Levi interrupted the two with, "Oh, there you are. Come along now, Levi, and Ms. Obermaier, the coach is here, and your things are being taken directly to the train station." Everyone said a last good-bye and waved each other off, and the two horse-drawn vehicles, their animals steaming in the cold air, headed out in different directions.

"So, my boy, she is quite a young lady, your friend Ms. Katherina Obermaier," Levi's father reflected as he settled into the red velvet bench of the couch. "And going to the Berlin Academy...quite impressive. Not many women attend, or even pass the examination to get in, you know. I just read in the *Münchner Abend Post* that just this year a women's group petitioned the Reichstag for admission to our universities. After all, it's a new century, modern thinking and all that, must look ahead." As the old man looked out the coach window he added, "And they've allowed women to attend university in England and America in some schools recently, so it should be allowed here, too. *Ja*, she's a clever girl, that one."

"Am I a clever girl, Papa?"

"Yes, my child," Otto Levi said with the warmest affection toward his daughter. "You're the cleverest of them all." She smiled broadly and hugged her papa's arm.

"Yes," Levi replied to his sister, "you're a clever girl, Ilsa, but Katherina's a woman!"

Ilsa sat up and challenged her brother. "Yes, and I saw how you looked at her, Levi. You like her, don't you? I mean you really like her, in that special way." She looked slyly at Levi with a mischievous grin.

"Now, now, daughter," her father admonished, "Levi can like whomever he chooses. And don't you like that soccer player at your gymnasium...what's his name? His father has the dry goods store across from the canal."

"It's Ewald, but he's just a boy," she said.

Levi looked at the two sitting across from him with renewed love for both. How he had gone away seeking adventure and exotic sights with the Bavarian army, which he certainly found, but after his experiences in China he found how precious life was. How precious his little sister was to him, now almost a woman…and dear Papa, always there, seeming to be all-knowing, ever-watchful, a safe haven to all the family. *And Katherina*, he was surprised by his certitude, *how I love that girl*.

CHAPTER XXVII

Laying Plans

MONTHS PASSED WITH letters exchanged, and photos, too. Both Levi and Markus applied to the University of Munich, receiving their acceptance letters only days apart. Levi began his studies in architecture and history, and Markus in engineering and languages. Both decorated soldiers were welcomed into their regimental club as heroes, drinking and sporting with others of Prince Regent Luitpold's Bavarian troops. Riflery, riding, soccer, gambling, and even outlawed dueling, which following the Polish dueling code of honor, were pastimes of these young rowdy men. But the two China veterans did eventually apply themselves to their studies, receiving commendations.

Katherina, welcomed by her Brandenburg relatives, soon enrolled in the Jewish Academy on the outskirts of Berlin, studying ancient languages, biblical archeology, music, and art. Tante Berti busied herself setting up housekeeping in their small apartment and dutifully writing to the Uruguayan Obermaiers with reports of their daughter's progress and the frequent visits to extended family and distant kin.

The summer break in studies afforded the young people an opportunity to arrange a mutual visit. "We're invited to holiday with the Levis in Munich for a week, and then we'll all travel south to Garmisch, and the Alpine lakes for an additional week," Katherina exclaimed to Berti.

They were soon on their way.

"Isn't it beautiful, Tante," Katherina said as she peered out of their sleeping compartment on the Berlin-Munich Express train. "It's just a picture postcard every time I look out the window…the lovely rolling farmlands, forests, and villages…and all the buildings in the cities! I just love that new style of building… What is it?" She hesitated a moment. "Yes, now I remember, it's called *Jugendstil*. I learned about it in my art class." She continued enthusiastically, "In France it's called Art Nouveau. It has all those swirls and curves, but here in Germany, it's more, sort of geometric."

Berti, also staring out the fast-moving train, commented with a slight air of concern, "Yes, well, but some of these new styles are vulgar and with all those questionable emotions flaunted in public. It's just not proper for young women to be exposed to such things." She looked across at Katherina facing her. "Why, we can't walk down the most fashionable street in Berlin, *Unter der Linden*, without seeing truly shocking posters and even in shop windows, in the best dress shops…" she was getting flustered, "those new styles are displayed everywhere." She straightened her dress and folded her hands in her lap.

Katherina exclaimed defiantly, "Well, I like that new style. Even jewelry and dresses are designed that way, that *Jugendstil*…and remember the new post office? Wasn't it just grand!" She looked across to her aunt, whose eyes were closed. Her soft, sonorous breathing revealed she was asleep.

"I like everything modern," Katherina declared to herself, aloud.

KALVARIANHOF

CHAPTER XXVIII

Kalvarianhof

"On the idle hills of summer,
Sleepy with the flow of (dreams)"
—A.E. Houseman

THE TWO-HORSE OPEN carriage from the village train depot creaked under the load of the five people: Katherina, Tante Berti, Ilsa, Levi, and Markus. "Of course, I invited Markus to join us for our excursion to the mountains. He got in this morning by train from his mother's Munich apartment," Levi explained.

Warm greetings and conversation continued as the northern visitors settled into their seats on the overloaded carriage. A pair of matching chestnut horses snorted as the narrow steel wheels cut into the dirt road that began at the edge of the forest just outside the village.

The Levi estate, called Kalvarianhof, was acquired by Levi's grandfather in the 1840s. The old gentleman, a veteran from the wars of German Unification and the Franco/Prussian war of 1870, had gained his true wealth late in life from investing early in the construction of the Munich to Augsburg railroad.

The estate itself, deep in the woods, consisted of a farm of many acres with tillable land beyond the forest, two barns, a smokehouse, several other outbuildings, and a tenant's cabin clustered around an enormous manor house. The three-story edifice, built many years before the Levis acquired it, was constructed in the traditional Bavarian style with ornately carved wooden balconies and stag heads mounted high on the outside walls. The exterior walls of the ground floor were painted white stucco with many little windows, each with green shutters and a flowerbox overflowing with red and pink geraniums. The upper structure was half timbered, also with flowerboxes and a profusion of blooms. This day, bed linens were seen hanging out several upper windows for airing.

Kalvarianhof got its name from the fifteenth-century abbey that once occupied the site. Only parts of several exterior walls remained, as they were incorporated into the later construction. However, deep in the cellar, virtually the entire house sat on a foundation of massive medieval arches from the original building.

Markus once asked Levi why his father kept the Catholic name, Kalvarianhof, since they were Jewish. Levi explained that his grandfather had insisted on retaining the name, both in the interests of history, and because the Levi family employed varying numbers of Catholic villagers to maintain the estate and to work the farm.

"It's what they know. It shows them that we Jews can respect their local Christian history, and besides," he added, "what's in a name? It's what's in your heart that matters. Am I right?" So the name remained, even though it referred to the hill on which Christ was crucified, Calvary, a crime the Jews had been blamed for through many centuries.

As the carriage rounded a bend in the dirt road and entered the clearing surrounding the house, Katherina gasped and her eyes widened. She rose a bit, taking in the view of the imposing estate.

Berti's eyes sparkled and a broad smile shone across her face. "Levi! You never told me your family had such a beautiful home. It's so big…and in such a wonderful setting."

It was all Katherina could do to stay in the carriage before it stopped in front of a massive wooden door under a portico on the side of the whitewashed manor. The afternoon sun made the red geraniums glow in the flowerboxes beneath each window.

"I love the smell of the forest here," she said excitedly as the group descended to the ground. Levi jumped down to stay the horses.

"I told you on the boat that Levi's house was grand, remember!" Markus teased, swinging the baggage down from the back of the carriage.

Otto Levi and his wife, Freidl, heard the carriage on the gravel road and were at the door to greet their guests. The housemaid-cook, Hilda, and a young farmhand simply called Willi stepped out from behind the Levis to help with the baggage. This was the first meeting for Frau Levi of the Obermaiers, and she was eager to meet these Uruguayan-Prussians she had heard so much about.

"Welcome, welcome to our home, Frau Obermaier… And this must be, of course, Fräulein Katherina. It is so nice to meet you at last. Do come in." The chatter of greetings continued as the guests followed through the front entry hall, hung with antlers, a boar's head, and swords on the wall reaching to the high ceiling. They continued to the front parlor, whose floor was covered with several oriental carpets under overstuffed chairs and couches. An enormous

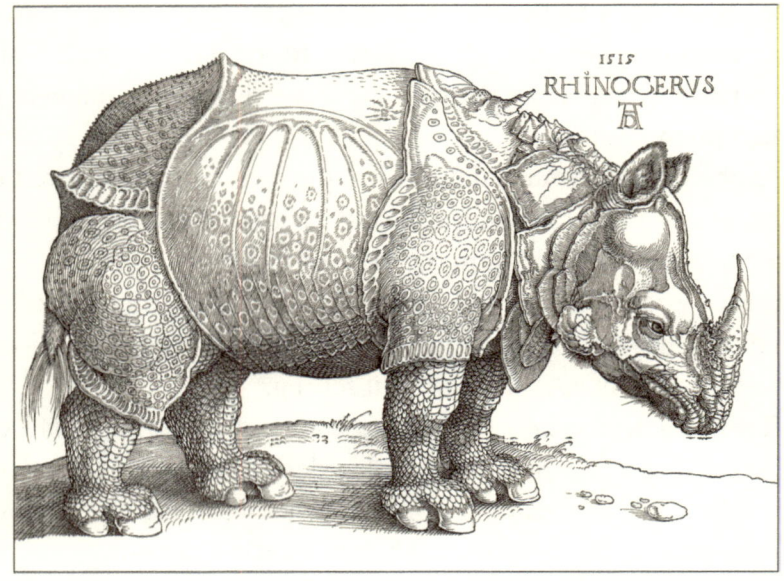

**LEVI'S CHERISHED ETCHING OF ALBRECHT DURER'S
RHINOCEROS OF 1515.**

bookcase ran the length of one wall. Opposite it, a collection of framed etchings, including several Rembrandts and an Albrecht Dürer engraving of a rhinoceros, hung on one side of a massive fireplace. On the other side were two baroque paintings in gold gilt frames: Luca Giorgione's *John the Baptist, Baptizing Jesus*, and a lifelike *Moses Descending Mount Sinai with Stone Tablets*. Everyone entering this stately home was struck by the beauty and opulence of what was, in essence, a prosperous family farm.

"What a lovely home you have, Frau Levi," Tante Berti commented as she settled into a silk upholstered chair. Coffee and small cakes were served on Meissen china, and the whole atmosphere was one of sumptuousness and elegance.

"Yes, we are very happy here. My husband's father was very fortunate to be able to acquire Kalvarianhof back in the 1840s." She turned her head toward her husband and smiled. "After our refreshments, you may wish to rest up a bit. Levi will show you to your rooms upstairs. Dinner will be served at seven."

Tante Berti was glad to stretch out on the bed in her private room, as Katherina, too excited to nap, eagerly followed Ilsa, Levi, and Markus on a stroll around the grounds. A small creek ran between the main house and the barns with a fish box in it.

"We like to keep several fish in there," Levi pointed to the submerged four-foot-long box, "so fish are very fresh for dinner. There's a pond over there," he pointed toward the woods, "where we raise them for our farmhands, too." He grinned. The four of them were four abreast, arm in arm as they walked the dirt road leading to the farm fields beyond the woods.

"See that big tree with all the branches all the way down to the ground? I used to climb that tree often for a view of the whole clearing and all the farm buildings...I could spy on everyone from up there." They all smiled.

"You climbed all the way to the top?" Katherina challenged.

"Yes, and I can prove it. I carved my initials way up near the top. I'll show you some time, if you're brave enough!"

They laughed merrily and Katherina said, "Oh you! You think I can't climb up there? Have you forgotten I have two younger brothers back in Uruguay?"

The forest was carpeted with dense grass and mature trees. There were signs of logging.

"We graze our cows in this part of the woods. That's why we thinned the trees hereabouts." The little group stopped beside a crude ladder nailed to a tree, with a small sitting platform twenty feet up.

"Papa and I would wait for deer from up there...then *bang*! Venison for dinner."

Ilsa spoke up. "Speaking of dinner, I think it's time to head back."

A sumptuous dinner awaited in the long dining room. The table sat sixteen but the seven diners were grouped at one end, with Otto and Freidl seated at the end. A white and blue linen tablecloth ran the full length of the table. A lovely summer bouquet of white, pink, and yellow roses with blue alpine thistle overflowed the cut-crystal bowl. Lit candles in crystal holders made the silver flatware sparkle in the evening light. Recently, Otto had the gas chandeliers wired for electricity, and the weak bulbs gave off a yellow glow above the table.

After Otto again greeted his guests and gave a short prayer, knives and forks and ladles rattled on platters and plates. Pickled tongue in jellied brine, slices of wurst floating in sweetened vinegar, cold potato salad, cucumber salad, tomato and onion salad, three types of bread with a large bowl of butter that sat apart on the buffet, and a tray of smoked fish completed the typical summer Bavarian meal. Liebfraumilch, Mosel wine, beer, and carbonated lemonade were also served. Everyone had a hearty appetite and between enjoying smoked carp and other taste treats, a lively conversation progressed well into the evening.

"Shall we continue to the middle parlor for coffee?" Frau Levi suggested.

"*Ja*," Frau Obermaier exclaimed. "After such a wonderful meal, it's good to get up and stretch our legs." The middle parlor had recent additions to its already beautifully decorated space. Some of Levi's Chinese antiques now adorned prominent places in the high-ceilinged room. A Ming painting entitled *Moon Viewing Pagoda in the Eastern Mountains* hung near two large carved ivory tusks of a seventeenth-century Ming emperor and empress. The ivories shared a small table with a rare Shang bronze ceremonial wine vessel near a golden Imperial household porcelain bowl with a green dragon design inside.

"Oh, Levi, these must be some of your treasures from China," Katherina marveled. "It's all so exotic...I'd love to visit the orient someday…after my studies, of course."

"I'm sure you'll get a chance," Levi offered.

Markus interjected, "And Levi and I could be your guides!"

With coffee served and a delicious, freshly baked Linzer torte consumed to the last crumb, everyone headed upstairs to end a most enjoyable day.

All the subsequent days at Kalvarianhof were equally pleasant. The following week the holiday travelers found the mountains as breathtakingly beautiful as any summer in memory—sunny days, clear skies, and dozens of sailboats on Bodensee or, as the Swiss call it, Lake Konstanz. Levi and Katherina had several opportunities to be alone at Kalvarianhof, and their feelings for each other rekindled with handholding, hugs, and secret kisses. With the two families now traveling together, however, it was harder for the two to be alone.

A mountain climbing hike near the Zugspitze finally allowed the four young people a chance to wander the upper alpine valleys in twos. Markus knew what Levi wanted, and made sure that at every opportunity, he escorted Ilsa off to some interesting sight or other. Of course, Ilsa knew exactly what was going on, but said nothing to her brother. However, Markus was peppered with questions about where they met and what went on aboard ship and what happened in all those ports of call on the way home.

Finally, Markus had had enough. "Enough with the questions!" he said good-naturedly. "I've told you everything three times over. Why don't you just ask your brother?" They were both quiet for a moment. "What do you think?" he asked.

"I think he's going to marry her. Don't you? Look at those two. Look." She pointed downhill. "Down below us, just to the right of that alpine hay shed." She leaned into Markus. "See. They're holding hands!"

"Well, that doesn't mean anything. We were holding hands as

we climbed over the rocky outcroppings."

"That's different," she explained. "You were being a gentleman, and…"

Ilsa was interrupted midsentence by a forceful spin around as Markus took her hand, pulled her to him, and kissed her. Her eyes were wide open in surprise. He let her go and she stepped back and looked at him intensely.

"You're the only man who ever kissed me like that," she blurted out.

He smiled at her, squinting in the bright sunlight. "Yes, and I'm glad to hear that. I won't want any other man to have kissed you… except your father, of course!" He laughed and looked away, but glanced at her to appraise her reaction.

"Well, it's not your decision who I allow to…who I choose to kiss…and you behave yourself. You're supposed to be a gentleman and treat ladies…well, you know what I mean."

"Yes, of course. I'll try to behave myself," he said in mock seriousness with a sideways grin on his face. "Shall we go catch up to Katherina and Levi?" As the two started down in the direction of their friends, Markus was sure he saw a controlled smile on Ilsa's face.

"Markus, my friend, I see how you and my sister are…" Levi hesitated. "…interacting." The two young men, back from the mountain hike, were in their shared room of the alpine guesthouse where the two families were staying. Levi shoved a ten-inch split log into the ceramic stove and latched the iron door. "I don't want either of you to get hurt…I mean, well, you see…I mean, you know Ilsa is Jewish, and you're Catholic. That's just an impossible situation. You know that, right? I mean, the two families would…"

Markus interrupted. "Aren't you putting the cart before the horse?" He looked at Levi, who picked up another piece of kindling. "You're not going to light that, are you? It's rather warm in here. It *is* July," he continued good-naturedly. "You have a beautiful sister. She's lots of fun. We have a lot of laughs together, most of them about you, as a matter of fact." He chuckled as he slipped out of his shirt.

"I just don't want to see Ilsa get hurt…that's all." Levi looked at his friend plaintively.

"Nobody's going to get hurt. We're just enjoying our holiday."

"Well, it looks like more than that…I saw you holding hands. Did you kiss her? Huh?" He was looking intently at Markus. "Well…?"

"Oh, for pity's sake! Can't I have a girl on my arm like you?"

"It's not the same thing. Katherina and I, we…" He stopped for a moment. "We have something very special, and…" He collected his thoughts. "And we can do something about it. We can be together. But you and my sister, you know that can never work. It's just not done. I'm telling you, leave her alone. All right?" It was more a plea than a command. "I mean, we can all just be friends together, have a good time, but…"

"*Ja, ja*, Levi," Markus said. "Friends it will be, just good friends."

CHAPTER XXIX

The Turning of the Tide

MEMORIES OF HER two-week holiday with the Levis in Bavaria were fresh in Katherina's mind as she settled into the hard wooden bench in her archeology lecture class. It was hot in Berlin this early September day, and it was easy for her to slip into daydreams of their time together, especially in the lovely alpine mountains. She imagined his face so close to hers, heard his deep voice, felt his strong arms and his smell...it was intoxicating.

"The tell at Beer Sheba has revealed significant new data on the transitional period between the kingdom of..." Her professor's voice droned on while she sat there in a haze of warm memory. Her young body reacted pleasantly to the visions floating through her mind.

Most times, Katherina would be enthralled with Herr Dr. Professor Bernhard's lectures on her most beloved subject. But this day she let herself be lulled in the pleasant daydream of her recent experiences.

"Fräulein Obermaier...Fräulein Obermaier, would you please comment on the assigned reading, beginning on page sixty-two, the results of the 1893 dig?"

She snapped back to reality on hearing her name. Because she was always fully prepared, she stumbled only briefly before recovering to give a satisfactory answer.

She was happy this day's lectures were over so she could retreat to her favorite fashionable milk bar with its lavish colorful porcelain-tiled walls and counters. It was the perfect spot for a proper young woman and her friends to meet before catching the horse tram to the station and home.

Life in the imperial city of Berlin was dazzling. The center of art and culture, the seat of the Empire, the crossroads of Europe, Imperial Germany had reached a height of power and prestige not seen in northern Europe for centuries. It rivaled Napoleon's Paris and King Edward's London. Vienna was its closest cultural rival but had been surpassed by Germany's industrial might and held back by the calcified conservatism of the Hapsburgs.

Even the Jews had made remarkable progress in spite of ongoing discrimination. The government had just announced that Jews "would be allowed to become judges but only in proportion to their numbers." This all seemed so abstract and far away to Katherina as she adjusted to her new life so far from Uruguay.

Tante Berti, on the other hand, deeply impressed by the position Jews had gained in Germany, compared Berlin to Imperial Russia, with its periodic pogroms and Cossacks.

Cossacks! thought Berti. *Those sword-swinging, barbaric anti-Semites.* She was glad they were through with them. Her brother and the family would be so happy to return to Germany. She must encourage them to hurry along with the selling of the house and land. It was so expensive in Berlin, but she was sure brother Fritz would find something nice. She looked out the window at nothing in particular. Karl always took such good care of them all.

Levi's letters were short but frequent. Katherina's most often included a pressed flower or an interesting description of a recent archeological find. In his last letter, Levi simply stated that he had to see Katherina and that he was coming during the Catholic All Saints Observance, a kingdom-wide Bavarian holiday at the end of October. It was a quick trip, just two and a half days in Berlin.

Berti was surprised and not particularly happy with the sudden appearance of Levi, and had ominous feelings about his visit. Her fears were fulfilled when her niece, having spent the afternoon in the English Garden with him, burst through the door of their apartment with Levi in hand. She was radiant and bubbling with enthusiasm as she swept into the small front parlor, her long fur-trimmed coat flaring as she came.

"Oh, Tante Berti, I've just received a wonderful present! Look, look what Levi just gave me." She stretched out her hand in front of her, with the ring thrust forward. "It's a ring, a beautiful amethyst ring! See…isn't it lovely?" She looked back at Levi, who was watching with some trepidation as he noted Berti's lack of enthusiasm.

The old woman made a studied examination of the gold ring with two little diamonds on either side of the bigger stone.

"Very pretty, Katherina, but it isn't your birthday or Hanukah. I'm concerned. It isn't proper for a young man, even such a nice young man as Levi," she nodded her head in his direction, "to present such a valuable gift…and a ring at that, with its symbolic meaning and…" She hesitated, feeling she had said too much, gone down the wrong road in protesting the gift. "I mean…that people could… would assume that it was possibly… You don't want to give the wrong impression." She hesitated again, looking at the two. Her features grew stern as she stared at the young couple.

"It's not an engagement ring, is it?" she blurted out, her eyes widening.

"Well, no…not exactly," Katherina offered, seeing her aunt's reaction. "It's a friendship ring!" she announced with a broad smile.

"But we have been talking about…things," she said, avoiding Berti's intense stare.

"Things? What things?" Berti insisted.

"Oh, Tante Berti, I don't have time right now, I'll tell you later. Levi has to catch the express train for Munich, and I promised to see him off. I'll be back in forty-five minutes, an hour at the most!" With that, she spun around and practically pushed Levi out the door. Berti said nothing, knowing Katherina's willfulness. She simply sat in silence, slapped her knee, and shook her head.

CHAPTER XXX

Uruguay

HERR OBERMAIER TRUDGED up the cow path to the barn, followed by José Theresa and his wife, Amelia, the new owners of the small farm the Obermaier family had recently put up for sale. Herr Obermaier had mixed feelings as he took one last look around at his family's safe sanctuary here in Uruguay. Karl Obermaier wrestled with the challenges facing him.

Uruguay was a long way from Russia, and now it meant another great migration for them. It was the family dream to return to Germany, to their traditional homeland, their ancestors. Now, with the wedding of his dearest child, Katherina, in the spring, he'd have to prepare for that long transatlantic journey. But selling the farm?

It had been a shock to receive the long letters, first from Tante Berti, warning of a growing relationship with Lancer Levi, and closely followed by Katherina's letters professing a true and enduring love. Katherina ignored their protests. Their objections were overcome by passion. Their subtle threats alluding to "funds for schooling" had had no effect. She had made up her mind as firmly as any highly intelligent twenty-year-old could have.

After much correspondence with the Levi family in Munich, and after learning of the quality and prosperity of the Levi household, begrudgingly acknowledged by Tante Berti, the Obermaier parents gave their approval on the condition that they would be present at the sacred ceremony.

Spring came early in 1903, with the snows melting away by early March.

"I am determined to finish my first year of studies at the academy before the wedding," Katherina told everyone. With the Uruguayan Obermaiers' arrival in late April, to the joy of Brandenburg and Pomeranian relatives, finishing touches were made for a small but beautiful ceremony.

The two families agreed the wedding would take place in Potsdam, outside of Berlin, as a convenience to the newly arrived immigrants settling in that town. The entire Levi family as well as Markus journeyed to the imperial city for several days of visiting and viewing the sights in Berlin.

"All this is happening so fast. It's very exciting," Ilsa exclaimed to Markus and her parents as the open carriage glided at a trot in front of the Kaiser Wilhelm Cathedral.

"And what a lovely day for touring. Imagine, my brother, Levi, getting married…and to such a lovely girl…woman. I can't wait to have a sister!"

"You all are growing up so fast." Ilsa's mother sighed. "But Katherina is from a good, respectable family, although I don't know how they will adjust to life here in modern Germany after coming from that little country."

"Now, now, Friedl, I'm sure Herr Obermaier and his family will adjust quickly. They're professional people, with resources, and their new rabbi will certainly assist in every way he can. Did you have a chance to invite them all for a visit this summer?"

"After the wedding, Papa, after the wedding."

The Ashkenazi (European Jews) had evolved their own variations and customs for weddings, and the Levi/Obermaier wedding conformed to that tradition. Two attendants holding candles led the procession to escort the bride and groom to the white canopy open on four sides. The bride's family lit unity candles and recited the seven blessings. Katherina, radiant in her modest but striking gown, caused smiles and sniffles to many attending. Several of Levi's closest friends journeyed to Potsdam and, of course, Markus, Anji, and his mother attended.

KATHERINA IN HER WEDDING DRESS, KALVARIANHOF 1903.

"It's a most beautiful, happy ceremony," Anji said. "Dance with me, brother."

"And may I dance with the bride, just like I did at the New Year's Eve party in Southwest Africa? Do you remember?" Markus teased Levi.

Katherina, bursting with joy, said, "Of course I remember, dear Markus, and we shall dance and laugh tonight just like on the ship and in Africa. They're wonderful memories, and so much has happened since then; it seems so long ago." As they whirled around the dance floor, she continued. "Have you heard? We are going to be practically neighbors."

"What do you mean?"

"So you haven't heard. I'm going to continue my studies at the University of Munich! They just authorized the admission of women!"

"That's wonderful, Kathi. It'll be like old times, the three of us."

Late the next morning, family and friends saw the newlyweds off at the Potsdam train station for the overnight express to Paris, and the beginning of their new life together.

אֲנִי לְדוֹדִי
וְדוֹדִי לִי

"I AM MY BELOVED'S AND MY BELOVED IS MINE."
SONG OF SOLOMON 6:3

CHAPTER XXXI

Honey and Salt

THE TWO LOVERS, when not swimming in each other's arms, took long strolls that ended with them easing into café chairs at some charming locale. The only disturbing intrusion into the lovers' lives in the gay city of Paris was the persistent clamor and virulent exchanges in all the Paris papers concerning the Dreyfus Affair.

"What do you think, Levi darling?" Katherina asked as they lounged over coffee in a green-canopied café. "Do you think Dreyfus was really a spy for Germany, as the French Military court said?" Her nose was buried in the afternoon edition of *Le Gaulois*. "I just can't imagine..." she hesitated, "but that secret letter they found from, who was that from? Some German official? And then it was published in the papers... It seems he really might be guilty."

"*Ja*, well," Levi slurped his cup of coffee, "his name is Count Munster, our ambassador here in Paris." Turning a page in *Le Journal*, he continued. "Between the anti-Semitism here in France, at least in these papers and in the army..." He stopped for several

moments and began again. "You probably know the French are beside themselves with anger and frustration over losing the Franco-
Prussian War, and that was twenty-two years ago!" He shook his
head. "They want revenge. It's all about their honor, and the honor
they afford their precious army." An air of contempt was in his voice.

"It's like the army is the symbol of the nation, and the army says
Dreyfus is guilty. To question Dreyfus's guilt is to attack the honor
of the army, and that's like attacking the integrity of the nation. It's a
real mess, and those two trials were a sham." He rustled his paper. "I
don't know if Dreyfus was a spy or not, or whether the French president will ever force the military to agree to a rehearing." He looked
intently at an article as he continued. "You know they found him
guilty again, but commuted his sentence to time served. Five years
on Devil's Island, that hellhole way off in French Guiana, South
America. I'm surprised he survived. At least he's back home now in
some little town outside of Paris."

His eyes brightened up. "Look here, there's a concert tonight at
the opera, and guess what's being performed?" He looked up to see
Katherina beaming.

"*Till Eulenspiegel's Merry Pranks!* I just read it, too. It's one
of my favorites. Strauss is such a marvelous composer and what a
conductor! He just stands there like a soldier at attention and moves
his baton ever so slightly, but he gets such a performance out of his
musicians." She gesticulated, to mimic Strauss. "Oh, do let's go,
shall we?" A pause, "And I read that the foyer of the opera house is
grander than most of the rooms in Versailles!"

"Of course, of course, we'll go if we can get tickets. Let's go
back to the hotel and see if some are still available." He winked at
her and looked at his pocket watch.

"Back to the hotel?" She smiled, and took his arm.

The week in Paris slipped through the newlyweds' lives like
sand through an hourglass. The warmth of spring and the gaiety of

the romantic city created the belief of all young lovers that their happy world would always stretch to the distant horizon. It bound them together in a shared tranquility.

"We have to be at the dock in Calais to catch our steamer for Dover by noon, my love." Levi spoke languidly across the candlelit table as he finished the last of the wine of their last dinner in Paris. "We really should get some rest before we storm the shores of the British Empire!"

They both laughed a warm, lazy laugh as they looked at each other in the elegant hotel dining room.

"To bed, to rest, if you insist, my darling," Katherina said in mock seriousness. "I am so looking forward to visiting London, and now with their new king…after all these years." She hesitated. "How long did 'the Empress of India' rule England? Do you recall?" She looked expectantly at her husband.

"I believe it was sixty-one or sixty-two years…imagine." He folded his napkin and prepared to get up. "There are few Englishmen alive today who can actually remember Queen Victoria's coronation."

"Well, my darling, I will always remember 'my' coronation," she whispered over her shoulder with a smile as Levi pulled her chair out from the table.

The train to Calais, the steamer to Dover, the train to London, and the carriage through Hyde Park, all passed under scattered white clouds, the shadows splaying patches of darkness on the spring green of the farm fields and parkland. London, the capital of the greatest empire since the Romans, exhibited its glories in monuments everywhere.

After a refreshing stop at their hotel, the two were off on a sightseeing tour—Trafalgar Square and Nelson Monument, the Wellington Arch, Prince Albert Memorial, and…

"Where shall we go next?" Kathi asked and then answered as she snuggled close to Levi in the open carriage. "Westminster Abbey

Cathedral…I want to see the tombs of all those famous poets and scientists, and it's said to be one of the most beautiful cathedrals in England…and the Houses of Parliament and the Tower of London, we can't skip those!" she bubbled.

"Wow! That's a lot to see…shouldn't we take a more leisurely pace, maybe go back to the hotel and draw up some plans, and a schedule, and a route on our map, and do some research in the guidebook? You know, plot our approach to experiencing all this history and art?"

"Ha!" Katherina laughed. "You are a clever one, sir, trying to lure me back to your cave, you naughty boy." She paused for effect. "But on the other hand, we may need a rest in the middle of the afternoon."

He smiled and looked into her eyes. "I was hoping you'd say that." He gazed at her and thought how wonderfully beautiful she was. And so it went for the rest of their honeymoon in England.

Back in Munich, both plunged into their studies and devoured each other in the luxury of youthful passion. Months went by in their world of laughter, beauty, study, and sensuous delight.

One cold, overcast evening in February 1904, they were sitting across from each other at the dining table in the alcove off the Kalvarianhof kitchen, their books spread out before them. Katherina reached out across the papers and texts and took Levi's hand. He put down his pen and looked up in anticipation.

"Yes, my love, what is it?"

Her face flushed, her eyes were brimming with tears, yet a smile was on her face. "I think I'm going to have a baby."

He stared at her for a second, and then the edges of his mouth turned up, forming a smile that broadened into a full grin, showing his white teeth.

"How wonderful…are you sure? Oh, this is just wonderful!" He reached across the crowded table with both hands outstretched and took her hands. They smiled lovingly at each other for a long minute, not saying anything, just looking into each other's eyes. Only the sound of the hot, crackling, thin dry pine logs emanating from the porcelain stove were heard. Finally, they rose and came together in a shared embrace as he whispered, "Wonderful!"

Little Rachel was born prematurely in November 1904 in an upper bedroom of the great house. The joy of this first born was celebrated in Potsdam and at Kalvarianhof with telegrams and crackly telephone conversations back and forth, and most especially by the young couple. Herr Doctor Rungi delivered the child and visited every day. When his visits increased to three times a day, an ominous mood settled over the house. Sadly, little Rachel's life slipped away, cut short by death's grip on the tiny premature baby. Gloom descended upon the family in spite of consoling words and assurances from the older women of many more opportunities for a child to such a young wife.

After long weeks of loving care by Levi and the entire family, Katherina was practically her young self again.

"I want to resume my studies in the spring," she said enthusiastically. Levi was so happy, seeing his beloved wife curious, smiling, and full of energy again. Markus visited often and regaled all with exaggerated stories of their adventures and happy times the three of them had together. Katherina enjoyed those visits and appreciated Markus' loyalty and friendship.

By the fall of 1905 the young couple, with Markus and his friends, were back to their studies, enjoying the gay university life in Munich and debating world events, philosophy, and the latest fashions. Ilsa, now newly enrolled at the university, joined in.

Levi and Markus, and their China veterans, noted disturbing news out of Asia.

"Look here, darling," Levi pointed out as he and Katherina perused the afternoon papers at a student-packed café on Isar Strasse.

"Imperial Japan and the Czar of Russia have finally signed a treaty to end that Russo-Japanese War. The American president, Roosevelt, got the two to sign the treaty. But this is the outrageous part." His voice rose in alarm. "The Japanese got Port Arthur! That's just across the bay from our colony at Tsingtao. And they got Korea as a colony, too!" He paused and Markus added, "And to think both of them were allies with us just five years ago in Peking!"

The newspaper shook with Levi's excitement. "Didn't I mention several years ago that those two countries were headed for a clash?"

"No, darling, you didn't mention that to me…it was probably one of your army buddies to whom you predicted the future." Katherina looked over to Markus and gave him an impish wink. She smiled at her husband as he looked up.

"Yes, right, probably," he said.

"Do you have any other predictions for the future, something wonderful or beautiful for the world?"

Levi stopped for a moment and looked at her, smiling. "I predict," he intoned in a funny, pompous voice, "that a certain lady I am acquainted with," he hesitated and looked at Ilsa, then Kathi, "will have a long and happy life, but…" He stopped for dramatic effect. "…she will first pass her examinations that are coming up in a few weeks and for which she must study!"

They all laughed as Katherina sat up in her chair, both hands on her hips.

"I want you to know, sir, that I am fully prepared now to do my examinations perfectly…" she also hesitated, "…with just a little more studying." Again, they all laughed and went back to their beers, sausages, and newspapers.

CHAPTER XXXII

The Past Is Prologue

HAPPINESS, SO FLEETING, soon escaped young Kathi and Levi again. In the spring of 1906, Katherina miscarried. The same sadness occurred again in late summer. Levi worried as Kathi slipped into a state of melancholia. Her university studies ended. There were no more lively talks of politics, art and music, books and philosophy. Katherina's mother, Frau Britta Obermaier, arrived from Potsdam for an extended stay, to nurse her only daughter.

Listlessness consumed Kathi's every waking hour, followed by long periods of restless sleep. Days passed in which she barely left their bed, and when she did leave their bedroom, she ate a pittance. Thin and weak and in a pitiable state, she was visited frequently by the village doctor, who finally recommended Vin de Mariani. It was one of the most popular imported products from Paris, and one of the leading wines of Europe in 1905. After winning a gold medal for wines in 1905, even Pope Leo the thirteenth endorsed it.

"It's a special wine containing tincture of cocaine. This should bring her spirits up considerably." Herr Dr. Rungi was sitting on the side of the bed as Levi, his mother Friedl, Frau Britta Obermaier, and Ilsa looked on expectantly. The doctor lifted a glass of the wine to Kathi's lips. She accepted it unknowingly as she lay there staring into space. An early autumn shower pebbled the window of her lace-curtained room, and leaves, heavy with rain, swirled in clusters toward the ground. She was oblivious to it all.

"This has a strong taste, but you see she doesn't even notice." The doctor shook his head ever so slightly. "I have reduced the use of Vin de Mariani for my patients as we learn more about the cocaine laced throughout this wine. But..." He hesitated a moment to frame his thoughts. "...it's usually very effective in cases such as Katherina's. However, it is also very addicting in some people, which has some very unpleasant side effects." He pointed to a slip of paper on the nightstand. "I've written down the directions, dosage, and frequency for administering this medicine, and it is a medicine—not dinner wine. Don't overdo it," he admonished.

Dr. Rungi looked up at Levi and then at the three women. In a comforting voice he said, "She should be better in a few days if she continues to take this. She's a strong young woman... You'll have a baby yet, Levi." He got up. "I must be going; I have other patients to visit today. I'll stop back tomorrow afternoon... Remember, don't give her more of this than I indicated." He nodded toward the wine bottle on the nightstand.

"Yes, Doctor, but do stay for dinner tomorrow," Friedl offered.

"We'll see. Good afternoon, Frau Levi, Frau Obermaier." He nodded to Levi and Ilsa.

"Thank you, Doctor, thank you so much," Levi said in a low voice.

"Yes, yes. Thank you, Dr. Rungi," Ilsa added. "I'll show you to your carriage."

Early the next evening, the family gathered, as they usually did, in the kitchen alcove, around the heavy wooden table with benches on either side. The doctor had left hours ago, after a full dinner of fried fish sprinkled with chives, boiled potatoes smothered in butter, salt, and pepper, and a stein of beer. The doctor's reassuring words were the focus of muted discussion.

Otto Levi, having his stein of beer, while Levi, his mother, Frau Obermaier, and Ilsa were sipping coffee, began nodding off. A half-eaten Linzer torte, cut into pieces, sat on a white porcelain plate in the center of the table.

Quiet small talk permeated the little room until Katherina appeared in her nightgown, her face gaunt beneath tangled hair. She stepped unsteadily from the shadows into the light. Ilsa, the closest to her, sprang to her feet as Levi scooted along the bench to get up. Everyone spoke at once, greeting Kathi and asking how she felt. They took her by her thin arms, on both sides, to steady her and guide her to a space on the nearest bench.

After she sat down and the chatter died down, everyone was astonished into silence as Katherina unsteadily reached the distance from her chair to the purple plum pastry in front of her.

"It's my favorite, you know," she said in a whisper, sinking her teeth into the fruity cake.

The next few days under the household's constant care, and with the careful administering of the prescribed amount of the medicinal wine, everyone saw a remarkable recovery in Levi's Katherina. Her spirits up, and her appetite much improved, she was eager to resume her studies, if first from home.

The atmosphere at Kalvarianhof bubbled with optimism. Frau Obermaier even felt secure enough in her daughter's recovery that she felt the pull of her two sons' needs and returned home to Potsdam. Over the next several weeks, Kathi continued to sip her several glasses of wine per day that Dr. Rungi had prescribed.

Levi's wife, back from dismal depths, soon plunged into every manner of her old pursuits. At first, there were short walks in the woods, but soon, as her strength and body weight improved, she dragged Ilsa, Markus, and Levi on robust excursions through the woods and across the farm fields of the estate. She pestered Ilsa to prod her archeology professor, Dr. Adelmann, to give her assignments and readings in the books her sister-in-law brought home from the university library.

Katherina engaged Levi and his parents in long conversations of all the topics she had loved to discuss before her recent illness. She spent hours writing long letters to her mother and father and her two brothers. Levi was surprised and delighted when Kathi took the initiative, prompting lovemaking in the stillness of their nights, together again in the same bed. "I'm so happy to be in your arms again, to feel your need for me," she said.

Her renewed energy seemed remarkable and brought relief and a warm happiness to everyone on the farm. It also allowed everyone to return to their own interests and responsibilities.

And yet, Levi sensed a change in his lovely wife. During the early weeks of her recovery, he was so relieved and happy for her that he embraced her every renewed interest. He smiled at her rapid talk on ever-changing subjects. The intensity of her undertakings made him laugh. It was as if she was trying to make up for the time she'd lost to her illness. He thought she had an overabundance of enthusiasm for life. But more than once, he'd shaken his head and asked her to slow down, as she was wearing everyone out.

And now, a creeping uneasiness was overcoming his early delight at her recovery. She didn't have to do everything and go everywhere at once…and her speech, that racing from topic to topic. She never used to do that.

But most disturbing of all was sex. Kathi had gone from a warm, enthusiastic, and passionate lover to a ferociously hungry being who wanted much more sex than they'd even had in the first glorious weeks of their honeymoon. It had become almost a violent act of uninhibited animal desire. Long after Levi was sated, she continued to engage in a frenzied quest for some unobtainable level of satisfaction, ending only when she was completely exhausted and dripping in sweat. She would collapse on his chest, from the position she most desired, exhausted at the conclusion of yet another session.

He tried to talk to her about her behavior, but she laughed it off or scolded him in her playful way. "I'm simply enjoying being fit and back to normal, darling."

Levi wanted to believe her. He suspected that the Vin de Mariani was responsible for her over-energized condition. He suggested they reduce the two or three glasses of wine a day to half that, and she agreed with no hesitation. Still, her disturbingly high energy level and nervous behavior continued.

Levi finally decided to have a private consultation with Dr. Rungi. He arranged an appointment with the doctor at his home office in the village.

"Good day, Herr Dr. Rungi." Levi reverted to his stiff military stance and crisp but shallow bow. "It's good of you to see me on such short notice."

"Not at all, young man, it's always good to see the young, healthy husband of one of my favorite patients. How is your lovely wife, Katherina? She must be fully recovered by now." He quickly perceived Levi's uneasy demeanor and added, "Or is it something other that is your concern?"

Levi was ushered into what had been the front parlor of Dr. Rungi's home, but was now the doctor's office. It was a lovely but modest Bavarian-style house, complete with wooden balconies and tiled roof, and on the white stucco exterior wall, a large brightly painted fresco of the *Mother and Child*, she standing on a slice of quarter moon and on her head the crown of heaven. The maid, in her white apron and lace bonnet, having escorted Levi in, stood expectantly inside the office door.

"Will that be all, Doctor?" she asked.

"Marta, would you kindly bring in an afternoon tray?" It was said as a question but meant as a command. Rungi turned to Levi. "Coffee or tea?" The doctor looked over the rim of his glasses.

"Tea is fine, thank you," Levi said distractedly.

Dr. Rungi nodded to Marta, and she left, closing the door quietly. "Now then, come, let's sit at the little table by the window; our tea can be served there."

The two men settled into the needlepoint-adorned chairs. There was a moment of awkward silence as the two looked at each other. The doctor shifted sideways in his chair as if to get more comfortable, but really to avert his gaze and break the tension.

"I have known you for, is it twenty-four years already?" He hesitated. "Yes, yes," a smile broadened across his face as he continued, "and I remember when your sister was born, a lovely child." Finally, he looked straight at Levi, but with gentle eyes. "Now then, I sense there is something troubling you, so how can I help?"

The doctor leaned back in his chair as Marta rapped on the door and backed in carrying a silver tray with a Meissen teapot and cups in the Baroque style. Small nut cookies were piled in a side dish. Both men watched silently as Marta poured the tea, set the teapot down, and then left the room.

"It's Katherina," Levi began. "She's so active...too active...and her nerves. She seems so nervous, so jumpy. I mean, she seems happy enough. Really very happy, I suppose, but something is wrong. Something is really wrong. She's not as she was before. I mean, you see, she's a very healthy woman...with all the energy and...but it's not the same. And when we are together, I mean at night, well..."

"Yes, go on," Rungi encouraged.

"She gets wild. Well, no, not wild exactly, but...she's just too... too passionate. When it's over, she's wet with sweat and completely exhausted. It's not like before. I think it's the medicine, the wine. She agreed to cut back to..."

"She's still taking the Vin de Mariani?" the doctor interrupted.

"Yes, but she promised to drink only two glasses a day and…"

"I recommended a stop of the medicinal wine several weeks ago. She should not be taking a drop of that now. I told Katherina," he paused, "and your mother was present at the time as I recall. When she finished that last bottle of wine in her room, that was supposed to be the last of it. She certainly did not need any further treatment since she was over her period of melancholia."

"But she has several bottles in our bedroom right now," Levi said in exasperation. "How…where did…"

With certain impatience, the doctor interrupted: "She must have gone to the village herself and purchased more."

He looked at Levi and in a sense was sizing him up for his next statement. "I'm afraid we have a serious problem on our hands. Your wife is probably addicted to the cocaine in the wine. How much, we don't know…yet."

Levi looked up. "Addicted, to wine, but…"

Again the doctor cut in. "Vin de Mariana is not just any wine, Levi. As I mentioned earlier, it has a significant concentration of tincture of cocaine in it. It can be addictive."

"So what should we do to get her over this, this addiction?" Levi asked. "I mean, can't she just stop drinking the wine?" He was staring out beyond the walls of the doctor's office, his hands fidgeting. "We can take it away from her, not let her have any 'til she's not addicted anymore. Wouldn't that work? I mean, just don't let her have any of it. Not a drop!" He turned to the doctor. "And isn't there some other medicine to help her? Well, Doctor…?"

Dr. Rungi got up and crossed over to his massive wooden desk. It was cluttered with papers, framed photographs of his family, and an extensive collection of small antique sculptures lined up in an arc in front of him.

"She may be able to withdraw from the wine, with our collective assistance, and still remain at home. I can give her medications that will relieve some of the withdrawal symptoms." Again he paused and looked across at Levi, sitting in the chair by the window.

"But I have to warn you, most addicts…that is," he corrected himself, "most patients with your wife's condition require institutionalization. A stay at an asylum with expert care and close supervision is usually required."

"Good God, I don't want to send her away. We must try to help her at home with Mama and Papa and Ilsa. Don't you think, Doctor?"

"Yes, yes, of course. I just wanted to share past experiences I've had with people in her condition. Of course, we will try treating her in her own loving environment, and it certainly would help her get through the withdrawal period." He spoke with genuine sincerity, but knew the chances of success were not good.

That evening, out of earshot of his wife, Levi talked with Ilsa and his parents about what the doctor had advised. With a real sense of foreboding, he broached the subject of the wine with Kathi, in as gentle a way as he could. They were in their spacious upstairs bedroom preparing to turn in. The rest of the expansive house was completely quiet.

"My love, it's simply not healthy to continue using…drinking that medicinal wine Dr. Rungi prescribed for you. He feels you should not be taking any more, and he thought you had already stopped."

"You talked to Dr. Rungi?" Katherina had slipped out of her floor-length linen dress and was standing in the middle of the room in a cotton slip, clutching the dress in front of her. The large mirrored door of an armoire stood open. She looked up from her preoccupation with undressing.

"Yes, I thought…"

"You talked with the doctor, without me? Without telling me?" she questioned in a surprised voice.

"Yes, darling. I'm concerned about you…your health, and your recovery after our sad experience, so I made a visit to Rungi."

"Darling, I'm perfectly fine. You don't have to worry about me. I'm completely recovered," she declared emphatically.

"Yes, of course you are, darling… I was just concerned about that wine. It's addicting, and the doctor said…"

"I'm not addicted! It just perks me up, and I enjoy it, that's all." She smiled at him, turned, and hung her dress in the polished wooden armoire. She walked over to their new dresser, which matched the Art Nouveau-styled armoire, bent over, and pulled open a drawer.

Levi followed her with his eyes and even under these circumstances, he was conscious of her beautiful body. Pulling a nightgown out of the drawer, Kathi strolled across the bedroom to a row of brass hooks on the back of the door. She slipped a housecoat off the hook, slipped into it, and left the room. Levi sat on the edge of the bed, his suspenders off his shoulders, and pulled off his shoes. He could hear his wife walking back down the hall to their room. She stepped in, closed the door, and hung her housecoat back on the hook. She placed her undergarments on a daybed in front of the window and strolled over to the washbasin stand with its floral patterned pitcher and bowl. Levi had slipped out of his things, propped himself up in bed with the goose down comforter covering him to the waist.

"You look handsome sitting there in bed. Are you waiting for someone?" She laughed as she gazed in the mirror at his reflection.

"Yes, I'm waiting for this Tyrolean beauty I've heard is rooming in this house. Do you know where she is?"

Kathi turned around and looked at him. "She's right here," she whispered, and pulled at the string at the top of her nightgown.

Levi felt the intoxication of her sensuousness and, in spite of his wanting to continue the conversation about the wine drinking, he felt himself yearning for her.

"You...you are so..."

"Shhhhh," she whispered from across the room.

She walked to the nightstand and turned off the lamp. Moonlight flooded through the windows and caught her nightgown slipping from her shoulders and fluttering to the floor. She stood there a moment in silence, knowing her husband was looking at her, drinking in every voluptuous curve of her young body. She slowly knelt on the bed and bent toward him. His hands raised and slid up her sides and ever so gently touched her breasts. She shivered slightly as he touched her hard nipples, and he knew she was consumed with the same desire as he. Levi slid down flat on his back and kicked the comforter down to the floor as Kathi slowly lowered her chest to his and moved back and forth, rubbing her breasts against his. She did the same thing with her lips, caressing his until he pulled her in closer, rolled her onto her back, and made love.

CHAPTER XXXIII

Into the Maelstrom

THE MORNING SUN streamed into their upstairs bedroom as Levi and Katherina stirred in the jumble of sheets, pillows, and comforter on the bed. Awake first, Katherina roused herself to a sitting position on the edge of the bed, her bare back turned toward her husband. Levi gazed at his wife while propping his head in his hand. "Good morning, my love," his gentle voice almost inaudible.

"Oh, you're awake," Kathi offered as she turned slightly, just enough for Levi to see the side of her breast. He stretched across and ran his hand down the spine of her back.

"No, no, no…" She laughed softly. "I've got lots to do today." She padded across to the hook, slipped on her housecoat, and left the room. A few moments later, returning, she walked to the washbasin, bent sideways, and looked to the side of the stand.

"I had a bottle of the Vin de Mariana here," she said. "Actually two bottles. The housekeeper must have moved them. I'll have to talk to her at once." Kathi turned and was about to leave again when Levi rose and met her halfway to the door. He gently touched her arm.

"Kathi, darling, she didn't take them."

Kathi turned toward Levi with a serious look of expectation on her face. "What?"

"I took them, darling…you must stop drinking the wine. Dr. Rungi gave me these pills for…"

"So, it's Dr. Rungi again?" she said with exasperation. "And you, you took them? Where are they?" She glanced around the room furtively. "You don't understand, darling. It calms my nerves." She pulled away from his touch. "I need…" She hesitated. "I want to continue using the wine, for just a little longer until my nerves…" Her voice had changed in seconds from a gay, happy wife, aloof and nonchalant, to a nervous, not quite desperate tone. She closed the distance between them and looked up into his face.

"Levi, darling." Her voice was half a plea. "Don't do this to me. Where did you put them?"

"Hell" is a good way to describe the next seven days for Katherina and Levi. Guilt, denial, embarrassment, betrayal, shame, helplessness, hopelessness, anger, rage, despair, sickness, pain, depression…and finally the asylum—it all happened in one week.

The private Jewish hospital for acute care, the asylum in Regensburg, was sixty-five miles from Kalvarianhof and run by the newly formed Jewish Mental Health Society of Bavaria. In the hours after Levi confronted Katherina, she began to experience what all addicted individuals experience: anxiety, shivering, shaking, delirium, severe cramps, loathing of all and everyone, pleading, begging, crying. Her body shook as if with fever.

Within a few days, deep, dark rings had formed under her eyes that appeared to age her a dozen years. Her hair was matted and disheveled. Her speech, the few times she spoke, was frightening to hear. Several times, she lay in her hospital bed soaked in her own urine. Her terrible suffering could be heard in her voice. She was a pitiable lost soul and it tore at Levi's heart to see her in such a deplorable condition.

Markus, his sister Anji, and Ilsa also visited and offered comfort to Levi as he watched over Katherina. She hardly sensed their presence that first week away from home. The days at the asylum with Levi sitting and waiting, waiting and watching, his eyes red from lack of sleep, were the most miserable he had ever experienced.

Dr. Rungi made the trip out to the asylum every few days at first, a major gift and a great inconvenience for a busy village doctor, but done mostly out of loyal friendship to the elder Levis. Katherina's parents came down from Potsdam, stayed with the Levis for a few days, and then took rooms at the BishopHof Hotel in Regensburg, to be closer to their daughter. After the second week, seeing slow but steady improvement in their daughter, the Obermaiers returned north to their boys.

Levi and his sister also took rooms at the BishopHof Hotel, even though Ilsa had to attend classes in Munich four days a week. She spent her weekends with her brother, often riding the two-hour train trip with Markus, who joined them on weekends. Ilsa insisted on getting Levi out into fresh air, and so the three of them, on occasion, would stroll the town parks, watch the Danube River flow under the ancient medieval stone bridge, and stop by Dampfnudel Bakery, a local favorite for coffee and cake. It went a long way to cheer Levi up and keep a certain perspective on Katherina's continuing recovery. Her intensive care brought Kathi far along, with the expectation that a month's stay in the asylum should complete her treatment.

CHAPTER XXXIV

Verboten

SEVERAL WEEKS OF sharing a train compartment also brought Ilsa and Markus a renewed interest in each other. Their shared stories, first of university classes, and then of future professions and goals in life, created an intimacy they both relished. The casual brushing by each other, the slight touching, soon led to discreet handholding. The weekend before Katherina was released into her husband's care, a rail repair delayed the train back to Munich. In early evening, in an outlying town, the train passengers were told of a two-hour delay, just time enough for dinner in a nearby restaurant.

"To celebrate Katherina's recovery, you and I are going to share a bottle of champagne with dinner." Markus smiled from across the checkered tablecloth.

"Oh, you shouldn't spend your money like that, Markus. Remember, you're a student...like me." She laughed. "This is a cozy little place, isn't it? How much time do we have?"

"Enough for me to enjoy dinner with you." Markus reached across the narrow table and put his hand on hers. She turned her head away but did not pull back. The waiter arrived with two orders of *sauerbraten*, but not before half the champagne was gone. Other passengers on the train were also dining close by and when, a little later, the two saw them leaving, Markus said, "We've got plenty of time, but we should start heading back to the station soon."

Streetlights lit the closed shop windows as they strolled along the quiet street hand in hand. A toy store window display, crowded with porcelain-headed dolls, stuffed animals, toy trains, and all sorts of boxed games, drew them into the recessed doorway.

"I had one of those!" Ilsa exclaimed, pointing to a dirndl-dressed cloth doll. "In fact, I still have it somewhere."

They both peered in closely, their heads almost touching the glass. Markus could smell Ilsa's perfume and in an almost unconscious motion, he turned her head toward his and kissed her. It was a soft, gentle kiss and when it was over, they both turned and resumed their walk in silence.

"When we get to the station I must call Mama; she'll be worried with me getting in so late."

They rode the almost empty train back home, mostly in silence, sitting opposite one another.

On occasion they looked at each other and smiled, and once or twice Markus moved his foot across to hers and rubbed her ankle with his shoe. She feigned offense, pulling back her ankle and ruffling her long skirt, but then returning her foot to the same spot.

With one station to go, Markus slipped across and sat next to her. He leaned his knee toward hers, it touched, and their heads came together in a long, willing kiss. They stopped a moment, looked at each other, and came together again with true passion. They were both breathing deeply when she spoke.

"My brother will be angry."

"Yes, I know."

She turned her face to his, her hand went up behind his neck, and their romantic moment continued until they heard from down the passageway the conductor announcing: "Three minutes to next station, three minutes."

The two intimate friends broke off and looked into each other's eyes, still breathing heavily. They gazed at each other, thinking and feeling the same thing. Finally, in a hoarse voice, Markus said, "We'd better get our things together; we'll be getting off soon."

The couple stepped off the hissing train onto an almost empty wooden platform at the village station.

"I'll walk you home."

"No, no, you've got to get home, too…and it's only a half mile through the woods. I can walk it blindfolded." She smiled at him and waited expectantly. He looked down the platform toward the waiting room. The conductor was talking to a baggage handler. "You've got to go, or you'll miss the train," she said.

He took her elbow and quickly pushed her into the shadows of the wall. They came together with a sureness and hunger for each other that caused a total surrender to desire. His hands coursed down and behind her and pulled her to him, lifting her slightly. Her arms were around his neck, her hand in his hair. The train whistle pierced the night air.

"All aboard!" they heard down the platform.

"You must go!" she whispered as she held his head in her hands. She kissed him again as he held her a few inches off the ground.

"Yes," he mumbled.

"Hurry!" she said, and he put her down.

The train jerked into motion with a clang and a chug, dense smoke blasting out of the smokestack, the sweet smell of coal in the night air. Markus turned and ran a dozen yards, grabbed the iron hand grip, and jumped onto the bottom step of the last car. He turned again and looked back, smiling. She was in the shadows, leaning against the station wall, looking his way.

CHAPTER XXXV

Katherina's Dream

"MAMA, DON'T PAMPER Kathi so much. I know you mean well, but she just wants things to be back to normal."

"Yes, well, I'm just so happy to have her back home again. She's such a lovely girl, and she's been through so much," Frau Levi got up from the table in the alcove of the kitchen at Kalvarianhof.

Levi continued, "It's been two months now. She's back at her studies, and I know she's very much enjoying them. In fact, she mentioned that Herr Dr. Adelmann was planning an archaeological expedition to the Middle East this summer, and she wondered if she could somehow go along."

"What? Go where?" His mother stopped slicing bread, turned, and with a startled look on her face, continued. "You're not going to let her go on some dangerous expedition to…to where?"

"It's to Palestine, I think around Jerusalem somewhere…sponsored by the Jewish Palestine Exploration Society…but she was just talking. I can't imagine her actually going…or Professor Adelmann allowing her to participate."

"I should think not! Your wife should be at home. It's enough that you let her be off to the university all the time." Frau Levi reflected for a moment. "I so wish she had had a baby. That would have settled her down and kept her…"

"Mama, I don't let her 'be' anything," Levi said. "Katherina is very strong willed. She does pretty much what she wants."

"Well, it's just not right. Maybe if she was not so…so active, she wouldn't have lost those babies." She saw Levi's reaction to her words. "Oh, I'm sorry!" she caught herself. "I didn't mean that. Not the way it sounded. I just want you two to be happy and have a family, like Papa and I, and live here at home, and, and…" She broke off as tears ran down her face.

"Oh, Mama." Levi stepped over to his mother and put his arms around her. "We are happy, and we are living here with you and Papa and Ilsa. And we will have a baby, I'm sure of it. Dr. Rungi said there is nothing wrong with Kathi. The next time she must just take it easy, and everything should work out fine." Levi kissed his mother on the cheek and wiped away a tear. "Now, don't you worry. Okay?"

A week later, on a beautiful spring day in a stroll out beyond the woods to the farm fields, Levi and his wife walked hand in hand. Levi stopped and picked up a handful of soil.

"I love the smell of the freshly plowed fields. The earth gives off such a rich, pungent odor. It's just waiting for the seeds to be pressed in, and the cabbage heads will be as big as soccer balls in two months."

"You really have the farmer in you, don't you, darling?" She smiled down at him.

"*Ja*, well, Grandpapa bought this beautiful land, and I have been on it, close to it all my life."

He was quiet a moment as he looked out across the flat field, way across to the tree-lined lane that led to the tiny chapel and burying ground.

"I've hunted it, plowed it, harvested it, and simply loved

Kalvarianhof for a long, long time." He looked up at her, smiling. "And I'm glad you're here with me to enjoy it.

He got up and they walked along the edge of the wall of trees that abruptly separated the tilled land from the forest.

"Let's sit awhile. The new grass is so soft," she offered.

They both found comfortable spots, Katherina leaning against a large pine tree and Levi sprawled out on the grass next to her, his hands behind his head. The white puffy clouds against the vibrant blue sky trailed off to the horizon.

"I'm so glad you're enjoying your studies with Professor Adelmann. I hear he's one of the best."

"Yes, he is, and yes I am!" She laughed, looking down on her husband. She paused a moment, thinking this was probably the best time to bring up a subject she felt would not be well-received. She looked away, her hand tracing through her hair. Finally, she turned back to him, moved closer, and laid her head on his arm.

"Darling, I want to tell you…ask you, well…tell you and ask you something."

"Yes, what is it, my love?" His words were lazy as he gazed up through the trees.

"Well, it's something I've always wanted to do." Again, she hesitated, turning her head slightly and looking at his profile. "I want to go on the dig with Dr. Adelmann, if he will have me…as his assistant." Her voice picked up speed. "I've seen the proposal to the Jewish Palestine Exploration Society, and it includes an assistant, and I feel sure, well, almost sure, that I qualify. I've always wanted to do this, and this is my chance!" She hesitated. "Don't you see?"

Levi turned toward her, looked her in the eyes, a slight smile on his face. "I was half expecting you to bring this up soon," he began. "I know you've been dreaming about an archeological expedition for a long time, but it's not like going to Paris. It's a long, strenuous trip just to get there…and there's God-awful weather, hotter than blazes, no conveniences. You'd be miserable most of the time." He stopped to let that sink in.

"And it's part of the Ottoman Empire," he went on, "very loosely controlled by the Turks, I understand. Most of the people are Moslems, not particularly friendly to Jews." He stopped again. "And the Bedouins...I've read how they sweep down the valleys and plunder the Arab villages. It's not a very safe place, even for the native peoples. You could be in danger. You might need guards."

Kathi was listening, formulating a rebuttal to everything Levi was saying.

He continued. "I've read that most of the villages are up in the hills and the mountains because it's safer up there, even though the best land is in the valleys. You know, there's little central authority to keep order." Levi shrugged his shoulders and added, "I think it's just plain dangerous."

Katherina would have none of it. "That's not a problem," she said quickly. "There are whole communities of Jews and other Europeans there, and archeological projects are going on all the time. And as for danger, Dr. Adelmann says that a lot of Arabs around the digs are happy to work with Jews because they get jobs."

The two of them sparred back and forth, with Katherina adding, "Dr. Adelmann was talking with his wife—she's going too, as his personal secretary and recorder of documents. I heard him say that the Turks were pretty cooperative as long as they got a little bribe and could examine what was found."

She became more excited, realizing she was not meeting immediate, outright rejection. "This really is my chance, my opportunity to do what I really always wanted to do! It's just for the summer, about two months...ten weeks, thereabouts."

"Do you really think Herr Dr. Professor Adelmann would agree to take you? And you've just recovered from a..."

"That's in the past. I'm through that...through with that," she said emphatically. "You're not going to hold that against me, are you?"

"No, no, my love, of course not. I just..."

"I'm completely recovered. I'm ready to do this...and it will advance my studies, really, to a professional level."

There was silence between them as they both thought about what had just been said. "Please, darling, say you approve," she said tenderly. "Tell me you'll let me go; you'll support me in this." She looked at him with great intensity. "I need your support. You know your mama will disapprove strongly and my parents, too. And... and I'll need some money," she continued, gazing at him. He gazed back in a noncommittal way. "I know Papa Levi will give me what I need...if I ask."

"Well, before you go asking my father for a trip to Palestine, you'd better find out if you will be included or not in this, this expedition." He was silent for a few moments. "Aren't there better qualified, that is, more advanced students that he would choose? And taking a young woman for two months, and into that harsh environment, it seems..."

She cut him off: "His wife is going. She could be my chaperone, don't you see? And if she can stand the heat, so can I. Really, Levi, I can do this...if Dr. Adelmann will have me."

"All right, all right, my darling, you do know that I object to this whole business," he said in exasperation, turning over. "However, I won't say anything to the family until you're sure you can go. Then we'll see what happens with Mama and Papa." His eyes found hers. "But I still think it's a bad idea, going off to Palestine!" He shook his head but was smiling.

She burst out into a wonderful broad grin and brought her arms up for a big hug. As they rolled around on the ground together, Levi thought to himself, *I can't imagine Dr. Adelmann taking my wife anywhere!*

CHAPTER XXXVI

Herr Doctor Professor Adelmann

OVER THE NEXT several weeks, Katherina became more and more disappointed. She encountered blunt opposition from Dr. Adelmann to her inquires about a possible assistantship on the archeological dig to Palestine.

"You have done fine work in your studies, Frau Levi, particularly the First Temple Period, but there are other considerations that must be taken into account." The bearded professor turned and stepped to a library table in his book-lined office. Talking over his shoulder, he continued.

"A young woman on such an expedition, it's very difficult." He stood, leaning over a pile of maps and other documents. Katherina sat in a straight-backed, leather-covered chair staring at Adelmann's back.

"But I could be of real assistance to you, Professor, and I mentioned that I could pay my own way. I really won't be any trouble, and I could help with the work of Frau Adelmann. Please, Dr. Adelmann, I so want to contribute, to experience and learn and work on a real site."

"Of course you do, Katherina, and you will have an opportunity someday, I'm sure. But this is just not the right time, and besides, there is no room for an additional person in camp. Now you must let me get back to my research. I leave in less than five weeks."

With that, he turned slightly and, with a wave of his hand, shooed his student out of his office. Katherina closed the door behind her, walked a few steps, and leaned against the wood-paneled hallway wall.

There had to be some way she could convince him she was worth it.

CHAPTER XXXVII

The Accident

NO ONE ACTUALLY saw the horse rear up and its hoof come crashing down on the woman who apparently had walked in front of the chestnut mare. They only heard her scream before she fell to the ground unconscious. Several bystanders rushed to her assistance and flagged a policeman making his rounds. He blew his whistle, which brought several more uniformed officers, and the horse-drawn ambulance arrived shortly thereafter. Someone else had caught the horse, harnessed to an empty carriage, as it ambled away.

A cluster of people stared down at the still body. Two uniformed ambulance attendants bent over the woman, examined the gash in the side of her face, and detected a broken collarbone. Two men and two officers lifted her onto the stretcher as she moaned in pain.

"I've seen the lady here at the university, but I don't know her name," someone offered.

"Here's her purse, Officer." The bystander was brushing the dirt off as she handed it over to the policeman, busy writing notes in a black book with a pencil.

"*Ja*, let's take a look for some identification." He pulled out a half-dozen calling cards.

"Frau Ida Adelmann," he read, half to himself but loud enough for a young student nearby to hear him.

"Why that's Professor Dr. Adelmann's wife...it must be!" the student gasped.

The injuries proved serious but not life threatening, and in weeks, Frau Adelmann was up and walking around, but with her right arm and her writing hand strapped to her body.

"You're making remarkable progress in your recovery, my dear," Dr. Adelmann said as he poured her a cup of tea. "The doctor thinks that in two or three months, you will be as good as new. How do you feel?"

"It seems so awkward, reaching for my tea with my left hand. I hardly know how to hold it." She slowly brought the cup to her lips. "How am I ever going to be able to help you this fall?" She hesitated. "Really, husband, I shouldn't go. I'll only be a burden. Certainly, you can find someone to take notes and do a lot of those things I usually do. And you will have Herr Professor Schellenberger, from the History Department, and that other man, what's his name?"

"Haidler, Jorg Haidler."

"Yes, Herr Haidler. Surely they would be of assistance."

Dr. Adelmann gulped his tea and put down the cup.

"First of all, Professor Schellenberger is not going to condescend to collate my notes for me. And besides, I wouldn't want him examining my unedited speculations. He would laugh at my wrong conclusions, and steal my right ones! And as for Haidler, he's a digger. He knows how to handle artifacts, but he's the last person I'd ask to transcribe my notes. Have you heard him speak? It's with a Polish accent. He's still got one foot in the dirt of a plowed field. He doesn't understand or know how to spell half the terms I use. No, he's a good man for what he does, but..." He stopped for a moment. "But I need you. Surely in two more months you'll be fit for the trip."

"Thank you, husband." She paused. "Oh, I'll be fit for the trip all right. But the doctor says it's going to be quite some time before my writing hand is back to normal...if ever. He says the muscles are atrophying as we speak, and the nerves may be damaged too." She looked across at her husband with an expression he knew all too well. When she looked that way, he knew she was convinced of her own opinion.

"So you had better find another assistant."

CHAPTER XXXVIII

Eastbound

"HOW CAN YOU allow your wife, our daughter, to take such a trip…such an adventure? And you're not even going with her!" The yelling over the phone could be heard by everyone in the room. The Obermaiers were furious.

"Do you think I brought my family from Russia to Uruguay and then to Germany for safety, so she could be shipped to…to the Ottoman Empire!"

"She's a grown woman," Levi offered lamely, speaking into the receiver. "She pretty much does what she wants, and it is part of her curriculum…and she will be supervised, that is, chaperoned by Frau Adelmann and her professor."

The voice through the wire replied, "That's not the way it's done!"

Karl and Helena had just received the long letter from their daughter. It explained the expedition in glowing terms, and how it was such an honor to be a paid transcriber to the distinguished Herr Dr. Professor Adelmann. It still did not go over well, with the resulting telephone call. It was the first of many.

"No, it would do no good to come all the way to Munich to try to dissuade her," Levi offered.

"No, I cannot go with her. I have my own studies to attend to, and my examinations are coming up soon.

"No, my father has agreed to assist with the expenses, and once he has pledged assistance, he will not retract it.

"Yes, these are changing times, and no, it's not for the worst."

Levi's father accepted the situation amiably, but his mother was more concerned than angry after Levi explained the honor and the chaperones and the pay. Ilsa was so excited about the trip that she wanted to go along. Markus, always the adventurous one, thought it was a marvelous opportunity and thought they should all go.

"I do want to experience that part of the world, Palestine and the Holy Land…and the whole Near East! Now that's something to see." The Obermaiers, finally resigned to the inevitable, hoped for the best. Their boys were so excited and proud of their big sister, they wanted to go too.

Hectic days followed with so many preparations to make. Dr. Rungi prepared an extensive medical kit, assuming there would be few medications available on the trip. The women went in to Munich several times on shopping trips, purchasing more garments than could possibly be taken along. Even Herr Obermaier assisted by visiting the Imperial Ottoman Embassy in Berlin to secure the necessary travel documents for Katherina.

The expedition had its choice of routes to Palestine: train to Bremerhaven and sail around the coast of France and Spain and through the Straits of Gibraltar, then on to the eastern end of the Mediterranean, or train to Venice and cut the travel time by almost a week, then on to Palestine by boat. It was an easy choice, although Katherina would have liked to see her family in Potsdam on the way to a boat in Bremerhaven.

Levi was determined to accompany his wife to Venice, and to see her off. The half-dozen archeological party members arrived in Venice on September 17 and had a wait of several days, as the freighter they were taking was loaded.

"It is a glorious day, isn't it, dear?" Katherina exclaimed as she opened the shutters of their hotel room overlooking the Grand Canal. "Let's go for a long walk and see all the treasures of the city, shall we?" She turned around and her nightgown swirled in a revealing way in the heavy, salty morning breeze off the Adriatic. She climbed onto the bed and gave a gentle shake to Levi, who was still half asleep.

"*Ja.* I'm getting up, just a few more minutes."

"You sleepy head! When I'm gone, you can sleep as long as you like. We only have today and the morning tomorrow, and we're in Venice!"

Levi's head lifted up.

"In that case," he whirled around and pulled Kathi to him, "we're staying in bed all day." He had a big smile on his face.

"No, no, no, you don't. We're going out!" She surrendered into his arms, but added, "Besides, we'll be back later, and then…"

"Yes, and then?" Levi questioned.

"And then…if you're a good boy the whole day, I'll give you a kiss."

"One kiss? Is that all I'll get for a whole day, one little kiss?"

"I didn't say it would be a little kiss," she emphasized with a smile.

He kissed her, she kissed him back, and then she rolled off the bed, saying, "Up and to breakfast!"

As the Italian freighter *Barbarini Majestica* pulled slowly away from the docks south of Venice two days later, Levi waved his outstretched arm high above his head. His lovely lady at the railing of the rust-streaked ship returned his waves with kisses blown to the wind. Frau Adelmann, her arm still in a sling, and the professor were at Katherina's side.

The white clouds against a blue, blue sky were like icebergs floating in an endless sea, all the way to the horizon. The ship picked up momentum through the water, and black oily smoke churned from its single funnel. As the *Majestica* grew distant and the passengers blurred by the sea mists, Levi remembered their first night in Venice.

They made love and made love, but the old way, gently and passionately. *It was wonderful*, he thought. It was probably the best lovemaking they had ever shared. Strange how love grows as hardships are overcome. He had a deeper appreciation of her when he realized he'd almost lost her. It was going to be a long ten weeks. He hadn't asked God for much. He began a prayer, but this time he asked that she be brought home safely. With a last long look across the sea at the column of smoke against a perfect sky, he turned and headed for the train and home.

**TOMB OF THE KINGS, OUTSIDE OF JERUSALEM BEFORE THE
ARCHAEOLOGICAL EXCAVATIONS.**

CHAPTER XXXIX

Jerusalem and the Desert

AFTER SEVERAL PORTS of call, their ship stopped at the ancient
Greek city of Ephesus. Several Christian pilgrims disembarked for
their goal, the pilgrimage shrine dedicated to the Virgin Mary where,
purportedly, she lived out her last days.

Finally, on September 29 the Italian freighter *Barbarini
Majestica* steamed into the crowded port of Jaffa. The docks, piled
high with crates of magnificent oranges and lemons, olive oil and
sesame, waited for export.

Professor Adelmann's five-member expedition met their hosts, the Jewish Palestine Exploration Society, at the docks. The Germans, always grateful, found their prearranged, temporary housing in Jaffa, in a crowded and noisy port city. Their sponsors apologized for the noise and talked enthusiastically about how some of them were going to found a new settlement next year and were going to call it Tel Aviv.

On leaving Jaffa, the Jewish Society gave the visitors a guided tour of the ancient walled city of Jerusalem, with its narrow, crowded streets, many dating to biblical times. The small group jostled their way along, passing the many merchants and religious sites of the Christians, Moslems, and Jews. They made a solemn stop at the Wailing Wall, with its massive foundation blocks of stone, all that remained of the second temple built by King David.

Professor Schellenberger and Jorg Haidler stood solemnly by as the Adelmanns and Katherina approached the sacred wall, and alone, and in their own way, spent a few silent moments. Each of the Jews had a tiny scrap of paper with names they pressed into cracks between the blocks of stone as a remembrance.

The expedition members also visited several Christian sites and walked the Via Dolorosa, Christ's walk of agony to his crucifixion. The predominantly Moslem citizens were friendly, but paid little heed to the Europeans, except as customers. The expedition moved the following day to a barren, rock-strewn site outside the walls of the city, in the Valley of Jehoshaphat. The dig and their tent encampment, which would be home for the next two months, was near a very ancient Jewish cemetery.

Dr. Adelmann secured a dozen local laborers for debris removal and other menial tasks, as well as a cook and cook's helper, a camp attendant, and of course, Abdullah, the crew chief. The camp itself began to resemble a small village. Canvas tents were erected with roof and walls, and for the five Europeans, canvas floors. A second shade tent, a few feet above the first, was also in place, even though the hot summer months had passed. Days were still hot and dusty, with cold, starlit nights.

Professor Adelmann had a large research and artifact tent complete with wooden tables and several camp chairs. Crates and boxes of all sizes and shapes were piled around the camp, having been brought on the backs of donkeys and hired bearers carrying a two-month supply of provisions.

My dearest husband, Katherina scratched in pencil, *another grueling day on our pile of stones as we call it. Found several coins, some Roman from different emperors, Claudius and Hadrian, and the latest one was a copper from Septimius Severus, dated about A.D. 200. It's an approximate way of dating the level we are at. It amazes me how many coins we find here generally. I hope to keep my pockets mended, so we don't lose our meager treasure!*

Katherina sat on a trunk at her little table next to a very hard cot that represented her private world in camp. She continued to write:

I do so miss you and dream about you most every night, when I'm not too tired to dream! Dr. Adelmann works everyone very hard including Frau Adelmann, knowing how short our time is here. No one seems to mind, as we are all excited by the work. The Ottoman army comes riding into our camp every few days, about a dozen soldiers. I think they come simply because they are bored out here on the edge of what seems to them to be nowhere. They are a pretty rough-looking lot, especially the way they look at me, but our Palestinian laborers have been very protective and always linger around

me when the troops are here. Now, I don't want you to wor-
ry about me. I am having such a wonderful experience. It's
more than I ever imagined. Just everything! The desert is so
beautiful. I'll tell you all about it when I am in your arms
again. Thank you, darling, for letting me come.
    P.S. Did I tell you I'm keeping a diary!

The dinner bell rang ten minutes before the evening meal. The
exhausted but animated group chatted as they gathered, as usual, to
eat outside with the tables brought out and with two kerosene lanterns at each end.

"Where does the cook's helper manage to find so much firewood
out here," Katherina wondered out loud, "and to keep a blaze going
well into the night. It's one of the mysteries of the desert, or what we
back home would call desert."

"It's a chilly evening again," Frau Adelmann commented as they
all sat down to the table that was moved closer to the fire.

"We'll have our meals in the big tent starting tomorrow, dear,"
offered the professor. "Work is going well. We should reach the base
of the foundation tomorrow and begin the interior sifting. Indications
are that parts of this site have not been disturbed since antiquity…a
very good sign." Adelmann shoveled a mound of curried rice into
his mouth with satisfaction. "Looks very promising." The twinkle
in his eye wasn't seen by anyone, but it was revealed by the sound
of his voice.

After dinner, small talk trailed off early as one by one the group
dispersed to their tents. It was a cold night. Katherina had added an
extra blanket to her cot, and she was sound asleep when it happened.

Someone or something pressed hard at the side of her tent and
popped stakes out of the ground. She woke to hear Moslems yelling, crates crashing, and general pandemonium in camp. Tents
began to light up as lamps were lit. Shouting commenced and

Professor Schellenberger charged from his tent, rifle at the ready. "What is it? What's happening?" someone shouted several times. *Bang!* A shot rang out in the dark. By this time, everyone was out and gathered by the fire, as more kindling was hastily tossed on to feed the blaze.

"Hyenas, several hyenas, or wild dogs!" Schellenberger huffed, trotting out of the dark. A wisp of smoke curled out of the barrel of his gun. "Came into camp looking for food; they're gone now...no danger."

"Well, of all things!" sputtered Frau Adelmann.

"Are they dangerous? Would they attack people?"

"They'll eat anything, but they prefer that it be dead first."

Several members let out exaggerated laughs, more in relief then in humor.

"Well, my tent is partially collapsed. I know I was tired but not dead tired!" Kathi exclaimed, bringing more genuine laughs. No one was ready to go back to their tents, so a bottle of schnapps was brought out, glasses poured, and everyone helped drain the bottle.

CHAPTER XL

The Dig and the Bedouins

"I TOLD THEM to pile the tailings further from the trenches; we don't want debris rolling back onto our work." The master of the Palestinian crew, Abdulla Mohammad Sidfardi, scurried around the open trenches directing his workers following Adelmann's reprimand.

Several more weeks passed in laborious efforts, as the quality of artifacts became more interesting and important. A large rectangular block of marble, with ancient Hebrew calligraphy, was unearthed next to the slag pile, of all places. It was only a few inches below the surface of the ground, also an unusual circumstance.

By chance and by order of Professor Adelmann, who insisted the slag piles be compact and not spread all around, one of the workers was shoveling debris back onto the pile when he exposed some text on a stone. For the archeologists, it was the most important discovery so far, with everyone poring over the inscription. It was ancient Hebrew with elements of Egyptian glyphs, a perplexing combination—a real challenge to decipher.

While Katherina joined in the excitement of this discovery, she had also made a secret but immensely important discovery for herself. She was pregnant again. She was sure of it.

Having been pregnant three times earlier, she knew how her body reacted…dizziness, sore breasts, just a hint of nausea, nothing that the others in camp would notice.

"I will not allow this to interfere with my work here," she mumbled to herself while on a break in her tent. "We're going home in several weeks, and I am seeing this great adventure through to the end. I want this baby, but she will have to wait until I'm done here." She smiled to herself and shook her head at her audacity.

I'm really being reckless, she thought, *but what if I'd told Frau Adelmann and the professor? They would send me home on the next boat!*

"That's not going to happen!" she said aloud.

"What was that? What's not going to happen?" It was Haidler. "I knocked on your tent post, but you didn't hear me over your own talking. I was asked to come get you; they're serving already… What's not going to happen?" he repeated.

"Jorg," Katherina practically shouted as she turned. "I was just…I was just having a private conversation with myself. Don't you have them, too? Now, what's for dinner?"

During the next week, Adelmann and Schellenberger pored over the two-foot by three-foot block of marble, trying to work out the translation of old Egypto-Hebrew. Kathi and Jorg and the others continued the excavation of the inner chamber of this most unusual archeological site which Dr. Adelmann had been studying from afar for several years.

It was a mysterious site as most archeological sites are, but what made it particularly significant to the professor was the fact that this supposed sepulcher strongly resembled those of the Egyptian tombs found in Thebes. Now, with the discovery of the Egypto-Hebrew block just unearthed and the Egyptian style of architecture of the outer structure, the parallels created a suppressed excitement of the potential possibilities.

Over the ages the site had several names; most were inaccurate. Known as the Tomb of the Kings, because of its elaborate carvings, it was thought by some to be the last resting place of ancient Jewish monarchs. Europeans from the medieval period, or possibly earlier, had given it its present name. Like many ancient monuments, successive dynasties modified or obliterated previously carved names and distinguishing features, making them their own. This was what Dr. Adelmann confronted at this site. It was once thought to have been constructed by Herod, appointed by the Romans to be King of Judea. This site, like most sites in Palestine, had been known and looted since ancient times, but for Adelmann, Katherina, and the others, it had answers and artifacts still to be found. They hoped to finish their discoveries and excavate down to the presumed floor of the tomb by December 11.

A large polished metal mirror, being used to throw light deep into the interior, was probably the same technique the ancient builders used thousands of years ago in all of the great construction projects of the civilizations surrounding the Mediterranean.

"We must be getting near the floor," Jorg commented as he carefully removed another shovelful of dirt for screening outside. "Look here, Kathi, along the wall. See how worn it is around the corner."

Katherina leaned in, turned, and without saying anything, directed the mirror bearer to adjust the aim of the light.

"See," Jorg continued, "people, many people over the years, maybe centuries, touched the wall here as they came around the corner. So we must be, what do you think, three or four feet from the floor."

"Yes, yes, of course," she replied, "that would be about right. We're doing two feet a day with debris removal, so we should finish this chamber on schedule. Then we can help with the sifting, and that should take us..."

She was interrupted in midsentence by the sound of faint screams from the camp.

"What's that?" she gasped, looking first toward the passageway and then to Jorg. Before either of them could move, the mirror bearer dropped the metal reflector and shouted, "Bedouins!" and then he ran out of sight.

Katherina and Jorg were plunged into darkness, with just the faintest of gray light seeping down the passage and around the corner.

"Wait! I'll light the lantern," Jorg exclaimed, fumbling in the darkness for his matches.

The Tomb of the Kings was actually several hundred yards from the tent camp, just over a rise in the ground. The two made their way to the entrance and peered out. Nothing…then more shouting…then several gunshots!

"If they're Bedouins, they're looting the camp!" Jorg stammered. "Better stay here." His arm came up in front of Katherina in a defense motion. "I'll go have a look. You stay here out of sight. Here, take the lantern, and watch, but stay out of sight," he repeated. "If any of them come, go deep in and turn off the lantern. They won't be able to see you." And he was gone.

Katherina shook with fright, her heart pounding as the long work skirt she wore billowed out from her body. She pressed herself hard against the sandstone wall. Quickly she gathered her skirt in and tucked it between her legs, and then she froze in place.

Nothing, she thought. Just muffled sounds and horses' hooves! She pulled back. The hoof beats were getting louder! She stepped back further into the deep shadows. *A horse!*

From her position, she could only see from the saddle down. A man's sandaled foot and swirling robes. Several more horsemen pulled up in front of the entrance, and Katherina stumbled backward into the blackness.

She cursed herself for making so much noise. She heard voices in Arabic! *Go deep*, Jorg had said, *go deep!*

It was pitch black, but she knew the way in from the many times she had entered. Now she was at the corner; now she felt along the wall to the furthest reaches of the chamber. She was still grasping the lantern. She set it down quietly. She stepped down into the two-foot-deep trench along the far wall and waited.

She was perspiring profusely. Her mind raced.

Hadn't she heard that Bedouins had an acute sense of smell? Could they smell her sweat if they came into the antechamber? If they could smell her, they could find her in the dark. What would they do to her? Rape! *Worse than death*, she thought. *Will they kill me? Where is Jorg? Where is anybody?*

She heard their voices. They had dismounted and were entering the passageway. She forgot the mirror! She almost shouted aloud, *Oh my God, I forgot the mirror!* Tears were streaming down her face. She wiped them away with the back of her dusty hand.

Pull yourself together, she thought. *What was that noise? Metal on stone. They've found the mirror!* She saw a light flash further up the passage. They were coming!

The marauders peered into the blackness. Once they'd found the mirror, they aimed it down the passageway. Two of them cautiously probed with their curved swords as they worked their way further into the deep excavation.

"Turn that shield so we have more light, you camel dung!" one of them shouted. They got to the corner and stopped. One of them placed his hand on the spot that Jorg and Kathi had examined a short time earlier.

In the dim light, from the poorly aimed and wobbling mirror, one of the men spied a glint of metal! "Weapon!" he shouted.

Both men leaped backward and thrust their swords out in front of them, while with the other hand they drew their daggers. Now, they were crouching low and prepared to fight.

"Where?" asked the other man.

"There, against the wall! Do you see it?"

"I see nothing...wait!" He slowly advanced in the almost black room. In a lightning move, he plunged his sword directly toward the faint object. Banging clatter and breaking glass reverberated against the stone wall as he pierced the lantern's globe and sent it flying against the far wall.

"Allah be praised. You're the camel dung! It's just a lantern." They lowered their swords and sheathed their daggers.

"Let's get out of here. Those thieves out there are getting all the good stuff!" The two robbers scurried out the way they came.

In the chamber, there was dead silence now. She listened for several moments. There was not a sound. Not a breath and then there was again the sound of falling glass shards. The lantern that had been thrown against the back wall had fallen directly on top of a thin pile of dust, dirt, and rubble. Under that pile, there was a two-foot-deep trench where Katherina had hastily buried herself. Now, her fear subsiding, she slowly dug herself out of the only hiding place in the chamber. She coughed several times and caught herself for making too much noise. Standing up, she shook her hair and dusted off her blouse. Her eyes had become accustomed to the low light, and she could move around freely. She shook out her skirt, slapped her thighs and rump, and dust rose in a cloud.

She made her way back up the passage, past the discarded mirror, to the entrance. As she cautiously looked out, she saw several members of her group rapidly approaching the site. She stepped out into the sun, closed her eyes for a moment, and leaned her head back, smiling faintly. Her near-discovery by the Bedouins had left her exhilarated to a point she couldn't remember feeling before.

The Ottoman soldiers had been less than a mile away and had

heard the several shots fired by, again, Professor Schellenberger. Contrary to their reputation with Europeans, the sultan's soldiers were good fighters and basically decent men, at least by Ottoman standards. They had come galloping into the archeological camp with rifles at the ready and exchanged shots with the Bedouins—who rapidly departed.

The only real casualty in the bandit raid was Jorg, who sustained a gunshot wound to his leg in the last minutes of the scrimmage. The Ottoman officer ordered that a doctor come, but it would be a full three hours. In the meantime, Jorg was bandaged and given his own bottle of schnapps along with the tender attention of Frau Adelmann and Katherina. After emptying half the bottle, he was thoroughly enjoying himself.

"That was clever of you, Kathi, burying yourself in that trench. Very quick-witted," Professor Adelmann said admiringly. "You have proven to be quite competent at the dig, also." He hesitated. "Congratulations!"

They were all in the dining tent. It was after dark. Four Ottoman soldiers had been assigned guard duty to the group for the duration of the dig, with two of them on duty outside the big tent.

"We return home next week…actually in five days…with several noteworthy discoveries, but 'the block,' as Professor Schellenberger has labeled it, is a truly remarkable find." Adelmann's eyes were twinkling as he spoke. "This discovery will be very well received in Berlin. As soon as we can translate its contents, we two will deliver a paper on our findings." He was referring, of course, to himself and Professor Schellenberger.

"We can all be proud of what we have accomplished here and our 'adventures'!" The entire group erupted in laughter. "And we still have five more days to finish what we started out to do."

"A toast! I propose a toast." Professor Schellenberger stood up and raised his mug of beer. "First, to the emperor and our glorious country and its many accomplishments in archeology in recent years." They all sang out agreement.

"Second, to my friend and colleague, Herr Professor Doctor Adelmann...and Frau Adelmann," he added, "for their tireless pursuit of excellence in their research." He turned to his friend. "This discovery, your discovery, will bring you fame and recognition in the empire and across Europe."

Everyone smiled and tentatively watched the speech giver.

"And finally I would add, well done to Frau Katherina Levi, for her efforts on this her first dig, and to her bravery and quickness of mind today. I salute you all!" Hurrahs and cheers broke out, with happy chatter into the night.

The next morning at breakfast, Dr. Adelmann called Katherina aside. "I'm putting you in charge of the final efforts of the dig for these last days," he said. "Under the circumstances, Herr Haidler is unable to work, and I have much too much to finish up here. Remember what you have learned in handling the site. You'll do fine." He smiled at her as Katherina burst into an open-mouth grin and thanked the professor profusely.

This was her first real archeological experience and she was officially in charge of the dig site! "I will do everything according to your standards, Professor."

CHAPTER XLI

Secrets Revealed

ON THE THIRD day of the last of the five days of work, Frau Adelmann was in the research tent with her husband and his scholar friend Schellenberger. She saw a curious thing and said, "Look!"

Professor Schellenberger looked up from his writing and nudged Adelmann's arm.

"Look who's coming. She seems in a hurry."

Katherina was heading straight for the research tent. Both professors stopped their work and as they watched her coming down the hill toward them, they both grew curious and apprehensive. Schellenberger briefly thought of going to his tent for his rifle, but immediately remembered the guards.

Before she had reached the tent, Katherina shouted, "I've found something. That is, I think I've found something. Please come have a look." Both men rose quickly, Adelmann knocking over his chair. He ignored it.

"What is it?" they said almost in unison. Schellenberger deferred to Adelmann.

"What have …what do you think you've found?"

Katherina was breathing hard as she entered the tent and was offered Schellenberger's chair.

"Here, have a glass of water."

"Well?"

"You'll have to come see, to see if it's what I think it is, Professor." She looked up at each man.

"*Ja*, and what is it?"

"I think it's a flight of stairs…but I'm not sure." The two professors' eyes widened. "You see, we haven't actually uncovered any stairs, but, but…you see, as you know, there is this band, a painted frieze, very faint, but visible. The design runs around the walls about three feet above the floor. Well, we just uncovered a new portion of it, and it turns down at about a forty-five-degree angle and continues downward toward the floor. But we're not down to the floor yet, so I'm not sure. But in the other excavations we visited over the last several months that had this same type of design, whenever it turned down at a forty-five-degree angle, the design followed the wall down a staircase."

Silence.

The two professors looked at each other without saying a word. Adelmann was the first out of the tent and at a quick pace headed up the shallow hill separating the camp from the site. Schellenberger was right behind, with Frau Adelmann and Katherina close behind him. Others in the camp, drawn to the activity, stopped working. The cook and his helper were talking and pointing as several of the other camp help came over to join in.

By the time the four arrived at the dig and proceeded down the passage and around the corner, the three men hauling debris had reached the floor level along the far wall. That is, they reached a patch of floor, a patch of floor with an edge that dropped down about four inches to a still debris-packed void.

"Bring a lantern in closer," Schellenberger exclaimed.

"By God, she's right! Look, Adelmann, the floor gives way. We should get everyone focused on this. We don't have much time, but this is something!" The two men were kneeling in the dirt, Adelmann scraping with a trowel he had taken out of the hand of one of the diggers.

"What do you think, my friend?"

Adelmann hesitated before answering. "This could be very significant. You see, there is no record of an additional room or level at this site. Nothing in the literature."

He turned his head to look at his colleague and continued in a scholarly tone. "My question is, why? Why a lower level? Assuming there is a lower level. Is it to a well? A tomb? A passage?" All four were silent for some time, digesting this new discovery.

Finally, Frau Adelmann, who had been on many digs with her husband, spoke. "This is going to take time, a lot of time. Time we don't have. We are supposed to meet the boat in Jaffa in six days. We can be late a day or two, but not…"

Her husband cut her off. "*Ja, ja*, I know, Mother." He rarely used such a personal expression in public.

"We don't know what we have here…how significant…or how long it will take to excavate," Schellenberger added. "We're going to need more help, more manpower, more money…and guards, and more time…a lot more time."

Katherina was trembling with excitement as she looked on at these two longtime professional archeologists discussing in animated gestures the potential of an additional discovery.

"It could be nothing…an empty room," Adelmann offered.

"True, true," replied his colleague, "but it is an unknown room. It shouldn't be there. The ancient scribes describe this as possibly a tomb, but make no mention of a staircase. We know this site was frequently mentioned as far back as Herod, before Herod. So, we have a mystery that needs solving." He was silent for a few moments as everyone sat quietly on the piles of rubble. "Do we extend the dig? Can we extend the dig?"

Adelmann finally spoke up: "*Ja*, we certainly could arrange things with the Ottomans…and the university…for time off and all that. But we need manpower and money. And we already have more research material than we can handle…and 'the block,' which is our most important artifact discovered here, at least so far."

"And that highly unusual combination of scripts," Schellenberger added. "We could just close it up. Fill it in and come back later; it's done all the time," he paused, "but I know you, Adelmann, you won't sleep until you know what's down there." He was pointing at the spot where the frieze disappeared into the dirt.

Finally, as if Professor Adelmann had made a strategic decision, he commanded, "So Frau Levi, continue to dig!"

Everyone's efforts were concentrated on what did turn out to be a staircase. In the next several days, through expedited digging, they finally reached the floor of the lower level. But in the end, Adelmann and Schellenberger agreed that they would, indeed, fill in the staircase with debris and save the site for another time.

Discussion took place over meals and into the evenings as to what to do with this discovery. Dr. Adelmann had even offered Katherina the opportunity to return in several months with a full archeological crew and continue the dig. Everyone was a bit surprised at her reticence to commit to another dig, especially since she was the first to discover this new find.

The day before leaving for the coast, and while workmen carefully filled in the staircase with dirt, Frau Adelmann visited Katherina in her tent.

"You have worked out splendidly, my dear," she began. "My husband is very proud of you and your rapid growth into a true professional archeologist." She leaned over and patted Katherina's shoulder.

"Thank you, Frau Adelmann," Kathi said. She sat on her cot folding clothes for packing. "It has truly been my dream of a lifetime to come here. I will always be grateful to Professor Adelmann and you, for your many kindnesses and trust." She smiled up at the older woman and touched her forearm.

"So you are packing, too. Over the years, I've got it down to a ritual I perform in the shortest possible time. All my dirty clothes in one trunk, and my clean clothes in a small satchel!" They both laughed heartily.

"Well, I don't have any clean clothes, except a few things which I can carry in my evening bag…if I had an evening bag on this trip!" They laughed at their mutual experience of not ever really being clean during the entire expedition. Katherina offered Frau Adelmann the only chair in her tent, but she declined to sit.

She looked around the little cloth world that was home to the lovely young woman beside her. "You must have missed your husband very much these past ten weeks, but you will be home again soon, probably in ten days or so."

"Yes, yes, I do miss Levi…I have so much to tell him. He won't believe half my stories!" Katherina smiled broadly as she lingered a moment and stared off in space. Her visitor was staring down at her.

"Yes, I'm sure you do have important things to tell him." Frau Adelmann waited expectantly for Katherina to reveal a secret the older woman felt existed. Katherina glanced up but said nothing.

After delaying the departure a full two days in order to close down the dig and transport their gear, research, and artifacts to the coast, Professor Adelmann had to offer a substantial bribe to export "the block." It was a truly significant find and the elder archeologist would have paid much, much more if need be.

Several days later, with a full load of olive oil, cotton, and handicrafts, the Moroccan tramp steamer *Berber Marrakesh* eased into the Italian port just south of Venice on a cold, rainy afternoon in mid-December. There was little harbor traffic so close to Christmas and even less activity on the docks.

Three figures stood bunched close under a black umbrella, looking up expectantly. As he looked out from under the umbrella.

She recognized Markus. She strained to see Levi, and caught his eye. So many feelings and emotions were bubbling in her, a tear trickled down her cheek.

"Levi! Levi!" she shouted from the railing, waving frantically at the little group. His strong arm waved the umbrella back and forth, and he threw her a kiss with his other hand. She thought he looked very handsome in his stiff white collar, fedora hat, and Edwardian suit. English fashion had become popular in Germany recently.

Finally on the dock and in her husband's arms, she gushed, "Oh, Levi, I so missed you, darling. I have so much to tell you, so very much."

CHAPTER XLII

Return 1908

TEARS...TEARS OF JOY, of happiness, of being almost home again, and tears of release from the stress of the secret...the secret that was not revealed to anyone on the passage back. It pressed in on Katherina as she lingered in Levi's arms on the Italian dock.

Cold wind whipped around the little group while they exchanged greetings and welcome home hugs. Markus and Levi's sister, Ilsa, were profuse in their gestures and comments to Professor Adelmann and his wife and Professor Schellenberger. That gave Levi and Katherina a few moments for private words and closeness.

A large, closed carriage was brought around for all and a second wagon for the many crates and luggage. They went to a hotel for a one-night stay before the train home. Gathering together for dinner, the group was led into a room of sumptuous surroundings that had once been a Renaissance villa of Venetians of noble birth.

Levi could not take his eyes off his lovely wife, with a wind-swept look about her. Tanned and athletic, Katherina looked fabulous to his eyes. She caught Levi staring at her and a faint blush pinked her cheeks. Her smile was met by his, and they held hands while the meal was served.

The eight of them sat around an oval table, heaped high with Italian cuisine, beneath an ancient crystal chandelier fitted out with gas. There were few people dining that evening, so the several waiters gave quick and attentive care to the party, pouring red wine into half-filled glasses.

Many questions were asked, with many animated answers, with laughter and waving arms, until Dr. Adelmann said, "Enough! Enough. It's time for bed! This has been a lovely welcome back, and we thank you," he nodded toward Ilsa, Markus, and Levi, "for greeting us here in Italy. An early train tomorrow, so I say good night. We shall all meet here early tomorrow morning." He got up and slid Frau Adelmann's chair out so she could rise.

The party broke up and everyone headed toward their rooms. In the upstairs hallway, more good nights as doors closed for the evening. They were in each other's arms with the click of the door latch.

"You have no idea how much I missed you, my love," Levi whispered, burying his face in Kathi's hair.

"Yes I do," she replied with her lips close to his ear.

"I missed you, oh so much darling, and now we are together again." They both giggled as they nuzzled each other, deliberately rubbing their bodies together gently in an ever-increasing arousal. "I prayed to God that you would be safe, and after hearing some of the stories at dinner, I must now thank Him for bringing you home safely. What stories! What adventures you had. They reminded me of my own experiences in China with the Boxers." He leaned back a bit and looked into her eyes with his gentle smile.

"How will you adjust to our simple, quiet life at Kalvarianhof? Won't you miss the exotic lands and the discoveries and your friends the Bedouins?"

They burst out laughing and swung out from each other, almost in a dance step, coming together again into a long and passionate kiss.

As their lips parted, Levi's hands slid across her body to the

buttons of her blouse. He could feel his passion rising, She let him un-
button and slowly pull open her white blouse as her eyes misted over
with desire. He gazed down at her white chest and the mounds of her
breasts beneath a light shift. Watching him watch her, her hand traced
down from his shoulder to his front below his belt. Through his clothing, she grasped his hardness. Both of Levi's hands rose to the top
edge of her shift and in ever-mounting passion, he forcefully pulled
the garment downward as her breasts popped out. His hands swept
up over her beautiful body, and she deftly undid his belt and buttons.

They enveloped one another with the fierceness of overwhelming
desire. They surrendered into uninhibited expressions of love, their
kisses roaming across each other's bodies and moaning with intimate
pleasure. And then their languid hands trailed across the landscape of
each other's body as they tenderly whispered their shared thoughts.

"Levi darling, I have a gift for you," she murmured, staring at
him with half-opened eyes. "A precious gift just for you," she hesitated a moment, "and for me."

Levi, smiling, looked into her eyes, their heads a few inches
apart. "Yes? A present, I love your presents!" He laughed gently
and quickly swept his hand from her knee, over her hip, up her side,
cupping her breast.

"No, silly!" She smiled as her hand slid on top of his. "This is a
most precious gift."

He sensed a subtle but serious tone to her voice, and he focused
his smiling face on her.

"We are going to have a baby, darling. And this time, I know it
will really happen. I just know it!"

Levi was taken aback. "What? Really, are you sure?"

"Yes. It must have happened here in Italy just before I left."
They kissed again.

"But, but…" Levi started.

Katherina interrupted him. "I didn't know until almost two months into the expedition. I didn't want to tell anybody or they would have sent me home."

"But, Kathi my love, shouldn't we…shouldn't I have been gentler just now, I mean…"

"Oh, darling, that isn't a concern; there is no danger this early in…in our being together like this…and I just know it's going to be all right this time. I'm sure of it. I feel it, darling."

"Oh Kathi my love, I am so happy, but you've been through so much before, I just don't want you to have to…"

"Levi, darling, I'm past that. What will be is God's decision. If it doesn't happen again, I am ready for that. But I just know I'm going to have this baby this time."

They came together in the shelter of their bodies, in the oneness of their love for each other. This time in a slow gentleness, a slow climb to the heights of their love, and in those long moments of joy, Levi again called upon God to deliver her from danger, from disappointment and despair…to allow her to have this one most precious gift.

Everyone at Kalvarianhof was surprised and apprehensive on hearing the news of Katherina's condition. But after Levi privately talked to his mother, father, and sister about Kathi's attitude toward this pregnancy, they all felt both relief and a certain reserved excitement.

Katherina, on the other hand, delighted in being fetched from the train station in Papa Levi's new automobile, the first motor car in the family. The 1908 Benz touring car chugged, sputtered, and roared toward the loading dock at the village train depot, sliding to a stop in the foot-deep snow. With open sides and a canvas roof, the Benz gave little protection from the frigid air whistling around five occupants. Even bundled up in buffalo blankets imported from America, everyone's cheeks were pink from the biting wind by the time the shiny maroon car skidded to a halt in front of their moonlit home.

"We're building a shed out back for my beauty," the elder Levi huffed as he clambered down from the driver's seat, then looking at the moon, said, "Markus, you must stay the night here. It's too late for you to go home again. Call your mother."

It was a bit strange for him, a Catholic, to see a home so close to Christmas with none of the traditional Christian trimmings. There was no Christmas tree, no Advent wreath, no *display of* the baby Jesus, Mary, Joseph, and the three kings, surrounded by hand-carved and painted camels and sheep. Absent were all the beloved objects of a Catholic tradition that his mother arranged so carefully in his home each December.

The Levi house, always beautifully appointed, had only a brightly polished silver menorah, with its nine candles, sitting in a prominent place in their dining room as evidence of Hanukah. However, as everyone hurried in from the cold to warm greetings, a festive mood prevailed.

"Mama, thank you for preparing this late evening meal for us," Levi said, hugging her.

After several rounds of beer and toasts of schnapps, the elders finally said their good nights. The four young adults sipped their drinks amid exotic tales of discovery and adventure.

Katherina pulled from her pocket several ancient coins that Professor Adelmann gave her as keepsakes. They all examined them closely, wondering who owned them, who dropped them, and the long-ago civilizations from whence they came.

"I have something very special here," Katherina said as she twisted sideways on the bench in the kitchen alcove where they all sat. From her other pocket she pulled out a tightly wrapped cloth. She slowly untied the little bundle to reveal a broken stone.

"It's only on loan to me from Professor Adelmann. I have to give it back. It's from the Tomb of the Kings in the Valley of Jehoshaphat, just outside of Jerusalem, where our dig is…was." All eyes were on the little bundle that she laid on the table for them to see. It was white marble, about six inches long, with a flat surface three inches wide. On that flat surface was carved ancient Hebrew calligraphy, with strange Egyptian hieroglyphic elements mixed in.

"We don't know what it means," she continued. "It hasn't been translated yet." Her audience of three leaned in for a closer look as Katherina leaned back. In a more serious, professional tone she said, "We don't actually know how to translate this early combination of Egypto-Hebrew writing; that is, we know some of the meanings of certain symbols, but not enough to decipher it all." In a more light-hearted voice she exclaimed, "But that's the challenge, that's the fun of all this, of archeology, of looking for the truth in the past, separating fact from legend." Everyone was enthralled by her exotic stories and her seriousness of purpose.

"How interesting it all is," exclaimed Ilsa. "You've had so many adventures and been so many places… It's so thrilling, Kathi. I wish I could do all the things you do," she looked up from the table at her sister-in-law, "and go to new and different places." There was a certain naiveté in Ilsa's longings, in her young, inexperienced life.

Levi and Markus, with their foreign adventures in China and the South Pacific, had gone from that sheltered life of youth, where Ilsa still dwelled, into the harsher world that Katherina had entered. They both, for different reasons, sympathized with Ilsa and knew how fleeting her protected world would be.

CHAPTER XLIII

Love in the Night

EVERYONE FINALLY TURNED in. It was a night of icy-cold floors, of bedrooms inadequately heated with small porcelain-tiled stoves and with frost-covered windows from which hung curtains that swayed with each change in the winter wind. Ilsa knew each floorboard, each squeak that could give away her presence in the long, dark hallway. She knew just how far to press down the door handle to slide the mechanism just far enough to swing open for her to slip through.

Without a sound, she crossed the floor and reached for the edge of the foot-thick feather bedding that covered Markus. As she pulled up the cover a few inches, Markus turned suddenly.

"Ilsa! No, you can't be here!"

"Shush," she replied. "Quiet!" She slipped in under the thick, warm bedding.

"You've got to go…now, before you're caught!"

"I'm here now," she whispered, snuggling in close to his warm body. "Everyone's asleep. I waited. No one heard me. I didn't make even one little noise," she said with a tiny giggle.

He was lying on his back; she was at his side on her stomach.

She reached up and slid her hand up to his face. He could smell her perfume. She stretched up and turned his head to hers and kissed him gently.

"Ilsa, darling, we can't be here like this. Your parents are just down the hall, and Levi and Kathi…"

She broke in, "They're at the far end of the hall, and with the wind howling…" She stopped talking to kiss him again. "I'll leave in a little while." She wiggled closer to him. He said nothing. Her leg slid up over him.

"Oh, Ilsa, my God, you…" Their lips came together with a passion. His hands coursed across her linen nightgown, following the curve of her back. He could feel her body pressing against him.

His hand found the edge of her nightgown and slid under and up her thigh. She was breathing as hard as he, as she moved her knees apart to let his hand find her. In rapturous moans his finger slipped into her, and a moment later, a second finger joined in stroking her soft loveliness. They both came together, now not kissing, but moaning in utter surrender to their mutual passions.

She collapsed next to him. They kissed and giggled as their sweaty foreheads rolled against each other. She wanted her darling Markus.

He read her mind. "Ilsa, we can't risk this, not now. You know what we talked about over the last few weeks. Our parents will never let us be together. And we're still in school and…"

She silenced him with a kiss, a series of little kisses, on his lips, his neck, his shoulders, and his chest. She looked up at him in the moonlight. She hesitated a moment, then sat up in bed and rose to her knees. She pulled her nightgown over her head and tossed it to the side, then laid her body on top of his. She raised up on her hands, enough so that she could sway back and forth, rubbing her breasts against his. She could feel his hips tightening and involuntarily pressing upward against her. She began to move her hips up and down against his cock as she continued to sway back and forth, her hard nipples caressing his chest.

Markus was alive with passion. Ilsa raised herself, her knees at his sides, reached down, and with her hand, took hold of his penis. She pressed herself against him. The head of his cock popped into her and then out. She was moving her hips in and out against him. She pressed hard and with thrust after thrust, she drove Markus into her. His hands were on her breasts and then her hips. He thrust upward into her, deep in, as she spread her knees apart, thrusting her hips into his. Finally she collapsed onto him, he still inside of her.

"No, no, don't move," she breathed into his ear. He lay there exhausted, feeling her wonderful body on his, with his hands stroking her back gently. He felt her body stiffen, her muscles tighten, as she rose to another orgasm. This time she quickened the movements. This time she thrust harder and faster. She was moaning "oh, oh" with each motion. She lay on his stomach, their bellies rubbing against each other. She was pumping hard as she neared her climax, perspiration flowing down her temples and between her breasts. Markus both kissed her breasts and, with his hands on her butt, rocked her forward and back. With a burst of moans, she shuddered with passion and fell to the hot body beneath her.

She smothered him with kisses. It seemed she couldn't stop kissing him, but finally she lay still. A few moments later, she turned her head toward his, her lips only inches away from his chin.

"Oh, yes, yes, yes!" she whispered forcefully, and she hugged him tightly. They lay together for some time but didn't speak.

She was smiling to herself, while Markus thought of the complexities of their situation. He loved her…he loved her body, and her unbelievable passion. He could feel himself stiffening just thinking about her for a few moments.

But what to do? It was just not possible to marry and live here happily with the two families. But to break it off? Did he want to do that? No, it was just too wonderful to be with her. It wasn't just the sex. They shouldn't have done it. He shouldn't have let it happen. What if she became pregnant? That would be a disaster…for both of them! What to do?

It was close to four o'clock in the morning. They had been together in his bed for at least three hours when Markus woke up with a shudder.

"You have to go, my dear. Ilsa, you have to go!"

She buried herself deeper into the pillows and the feather bedding, her hair spread across the pillows. He rocked her gently. "Yes, yes, I know. I must go back to my cold, lonely bed. I don't care what anybody thinks, I want to be with you, darling."

They kissed again, and Markus reached for Ilsa's nightgown. "Here, let me help you with this."

"I love the feel of your hands on my body," she whispered as she slid the nightgown over her head. "I want to be with you every night…like tonight." They kissed again.

"Me, too, but not now…"

She slipped off the high bed onto the cold floor. Her bare feet, shocked by the cold, caused her to grimace and mouth "Ouch!"

Before she turned to go, she leaned in to kiss Markus again. It was a strong, passionate kiss and Markus' hands found her breasts and lifted them gently through her nightgown. Again, they rolled their foreheads together. He let out a low growl. "Go!" he said.

The afternoon of the next day, Katherina was quietly informed by the maid of the "soiled" sheets with their telltale signs of lovemaking. Now, Ilsa sat on her bed, her eyes red with tears, looking up at the frowning face of her sister-in-law and begging. "Don't tell, please don't tell!"

Markus and Levi had taken the train into Munich, while Papa had taken the young stable hand Willi into the village to purchase wood for the motor car shed. Mama was taking her afternoon nap.

It was a brittle cold day, with gray clouds hanging low in the sky. The house was very quiet, with once-in-a-while muffled sounds from the cook's dinner preparations in the kitchen. Smells of cooking and fresh bread wafted up from the first floor as the two young women confronted a profound moral and emotional dilemma.

"How long has it been going on?"

"Last night was the first time. I mean the really first time we… we…"

"Intercourse, did you?"

"Yes, but it was the first time…I mean the first night together."

"The first night, or the only time? Never mind, I don't want to know."

"It was the first night and the first time, but, but," Ilsa was immensely embarrassed, "several times…" Her voice trailed off into more tears.

"Did you use anything…I mean protection?"

"Protection?"

"Oh, for God's sake!" It was the first time Ilsa had ever heard Kathi use God's name in anger. "It's probably too late, but take a hot bath. Now!" Ilsa could hear the frustration tinged with disgust in Katherina's voice. "And wash yourself, deep."

Kathi, suddenly aware of her tone, said, "Come along," in a much more gentle voice. "We'll talk as you bathe. Now get undressed, and I'll meet you in the tub room. I'll go run the water."

The bathing tub was located in what had been a storage room, but now served its new purpose with hot water pumped from a small boiler in the basement. The room had not been altered much, except for the plumbing pipes to the galvanized tub. The bathtub was in the center of a large room of no windows. An oriental carpet partially covered the wooden planked floor and on it stood a straight-backed chair, a freestanding towel rack, and a small dresser. A single gas fixture, converted to electricity, hung from the ceiling.

Steam rose in billows in the cold room as Ilsa, wrapped in a long housecoat and carrying several towels, stepped in and closed the door. Katherina stepped toward her and took the towels.

"You'll feel much better after your bath," she said gently. "I put bubble soap in for you. I think it's just the right temperature; at least it's the way I like it." Kathi was trying to make amends for her harshness earlier.

While she waited for Ilsa, she thought about her first passionate embraces with Levi and about how wild and abandoned they were. Ilsa was simply experiencing what she had experienced herself. Of course, it did not make up for poor judgment, or the violation of the taboos of religion and tradition. But now, what was done was done. It was time to look for solutions.

Ilsa stepped toward the tub and opened her housecoat. She looked at Kathi looking at her, and she was obviously embarrassed to be naked in front of her sister-in-law.

"Oh, step in, silly. I have a body just like yours!" They looked at each other, smiled, and then burst into giggles. Kathi took Ilsa's robe and watched as the beautiful young woman stepped gingerly into the tub. She couldn't help noticing the lovely body standing in the water. Ilsa slowly bent over and lowered herself. With every movement her breasts swayed and the curves of her body were accentuated by the single overhead bulb and the darker shadows of the room.

It's easy to see why Markus is in love with this beautiful girl, thought Kathi as she folded the housecoat and put it on top of the towels on the stand. She sat down and Ilsa, now accustomed to the water temperature, slid beneath the bubbles, with just her head showing. She turned to Kathi and asked, "You're not going to tell, are you?"

"Of course not, silly." She used that term again because it took the seriousness of the question down a bit. "You've got a serious problem that so many women face. We sometimes fall in love with…"—she was going to say "the wrong man" but she changed it to—"with love." Even she thought that sounded corny, but it was better than saying "with the wrong man." She hesitated a moment, and could see Ilsa washing herself beneath the bubbles.

"You're young and experiencing adult life and feelings, feelings for a man, intense feelings, for the first time. It's very romantic, and it's easy to become swept away by passion." She let Ilsa think about that for a moment.

"Love is wonderful, but love can also be painful and…"

Ilsa interrupted her. "I know, I know, but I love him! I want to be with him, and he loves me. I know he does," she said passionately.

"Of course you do and he too, but sometimes love is not enough, Ilsa." She leaned forward in the chair. "Think what pain your relationship with Markus will cause if it became public. Mama would have a broken heart. Papa would be angry, very angry, and disappointed. What would Levi do? Would their friendship survive such a breach? I really don't know what my husband, your brother, would do."

They were both silent for a long time. Ilsa slowly fanned her hands through the water as she stared into the shadows. "I know it's not right," Ilsa finally said. "But I love him." Tears were mingling with the beads of water on her face. She began to cry softly and she sat up in the tub, her head hanging down. Katherina got up and knelt down beside the tub and put her hand on Ilsa's head. Ilsa leaned toward her and rested her head on Kathi's shoulder, sobbing into Kathi's white blouse. Her body shuddered with grief as Kathi gently stroked her back.

"I am so sorry you have to feel such pain, my dear sister," she said, a tear running down her cheek. "I, too, have experienced pain—deep, unrelenting pain—in the loss of my babies." Kathi began to cry, too. It was so unexpected, but she couldn't stop. Tears flowed as she sobbed, clutching Ilsa tightly. The two women, both overcome with grief for vastly different reasons, held each other in their arms. Ilsa soon recovered, and Kathi continued to tremble between forlorn moans. She turned to allow Kathi to rest her head on her shoulder.

"There, there, Kathi dear, you are going to have a baby this time. I'm going to help you."

CHAPTER XLIV

Christmas 1908

"WE'RE OFF TO Munich. Let's not miss our train." This trip had been planned for weeks. The two families would meet at Markus' mother's apartment, have tea, and from there, walk to the Marianplatz and the Winter Market. It was December 21, 1908, three days before Christmas Eve and the third day of Hanukah, which started on the 19th that year, and everyone was looking for that last present.

The Winter Markets had a long tradition, evolving through a thousand years from medieval times. While these festive markets had a decidedly Catholic holiday atmosphere, there were so many secular booths and stalls that the Jewish Levi family always felt it was more of a German tradition than a Catholic celebration. They came several times each season, particularly for the many holiday musical programs. This year was no exception.

"We have tickets to the Mahler Symphony this evening!" proclaimed Otto Levi. He had conspired to secure tickets to Gustav Mahler's Seventh Symphony for both families. It had had its premiere performance just two months earlier in Prague, for the sixty-year reign and celebration of the Austro-Hungarian Emperor Franz Josef.

There were thirteen tickets purchased in all, for each member of both families, including the Obermaiers, their two boys, and Tante Berti, who came down from Potsdam for the holidays.

"Isn't the Winter Market enchanting," Frau Mathias said to the other two senior women. "I just love the smells and the lights and all... My dear husband loved it so."

Frau Levi squeezed her hand in sympathy as they strolled by street musicians, sellers of hot wine, and dozens of vendors selling Christmas candles, ornaments, lace, and hand-knitted scarves. Dinner at the King Ludwig Hotel, always sumptuous, featured a special holiday offering of roast stag.

"The Seventh Symphony was just marvelous, Papa. Thank you!" Levi said. Everyone agreed, and a toast was made to everyone's good health.

"I'm so happy to see my family again, and to see my younger brothers growing into their teens," Kathi said the next day at breakfast. With the Obermaiers staying at Kalvarianhof, the large old home resounded with chatter, laughs, and wonderful smells from the kitchen. No one noticed Ilsa's slight listlessness, her usual exuberance much diminished, no one except Levi.

When he had the opportunity, Levi took her hand in the upstairs hallway and guided her into the music room. He quietly closed the door. Ilsa walked to the window and looked out at the new fallen snow in front of the manor house. The trees looked black against the undulating blanket of untouched whiteness. She was expecting someone to notice...at least that's what Katherina had warned her would probably occur. "You can't hide your feelings completely," she said.

Earlier, Ilsa had prepared for her brother's concerned inquiry. She turned to face him as he asked, "Is something wrong, Ilsa? You haven't seemed to be yourself these last few days. What's the matter?" His voice was kind and full of empathy.

"Really?" she said matter-of-factly. "Everything's fine...well, except…" She turned her head away. "I've had several days of mild discomfort…lady's troubles." She tried to act slightly embarrassed. "It's nothing, just part of…"

"Oh, yes, of course," Levi quickly interjected. Now he felt awkward. "I'm sorry. I was just a bit concerned about my little sister." He tried a smile. She stepped up to him and gave him a hug.

"You're such a good, kind-hearted brother, I love you so. But you know, I'm a woman now, with all that life brings with that."

"Yes, yes, of course." He hugged her back and held the hug a moment.

"Let's join the others downstairs," she offered.

Katherina was preoccupied with her parents and her two brothers, Moses and Benjamin. Markus' mother, Levi's parents, and the Obermaiers spent the evening exchanging tales about their children and politics and the changing times. Levi, Ilsa, Markus, and his sister Anji spent the evening talking university and the latest cultural events in Munich including the sensational exhibition of Vladimir Kandinsky and a new group of artists called Expressionists.

"It's all about feelings and what you feel about things," Anji began. "It's not so much about how things look in real life. They think color has feelings and so they use it to express emotions."

The conversation was carried along by Anji and Levi mostly, with a comment here and there by the other two. Markus glanced at Ilsa often, but she rarely returned the look. He tried without success to get Ilsa's attention long enough to plan a meeting. He sensed the tension between them and held himself responsible for the night of passion that he now supposed Ilsa regretted. He felt guilty and yet, having had other experiences with women, he knew deep down that Ilsa had been very willing to participate in their lovemaking.

He was torn between guilt and desire. He loved her; at least he thought he did. He had examined his feelings earlier. It was more than lust, more than that lovely body and all it offered him. She captivated him, and he thought she felt the same way. However, now she was unresponsive to his signals, his gestures. In frustration, he excused himself for a few moments of solitary thought in the toilet room. Later, Markus finally whispered a desperate plea.

"Meet me in the village *bierstube* next to the train station, tomorrow after lunch, about two. Please!"

Early the next morning, after a night of restlessness and little sleep, Ilsa, overcome with guilt about avoiding Markus while longing to see him, was moved to call him at his parents' apartment in Munich. She went downstairs to the front entry hall where the wooden telephone hung on the wall. She cranked the lever and gave the operator the Mathias number in Munich. Frau Mathias answered the phone and was surprised and delighted to hear the young woman's voice. Ilsa was both relieved and disappointed in hearing that Markus had stepped out to do some last-minute Christmas shopping with several of his army buddies.

"Would you please give Markus a message for me, Frau Mathias?" Ilsa hesitated a moment to collect her thoughts.

"Yes, what is it, my dear?"

"Please tell Markus that I can't meet with the group tomorrow afternoon, as we are celebrating Hanukah. I can get together with everyone in a few days. Please thank him for inviting me. Good-bye, Frau Mathias, and Merry Christmas to you and your family."

"Thank you, Miss Levi, and a Merry Christmas to your...or should I say Merry Hanukah?"

"Happy Hanukah is the usual expression, Frau Mathias."

"Yes, well then, Happy Hanukah to you and your family. It was such a pleasant evening with Mahler's music and dinner with everyone and all the wonderful conversation. Good-bye now."

Ilsa placed the earpiece of the phone back on the hook, next to the crank. A tear rose in her eye as she thought about how sweet Frau Mathias was.

Katherina had been watching Ilsa closely. She was concerned that Ilsa would not hold up to the entreaties of Markus. It had to be difficult to be young and in love with someone, especially after having intimate relations with him…and now to let him go, to walk away from someone she truly loved. That had to be devastating.

Finally, Katherina suggested that Ilsa get away for a while, possibly to an aunt or to cousins in the country near Schliersee.

Ilsa did not warm to that suggestion. "What would I do at one of my relatives'?" she speculated. "After the usual conversations, they would all wonder what I was doing there. Too many questions!" The two women were in the music room sitting on the couch, each with a book in her hands. It was mid-afternoon, and already lights were turned on, as the sun had passed below the horizon out beyond the dark forest surrounding Kalvarianhof.

Finally, Katherina sat up and placed her hand on top of Ilsa's. "I've got just the solution, dear sister." They turned their heads toward each other. Ilsa, with reddened eyes, looked up expectantly. "Why not go home with my parents, and I will go along, too. I've wanted to go to my parents home again for a while to see my relatives, and it would be a perfect solution for you. Mama and Papa would be thrilled. They won't need much of an explanation either. You can return in a week or so…whenever you like!" She paused. "What do you think?"

Ilsa looked into Katherina's eyes and thought for a few moments.

"Yes, let's do it! But in your condition, I mean the baby…"

"Oh, I'm fine, and I'll be back in a week or so. I'll convince Mama and Papa."

There was little concern among the Levi family with Ilsa and Kathi accompanying the Obermaiers home to Potsdam. It seemed like a kind gesture and, of course, the Obermaiers were thrilled. They even called home to the housekeeper, to arrange everything for the additional two family members.

New Year's Eve was awkward, but both Ilsa and Markus got through the holidays by being friendly, formal, and seldom alone with each other for more than a few moments. Markus, perplexed and hurt by Ilsa's abrupt coolness, believed she just needed time to be alone, to come around again to a closer relationship. Ilsa, on the other hand, simply wanted to get through the holiday week without running to Markus.

She told herself that she just wanted to tell him how much she loved him. If it wasn't for Katherina's support, Ilsa felt she could not endure this tragedy. Many a private tear streaked her cheeks before she departed Kalvarianhof.

Levi, usually very sensitive to the undercurrents in the family, seemed oblivious to the emotional storms in Ilsa and Markus' lives, but he was soon confronted with the tragic events unfolding in his sister's life.

CHAPTER XLV

The Letter Unfolds Before the Crash

THE DAY OF departure for the Obermaiers arrived.

"Good-bye, everyone! We'll take special care of Katherina now with a baby on the way."

Papa Levi hugged his daughter, and his wife handed Ilsa a basket filled with fresh rolls, butter, and several varieties of sausages. "For the train," she said.

Both the automobile and a carriage were loaded with baggage and people. To save space, Levi was the only family member to accompany those departing. Young Willi drove the carriage. The train was on time, tickets purchased, and there was another round of good-byes.

"See you in a week or so!" Levi hugged his sister. He didn't notice the tear on her cheek. She did not want to let him go. He kissed Kathi good-bye and whispered gently, "Now take it easy. No heavy lifting, don't get overly tired or excited, and come home soon."

"Yes, yes, my dear."

Katherina had struggled within herself as to how much to tell her husband before departure. She finally decided to say nothing about his sister's affair with Markus, letting events reveal themselves in due course. Just as the train bell clanged and the "All aboard!" was announced, Kathi handed Levi a letter, to be delivered to Markus, at the train station *bierstube* after the northbound train departed for Potsdam. She ended with, "I'll explain everything later, my dearest; just be patient as you always are." With a quick kiss, and "I'll see you in a week," she turned and stepped into the wood-paneled first-class compartment.

Levi looked perplexed as he held the stiff cream-colored envelope in his hand and said, "Markus, here?"

"Yes" was her only reply.

The train pulled out in a cloud of smoke and steam, and the two young women leaned out the rolled-down window, waving. Levi was brought back to the excitement of the moment, smiled at the two women, doffed his hat, and returned their waves.

He stood there a long time in the noonday haze, watching the train grow smaller and smaller and thinking about what his wife said. She'd explain everything later, he told himself. They always talked about everything. What could this be about?

He looked down at the envelope in his hand and for the first time recognized Ilsa's handwriting. An apprehensive feeling flooded his body. A swarm of half-remembered places, events, comments, gestures, and looks swept through his mind. Ilsa and Markus were in all of them.

He examined the envelope again, closer this time, turning it over in his hand. He was half tempted to open it.

No, that was out of the question.

"What is going on?" he said aloud. Had he been blind to something?

If there was something going on between the two of them, why didn't Katherina tell him? She said she'd explain everything later.

So there was something to explain…and he was beginning to see what it was. A frown creased his face. He turned his body away from the frosty breeze and slapped the letter against his pant leg.

He'd told Markus not to get involved with Ilsa. He distinctly remembered telling him it would not work; it could not work…that's what he'd said. And now this! He looked at the letter again as he walked back toward the station house; his eyes darted back and forth as his mind explored unpleasant possibilities.

"This better not be as bad as I think it is," he said under his breath. "I know Markus and women!"

He entered the small waiting room, its coal-fired potbelly stove radiating warmth. He opened his coat and pulled out his pocket watch from his vest pocket. One thirty-five. He glanced up to the large clock on the wall: one forty. He advanced the minute hand five points on his twenty-four-hour timepiece. She'd said to meet Markus at the *bierstube* after her train left.

He'd better get over there. It was only a short walk out the station door and several buildings over to the rustic railway restaurant. He walked into the smoke-filled, overheated drinking establishment and stamped the snow off his boots. With its loyal group of locals and young students from the newly created flying school a quarter mile away, the little *bierstube* did a surprising business.

It took a moment for Levi's eyes to grow accustomed to the dim light, but he quickly recognized his friend. Markus was sitting across the room, in a half booth with his back to the door. Several chairs were on the opposite side of the table, on which sat a clear beer mug fully filled with the golden liquid.

As he hesitated a moment looking at Markus, Levi realized he had not thought through what he would say or, more importantly, what his attitude should be…or what it *was*, for that matter. He really didn't know enough to know what to do. Better he just deliver the letter and go from there.

He walked over to the heavy wooden table and sat down.

Markus was shocked to see his friend slide into the chair across from him. He quickly looked around for Ilsa.

"She's not coming, Markus," Levi said, watching the expression on his friend's face. "She and Katherina and the Obermaiers just left for Potsdam on that last train. They'll be gone a week or so."

"What? Levi, I…we…" His face grew ashen. "Why isn't she here? She agreed to meet me," he said in a broken voice. "We were…"

"Here," Levi interjected, pulling the letter out of his coat. "I was asked to give this to you. I only received it myself as the train was pulling out. It's all I know about…" he searched for the right words, "about your relationship with my sister."

Markus reached out and took the letter, almost as if it were some dangerous, frightful thing that could only lead to pain and despair. He held it with both hands and looked at the front of it for a long time. Levi could see his hands trembling.

He had never seen Markus in such a state of painful anxiety, not even in the worst situations in China. Levi was confused and torn by his mixed feelings. Between a rising sense of anger and what… sympathy, empathy? It was almost like the feelings he had in China, seeing the withering bodies of Boxers on the ground, injured and dying, scratching and clawing in the dust at their mortal wounds. Fear and hatred gave way to compassion for the dying Boxers, seeing other human beings in such hopeless straits.

Now the letter was in the hands of the recipient, and those hands slowly tore open the envelope, his finger poking and pushing, creating a jagged opening. He could smell her intoxicating perfume rising, as if in a dream. He pulled the single folded sheet out into the light. Levi thought it best to leave Markus to read his sister's letter alone, and began to rise. Markus' hand swiftly crossed the table to Levi's arm.

"No, don't go. I…I want you to stay." His companion settled

back down into the chair and sat quietly. Markus flipped open the letter with his thumb and began to read.

My dearest beloved:
It has taken all my courage, all my strength to pen this farewell note to you.

Markus stopped reading. He was holding the trembling letter with both hands resting on the table. He dropped his head low for a moment, not looking at the note, and continued with tears brimming up.

I know you love me as I love you, but we both know this cannot be. My rabbi wouldn't permit it nor your priests, nor our parents and families. It's my fault, I know it is. I led you on; I came to you in the night. And now God is punishing us both.

I am so sorry for the pain I have caused you. I cannot understand why this is bad, why it is forbidden. I know in my heart what we had, our love, was the purest, sweetest experience I will ever know in my lifetime. Please don't be sad for long, we must go on with our lives, but separately.

I will be gone for a while, up north in Prussia, in Potsdam, with the Obermaiers. Kathi is coming with me, or I would never leave. I am so fearful that your long friendship with my dear brother will be hurt by our now, past relationship. I will do anything to help repair the damage I have done to my two most cherished men (not counting Papa).

Please do not come north to me. I could not bear it right now. They say time heals all wounds. I pray it's true. Goodbye, darling. We will meet again, but it must be different.

Ilsa

P.S. Only Kathi knows. I didn't tell Levi.

Markus didn't realize tears were streaming down his face and his nose was dripping into his lap. He half crumpled the letter, then released it onto the table, where it sat heavy as stone between them. Levi had been intensely watching his friend as he disintegrated emotionally before his eyes. Markus stifled a moan and dropped his head into his crossed arms on the table. Several locals and pilots had taken note of the upset stranger in the booth and tried not to watch, but took furtive glances at the two men.

He finally spoke. "She's wrong. It's my fault. You were right. I never should have let it go on…to this." His head was swaying back and forth. His hand and forearm wiped his nose. He fumbled for his handkerchief.

On hearing Markus' comments, Levi grew apprehensive and asked, "To what? You never should have let it go on to what?"

Markus, regaining a bit of composure, stopped and looked at Levi. "You really didn't know, did you?" He slowly pushed the crumpled letter across the table.

"You want me to read it?" Levi asked.

Markus said nothing, but closed his eyes and nodded in the affirmative. Now Levi looked at the letter before him before picking it up. He laid it back down onto the table and swept one hand across it to flatten it out. He began to read. Markus watched Levi's eyes move across the page, then drop down to the next line and repeat the process. He knew what was on almost every line, and waited for Levi's response.

Levi got to the line "I came to you in the night." He stopped. He read the line through several times. He took note of his sister's beautiful handwriting. He could smell her perfume. His eyes left the letter momentarily, and he stared at the floor.

Back to the letter, he finished reading it. He carefully, almost lovingly refolded the single sheet, reached across the table for the envelope, and slid the letter inside. Markus had been watching him and now accepted the letter back. They sat there in silence for a long time, not making eye contact.

Finally, Levi called to the bartender, "Schnapps!"

The man in a white apron came over with a bottle of Jägermeister and two glasses. He put one glass down in front of Levi and poured a shot. He looked at Levi without saying anything, and Levi nodded his head toward Markus. The barkeep put the second glass down and poured. As he turned to go, Levi told him to "leave the bottle." They both drained the shot glasses. Levi filled them again. He looked at Markus. "It's over. Done. You know that."

Markus, his face puffy with swollen eyes, nodded yes. "Levi, I am so sorry, I…"

Levi interrupted him with a silent gesture of "stop" by turning his head sideways and putting his hand up. Again, he said, "It's over."

They were silent.

"So what are your plans for the future?"

Markus hesitated a moment, collected himself, straightened his jacket, glanced around at the other patrons who were busy in their own conversations, and cleared his throat. "We, that is, Ilsa and I, were planning to go to Southwest Africa. I guess I will still be going there." Levi was surprised and startled to hear how the two had made such advanced plans.

Markus continued: "The army offered me officer rank to go to the colony and work on that wireless station they've been building…as soon as I finish my electrical engineering studies in a few months. And I want to finish my pilot's license here at the airfield. There's a rumor that King Ludwig is going to start a Bavarian Army Air Corps soon."

His voice strengthened as he focused on his future, momentarily distracted from Ilsa's letter. "At university we've been testing a portable wireless that can be installed in an aeroplane. But right now, it's too heavy for present aircraft. Either the aeroplanes have to get bigger, or the radio transmitter smaller. Our experiments and the technology are changing so fast, it's just a matter of time."

He stopped talking and stared at the center of the table. "It's going to be strange," he paused, "leaving everyone. I mean, when we all went off to China, you and I, we went together with the other guys. This is going to be different. I'll be going out there alone this time."

Between several more rounds of schnapps, Levi stared at his friend. He still had mixed feelings about the obvious affair Markus and his sister had. But after reading the letter and seeing how deeply and genuinely both of them felt, he couldn't help having a degree of sympathy for both.

"Well," he finally said, "here's to your future plans." He raised his schnapps glass. Markus did the same. "*Prost!*"

As the afternoon dragged on, the two men, such close friends from childhood, were brought back toward that close friendship. They talked about life, their lives, and their experiences abroad in those exotic foreign cultures with such different morals. Levi also could not help noting the parallels between Markus' love for Ilsa and his lost love, Li Ling. That relationship had also ended badly for Markus.

By late afternoon, having finished off the bottle and several rounds of beer, they were both drunk.

"Come on back to the house with me," said Levi. "You're not in any shape to go back to Munich. Besides, I have the Benz outside. You wanna go for a ride?" Arm in arm, they made their unsteady way out into the evening snow. After several awkward attempts at cranking the engine to life, the two drunks piled into the automobile. Gunning the engine, Levi throttled his father's car into motion, making a complete circle in the loading area in front of the train station, scattering several villagers in the process. Markus almost flipped out of the auto, but Levi grabbed his coat and pulled him back in.

They both thought that was funny.

Few vehicles, horse-drawn or otherwise, were on the narrow village lanes, or the dirt road leading through the woods to the manor house. The sting of the icy wind made Levi's eyes squint and water as he swung wide around curves, causing the Benz to sway back and forth down the dark forest road. Fortunately, hardly a soul was seen. Markus, in a stupor, slumped down in his seat in the open-air car.

Levi hardly knew what hit him when the auto slid off the road and into a pine tree. Snow, knocked off the branches from the impact, poured down and covered the car and the men several inches deep. Markus was out cold and sprawled on the ground, where he had been thrown by the crash.

Levi sat stunned, gripping the wheel for a few seconds, staring at the black, foot-thick trunk of a pine tree. He shook his head several times trying to clear his mind. He turned to check on

Markus. Gone! Fear gripped him as he struggled with the bent door, finally tumbling out. Picking himself up, he ran around the back of the Benz and saw Markus lying still on the ground several yards away.

"Markus! Markus!" he shouted and ran to him. Rolling him over in the dim light, he saw red blood on his face. "Oh my God!" He shook him gently. Several moans emanated from deep within. "Markus, are you all right?"

"Oh, what happened?" He tried to sit up. "Oh, my head." Markus raised his hand to the wound and looked at Levi. "Jesus, are you trying to kill me?" He fell back prone on the ground.

"I'm sorry, I'm sorry. Here, let me help you up. Are you hurt anywhere else?"

As the two men struggled to rise, Levi saw a light coming down the road from the house. Young Willi was coming with a lantern.

"We heard the crash. What happened? Oh my, he looks really

hurt. Let me help." Fortunately, the crash happened in the bend in the road just before the clearing and the house.

Otto Levi and the cook were trudging through the foot deep snow toward them. "Is everyone all right?"

Willi spoke up. "They missed the curve and crashed. Herr Mathias is injured."

With both men now on their feet, Levi on one side and Willi on the other, they supported Markus as best they could.

"Quick, get him to the house," Otto said. "Willi, soon as we get Markus to the house, take a horse and go get the doctor."

"Can't we call him?" asked Levi.

"No, the telephone has been out all day because of the storm."

Friedl had already prepared a bed of sorts in the middle parlor as it had the biggest sofa. She brought pillows, sheets, and blankets, and when she saw Markus' face in the light, after an involuntary gasp, she sent the cook to prepare hot water and towels.

"How bad is he?" she asked.

"Don't know, dear. Willi is taking a horse to get the doctor."

"Here, ease him on the couch. Be very careful of his neck," Friedl commanded. "Support his head."

She pushed a pillow under his head just as they lowered him. Markus was half-conscious and mumbled several times. The cook came back just as he began to throw up. Friedl grabbed the pan of water, dumped it into the potted palm, and quickly placed it so as to catch most of the vomit.

"Turn him so he can finish," she said forcefully.

Levi obeyed.

"Bring a fresh pan, please, Hildi." Friedl assessed the situation. "When the doctor comes, he'll need better light. Bring that lamp over here…and he will need a table for his things."

Everyone scurried around to fulfill Friedl's directives.

"Is Markus injured anywhere else?"

"I don't know," said Levi. "I don't think so, but…" He didn't finish.

The doctor arrived, examined Markus thoroughly, and determined that, besides the head injury and a few contusions, the patient was otherwise all right.

"With these head injuries, we never know for a few days if they are more serious than they look." Getting up from the chair next to the makeshift bed, the doctor continued, "We'll wait and see. He's going to have a real headache in the morning. I'll be back early…about seven."

The telephone rang later that evening. "Oh, the telephone's working again," someone said as Otto woke up from a doze and answered it.

"Hello, Katherina . *Ja, ja*, so everyone arrived fine, and you had sun? Wonderful…give my greetings to your parents. We enjoyed having them and the boys. Levi? Yes, he's here, just a moment.

"Levi, Levi, your wife is on the telephone. Here he is." Otto handed the earpiece to Levi.

"Hello, my love," Levi said quietly.

"Yes, hello dearest. We arrived on time; everyone was exhausted from the trip and went to bed, except me. I wanted to call you. Ilsa is holding up well, at least so far. A few tears in private. How did Markus receive the news, the letter?"

"Fine, fine…I mean…Katherina, there's been an accident."

"What? Who? Is anyone hurt?"

"Yes. It's my fault." His voice was cracking. Katherina knew her husband. He seldom got emotional.

"What, darling? Tell me."

"We had an auto accident…it was my fault…we were coming back home when I lost control, I was drunk…it was my fault, and now…" He was practically in tears. "If anything happens…"

"Drunk? You? Who were you with? It couldn't have been… Markus? You and Markus?"

"Yes, you see, we were drinking all afternoon…after I read the letter and…"

"You read the letter?"

"Yes, after he read it. Anyway, we decided he would spend the night here. We were driving back…I hit a tree. The doctor just left."

"The doctor just left? What did he say? How bad is…" she lowered her voice. "How bad is Markus injured?"

"He hit his head when he was thrown out of the Benz."

"Thrown out? Oh my God!"

"The doctor says we'll know in a few days if it's more serious than he thinks it is right now."

"Where is Markus now?"

"He's asleep. The doctor gave him something. He's in the middle parlor. Mama made a bed for him there. We'll move him upstairs tomorrow if the doctor says it's okay."

"Did he say anything? Was he conscious after the accident?"

"Yes, for a few minutes."

"A few minutes?"

"Yes…then he passed out."

Kathi clenched her fist and bit her knuckle. "Did he say anything?" she repeated.

"Yes." Levi was reluctant to say it. He wished he had said no.

"What?"

"He said, *Are you trying to kill me?*" Levi had tears on his cheeks as his voice crackled into the receiver. "I didn't mean it…but it's my fault, I was drunk and driving too fast in the snow."

There was a long silence at the other end of the line. Katherina's mind was racing to sort out a response to her traumatized husband. "Do you want me to come home, dearest? I can take the morning train home."

"No, no…it's just that if anything happens to Markus…"

"Markus is going to be okay. He's a tough, strong young man.

He'll recover, you'll see."

"Yes, I hope you're right." Levi's voice betrayed doubt.

"But don't tell Ilsa. I don't think she could stay away if she knew what has happened." There was silence again.

"What am I going to tell Ilsa if…"

"Don't think about that now, dearest, you don't know what's to happen." She paused. "I love you, my dearest. I wish I could be with you this moment."

"No, no, you have to stay and take care of Ilsa, for now. I'll call you tomorrow. What time is good?"

"I'd better call you, when I can be alone by the telephone."

"All right then, good night."

"Yes, good night, dearest…and get some sleep. Everything will be better in the morning."

Several days, lots of rest, and eleven stitches in his head brought Markus pretty much back to normal, or as normal as a young man can feel after losing his beloved girlfriend. His mother and sister came out and took him home, assuming the accident was the result of youthful recklessness. Levi took the train in to Munich, to Frau Mathias' apartment two days later. The two young veterans patched up their longtime friendship, with Markus again asking, "Levi, what should I do?"

"Your plan is a good one, and I think you should take advantage of the army's offer. Sure, you'll be gone a year, but that may be just what you need. Besides, it'll be good for your career."

**KING LUDWIG III OF BAVARIA AND OFFICERS INSPECTING
AN AEROPLANE.**

CHAPTER XLVI

Potsdam

ILSA SPENT THE week acquainting herself with the Obermaier family. Katherina took her around Potsdam, and to the magnificent Sans Souci Palace.

"It's a lot smaller than I imagined it to be, but so beautiful," Ilsa commented as they trudged through the snow-covered gardens.

"Yes, well, it was meant to be the summer retreat for Frederick the Great, and it was. Even closed up for the winter, it's really magnificent, isn't it?" Taking Ilsa's gloved hand, they walked along the ice crunchy garden pathways, bundled against the cold.

"The name, Sans Souci, means 'without a worry or a care in the world.' It's perfect for you, Ilsa, because you are beginning a new chapter in your life, and you're free of worries, right?" They both laughed a little.

"I hope so," Ilsa replied.

"Come. Let's see the magnificent golden Rococo sculptures at the Chinese Tea House."

Katherina and Ilsa stayed on an additional week, visiting Berlin several times. Of particular interest for Ilsa was Humboldt University, because Kaiser Wilhelm had approved the admittance of women to the University recently. Humboldt offered a highly re-garded Department of Medicine that Ilsa was particularly interested in. With encouragement from Katherina, Ilsa decided to ask her parents if she could transfer from Maximilian University in Munich, to Humboldt University in Berlin.

One of the first questions Ilsa received on arriving home, after asking to transfer, was:

"Tell me again why you want to transfer way up north to that University in Berlin? It wasn't clear to me on the telephone." Friedl Levi looked at her daughter with sad eyes. "You have such a won-derful university right here in Munich."

Ilsa's mother was obviously upset at this sudden request of her daughter. She kneaded the lump of bread dough more vigorously, stopping momentarily to sprinkle in caraway seeds as she thought about this major development.

"I don't like you living alone in a strange city. It's just not lady-like." She paused. "It's just not to be done."

She stopped her labor and turned toward her daughter.

"Besides, I'll miss you not being here for our little talks, and I just like knowing you're around the house." Her voice broke a little with this last comment.

"Mama, I won't be living alone," Ilsa said gently. "The

Obermaiers invited me to live with them. I'll simply take the train into Berlin four days a week. I'll be coming home frequently. I promise!" She was smoothing a thick pat of butter onto a roll followed by a dipper of honey.

"It's dripping. Here, put this towel on your lap. That's such a pretty dress."

"Besides," Ilsa continued, "it's the best medical program in the country. Papa said if it is what I really want, he will support me on this." She hesitated. "He said we need a doctor in the house, even a woman doctor…just in time for his old age!" She began to chuckle, and her mother's mood changed as she first smiled, thinking about her husband, and joined in with a light laugh.

"Your father! You can get him to agree to almost anything, young lady." Her mother laid the wooden stirring spoon down on the kitchen counter. "You already have almost four years at university here. Why start over?"

"I don't have to start over, Mama. Mr. Obermaier has contacts at Humboldt University, and he can arrange for me to transfer there with no loss of credit." There was a long silence.

"Mama, you and Papa can come visit me," she said lightheartedly. "We can have a wonderful time in Berlin…maybe we will see the kaiser!"

Friedl, feeling defeated, said, "I don't need to see the kaiser, or Berlin, for that matter. I just want to see my little daughter."

Ilsa got up and hugged her mother. "You will, Mama, you will."

Over the next few weeks, between several teary-eyed intimate conversations with her brother, and preparations for her move north, Ilsa had only one encounter with Markus. Levi arranged the meeting at Kalvarianhof, while the elder Levis were in Munich viewing a new phenomenon, the silent motion picture. Markus requested one last meeting before Ilsa left, and she reluctantly agreed. The several weeks since their last strained meeting had given them enough time to become slightly detached from their previous feelings.

Markus arrived soon after the dinner hour in early afternoon, and joined Ilsa and Levi in the front parlor. After a brief awkward few moments, and a discussion of the fresh pink scar on Markus' temple, which he ascribed to a minor accident, Levi said, "I'm off to the kitchen for some coffee. Join me later if you like."

Forty-five minutes later, the two ex-lovers strolled into the kitchen hand in hand. Levi had a sudden flash of anxiety at seeing the handholding, but was relieved when Ilsa slid into the bench next to him smiling. Markus sat across the table from them.

"We will always love each other," Ilsa began, "but in a different way than before. We will always be friends."

CHAPTER XLVII

Flight

ILSA OCCUPIED A spacious room at the Obermaiers' in Potsdam. Her enrollment was secured at Humboldt University in Berlin through Professor Obermaier's efforts.

"I can't thank you enough, Herr Obermaier. I'll always be grateful to you for your kind efforts on my behalf."

"Well, it's what we do for family, *ja*? Now study hard and make your parents happy." Ilsa enthusiastically applied to the medical school and was accepted for the autumn 1909 class.

In the meantime, Markus poured his passion into his flying lessons, such as they were.

Young men, about his own age and with modest flying experience themselves, taught him all they knew. One day, he invited Levi out to the cold, grassy airfield in the village to watch his first solo flight.

"As you know, Levi, this airfield we use is the parade grounds for King Ludwig III's cavalry regiment… It's plenty big enough for takeoffs and landings!"

The flying school attracted many young men from the fencing club that the two friends enjoyed. There was the same sense of chivalry, daring, and skill involved in both. Fencing, the very popular sport of dueling to draw blood, had parallels in danger and glory that flying offered. It easily drew in these young men, including Markus.

Lifting off the ground in cloth-covered wooden flying machines, with sputtering engines and leak-prone gasoline tanks, caused reckless youth to risk injury or death for the chance to soar like eagles across the countryside. There had already been several injuries, mostly in hard landings made by inexperienced pilots.

"So are you and your mechanics ready for your first solo flight?" Levi asked as the two men walked through hard-packed frozen grass toward the open-sided stable used as a hangar.

"We'll see!" replied Markus as he pulled his scarf tighter around his neck. Five aeroplanes were in and around the wooden structure, along with a completely crumpled-up wreck that was beyond salvaging. No two flying machines were alike, and only one was thought flyable that morning.

The development of flight was so new and experimental and changes so rapid, that new or modified aircraft rolled out of crude hangars every several weeks. Many of these experimental aeroplanes crashed, their sheer cloth skins and thin wooden struts tearing and splintering with every mishap. Most were repaired within days and sometimes hours. There was not a single aircraft company in Germany manufacturing aeroplanes in 1909.

As the two friends approached the hangar, Markus pointed. "That's the one I'm taking up today." He surveyed the field and the row of trees running along the far side. He turned and looked at the windsock on a pole near the barn hangar. "So I'll head into the wind on liftoff and head down the field toward the church steeple. Maybe Our Lady will bless my flight!" He chuckled.

"Who is that saint that loves the birds and animals, Saint... Saint...?" Levi asked.

"Saint Francis of Assisi," Markus responded. "You think I'll need his help?"

"Well, you have all those saints for just about everything. Maybe you could use one for flying, too." Both men were smiling.

"It's a good thing you're not Catholic. You would probably have to go to purgatory for demeaning our saints."

"We Jews have enough problems here on earth; we don't need a purgatory halfway to heaven." They both laughed again, each shaking his head.

"Markus!" someone shouted from the shadows of the hangar. "We got her running, and we cut the vibration down a lot with a couple of wire stretchers off the cowl." It was Theo, a mechanical engineering student and one of the volunteers. They were the erstwhile mechanics for the flying machines. "She should be fine, but remember to ease up on the choke just a bit if she sputters." He walked out of the hangar into the bright sunlight. As he wiped his hands on a rag, he looked up at the windsock. "Wind's picking up. You should probably take her up before too long. Never know about the weather." The weather, in fact, was mild for late March, foretelling an early spring.

"I should be back in fifteen or twenty minutes. It's pretty cold up there, even with the exhaust piped into the cockpit!"

Markus went inside the hangar with Theo and another young pilot, who was the official observer for the flight. "Levi, come on in and help push this baby out."

It was surprisingly light and Levi thought very flimsy. The four men lifted the tail and pushed on the wings to roll it into the field. He was used to carriages and farm wagons, built strong and sturdy. His father's Benz was solid and heavy. Everything on it was made of cast iron, steel, or brass. This machine was light and delicate, almost like a giant kite, like the little kites he flew as a child.

"It seems pretty shaky. Are you sure this thing will hold together with a man in it?" Levi was only half joking.

"Just watch, my friend," Markus said as he carefully stepped up onto the wing and slid into the wicker basket-like seat.

"We were running the engine a bit earlier so it's still pretty warm," Theo said as he walked around the wing toward the propeller. "She should start right up." He reached up and slowly rotated the propeller into position.

Markus adjusted his goggles, tightened his scarf again, looked back at the ailerons as he moved the stick to check their movement, and finally looked forward and gave a thumbs-up.

Theo, seeing the signal, braced his feet in the proper position and pulled down hard on the propeller. The engine coughed several times and died. "A little more choke!"

Markus looked down and made the adjustment. Theo stepped up to the propeller again and positioned himself as before. Receiving the signal, he pulled down hard and stepped away from the whirling mahogany propeller as the engine roared to life.

The observer and Theo each held onto a wingtip, waiting for Markus to signal release. Levi watched with fascination the entire procedure and stepped forward to help hold back the trembling machine. Markus gave the hand signal for release, and the aeroplane leaped forward, its tail fishtailing across the frozen ground as it sped across the grass. In a matter of seconds and in a very short distance, the plane appeared to jump off the ground and rise swiftly into the cold air. A breeze seemed to sweep the small craft sideways as Markus easily cleared the trees and headed toward the church steeple. Several people walking along the road that paralleled the field and a number of carriages stopped to watch the dramatic and unfamiliar sight.

What a marvel! Levi smiled, thinking about his friend high above the treetops. He must be thrilled to pieces to be up in the sky looking down on the world. It was an amazing achievement. Levi slapped his arms across his chest to keep warm, and the little plane seemed to almost disappear behind rooftops and tall trees at the far end of the field.

This is the perfect sport for Markus, thought Levi. He strained to see Markus' aeroplane reappear. Four or five minutes went by, and he had not returned. Levi was standing by himself, but now looked over to the observer. He was busy writing in a logbook and looking at his watch. "He should be coming back pretty quickly, shouldn't he?" Levi asked.

"He's got a good twelve to fifteen minutes of fuel left…depends on how high and fast he's flying," said the observer. He looked up from his writing. "They always want to stay up as long as they can, especially on their first flight. As long as everything's going all right, they're as happy as a bird." They both were looking downfield. "It's when a guide wire snaps or the engine starts to act up that they want to head home and put her down."

"Does that happen often?"

"Pretty much to all of them, eventually. Aeroplanes are new and just being developed, not like that Benz your papa drives around town. I'll bet a hundred engineers and skilled craftsmen worked on that Benz and its parts. We've got, what…three dozen volunteers who come in when they can, to work and fly. But in a few years this is going to be big business." He stopped talking and appeared to be listening intently, turning his head to catch any faint sound over the wind. "We heard King Ludwig is interested in what we are doing right here at this airfield," he said enthusiastically. "They say he wants to form up a flying corps for the army." He stepped forward a few steps and looked down the field toward the steeple. Without turning toward Levi, he exclaimed, "I'd be the first to join if the old king really does that!"

Levi and the observer, standing on the cold, frozen ground, fell silent and waited. After a short time, the observer spoke almost to himself. "He's got four or five minutes of fuel left." As he jotted something in the flying log, the wind caught the pages and ruffled them. "Wind's picking up," he said.

The two men turned their heads into the wind in unison. Heavy gray clouds had moved in, covering a quarter of the sky behind them.

"He should be back, right? I mean, how much fuel does he have?" Levi asked.

"They seem to always do this…fly until they're dry. That wreck over there," the observer nodded over his shoulder, "ran out of gas. Lucky he only broke his leg and cut himself up some."

"*Ja*, so, how much time does he have left?" Levi's voice was low and almost inaudible in the rising wind.

"I filled the tank myself, right up to the cap…so I figure he has a few minutes…but in this wind," he looked across the field at the swaying trees, "he's using up fuel fast. Just to hold her steady, it takes more fuel in this." He looked up into the sky again.

"He's not back yet?" huffed Theo, jogging up to the two men. "In this wind he should be coming in over the hangar. Hope he's not trying to come up from the far end. How much fuel does he have left, Franz?"

Franz, the observer, replied, "None."

"Should I crank the siren?"

"Let's give him a few more minutes…he might have been riding the currents a bit and saved fuel that way."

Levi was getting very anxious, remembering Mathias' near tragedy in the auto crash. He did not want to experience that again.

"*Ja*, it's time," Franz said with a certain finality. "Crank the siren."

"Oh, for God's sake!" Levi was pacing back and forth, craning his neck to see and listen, hoping to hear the engine of the fragile little plane.

The crank siren was used in emergencies at the airstrip to summon help from any pilots and mechanics who were within earshot. While an agreement had been worked out with the local fire brigade that the siren would be used for an aeroplane emergency and not a fire, a contingent from the fire brigade usually did come out to the hangar if not occupied elsewhere.

Levi heard, off in the distance, the clanging of the fire bell on the horse-drawn fire brigade wagon. Within five minutes, several men on horseback and two in a buggy pulled up near the hangar.

"Who's up? When did you last see him? What direction?" The buggy made a wide circle, the narrow wheels cutting the frozen grass as white puffs of breath filled the air with every snort of the horses. The buggy headed in the direction of the steeple, just as the fire brigade arrived with three men.

After a brief conversation the lead man said, "We'll circle around the park canal up past the old hunting lodge and then back beyond the tree line over there." He pointed across to the swaying trees. "It's easier in the winter. If they come down in the trees, we can find them easier." Climbing back behind the reins, he said, "He couldn't have flown too far, unless he traveled in a straight line." The heavy fire wagon made a slow circle in the frosty ground and headed off the field.

"What should I do? How can I help?" Levi pleaded.

Franz, the observer, said in a concerned voice, "Well, you could go on foot, but Markus could be in any direction, so that's not... Why don't you get your father's Benz? You could cover a lot more area that way."

"Yes, yes, of course. That's it." Levi started a brisk jog off the field, realizing it was a very long way home.

"Wait, Levi!" It was Theo. "Why not call your father and have him drive over here?"

"Yes, of course...do you have a telephone here?"

"It's in the hangar, in the little office room in the back. It's unlocked."

Levi headed for the hangar at a trot. Just as he entered, with Franz and Theo following, the telephone began ringing. Franz overtook Levi and disappeared into the office.

"*Ja*, hello. What? What? No? When? *Ja, ja*, he's here. Levi!" he shouted, but Levi was right behind him. "It's your father."

Levi grabbed the telephone earpiece out of Franz's hand before he could say another word.

"Papa? Papa, Markus is down somewhere in his aeroplane and… What? Where? When? Thank God! Did he crash? No? He's okay? No injuries? Ha! He had us all scared to death! We thought he crashed somewhere over beyond… What? No, no. I'll be home shortly… *Ja*, good-bye."

Levi placed the earpiece back on the cradle and slumped down into the swivel chair. Franz and Theo were waiting expectantly, but were relieved to see Levi's mood change to one of happiness and relief.

"He landed at Kalvarianhof, in a meadow just beyond the barns. My God! He had me scared."

"Kalvarianhof? That's in the middle of the woods. Is there enough open land to land an aeroplane there?" asked Theo.

"Apparently…I'm glad it worked out so well for Markus' first flight. And we don't have to scrap or repair another aeroplane!" Franz turned and looked out of the hangar. "Look at this storm coming in." The sky had completely darkened over, and a real wind was blowing. "Crank the recall, Theo. And then we'd better wheel those other two aircraft into the hangars. Want to help, Levi?"

After the two planes were covered, there were thanks, handshakes, and pats on the back, and Levi headed out alone across the hard ground in the direction of Kalvarianhof.

A strong wind whipped around him. He felt exhausted as he

trudged along, so grateful that Markus had landed safely. The wind and gathering storm caused tears to form in his eyes. As he neared the trees and hedgerow, he stopped and leaned against a fence post. His throat tightened inexplicably and he wiped a tear from his eye. He rested his head on his arm, which rested on the post.

If anything had happened to Markus, he said to himself. He pulled out his handkerchief and blew his nose. *But it all worked out, it's okay, Levi.* He was distracted momentarily by a carriage going by.

He thought again of Markus, and of how he felt about Markus' flying. The whole uncertainty of it, the danger. It was all very exciting, but it was a deadly serious business, this flying.

DAUGHTER

CHAPTER XLVIII

Ambitious Plans, Distant Fears

SPRING FINALLY ARRIVED with the smell of wet forest and with crocus and daffodils sprouting up, seemingly overnight. Katherina was large with child as April drifted into May. A June delivery was expected and all was readied in the dressing room converted to a nursery.

Levi was so happy to see his wife coming to a healthy full term this time, and with frequent visits, the doctor reassured the family that all was normal. Kathi was serene in her confidence and truly enjoyed this pregnancy. Markus had even presented the soon-to-be parents with a beautiful pram, chosen for its big wheels, well-suited for strolls down country lanes.

Ilsa made a special effort to return home each month and had promised her dear sister-in-law to be home before the delivery. Her separation from Markus grew less stressful as she delved into her new university studies and was fawned over by the Obermaiers, particularly Moses and Benjamin.

What an exciting time to be in university in Berlin. The imperial city was throbbing with life. The museums and cafes exhibited new and startling art. Revolutionary musical works were performed alongside the most beloved classical compositions. Intellectuals, writers, poets, philosophers, revolutionaries, and scientists of all fields were drawn to the vibrant metropolis. Scholars like Freud, Planck, and Einstein made frequent visits. The art and artifacts from the empire's colonies flooded into shops and museum exhibitions. Antique dealers did a brisk business in valuable antiquities spirited out of Mesopotamia, Egypt, and other exotic realms and from Germany's colonies. All this was at Ilsa's feet, and she absorbed the cultural offerings with relish.

Markus also advanced his skills in flying with new and more powerful and more airworthy aeroplanes rolling out of hangars at an accelerating rate. His electrical engineering studies consumed all his time not spent flying or advising modifications to aircraft. Although he saw less of Levi, with both men finishing their studies, their relationship had returned to a closeness reminiscent of their China days.

Levi enjoyed his mechanical engineering and architecture studies and was working on designs for railroad bridges as part of his graduate work. He had even worked on plans for the replacement of several antiquated rail bridges on the Munich-Augsburg line. It was the investment in that line by his Grandpapa Levi that made possible the purchase of Kalvarianhof.

With the soon-to-be completion of his studies, Levi was eager to find an engineering position that offered opportunities to advance his career. Imperial Germany was in a major expansion of its economy and its empire. This growth created potential jobs both in the country and in the colonies. With a baby due next month, Levi's top priority was to work close to home. He and Katherina agreed on that.

"Just because I'm having a baby doesn't mean I'll give up my archeological work." She was adamant. "I'll take a break for a few months, but don't think I'll sit home forever!" She looked down her nose at Levi. He had a big grin on his face, and she couldn't help smiling broadly back at him. "I mean it, I love my work and I won't stop."

"Of course you won't, my love. Now give your husband, soon-to-be-a-father, a kiss." They were in the kitchen alcove, at the big wooden table sitting side by side on the bench. She had her arm around him as she leaned her head on his shoulder. He reached under the table across to her bulging belly.

Kathi looked at him. "Can you feel our baby move? She kicks all the time now."

"She?"

"Yes."

"How do…"

"Her name is Rebecca."

The room was white, lacy white. Even Markus' gift pram was only slightly off-white, but the pillows and little blankets were as pure as snow.

"Oh, I just can't leave her be," Kathi said, bending over the crib.

"She's asleep, my love. Better you rest while you can. I'll stay with her for a while." It was the first time little Rebecca was in her own bed. The crib sat next to the door leading into her parents' bedroom, the room in which she was born on June 14, 1909.

So began a long, happy interlude in the Levi household. Rebecca was a healthy baby, Ilsa was a happy medical student, and Levi's parents, still healthy and hearty, were giddy with their grandchild.

"You're invited for an extended stay during the summer, Mama." Katherina had just received a congratulatory telegram and flowers and was enjoying a long, happy phone call from her parents.

Dr. Professor Adelmann and his wife sent a beautiful ancient Egyptian cartouche of the female pharaoh Queen Hatshepsut as a birthday gift to baby Rebecca. The professor also requested Katherina schedule an appointment with him at the university with the possibility of a lectureship in Middle Eastern Archeology for the fall term. Kathi had also heard from Dr. Professor Schellenberger that there was a possibility of another expedition in late 1910 or early 1911. The implication being that Katherina would be invited to participate as a principal archeologist.

"A lectureship at the University and maybe another dig!" she exclaimed in her animated way.

Life at Kalvarianhof was good, with farm prices steady, a continuing demand for milk, beets, cabbage, hops, cattle, and timber. All were products of the Levi holdings. Young Willi, the orphan farmhand, had taken on more and more responsibility, and he was now supervising other village farm workers.

Levi was feeling good about his career too, having just finished his university studies and having received several job offers from leading architectural firms. He was also approached by the military looking for engineers and architects for the vastly increasing colonial enterprises across Africa and the South Pacific.

"It's alluring to remember the beauty of the South Pacific and the potential to work on big projects in the four German colonies in Africa," he told the family, "but I really want to stay close to home." Kathi smiled at him from across the room.

"Kaiser Wilhelm has an ambitious plan to expand the railroads here in Germany, and that means plenty of work for bridge builders and the like." He smiled to himself, hesitated a moment, and continued. "It's really for the military, I mean the railroads. He fears France on the west and Russia on the east. He has a point." Levi was looking at his father in the overstuffed chair in the front parlor. Mama and Kathi were sitting nearby with little Rebecca.

"He remembers that France invaded Germany twice in the last one hundred years, first Napoleon and then that other, that Napoleon the Third in 1870. You were in that, Papa…and Markus' father was wounded by the French." Otto nodded his head as Levi continued.

"The kaiser is building rail lines that lead directly to our borders so he can move troops quickly if need be. It's not bad insurance and it makes lots of work for us builders."

Otto Levi had sat quietly, listening to his son. He finally spoke up.

"You haven't mentioned our eastern border. We're building rail lines to the edge of our country in that direction too, and again, it's for the troops. Some of those expensive rail lines end up at small farm towns, but on the border. It's not about commerce." He took a pull on his pipe and blue smoke puffed out of both his nostrils. The smell was sweet and pleasant.

"Remember the Crimean War, just fifty-five years ago or so? The British and French wanted to stop the Russians from expanding their empire westward and southward to warm water. It was a threat to the British Navy, and therefore her empire, and to French interests too. So they fought a war over it." More smoke puffed from his nostrils.

"Our kaiser feels the same threat from Russian expansion westward today, especially since the czar of all the Russia's, annexed Finland and other lands......and now has a mutual defense treaty with the French, I'm told. And they're right on our eastern border!"

"Now Otto, don't get too worked up over politics. You can't do anything about it," admonished his wife, Friedl. "And besides, it doesn't affect us."

"Yes, well, it doesn't affect us now, but in the future?" Otto shrugged his shoulders.

IMPERIAL GERMAN SHIP THE LIGHT CRUISER SMS KONIGSBERG.

CHAPTER XLIX

Bye to What Was

ONE DAY IN late summer, Markus telephoned. "I've got an announcement to make, and your family is my chosen audience!"

Levi invited his friend out to Kalvarianhof for dinner. Markus arrived in his new custom-tailored officer's uniform, with warm greetings by Otto.

"Come in, my boy. Don't you look smart? Congratulations on your promotion to officer."

Markus Mathias was now officially an electrical unit officer of the First Bavarian Army Corps, for Lower Bavaria, with headquarters in Munich. His hand-tailored uniform was a perfect fit, a tradition of the more wealthy military families who could afford finer cloth and finer craftsmanship than government-issue uniforms. His spiked helmet gleamed, with its silver helmet plate depicting the Royal Bavarian coat of arms. His gray tunic, with red piping down the front and the same red piping down the outside seam of his trousers, terminated in knee-high black riding boots brought to a shiny polish by his assigned officer's assistant. It was the equivalent of a manservant in civilian life, except in this case it was an enlisted man of corporal rank.

Markus' Iron Cross First Class and his Iron Cross Second Class were pinned to his uniform as per regulation. On his light gray shoulder straps was the newly authorized Electrical Services device of forked lightning bolts in gold.

Otto Levi ushered Markus into the front parlor, where Levi was bouncing his daughter on his knee. Katherina, radiant as ever, sat next to him on the couch. Friedl was nearby, busy knitting something in pink wool.

"Markus!" Levi exclaimed as he handed Rebecca to his wife. "Oh, very impressive! I see you've got your new uniform…and all be-medaled yet."

"Yes, and you have one of these, too." Markus pointed to his Iron Cross Second Class.

"Yes, well, it's in a drawer somewhere since I don't have a uniform to put it on," Levi retorted.

"I'll see what I can do about getting you one, if you like." Markus had a big grin on his face and they both laughed.

"No, I think not. I'm a happy civilian engineer. That's the way we like it." He looked over to Katherina.

Kathi got up with the baby in her arms and greeted Markus warmly, and Markus cooed for the baby and then greeted the senior Frau Levi with a kiss on the hand and a click of his boots.

Friedl offered: "Do sit down, Markus, and join us. What news do you have for us today?"

Everyone settled into the comfortable furniture as Hildi, the cook and housekeeper, brought in a tray of wineglasses and two bottles of Rhineland Riesling. Markus had pulled up a straight-back cushioned chair. "*Ja*, well," he began. "I received my orders, and they are as I requested. I ship out to our colony in Southwest Africa in ten days. That's when the light cruiser SMS *Königsberg* sails. I have to be in Hamburg in one week. I'm taking the train up in a few days."

"So soon? Oh, Markus, we will miss you terribly," Kathi said with genuine concern.

"I know we've talked about your going down to Southwest Africa for a year of duty, but this makes it all too real, my friend. What are you going to do without us?" Levi asked.

The whole room broke out in peals of laughter.

"Yes, well, I'll manage somehow, but if I get into real trouble I'll send for you!" More laughter.

Kathi joined in the joking: "Don't worry, Markus, I'll send him right along to you, just telephone!" Now more laughs.

"As a matter of fact, Katherina, you are not so far off the mark. I'm going there to help expand our wireless radio transmitter. It's a powerful setup and can actually broadcast and receive messages from our colonies and ships in a huge region of the South Atlantic and a big chunk of Africa." He was looking at Kathi, but his eyes darted to all the others in the room. "And, through relays we can send messages all the way back to Berlin." Everyone was duly impressed.

Otto spoke up with a twinkle in his eye. "We will all stay by the telephone for your call, Markus." Again everyone had a grand laugh. "Now to dinner!"

A few days later Markus arrived at the military transit base in Hamburg with several other officers and was quartered with them. They were all shipping out to the African colonies. Markus had several days before the SMS *Königsberg* sailed and took advantage of his free time to tour the ancient bustling port city. His billet was changed several days later to quarters on the *Königsberg*. As he left the ship one morning, he noticed with special interest three long crates on the dock with markings labeled "fuselage." He smiled as the crates were hoisted on board the ship. "Aeroplanes!"

After much soul searching, he had telephoned Ilsa from Munich several days earlier. Somehow, he wanted to both reestablish contact and at the same time to finalize their relationship. At least that was what he thought at the time.

She was surprised to hear from him and was cool and unemotional in most of their long conversation. She felt his voice pulling at her heartstrings and at the same time knew it only meant more pain for her, and for him. Yet, he was truly leaving, knowing his going was because of their ill-fated relationship. She felt a pang of guilt and pity, a pain for what was lost, and a knowledge that it could never be. They both tried to explain, tried to convince the other that what they had had was wrong, or at least unworkable, and that what they were doing now was right.

The conversation stirred up past emotions, and Markus felt at the time that maybe he shouldn't have called Ilsa. There were long silences on the telephone, each sensing the other's distress.

"I'm sorry. I'm sorry I loved you," he said finally. "I'm sorry I pursued you 'til you came to me in the night. I should have been stronger. It's my fault, the pain I caused you. I'm older. I've had more experience in life. I'm truly sorry, Ilsa."

Tears were streaming down her face, but she was able to maintain some control. "It was no one's fault. It's just the times we live in. It could not be…so now we are both moving on, as it should be. You will always have a special place in my heart and in my memories, but now you are going away as I have already left that life behind me. It was hard at first but the busyness of life seems to push pain away."

She had stopped and listened. There had been silence for a long time with only a faint sniffle to be heard.

"Are you going to be all right, Markus?" she said and hesitated, then answered her own question. "Yes you are, my dearest friend. What an exciting life you will have in Africa! Think of it!" Her last comment broke the somber mood, and the telephone conversation turned into a completely different exchange. They talked additional minutes, ending on a decidedly upbeat tone, of wishes for happiness and success.

"And we agree we'll see each other again next year at Kalvarianhof!" That was the final, healing thought Markus was seeking. Relaxing during his last days in Germany, he reflected on his lost loves, both for Ilsa and Li Ling.

Ahead lay the vastness of Africa—a new beginning, full of unknown adventures, hope, and love—titanic dangers unforeseen, and World War I.

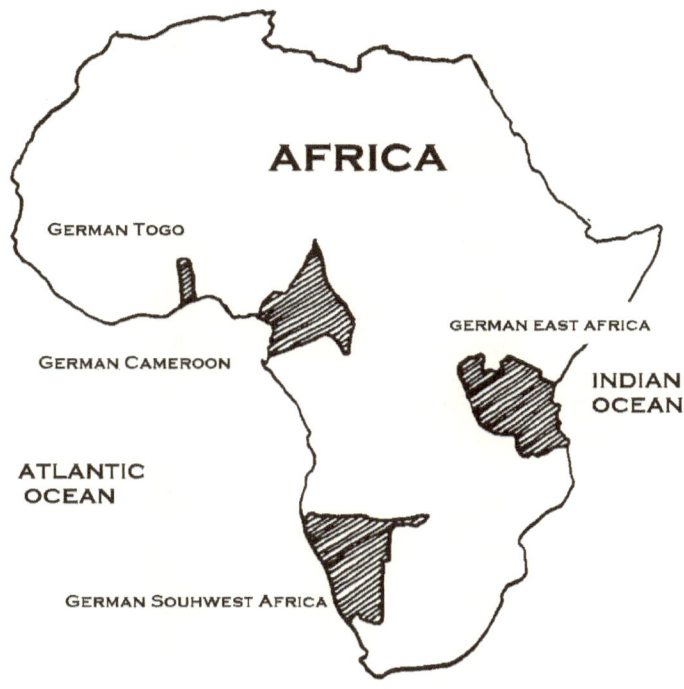

IMPERIAL GERMAN COLONIES IN AFRICA 1909

Lists of Historic and Fictional Characters

Historic Characters

Lieutenant Angelo Olivieri, Commander of the Italian Bersaglieri

Corporal William Gregory, British Royal Marines

Sir Claude MacDonald, British Minister to Peking

Baron August von Ketteler, German Diplomat

Captain Hall, United States Army

Sub-Lieutenant Henri, French Navy, Commander in Peking

French Bishop Favier, Rector of the Peitang Cathedral in Peking

Giuseppe, Amato, Italian Navy Medic

Facchinetti, Alfredo, Italian Navy Deckhand

Sergeant Saldinari, Italian Navy Quartermaster

Bugler Panelli, Italian Navy

Kaiser Wilhelm II, King of Prussia and Emperor of Germany

King Ludwig III, King of Bavaria

Sun Yat Sen, Chinese Revolutionary Leader

Reverend Stonehouse, Missionary in Peking

Major Shiba Goro, Japanese Imperial Navy Commander

Warrant Officer Okado Takitaro, Japanese Imperial Navy

Field Marshall Count von Waldersee, Imperial German Commander

General Chaffee, United States Army Commander

Prince Regent Leopold of Bavaria

Doctor Solf, Governor of German Samoa

Fictional Characters

Lancer Markus Mathias, Imperial German Army

Frau Fanny Mathias, Markus' mother

Anji Mathias, sister of Markus

Lancer Solomon Levi, Imperial German Army (called Levi)

Lancer Bauer, Imperial German Army

Sergeant Brandenburg, Imperial German Army

Captain Bernard Mayerling, German Commander in Peking

Count Molenofski, Russian Commander in Peking, cousin to the Tsar

Chou Lee, Aristocrat and Chancellor of the Imperial Observatory in Peking

Chang Pao Fu, Eunuch servant to Chou Lee

Wan Ling, father of Li Ling, scribe, artist, Chinese intellectual, revolutionary

Li Ling, daughter of Wan Ling

Norbert, German soldier

Günther, German soldier

Heiner, German soldier

Peiho, tavern owner

Otto Levi, father of Solomon Levi

Frau Freidl Levi, wife

Ilsa Levi, daughter

Rebecca Levi, baby

Ewald, gymnasium soccer player

Hilda, cook at Kalvarianhof

Willi, orphaned stable boy and farmhand

Doctor Rungi, village doctor

Marta, housekeeper to Dr. Rungi

Karl Obermaier, father of Katherina

Frau Britta Louise Obermaier, wife

Katherina Louise Obermaier, daughter

Moses Obermaier, son

Benjamin Obermaier, son

Tante Berti Obermaier, aunt

Doctor Adelmann, Professor of Archeology, University of Munich

Frau Ida Adelmann, wife

Jorg Haidler, expert archeological digger

Abdulla Mohammad Sidfardi, Master of Palestinian laborers

Doctor Schellenberger, Professor of Ancient and Mid-Eastern History

Levi (Obermaier) Genealogy

LEVI FAMILY GENEOLOGY

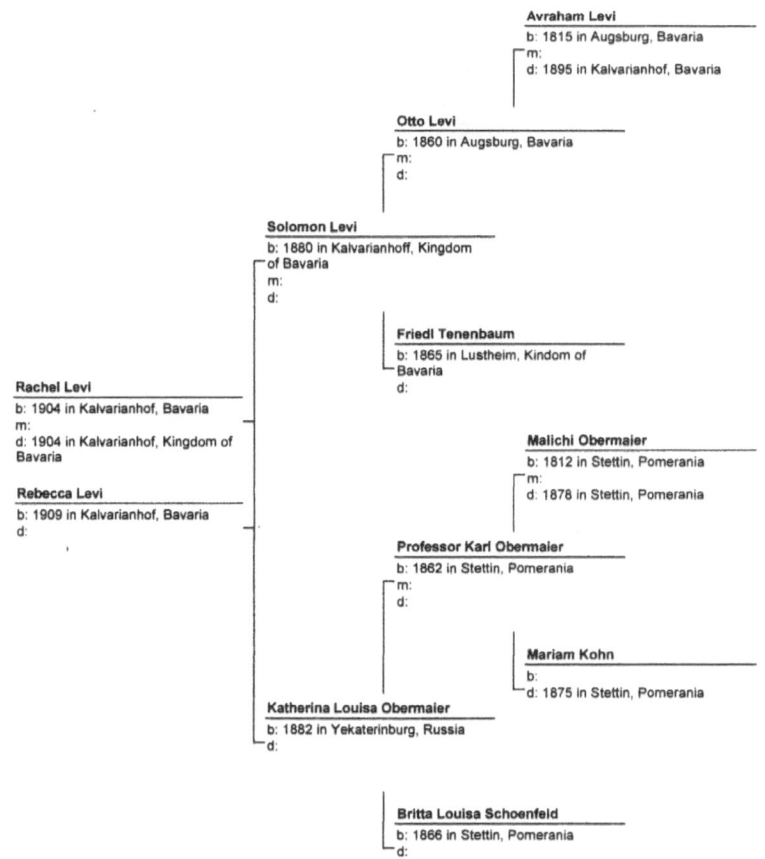

Avraham Levi
b: 1815 in Augsburg, Bavaria
m:
d: 1895 in Kalvarianhof, Bavaria

Otto Levi
b: 1860 in Augsburg, Bavaria
m:
d:

Solomon Levi
b: 1880 in Kalvarianhoff, Kingdom of Bavaria
m:
d:

Friedl Tenenbaum
b: 1865 in Lustheim, Kindom of Bavaria
d:

Rachel Levi
b: 1904 in Kalvarianhof, Bavaria
m:
d: 1904 in Kalvarianhof, Kingdom of Bavaria

Rebecca Levi
b: 1909 in Kalvarianhof, Bavaria
d:

Malichi Obermaier
b: 1812 in Stettin, Pomerania
m:
d: 1878 in Stettin, Pomerania

Professor Karl Obermaier
b: 1862 in Stettin, Pomerania
m:
d:

Mariam Kohn
b:
d: 1875 in Stettin, Pomerania

Katherina Louisa Obermaier
b: 1882 in Yekaterinburg, Russia
d:

Britta Louisa Schoenfeld
b: 1866 in Stettin, Pomerania
d:

Mathias Genealogy

Bernhard Mathias
b:
m:
d:

Captain Georg Mathias
b: 1850 in Munich, Bavaria,
Germany
m:
d: 1899 in Munich, Bavaria,
Germany

Markus Mathias
b: 1881 in Munich, Bavaria,
Germany
m:
d:

Fany Hildebronn
b: 1856 in Ismaling
d:

Anji Mathias
b: 1888 in Munich, Bavaria,
Germany
d:

Bibliography

Daniel, Clifton. *Chronicle of the 20ᵗʰ Century.* New York: Dorling Kindersley, 1995

FitzLyon, Kyril. *Before the Revolution.* Woodstock, NY: Overlook Press, 1978

Konstam, Angus. *Yangtze River Gunboats 1900–49.* Oxford: Osprey Pub, 2011

Tolley, Kemp. *Yangtze Patrol.* Annapolis, Maryland: Naval Institute Press, 1971

Ehrhardt, Ingrid. *Kingdom of the Soul, 1890–1920.* Munich: Prestel Verlag, 2000

Barzun, Jacques. *From Dawn to Decadence.* New York: HarperCollins, 2000

Inman, Nick. *Jerusalem & the Holy Land.* London: Penguin Company, 2007

Warner, Philip. *The Crimean War: A Reappraisal.* New York: Taplinger Pub., 1973

Embleton, G.A. *The Crimean War 1853–56.* London: Almark Publishing, 1975

Pick, Robert. *German Stories and Tales.* New York: Alfred A. Knopf Inc., 1959

Oliver, Douglas L. *Native Cultures of the Pacific Islands*. Honolulu: U.of H., 1989

Swinton, E.D. *The Defense of Duffer's Drift*. London: Octopus Publishing, 1990

Ellis, Peter. *Rider Haggard, Voice from the Infinite*. London: Routledge Paul, 1978

Barthorp, Michael. *The Zulu War*. Dorset, England: Blandford Press, 1984

Lewis, Jon E. *Eyewitness History 2000*. New York: Carroll & Graf Publishers, 2000

Fleming, Peter. *The Siege at Peking*. New York: Harper & Brothers, 1959

Wheatly, Weaver & McDowell. *The Boxer Uprising*. California: O.M.S.A. Pub., 2000

Harrington, Peter. *Peking 1900: The Boxer Rebellion*. Oxford: Osprey Pub., 2001

Preston, Diana. *The Boxer Rebellion, War on Foreigners*. London: Robinson, 2002

Stratemeyer, Edward. *On to Pekin*. Boston: Lee & Shepard Publishers, 1900

Shaughnessy, E. L. *China: The Land of the Heavenly Dragon*. London: Duncan Baird Pub., 2000

Hackenberger, Willi. *Deutschlands Eroberung Der Luft*. Berlin: Montanus Pub., 1915

For your pleasure, here are the first three chapters of book two, 'Kalvarianhof, The Storm That Shook The World', from the four book series of 'Kalvarianhof'.

KALVARIANHOF
THE STORM THAT SHOOK THE WORLD

CHAPTER I

German Southwest Africa,

Autumn 1909

SAILING FROM THE city of Bremerhaven, a major port for Imperial Germany, south, in a reverse route Markus traveled seven years earlier, the young Imperial German officer leaned on the familiar railing of a naval cruiser and watched the coast of France slip by.

The SMS *Königsberg*, loaded to the gunwales with supplies for Germany's four African colonies, plowed through late September swells bringing troops, military supplies, settlers, food and beer-- lots of good German beer--to the thirsty colonials in Africa.

Markus Mathias, newly-minted lieutenant of the German Emperor and King of Prussia William II, was bound for the Imperial German Colony of Southwest Africa. This was Markus' third trip to this wild and primitive land on the southwest coast of the Dark Continent. He enjoyed his first trip with his friend Levi in 1898 as teenagers on an adventurous holiday. His second, Christmas, 1900, was the coaling stop on the return of his military unit after the Boxer

Rebellion in China.

Now, in the autumn of 1909, this third journey was to be the start of a new life for himself after the tragedy of his lost love with Levi's sister, Ilsa. Yes, they agreed, both teary-eyed, that it could never be- -a Jewish girl and a Catholic man. Catholic Bavaria in general and their social and professional circles were not ready to accept a union so mixed, no matter how true the love. And of course, the families would have had none of it, if they had known.

So Markus, now twenty-seven, found himself alone on a long and important military mission, and for the first time, without his close friend Levi.

I've always relied on Levi to give me good advice and encouragement, and he had a way of tempering my more reckless impulses. This trip is different; I'll be alone and with some serious responsibilities. He thought of these things as he jostled other soldiers crowding the railing on a sunny, blustery day off the coast of France.

"Well, young man, what do you think of our ship? It's one of your navy's finest, I imagine." The speaker was a stout man with a quick smile, speaking in a heavily accented German and wearing a perfectly tailored civilian suit. Markus turned to respond to the hearty questioner.

"*Ja*, it is a fine ship, and fast, but these cruisers are being superseded by a new class of heavier more advanced design and with better armor." He hesitated, "And who, sir, do I have the pleasure of addressing?"

"Warner Lange, Professor Warner Lange", he cleared his throat, "from California."

They both blinked in the gusty wind. "And I see you are a captain... and with lightning bolts on your epaulets. You must be in some kind of communications outfit?" He looked expectantly at Markus, waiting for an answer.

"Yes sir, that's correct." Markus stood erect, clicked his heels and said, "Lieutenant Markus Mathias, Electrical Unit Officer of the First Bavarian Army Corps for Lower Bavaria with headquarters in Munich, currently assigned special duty to the Kaiser's colony in Southwest Africa." They nodded to each other in mutual recognition.

"So Professor Lange, what brings a professor from far off America… California you say, aboard a German cruiser heading for Africa?" It was an intriguing question, and Markus focused intently on the American.

"I have been invited by your government to assist in the upgrade and testing of the long range wireless telegraph installation in your Southwest African colony. So we are headed to the same destination…how interesting." They both eyed each other with growing professional interest. "And you, Lieutenant, what is your purpose in this long sea voyage to the southern hemisphere?"

"It appears we are both going to the same facility. I am bringing our latest wireless equipment for installment." There was a long pause as the two men, pressed momentarily against the railing, let other passengers through the crowded deck. Markus continued,

"You say you are from California? I just read about Marconi's radio broadcast from some little town over there. Very impressive!" he grinned and shook his head slightly before adding: "And exciting for the future of direct spoken wireless communication."

They both smiled broadly with the knowledge that it was indeed the future direction in their field.

"Well… Markus, is it? Markus, I've just come from that little town, it's San Jose, San Jose, California, and I was with my friend and colleague Gugliermo Marconi when he made that transmission. A wonderful scientific event! We were both teaching at the college there until he left to develop his business interests."

Lange stared out to sea. Markus, so impressed with the stranger he had just met, thought: *He's a friend and colleague of Marconi, and apparently he participated in the first voice radio broadcast ever!* He didn't know quite what to say. Warner Lange solved that by offering:

"Lieutenant, would you join me and my family for dinner at our table this evening? Say, seven? It's in the first class dinning salon. We can continue our conversation over a nice meal."

"It would be my honor and pleasure, Professor Lange." With that Warner Lange took his leave with a tip of his hat and disappeared into the crowd on deck.

Dinner was served separately in a dining salon reserved for civilian passengers and high ranking officers. It was a plush ornate room, with deep carpet, curtains on the windows and the dinnerware had the ship's own motif with SMS *Königsberg* prominent on each plate and bowl. Markus felt a bit on display as he walked very upright through the tables of military and civilians. Most officers, who looked up, immediately fixed their eyes on the two Iron Crosses on his uniform, earned by his daring actions in China.

He spotted Lange across the room at a round table for six. Two naval officers were already seated with the Langes. As he approached, Warner's eyes lit up, and he rose slightly as he greeted his new acquaintance.

"Lieutenant Mathias, glad you could join us. Dear, this is Markus Mathias, Bavarian Lieutenant, assigned to the same project I will be working on." All eyes were on Mrs. Dorothy Lange, a strikingly beautiful, willowy woman of about 40.

Next, Lange introduced his daughter, who was sitting with her back to Markus. He stepped to her side as she offered her hand as her mother had done. Diana Lange smiled but said nothing as the two naval officers rose from the table.

"Lieutenant, this is Captain Spencer, the chief medical officer on board, and Captain Becker, the Purser." Markus saluted and received salutes and greetings in return. Dinner was served and pleasant conversation was had around the table, when Professor Lange inquired,

"What can we expect when we get to port in Africa?"

The two naval officers commented that each had been to other German colonies, but not to German Southwest Africa.

"And you, Lieutenant, have any ideas?"

"*Ja*, well, this will be my third visit to this colony."

Thus began a series of lively questions from all around the table, after most were taken aback that such a young officer could have visited this far distant and impoverished corner of the world twice all ready.

Questions about Southwest Africa led to the *whys* and *wherefores* which led to Markus' experiences in China and finally to how he managed to receive two Iron Crosses, some of the most prestigious honors in the German military. The conversations were brisk and entertaining, and progressed long after most guests had left the dinning lounge.

Finally Mrs. Lange suggested it was time to retire. Everyone agreed, with chairs pushed away and cloth napkins dropped onto the table. Parting words were exchanged and everyone headed toward their rooms. Warner caught the cuff of Markus' uniform.

"Shall we retire to the bar for a final toast to our joint venture?"

CHAPTER II

Swakopmund and Windhoek,

GSWA

(German Southwest Africa)

MARKUS WAS SURPRISED to see how much progress had been made in developing the port and town, as the SMS *Königsberg* eased into a berth at Swakopmund. The railroad to the capital, Windhoek, had been completed and expanded to other parts of the colony.

Over twelve thousand German missionaries and immigrant farmers flowed into the back country fifty miles beyond the desert terrain of the coast for free land, and in the process, transplanting German culture to the wilds of Africa.

There was the usual excitement and confusion of disembarkation with piles of civilian luggage next to tons of government equipment. Warner Lange, followed by his family still aboard ship, managed to spot Markus and exchanged lodging addresses.

"We are staying here in Swakopmund for a few days to see the sights and get our land legs before moving on to the capitol next week. And you?" Lange was practically shouting because of the stiff wind howling around the superstructure of the ship. Markus replied in kind.

"I'm off by rail to the military base at Windhoek tomorrow morning. I'll be bunking here on the ship this evening, although I thought I would walk the town to see what's new. Can I help you with the luggage?"

"No, no, Lieutenant, but we are staying at that new hotel over there, the Bismarck. It's the building with the ladders leaning up. Join us for dinner if you like, about seven."

"That would be delightful, Professor. I'll see you then." He did a half salute with a smile to the two ladies and said, "Ladies," and left. Dorothy Lange, in her gracious and subtle way, said to her husband, after Markus left, "You seem especially taken by that young officer, dear. Could our daughter have anything to do with your interest in him?" Fortunately, Diana was peering over the side of the ship watching all the activities.

"Now Dorothy, the man's in my same field of work, and very bright...and you saw his two Iron Crosses. They don't give out those honors except for exceptional reasons. He wouldn't be a bad match for Diana." He hesitated and took his wife's arm, turning her slightly.

"Look at her, so lovely and smart. She's got a head on her shoulders, that girl, but she's already twenty-two!"

"Twenty-one, dear, twenty-one."

"Yes, for another eight weeks!"

"But a foreigner? You can't be serious. And we know nothing of his family."

"He's German. You can't beat that for a foreigner. They're some of the smartest people on the planet. Look how many successful Germans there are back home."

"That's my point, dear. They're back home." She finally added, "And there's that Andrew Hopkins. I'm told he's going into his father's business in San Francisco."

"Really?

"Railroads and banking."

"Are you sure about that?"

"Yes, dear."

Markus arrived at the Bismarck and found his way to the dining room while sniffing the fresh paint in the lobby. Black servers, obviously well trained by the hotel staff, and impeccably attired and with white gloves, were busy serving guests. He came up behind the professor and faced the two women across the table. "Greetings, again, *Frau* Lange and Diana. I hope you are well settled here in this lovely hotel." He did a quick sweep of his arm around the dining room.

"Professor," Markus nodded his head to him.

"Yes, Lieutenant, welcome to our little home away from home… very nice quarters."

He picked up the menus.

"Now let's see what they serve in one of the Kaiser's colonies, shall we?"

As everyone studied the menus, Markus related:

"The last time I was here in Swakopmund was Christmas 1900 on the way home from China. Governor Theodor Leutwein gave us a wonderful New Year's Eve party just down the street at Government House. The food and music and dancing were excellent. Everyone had a grand time!"

"You mean there were ladies to dance with here in 1900?" Diana asked. Markus delighted in answering the lovely young daughter of the Langes.

"Why yes, there were, but not enough of them." The Langes burst out laughing in unison. Flustered, Markus quickly added, "What I meant to say was that I was on a troop ship so there were a lot of men and they all wanted to dance, so the ladies were really put upon to dance most every dance."

He regained his composure and smiled broadly before adding, "My good friend Levi, who I served with in China was also with me. Our ship stopped in Uruguay, and we met a very nice family whose daughter, Katherina, was on her way to Berlin with her aunt, for her studies. She danced and danced, and it was all great fun. Levi actually married her several years later. They just had a pretty little girl." Warner Lange looked across to his wife who exchanged *the look*.

Markus was staring at the center of the table in a fixed way, lingering in his private thoughts. Diana looked at her mother. Finally, Dorothy looked intently at Warner. He caught the unspoken signal.

"Yes, well, an interesting story, and nice to hear everyone had such a splendid time. And your friend Levi, is it? You must be very happy for him and his family." Markus snapped back to the here and now.

"Yes, it's a wonderful family. They deserve all the happiness in the world."

"So let's order!" Lange said with a flourish, I could eat a longhorn!" The two women laughed while Markus looked puzzled. Diana spoke up.

"A longhorn is a cow, well actually a steer, and most of them are wild! You will find them in the West... of America. They have big, long horns, each one this long!" She stretched out her arms full length, almost reaching from her mother's shoulder to Markus.

"That must be some animal. I'll have to come to California and see one someday."

Mrs. Lange said, "Diana, put down your arms!"

"I was only showing *Herr* Lieutenant, I mean Lieutenant Mathias how big they were." Diana blushed in embarrassment.

"*Frau* Lange, your daughter has really quite a wide reach. Those cattle must truly have big horns." Everyone chuckled as their dinners arrived.

CHAPTER III

The Ranch,

The Hunter and The Huntress

THE NEXT FEW weeks found Markus settling into his quarters in
Windhoek, getting acquainted with the existing military staff of the
wireless station and uncrating the delicate wireless equipment. The
Langes also found their accommodations in Windhoek and Warner
and Markus began their collaborative efforts of installing and testing
the new equipment Markus had brought from Germany. Governor
Leutwein expressed great interest in the wireless station and its vital
military and commercial value by staying in close consultation with
Lieutenant Mathias and Professor Lange.

At one of the frequent long lunches held by the governor to discuss progress and technical problems of the wireless, several leading business men also attended. One of them was a large landowner,
rancher and an early settler in the Southwest African colony named
Tomas Conrad. After one of the luncheons, *Herr* Conrad invited the
Langes and Markus out to his ranch for several days of relaxation
and hunting.

The sprawling Conrad holdings encompassed several thousand acres of grasslands, salt pans, upland forest, a few year-round streams and, during the dry season, dry river beds. With several blacks in his employ, Conrad and his seven children lived as isolated landed gentry. Conrad was one of the lucky ones, or rather he got in early, got good land, and diversified his enterprises. Some of his fellow German farmers and ranchers weren't so fortunate in the harsh land.

"We raise cattle, some sheep, and the orchards do quite well for us. The railroad makes it easy to transport our livestock and fruit." Conrad was obviously proud of his accomplishments and of his family.

"We've just started doing a bit of mineral exploration up along the escapement."

As the four guests settled into overstuffed, slip-covered couches in the parlor of the ranch house, Tomas proceeded to introduce his seven offspring who had filed in. They were lined up as in a military formation but with bright smiles for their visitors.

"My oldest, Wolfgang, now twenty-six, Arnold, next twenty-five, Humboldt, twenty-four, Helena, twenty-two, the twins, Michael and Norbert, nineteen, and our little angel, Christiana, eighteen." Everyone exchanged greetings before several of the Tomas boys excused themselves.

"Always lots to do around here," Arnold said, staring at Diana, as he took his leave.

The two daughters stayed and were delighted that there was another young woman, Diana, to talk to. After many questions about ranch life, Tomas said,

"Petre, our houseman, will show you to your rooms. We dine at seven and retire early as we will head out just after sunrise tomorrow. The wagons, guns and equipment will leave at five, and your horses will be saddled by six. It should be good hunting."

Talk at breakfast was all about the hunt. Wolfgang began,

"We will be after antelope today, several types actually, but we may see elephants, zebras, giraffes and hyenas, lots of hyenas. If we're lucky, we may spot a desert rhino, the black one… that would be a bit of luck."

Michael added, "With real luck we may spot *die strandwolf.* Now that would be something!" He concluded with a grin.

"At least we won't have to worry about the Nile crocodiles, we aren't going as far as the river today." He chuckled at his own joke. Warner spoke up.

"You have crocs here? In the U. S., we have alligators, thousands of them, but not in California!" Everyone thought that was funny.

"*Ja*, I know about your alligators," Conrad said, looking across the table at Warner.

"But these Nile crocs are something else again. They get to eighteen feet or more, live for seven or eight decades, are surprisingly fast over open land and are man eaters. We always stay clear of them when we're down by the river. They take cattle, sheep, antelopes, anything that goes near the river." He looked serious and sounded serious.

"All the animals out here are dangerous in one way or another, including the wild dogs. We had a visitor to the ranch once who went out early one morning. He saw a wild dog and decided to feed it a breakfast roll. He came back with a bad bite on his hand... very lucky there weren't several other dogs. They would have taken him down, gone for the throat, and that would have been the end of it."

Michael added, "And that's not even mentioning the snakes!"

"Now, now, let's not scare our guests. No one in the family has had a bad experience with snakes."

"What about Mobuto? He…" Arnold spoke up but was interrupted by his father, who gave him an exasperated look.

"He wasn't part of the family."

After a morning blessing recited by a very devout Helena, the breakfast table was abuzz with chatter about the animals. The hungry hunters devoured fresh baked Kaiser rolls with honey and butter,

African coffee and an assortment of fresh fruit, sausages and hard boiled blue eggs.

"Everyone finished... good, let's saddle up."

The Langes and Markus were fascinated by the topography of the ranch--so different from California or Bavaria.

"You warned us it would be very warm out here in open land. You're right" Lange said, as he used is riding crop to swat off a horse fly on the mane of his mount.

They had been riding for over an hour, away from the tall trees and cool shade surrounding the ranch house. Markus was glad he now wore the cowboy-style hat with one side pinned up that the German army had issued to its African troops. The wide brim all around kept the blazing sun off his neck and out of his eyes.

Better to see the lovely Helena, with a silver crucifix rising and falling with the rising and falling bounce of her white blouse.

Their horses trotted through the vast grass lands that swept to the distant shimmering blue gray hills miles distant. Diana, obviously an expert rider like her mother, rode on the other side of Helena. The entire Conrad and Warner families and Markus were riding out, but only several were actually to hunt. The rest would stay in the day camp already set up for them before dawn.

Tomas and Warner lead the twelve riders plus three black rifle bearers. The tracker was several hundred yards ahead of them all. Tomas made sure all were kept far behind the tracker. He pulled back on his rains and brought his horse to a stop. The others caught up and also halted.

"From here on I must ask you all to refrain from talking. Our tracker has signaled that he found traces of game nearby." On signal, the rifle bearers quietly rode up, slid out of their saddles, and distributed a half dozen rifles out of large saddle bags, one to each of the lead riders, and one to Helena.

"They're loaded, but no rounds are in the chamber." Tomas said quietly. The metallic click and counter-click sounded six times simultaneously as each hunter opened and closed the bolt, sliding a round into firing position. Markus held his rifle across his lap behind the saddle pummel, as did most others.

"So, Helena, you're to be a hunter also today." Markus was smiling.

"Of course, why not. I often hunt with papa and my brothers. It's fun. I like to get out into the open country and see what surprises God has for me today." With that, Helena spurred her horse forward and joined her father.

Most of the hunting party without rifles, broke off after the rifles were distributed and headed to the camp. The hunters walked their horses quietly for several hundred feet through high grass interspersed with thorny bushes twelve feet tall.

While khaki-colored dust was everywhere, there were patches of dark--almost black--spiky leaves on the bushes and faint traces of a lighter green at the base of the straw-like grass. All around were shades of tan, brown, gray and black. Only the cool blue sky broke the deathlike colors of the arid landscape before them.

Tomas raised his hand and all stopped in their tracks. He did a hand signal, twirling his finger held out to his side, then raised it to his lips for silence. Everyone knew the hand signal meant "dismount." The rifle bearers came up without making the slightest sound and took the reins of the horses. The five hunters with both hands on their rifles, cautiously moved forward toward the tracker, trying carefully to avoid stepping on dry sticks and other debris.

Without turning around, Conrad brought his left hand directly out from his shoulder and rapidly spread his fingers out twice. Everyone stopped in their tracks and remained motionless. They stood like statues for at least three minutes when the tracker, in line of sight of them all, raised his hand slowly and signaled three times with his hand and pointed off to the left.

Fifteen, everyone thought. By rotating his wrist he communicated for the five hunters to come forward into a firing line. The group had been briefed that when the tracker found antelope, each hunter was to pick out one as a target but not shoot till Tomas fired the first shot.

The party members in camp heard the crack of rifle fire... ten, eleven, thirteen shots in all. Flocks of birds flapped into the air near the fallen antelopes. The crashing of thorn bushes and branches was heard as the rest of the frightened animals sprinted, in great leaps, for their lives.

"How many did we knock down?" Warner practically shouted as the group moved forward. One of the antelope lay on the ground but still kicked its legs in an effort to get up. The tracker, with a quick shot, dispatched the wounded animal.

"Looks like we have seven fine kills." Tomas declared as the others walked around, prodding and poking and debating who shot which antelope.

"This one's mine!" several said.

"How many shots did you get off?" asked Warner.

"One." Markus replied.

"One? Only one?"

"It's all I needed"

"But didn't you try for a second kill...I mean, there were a whole herd of them?"

"It wasn't my intent to shot the whole herd," Markus said, as he examined the chamber of his rifle.

"Breaches open everyone." Tomas ordered the safety procedure, and added with a big smile, "Time for lunch!"

Back at the ranch house after a lunch at the day camp, a late dinner was prepared that included antelope steaks, roast antelope, and a wonderful cream-based antelope stew.

Following the leisurely meal with tales of past hunts and famous

African hunters, everyone strolled into the parlor for a surprise that Tomas was eager to share.

"This just arrived on the same ship our guests sailed on, the *Königsberg.*" He said, primarily addressing his family. Tomas walked to a small table and dramatically pulled a cloth away, revealing a beautifully finished wooden box.

"It's a gramophone! See here," he opened the lid. "I ordered several dozen of these musical cylinders. Helena and Christiana selected the musical pieces. Shall we try it?"

As the Edison gramophone was cranked and a cylinder recording of Brahms piano lullabies wafted through the parlor, Michael asked Diana if she would like to stroll the garden, just outside the double doors of the parlor. Several others joined them, including Markus, Wolfgang and Helena.

"The last time I was here the Boer War was still being fought. Of course, that was eight years ago. I'm interested to hear what impact the war had on your family and the ranch?" Markus directed his question to Wolfgang with Helena listening.

"Yes, well, actually it had a positive effect." Wolfgang began. "After the war both the British and the Boers purchased our crops: beef, sheep and, of course, fruit from our orchard. We had a lot of sympathy for the Boer's cause, actually. After all, they were ranchers and farmers like ourselves. As soon as gold was discovered in the Boer territories, the British jumped in to take control of as much land as they could… and expand their empire." Markus listened intently.

"Of course, the Boers weren't blameless. Up until around 1900 they still supported slavery!"

A calm silence enveloped the threesome as they looked at the dazzling night sky blazing with a million stars against coal black infinity. Finally, Wolfgang added,

"But we get along with our British neighbors all right. They're good customers!"

A little laugh and smiles warmed the star-studded heaven gazers.

"This is one of my favorite times, I mean at night, like this," Helena spoke to no one in particular.

"I often stroll in the evening, after dark. It's like I feel closer to God when I am alone and it's quiet and with the vast heavens above." She was looking up at the shimmering sky. Markus paused and lingered, looking at her staring up, her head back and the faint light from indoors just lighting her white neck and the side of her face. Wolfgang again broke the silence.

"Helena already has a reserved seat in Heaven, if she can get one of those for her devotion. A good Catholic she is, always in church and always praying for everyone in the family!"

"Don't mock me, Brother. God can hear every word you say." With that she turned and walked off.

"I'm sorry, Sister. I was just making a joke for our guests!" There was an awkward moment, then Markus offered,

"Maybe I'll join her for a few minutes." With that his turned and stepped lively in the direction Helena had taken. The young woman stopped by a small groove of fruit trees her father had planted.

"May I join you, *Fräulein* Conrad? Markus spoke softly.

"Oh, I thought I was alone."

"I'll leave if you like."

"No, no. Stay if you wish." She paused. "My brother, it's disrespectful how he talks. I don't have any unrealistic expectations about his beliefs, but he shouldn't have…"

"Of course he shouldn't have. It was just an inappropriate attempt at humor. I think he was just trying to entertain his guests."

"Yes, well, it wasn't the first time." They were both silent for a few moments.

"I think I know how you feel…I mean about God…and religion." A few moments of silence as Helena turned slightly toward him.

"Back home in Bavaria, we… I mean my mother and sister and

I, go to church every Sunday to the Mariahfkirche in Munich. It's a big beautiful church with a wonderful organ."

She turned more toward him.

"We don't have a big church like that, like the ones in Germany, but we do have a good choir, and an organ…I'm in the choir." She was looking at him. "If you like, you can join us next Sunday. We go to the later Mass, the High Mass at ten. It takes us a while to get into town."

"Fine then, I'll meet you at the church. Which one is it?"

"It's the only Roman Catholic church in Windhoek, Saint Mary's. The other church is Lutheran, and there is a Dutch Reformed congregation, but they don't have a church."

They walked on awhile when he spoke again.

"I'm glad it's to be a High Mass. I love the pageantry of the music, and candles and bells, and the processional. It's all so beautiful… and the incense, I like that, too." They were both smiling.

"Maybe we should turn back." she said, touching his arm.

"Must we? This is a piece of Heaven you have here, all to yourself."

"It's for everyone. All they have to do is look up to the heavens."

Markus could not resist himself. He raised his hand to her cheek and gently turned her head to his. He leaned in a bit closer to her and looked into her eyes.

"Lieutenant, you are too forward!" As his dropped his hand, "I am so sorry, *Fräulein*. I didn't mean to offend you. It's just such a beautiful night and such a beautiful place,…"

"Just because you've been to China and in the army and all those places, and medals and such, don't think you can, you can…"

"I said I'm sorry, and I am sorry, truly." They were silent again standing there in the dark. He with a passion built up over months, she with mixed emotions, but with a warm stirring. "May I still meet you at church this Sunday?"

"Of course, of course, you can." She had involuntarily touched his arm. Again stillness, a beautiful stillness, with energy in the air between them that they both felt separately. Finally Markus spoke.

"Do you have a favorite star, somewhere up there?"

"Why yes, it's at the tail end of Cassiopeia. See? Up there near that bright one."

She was pointing. He pointed, too.

"No, no, you're too far over to the left…this way. See where I'm pointing? Below that fuzzy bunch of little stars, see?"

"Which fuzzy bunch of little stars? There are dozens of fuzzy bunches of little stars!"

They both broke out in laughter, and it took several minutes to recover.

"Oh, you are such a slow learner." She said in a feigned exasperation. "Now, let me show you exactly where my star is. Now, point up where I am pointing. Now, sight straight up your arm and off your finger…keep it straight! Fine." She walked around him to his upraised arm.

"No, No, don't move. Now a little over that way." She was close behind him and raised her arm to his and gripping his wrist, moving his arm a bit down and to the right.

"Now do you see my star?"

"Oh, that bunch of little fuzzy stars."

"Now, don't you get started again." she scolded him with a smile. "It's just there!"

She squeezed his arm for effect. "Do you see it now?" After a moment's pause he replied in a soft quiet voice,

"Yes, yes, I see it, and it's beautiful…very beautiful."

They hung there in silence, in the dark, not moving, with only a million stars glowing down on them for light. She could smell him, his manly smell, and it stirred her. Her hand was still on the back of his wrist and being so close to his back she could feel his body rise and fall with each breath. He realized her hesitation, her silence, her hand still on his wrist. He slowly lowered his arm, turned toward her and in a husky whisper,

"Beautiful, it is truly beautiful."

Her arm came down with his and they stood there close together, she not looking up but staring almost through him, in the dark. This time she could feel his hand slowly raising, coming between them, and just brushing the front of her blouse as it touched her chin. He lowered his head slightly as he raised her chin. Their lips barely touched. Each could hear… feel the other breathing. He moved his lips away an inch perfectly still.

She was rigid, but he could hear her exaggerated breathing. His hands slide around to her back and pressed her to him. Each was swimming in their own emotions. He could feel her voluptuous body against him, he was totally aroused.

This was too much for her, and she broke off from their embrace.

"No, no, you mustn't. I must go!" With that, he released her. She moved swiftly down the dark, well-worn path.

"Gute nacht." he said.

I hope you have enjoyed book one of 'Kalvarianhof, The Perilous Journey', and the first three chapters of book two:
'Kalvarianhof, The Storm That Shook The World'.

Follow the author on:
Facebook and on the Web at waltersoellner.com